John insisted on seeing his father's body before the coffin was locked.

"Either I look at him, or I'll raise such a stink that you'll never hear the end of it. Jack Anderson would love to get hold of a story like this."

"Like what?" McBundy asked sharply, something hard in his eyes.

John almost blurted out that he had read his father's notes, almost said that he knew everything about the network now. The incidents, the places, the names— McBundy's name near the top of the list. But he held his peace.

"I just want to look at his face, that's all."

McBundy brought John and his wife to the rear of the chapel, where he had one of the assistants open the top half of the coffin.

John could clearly see his father's face now. It was powdered white, with a dab of rouge on each cheek and a touch of lipstick. He looked almost as if he were sleeping, and not dead.

"Dad?" John had choked out the single word. He reached out to touch his father's cheek, but Liz held him back as McBundy motioned for the attendant to close the coffin.

FALSE PROPHETS

SEAN FLANNERY

CHARTER BOOKS, NEW YORK

FALSE PROPHETS

A Charter Book / published by arrangement with
the author

PRINTING HISTORY
Charter Original / December 1983

ISBN: 0-441-22694-9

Charter Books are published by The Berkley Publishing Group,
200 Madison Avenue, New York, N.Y. 10016.
PRINTED IN THE UNITED STATES OF AMERICA

This book is for a lot of people: for Lorrel Elizabeth, my wife; for Tammy Lynn, my eldest daughter; for Kevin and Justin, the boys; and for Travis and Gina, the babies. I love you all.

XCIII

Indeed the idols I have loved so long
Have done my credit in this world much wrong;
   Have drown'd my glory in a shallow cup
And sold my reputation for a song.

XIII

Some for the glories of this world; and some
Sigh for the prophet's paradise to come;
   Ah, take the cash, and let the credit go,
Nor heed the rumble of a distant drum.

—*The Rubáiyát of Omar Khayyám*

FALSE PROPHETS

It was late Tuesday evening in Washington, D.C., when Darrel Switt finally looked up from his reading. He was still dressed in his dark suit from the funeral, only now his tie was loose and his shirt sleeves were rolled up.

"You say that you've read this?" he asked.

John Mahoney nodded his head very slowly, almost as if he were afraid of breaking something. "What do you make of it?"

"I don't know what the hell to make of it," Switt replied. He stood up and laid the thick bundle of notes on the coffee table, then stretched.

"My father was a very pragmatic man. He wasn't given to flights of fancy."

"Were you aware of what he did for the Agency?" Switt asked.

"In a general way," John Mahoney said. "Not the specifics, of course, but sometimes we knew where he had gone. And we

1

loved him all the more for his attempts to keep us insulated."

"Have you discussed this with anyone?"

"No."

"Not even your wife?"

"No one. My father trusted you. In his letter he told me to make absolutely sure no one but you was to get this package."

Switt seemed lost in thought.

"What are you going to do about it?" Mahoney asked.

"I don't know . . . yet," Switt said. "When are you going back?"

"We're not going directly home. We'll be leaving Washington the day after tomorrow for Minnesota. We have to close down his cabin. The children are with us, so we'll probably stay there for a few days."

Switt seemed to draw inward again for a moment. Then he asked, "Are you staying at the Marriott?"

Mahoney nodded.

"Fine. I'll call you there before you leave. I'm going to have to think this out for a day or two. I need some time."

"Good enough," Mahoney said, rising. "Thanks again for your help."

"I don't know if I will be able to help."

"My father thought you were the man for the job." Wallace Mahoney's confidence went deeper than that, John knew. Switt had become for his father a son of a sort his own two could never be. During his last years with the Agency, John and Michael had lived far from Washington, while Darrel Switt often saw Mahoney daily. They could discuss their work openly; the normal activity of talking about the office to one's family was closed to men in the intelligence field. If the career to which his father had dedicated his life could be thought of as a family business, then Darrel was the heir to that business. John felt no jealousy; rather, he was grateful that another man had been able to give his father the sense that what he considered so important would continue to be done with love after his time.

"I'll call you before you leave," Switt said, walking John to the door and shaking his hand.

For a full five minutes Switt paced the room, every now and then glancing down at the bundle of notes he had been given shortly after the funeral, until he finally went to the phone and dialed an overseas number.

It took ten minutes for his call to go through to Geneva, and by the time it did he was sweating.

"Yes?" a long-familiar voice said over the transatlantic line.

"This is Ferret," Switt said. "The Mahoney business isn't finished yet."

"He's dead."

"I've just come from the funeral. His son was there. He handed me a manila envelope filled with notes. Your name is there, along with the entire Malecki-Larsen connection. Christ, he had everything."

There was a silence on the line. Then: "Has he shown them to anyone else?"

"He said he hadn't."

"You had best come here then. Can you get away without suspicion?"

"I'm on compassionate leave. Mahoney was a friend."

"I wanted to be his friend, but it was not possible."

"It'll take me at least forty-eight hours to get away," Switt said heavily.

"Don't take any chances. Just a little longer and we'll have this bloody mess cleared up."

Switt hung up the telephone, slowly crossed the room to a sideboard, and poured another drink. The bloody mess would have to be cleared up, and at the moment Switt could think of only one way to accomplish that.

THE RESURRECTION

Chapter 1

ARCHIVISTS WHO LATER put all the pieces together said the outcome was inevitable and had for its genesis two events that, although closely related, should never have happened.

No one on the outside, however, really ever had the complete picture. There were those, such as Ezra Wasserman, the former head of Israeli intelligence, the Mossad, and now in retirement at Gan Haifiz, who knew or guessed a great deal. And Carl Margraff in Berlin who had helped, in his own way, to ferret out the Israeli mole, had been having gut feelings about it all since his son's death years earlier. And finally a certain groundskeeper in a Missoula, Montana, cemetery who received the shock of his life and talked about it for years afterward.

There were others—legmen, contact teams, technicians, drivers, spotters, and a host of experts—who, if they could all have gotten together, perhaps in some dark corner of an obscure bar where the music was soft and the drinks mellow, might have come close to understanding.

And there were stunned men and women at high levels in the secret services of a dozen countries who each thought they knew. Of course, none of them wanted to think about what had happened, much less talk about it openly or even among their colleagues.

But at the time—a certain late, balmy summer—absolutely no one could have predicted the startling outcome.

It was an early Saturday morning in mid-August. The city of Geneva, Switzerland, lay under a thick pall of haze that, because of a rare temperature inversion, was a combination of fog and automobile exhaust. The pale wisps and tendrils had crept down from Hermance and, on the opposite shore, from Céligny, Coppet, and Versoix like some vital creature, infecting not only the atmosphere but the very fabric of the great city.

The sun, still low in the eastern sky, which would later sparkle on the wavelets on the south bay of the lake, was this morning only a dull ball that could be stared at with no discomfort.

Geneva was not normally a dark city. Its people, though stoic by reason of their Swiss heritage, had nevertheless learned to be good hosts to the thousands of tourists who descended annually. But today the haze seemed to carry a hint of something dark, foreboding, which Darrel Switt found disconcerting. He was a well-built man in his mid-thirties, dressed comfortably in a navy blazer, gray slacks, and a loosely knotted tie. He was obviously travel-weary, and from time to time during the cab ride he pulled at his long, drooping mustache, an unconscious gesture he had developed over the years.

He had taken precautions this morning, riding a tram past the Voltaire Museum to the Cornavin railway station, where he had walked up to the post office before hailing this taxi.

There had been no shadows, no tails as far as he had been able to determine, and yet he still had the over-the-shoulder feeling that nearly screamed in his brain for him to turn suddenly, to double back, to look for chance reflections in glass windows.

Paranoia. He thought now about the words of one of his tradecraft instructors.

"It'll strike you sooner or later. No getting away from it, gentlemen," the man (Margolis was his name?) had told them.

He leaned forward over the podium, his eyes flashing. "But if you understand it, the very fact will become your ally. Point: You've succumbed, and you're jittery. The other fellow is looking for it. And he sees all the signs. He'll expect you to run like a rabbit. Jump every which way. You can play him then, like a fish on a dibble pole. Bounce him all around. Jack him up so badly he's bound to make a mistake."

"But your counterpart is going to be paranoid as well, sir," one of the younger recruits had piped up.

Margolis leaned back, a broad grin creasing his craggy features. "A bright boy," he said. "But quite right—unless, of course, your mark is jacking you around."

They had all laughed at the time, but it wasn't funny in the field. Nothing was funny out in the cold.

The cab crossed the Rhône River on the Pont de l'Ile and turned up toward the Eaux-Vives section of the city. Switt sat up a little straighter in his seat as he redid the top button of his shirt, snugged up his tie, and smoothed his hair with his fingers.

He had always been a young man. The baby of every group he had ever been a part of. From high school in Des Moines to college at Northwestern and finally the Company, his had been the baby face.

He sat a little further forward now so that he could see his own reflection in the rearview mirror. Not young any longer, he thought. Lines around the eyes, which were no longer so bright and innocent. Creases at the corners of his mouth, which smiled less than before. And a few flecks of gray at his temples and even in his luxuriant mustache.

Not age, but pressure. He had always been a high-pressure man. In college he had thrived in the competition for grades; no matter what the objective, he always seemed to come up with a way to meet it that often didn't include studying. Later, with the Company, he had shone in his work. Moscow had been a veritable playground for him, where, no matter the intrigue or complexity of a situation, he could not seem to get enough.

All that, however, had had its effects, some of which he could see now in his reflection.

They had come to an area of residential streets, and the cabby, an older man with several teeth missing and the others crooked and nicotine-stained, turned and scowled.

"The street number, *monsieur?*"

"Right here is fine. On the corner."

"But the number you wish..."

"Here on the corner is fine," Switt said, handing over a fifty-franc bill.

The cabby pulled up at the corner of the Rue du Lac and Quai Gustave Ador, and deftly flipped the meter flag up with one hand while digging in his leather purse for change with the other.

But Switt jumped out of the cab and headed into the mist. The cabby looked after him with wonder at Americans and their senseless behavior.

Switt worked his way east and south as if on a walking tour of the city, although there wasn't much to see at this time of the morning under these conditions. At length he arrived at Route de Frontenex, a major city artery, where he got lucky with another cab almost immediately.

This time he directed the driver to take him to an address a dozen blocks deeper back into Eaux-Vives, where he got out half a block from his destination.

Turning down a narrow side street in an area of old, elegant homes, Switt hurried through a wide stone gate into a mews fronted by small apartments that had once been stables. They were backed by a line of a half-dozen huge, ornately decorated, three-story homes, each penetrated by a narrow tunnel driveway that led to the rear.

Switt went directly to the largest of them, ducked down the tunnel, and at a side door mounted the one step and rang the bell.

He had been here only once before, several years earlier. He had been full of pride and ambition then, filled with expectations and purpose, filled indeed with a self-righteousness that had been greeted with wholehearted acceptance. This time, however, Switt admitted to himself that he was frightened.

As he was about to reach out and ring the bell again, the heavy oak and glass door swung open. An older man, partially bald, wearing wire-rimmed glasses and dressed in morning coat and trousers, stood there blinking a moment before he stepped back.

"Won't you come in, sir?" he asked, his voice soft, British.

Switt went inside to a wide foyer. Beyond, he could see the main corridor off which were the living room, vast dining hall, and, to the left, toward the rear, if his memory served him correctly, the master study.

The butler closed the door and stepped ahead of Switt. "Just come with me, then, sir."

Switt followed him across the hallway, where a huge portrait of an old man with muttonchops and gold pince-nez stared severely down at all who dared enter what was obviously his domain.

The study was huge, with tall, stained-glass windows and French doors that would have afforded a view of the rose garden but were covered with heavy, wine-red drapes. Three walls were almost completely covered with floor-to-ceiling bookcases filled with leatherbound volumes, a ladder on tracks in one corner. The center of the room was dominated by a leather-topped desk, to one side of which stood a mammoth globe with ornately carved gimbals and legs. On the opposite side of the room, just in front of an oak sideboard built into the bookcases, was a grouping of soft leather chairs, a wide couch, several lamp tables, and a matching coffee table. A thick Oriental rug covered the floor.

"Please have a seat," the butler said. "May I bring you some coffee?"

Switt had been staring at the books and at the bric-a-brac in every nook and cranny. He glanced up. "Please," he replied. "And maybe some brandy with it."

"Of course, sir," the butler said. He turned and left the study, softly closing the door.

Switt stood where he was for several seconds, then moved across the room and sat down in one of the leather chairs, avoiding the temptation to go to the desk and look through it.

Missed opportunities never return, their instructors had hammered into their heads. "You let the golden moment slip by, and it'll never come again."

He stared at the desk, but his thoughts were elsewhere. Back at Wallace Mahoney's funeral. Back to Mahoney's son, John, and the man's wife and children. Back to what he had set in motion. He shuddered with a sudden chill.

The butler returned shortly with a tray upon which was a silver coffee service and two cups and saucers. Without a word he set it down on the coffee table in front of Switt, poured two cups of coffee, then went to the sideboard and brought back a bottle of cognac and two snifters. He poured a generous measure in each glass before he straightened up and left the room.

Switt watched the door for several seconds. Then he picked up the snifter, drained it, and poured another.

From outside he heard voices. He got to his feet as McNiel Henrys entered the room.

"You took the usual precautions, I presume," Henrys said. He was a tall, distinguished-looking man in his late fifties, with a touch of gray at his temples and in his neatly trimmed mustache. He wore freshly pressed slacks, a light-colored shirt with an ascot at the neck, and a linen smoking jacket.

"Yes, sir. Flew in last night and did a lot of jumping around this morning."

They shook hands, and Henrys motioned for him to sit down.

"How was the funeral?"

"There was hardly anyone there," Switt said. "McBundy and a couple of his cronies from the Company. And of course John and his wife and three kids."

Henrys was nodding as if Switt were giving him sage advice. "How have you been these past few days?"

"Nervous. And I'm not afraid to admit it."

Henrys sat down, looked with surprise at the cognac, then picked up his coffee, crossed his legs, and sat back, balancing the cup and saucer on his knees. "Did you bring the notes Mahoney's son passed to you?"

Switt nodded, got to his feet, loosened his tie, and unbuttoned his shirt. He had the notes strapped to his chest. He handed the package to Henrys and restored his clothing before sitting down again. "It's all there, including Mahoney's conversation with you."

Henrys set down his coffee cup, removed the notes from the envelope, and thumbed through them. "Whom had he finally pegged as the CIA liaison?"

"McBundy."

Henrys shook his head. "His only serious mistake, trusting you," he said, an odd edge to his voice.

A sudden bitterness at the way things had turned out welled up in Switt. "He didn't make many. He was a fucking legend in the Company."

"He was a bloody saint, for my money," Henrys said without looking up. "Malecki, Larsen, and Arlemont are all out of the network now."

"He had your name, and Zwiefel's in Bonn, and Rubio's in Rome."

"At this point it's nothing but the conjecture of a dead man."

Again the bitterness rose at the back of Switt's throat. "In there he mentions that you agreed to tell him everything. He said you met. Here at the house." He wanted to take a shot at Henrys, to jar him loose somehow from his apparent complacency. "Would you have told him everything?"

Henrys looked up, a harsh expression in his eyes. "That would have depended upon him. If we had had a little more advance warning that Mahoney was in Israel, working for Wasserman, things might have worked out differently. But he did go back and divert the Mossad from our track."

"For all the wrong reasons."

"Yes!" Henrys spat. "But the result was the same now, wasn't it? Wasserman may have had his suspicions, but he wanted to believe that there was nothing more to it than a spy ring passing Israel's secrets back to the Russians. 'Another Israel Beer mess' was the way he referred to it, I think."

"Then you would have brought him in?"

"Into the fold?" Henrys asked. "I think not completely. He was an old man—"

"But the best," Switt interrupted. "I loved that old man."

"I have no dispute with you, my dear boy. But Wallace Mahoney was—how shall I put it—an idealist who hadn't the foggiest idea what the term meant." Henrys shook his head and sighed deeply, then got to his feet and went to the door.

The butler was waiting on the other side, and Henrys handed him the notes. "Have these run through analysis. I want to know if they've been photocopied." Henrys walked back to his chair, picked up his cup and saucer, and looked at the American.

"I want to know why you had him killed," Switt blurted out. It had been on his mind for days.

"Mahoney?"

"Yes. If you were considering telling him everything—or at least some of it—why did you have him killed?"

"I didn't," Henrys said. "You thought that we had?"

"Who, then?" Switt asked. He wanted to believe Henrys. He had worked with the man for several years now, and he truly believed in what they were doing, what they and their predecessors had accomplished over the last four decades. And yet there were times like this—and they had happened before—when he just didn't know.

"The Israelis, I should expect. They knew that his own government had been watching him, and it would have been a disaster for them had he told his own people that the Mossad had been an open book for years."

"He died on an El Al plane," Switt said in amazement. The connection had never entered his mind.

"Of course. And we'll have to stay away from it. At least for the time being. They're too skittish now. When the dust settles, we'll find out."

"And then?"

"And then nothing, Darrel. And then we file it and leave it lie. It's all over." Henrys glanced toward the door. "Except for young John Mahoney. We're going to have to do something about him. Immediately."

The moment he had most dreaded had come. Switt glanced at his watch. It was shortly after eight o'clock, which made it one in the morning in Minnesota. Soon now. Any moment.

"Did you copy Mahoney's notes?" Henrys asked, his voice soft.

"No. I had no reason to."

"But you did read them?"

Switt nodded, off guard, wondering what the man was getting at. Company operations were his responsibility. That division had been made patently clear to him from the beginning.

He would act as absolute liaison from the CIA, just as Per Larsen with ININ had covered NATO; Arlemont had covered the French SDECE; Rubio, the Italian SISMI; Zwiefel, the West German BND; Sergovich, Russia's KGB; Yon Sieu, the mainland Chinese. And all the others.

Henrys acted on behalf of the British, but he was also the overseer. Still, no one, not even Henrys, overstepped his own boundaries. Too much confusion if we all muddled about on each other's turf, as he put it.

"You did read them, then. Mahoney was here. Did he pass this location on to his son?"

"It wasn't in the notes."

"I see," Henrys said thoughtfully. He got to his feet again, placing his empty cup on the coffee table. "Are you hungry? Would you like some breakfast?"

"I could use something," Switt said, getting up. Maybe he

wouldn't tell Henrys what he had ordered.

"I must attend to another matter. Meanwhile, I'll have Robert show you to your room. You can freshen up if you like. When you're ready, come back down. We'll eat outside. The mist may have cleared by then."

Upstairs, Swift was ushered into a large, airy bedroom with its own vast bathroom and tall windows overlooking the mews. The mist still hung over the city, but the sun had climbed higher and shone brightly.

He had brought his cognac with him, and he set the snifter down on the windowsill while he lit a cigarette.

Alone again as he had been for most of his adult life, Swift tried to settle his mind, tried in some measure to make sense not only of what Henrys had told him, but of what he had himself set in motion back in the States. When you looked at the big picture it was all very clear, although their methods— his own included—frightened and sickened him at times.

Christ, Mahoney had never even suspected who the real operative was within the CIA. It hurt now, the deception. And it did not make Swift very proud. It hurt that he had lied to the old man all these years. Since Mahoney and he had been stationed together in Moscow four years ago, and had gotten to know each other, the lies had continued.

Here and now, looking out across the mews, the mist clinging to the eaves of the buildings, almost rolling along the cobbled streets, it was next to impossible to assign any reality to the things he had done in the name of the network over the years. The lies he had told. The lives he had ruined. He didn't know if he understood reality any longer.

The reality, of course, was Wallace Mahoney's death at the hands of the Israelis. He knew too much.

The reality was John Mahoney, his wife, and three children out there with nearly all the evidence they needed to bring the entire network to its knees. If it got out, there would be no going back. No picking up the pieces. Everything they had worked for, all of it, would go down the drain.

Swift finished his cognac and carefully set the glass back on the sill.

Despite all that, it was nearly impossible for him to justify what he had ordered. *Nearly* impossible, he thought morosely. Not *totally* impossible.

He went into the bathroom and splashed some cold water on his face, straightened his tie, and brushed his hair. He stepped lightly down the richly paneled corridor with its paintings and antique tables. The staircase faced three gigantic stained-glass windows, beautifully illuminated now that the sun was coming up, but lending a somber, churchlike atmosphere to the house, so that by the time Swatt had reached the bottom, his mood once again was dark.

The butler who had let him in was there. With his usual deep scowl on his face, he led Swatt down a corridor past the study and out a rear door that opened onto a wide patio overlooking a rose garden. A half-dozen thickly padded outdoor chairs were grouped around a glass-topped, wrought-iron table. To the right a staircase led down to the vast garden.

"Mr. Henrys is below, in the garden. He asked that you join him. Breakfast will be served momentarily, sir."

Swatt nodded absently and went down into the garden, where a series of white stone pathways meandered through various species of rose plantings, shrubs, and trees. Some of the flower beds were raised above the general level of the garden, held in place by stone retaining walls; others were sunken; some were surrounded by lovely, shimmering pools of water; and still others were kept under glass in miniature greenhouses.

There was a miasma of rich odors from the damp earth and flowers that, although not unpleasant, seemed somehow confining to Swatt. The mist clung here, and twenty feet away from the stairway Swatt was isolated.

Henrys was nowhere in sight. "Mr. Henrys? Sir?" Swatt called out.

"Over here." Henrys's voice came faintly from deeper within the garden.

Swatt looked around a moment, then moved forward down one of the winding paths. The place was putting him on edge, but he resolved that now was the time to tell Henrys about the team he had ordered from New York.

It would be almost time now. Within the next hour, John, Elizabeth, Carl, John, Jr., and Cindy Mahoney would cease to exist.

There was no other way, he had told himself, and he repeated it now. The end justifies the means. Henrys would have to be made to understand that no questions would be raised.

It would all be done neatly. Accidentally.

Wallace Mahoney was dead and buried. His son Michael had been killed several years ago. His wife had died of cancer last November. And now his remaining son and grandchildren would be gone. The end of the Mahoney line. But it was war, wasn't it?

Henrys was seated on a low stone bench in the middle of the garden, and Switt almost walked past without noticing him. He stopped short. Henrys was pointing a pistol at him. A large, bulbous silencer was screwed onto the end of the barrel.

"You overstepped your bounds, Darrel," Henrys said, his voice still eerily soft. "It's probably too late for me to stop what you have ordered, but I am trying."

Switt backed up a step. "Why?"

"Why what, my boy? Why do you have to die?"

Switt could feel his bowels loosening, and he looked wildly over his shoulder toward the house. He saw only the mist.

"There is no one at the house except for Robert. My daughter has gone to the mountains for a few days. And there certainly is no one to hear you if you cry out."

It didn't make sense. He had worked for them for so long. He had done things for them that were almost unthinkable. He had betrayed his own country. And his friend. The one man he had most admired. His role model, insofar as a man brushed by the cynicism of his kind of work allowed himself such a thing.

"Why?" he asked again.

"You are a loose end, Darrel. An embarrassment. Mahoney trusted you, his son ran to you. Too many leads and connections come to you. The network must remain intact at all costs, you know that. You've been to school on that subject. In fact, I'd venture to say that if you were thinking rationally you'd do the same thing."

"But . . ." Switt started to speak when a huge fist slammed into his chest, driving him backward into a thick line of rose-bushes.

There was no sound, no pain. Switt's entire body felt merely numb, detached from his brain, which seemed to be functioning in a dreamworld. He opened his mouth in an attempt to speak, but nothing came out. He could not even breathe.

Henrys's figure appeared above him, and Switt was looking

into the barrel of the pistol. He opened his mouth again. Suddenly there was a tremendous thunderclap in his head, and then nothing.

Chapter 2

Ashes to ashes, dust to dust. The words kept running through John Mahoney's brain. He lay in the small bed beside his wife, listening to his own heart beat, seeing in his mind's eye the coffin being trundled out of the chapel for the ride to the airport, and then the long trip out to Missoula, Montana.

His brother Michael had been buried out there, as was his mother. There were other graves waiting for him, for his wife Elizabeth, and for the children. He could see the windswept hill, the trees sighing, almost calling for him to come join his family.

John had been at work at Monsanto Chemical in Los Angeles the day the two FBI agents had come for him to tell him about Michael. They had picked up Elizabeth and the kids and had driven down to the Presidio in San Diego where a crusty lieutenant colonel, with more gentleness than even the man himself suspected he possessed, informed John of Michael's death.

"A car accident outside Missoula," the officer had explained, but he would not tell them why they had been picked up by the FBI and were being held on a military base simply because his brother had been killed in a car wreck. It had something to do with his father's work, he knew that, but nothing more.

Liz had held him then, and they had cried together, but the colonel had been adamant about his orders. John and his family were to remain on the base and not make any contact with anyone for any reason.

That had been on a Tuesday afternoon. Friday night he received a call from his father, and on Saturday they all flew to Washington, D.C., to meet him. He had looked gaunt, a haunted expression in his eyes, and John had had a hard time trying not to break down. On the way from the airport to the hotel his father explained that an operation in Moscow from the U.S. embassy had gone sour. The Russians had placed an order to kidnap Michael. It had somehow backfired, and Michael was killed. The order had also gone out to kidnap John and his wife and children, but the FBI had managed to get there first. It had been a tight squeeze, however, and his father kept saying how sorry he was . . . repeating it over and over, so that Liz had become embarrassed, and John had almost cried.

All during the time John and Michael had been growing up, their father, when he was home, presented the strong but loving figure. It wasn't that he had been autocratic; everything he did for the boys and for his wife was done obviously out of love. It was that he had been so damned smart. Without a hint of braggadocio, Wallace knew everything . . . or could figure out what he didn't immediately know. As a result John and Michael worshiped their father. They loved their mother. They had always felt a tenderness toward her. But with their father it was nothing short of adoration.

When they finally got to the hotel, John's mother had been her usual self, more concerned about how her husband and son were taking the death of Michael. And the only way John had of knowing how badly she was taking it was from the especially tender manner in which his father was treating her.

* * *

It was cold in the cabin. Fall came early to northern Minnesota, and John had let the fire in the fireplace die down before they had all turned in for the night.

He raised his left arm in front of his face so that he could see the luminous dial of his watch, although its luminosity wasn't really necessary with the full moon shining in the windows. It was nearly 2:00 A.M., but despite the emotional battering he had been giving himself, he was not sleepy.

Carefully, so as not to wake up his wife, he pushed back the covers and slipped out of bed. Across the tiny room, he found his clothes where he had tossed them, and pulled on his trousers, a sweater, and his sneakers.

Before he went out into the main room he stopped and looked down at the figure of his wife curled up in a ball beneath the covers. Only the top of her head was visible, her long blond hair spilling out over the pillow.

Ashes to ashes, dust to dust. Two years earlier, after the Moscow assignment, his father had been placed in Bethesda Naval Medical Center, where the varicose veins in his right leg had been stripped. It had taken nearly three months for him to mend, and a couple of months later he had bought this cabin on Shultz Lake, just north of Duluth.

Liz had been surprised at how ramshackle the place was, but the kids loved it, and John had understood his father's buying it. When they were little, he often told them about his Uncle Fred, whose cabin had stood on the other side of the lake. As a young man, Wallace Mahoney had spent many summers here with his uncle. The happiest days of his life, he had proclaimed more than once.

A few months later his mother telephoned from Washington, this time informing him that his father had been injured and that they were to come immediately.

Everyone at the hospital had been tight-lipped about it all. Before they were allowed to go into the room, Robert Mc-Bundy, his father's control officer, had cautioned them not to ask what had happened.

"I thought he was retired," John had shouted in the busy hospital corridor. His fear made him angry.

McBundy had looked him directly in the eye. "I'm going to ask you something now—and I sincerely hope you won't give me the wrong answer. Retired from what?"

"John?" his mother had said fearfully.

John woodenly gave the stock answer. "From the European trade desk at the State Department."

McBundy nodded, and John's mother seemed relieved.

"He is retired. We brought him out to clear up a simple matter. He was injured in the line of duty. Nothing serious, I assure you."

In the hospital room, it had been his father comforting him, telling him everything would be all right, instead of the other way around. And despite the fact that John was an adult, with a family of his own, he did take comfort from his father.

"I thought maybe . . ." John started. There was a blue tinge to his father's face.

"Thought what, John? That you'd lost me?"

John nodded. His father smiled.

"Not a chance, son."

John went out to the screened-in porch where the three children were bundled up in their sleeping bags. John, Jr., who had always been a restless sleeper, had pushed himself halfway out of his bag. John covered him, then kissed him on the forehead. At ten, he was the middle child, full of curiosity about everything, barely holding on for the day he too could go to high school like his fourteen-year-old brother Carl, the serious one of the family. Carl, they all said, was nothing more than a younger version of his grandfather, whereas Cindy, the baby of the family at six, was the opposite—bouncy, bright, without a care in the world.

For a long moment he looked at them all, love and pride welling up in his heart. They represented all that was good and real in the world, just as this cabin on the lake had represented the same values for his mother and father.

Ashes to ashes, dust to dust. His mother's cancer had been advanced before she would allow John to be told about it.

On that late fall day the weather in Los Angeles had been heavy and still, as it had been all through the week, a deep overcast almost portending the news from Duluth where his parents lived in the cabin.

His father had telephoned and suggested that they leave the

children with a babysitter. It wasn't something they should see,
he said. And standing there now, gazing down at his children,
he knew that his father had been correct, although at the time
he had thought it important for them to see their grandmother
while they could.

She had been waiting for him and Liz to arrive, and earlier
she had had one of the nurses help her with some makeup.
Outside it was bitterly cold, near zero with a strong wind across
Lake Superior, but in the hospital room the atmosphere was
stiflingly hot, with the odors of illness everywhere.

It was all he could do when he walked into the room to
contain himself. There had been so much tragedy in the family
during the past year or so. And now his father seemed near
collapse, and his mother looked terrible. The skin hung in folds
on her face and arms. When he bent down to kiss her, he could
hear her breath rattling deep in her chest.

His father had lost weight as well. Apparently he had not
been sleeping or eating; his eyes were red-rimmed and puffy,
and his hands shook.

Liz took in the situation instantly. She literally dragged her
father-in-law from the chair and forced him and John out of
the room.

"Get out of here, both of you. Get yourselves a cup of
coffee. Or better yet, get out of the hospital and find a drink
somewhere. Marge and I want to talk for a bit."

John hesitated, and his father seemed rooted to the spot,
unable to decide anything.

"Get out of here," Marge echoed from the bed, her voice
like a soft breeze across a field of dead leaves.

When they had come back an hour later, Marge was sitting
in a chair by the window. Liz had fixed up her hair and redone
her makeup, and she looked splendid.

Three weeks later she was buried next to Michael in the
cemetery on the hill above Missoula.

John looked through the screen down toward the lake where a
long streak of yellow from the brilliant moon cut across the
nearly still water. He went out of the cabin and walked across
the dew-wet lawn to the small dock where his father's fishing
boat was still tied.

They had arrived late that afternoon. John had telephoned
his father's Duluth lawyer yesterday, and he had cleared the

way for Wallace Mahoney's car to be released to John from the airport's long-term parking area; the car keys had been given to him, along with his father's other personal effects, in Washington. By the time they had gotten to Shultz Lake, they weren't in the mood to do anything except open the cabin, have a little supper, and go to bed. Except for a suitcase for the children and an overnight bag for themselves, the luggage was still in the car.

In the morning they were going to start packing up everything. The real estate agent was coming up from Duluth on Monday to appraise the place. On the telephone he had assured them that the cabin was in just the right price range for a quick, easy sale.

John walked out to the end of the dock and fumbled in his pockets for his cigarettes. When he found them he lit one, flipping the match out into the water. A second later a fish jumped, its splash sending ripples in widening circles across the yellow streak of light from the moon.

Ashes to ashes, dust to dust. McBundy had called on Sunday with the news. A heart attack, he said.

During the previous two weeks John had gotten a bit frantic about his inability to contact his father. There was no answer at the cabin, and his repeated efforts to get in touch with McBundy at the Central Intelligence Agency had produced no results. There was no man by the name of Robert McBundy who worked for the Agency. And no, there was no one named Wallace Mahoney on the payroll either.

"A heart attack, or was he shot again like in San Antonio?" John lashed out bitterly.

"I'm sorry, John, but he died of a heart attack. He had gone on a vacation to Israel. He died on the return flight."

"I'm going to call for an autopsy."

"No, you're not. Your father is dead. We've already made the funeral arrangements here. There'll be a memorial service at Arlington on Tuesday, and then his body will be transported to Missoula. It's what he wanted."

"How do you know what he wanted?" John had shouted, tears streaming down his cheeks.

The next morning, before they had driven out to the airport for their flight east, the thick manila envelope from his father had arrived, postmarked Paris. And everything changed.

* * *

"What are you doing out here?" Elizabeth asked, startling John out of his thoughts. His wife came onto the dock. She had thrown a jacket over her nightgown, but her feet were bare and wet from the dew.

"You're going to catch cold running around like that," he said.

She saw that he had been crying. She came into his arms, and they kissed deeply. When they parted, she looked up and gently brushed the tears from his cheeks with her fingertips.

"It's hard, my darling, I know," she said softly.

"They killed him," John said.

"We saw him..."

"Oh, Christ," John said, turning away, unable for that moment to speak.

McBundy had wanted a closed-coffin funeral, but John had insisted on seeing his father's body before the coffin was locked.

"Either I look at him, or I'll raise such a stink that you'll never hear the end of it. Jack Anderson would love to get hold of a story like this."

"Like what?" McBundy asked sharply, something hard in his eyes.

John almost blurted out that he had read his father's notes, almost said that he knew everything about the network now. The incidents, the places, the names—McBundy's name near the top of the list. But he held his peace.

"I just want to look at his face, that's all."

McBundy shook his head, but finally brought John and his wife to the rear of the chapel, where he had one of the assistants open the top half of the coffin.

John could clearly see his father's face now. It was powdered white, with a dab of rouge on each cheek and a touch of lipstick. He looked almost as if he were sleeping, and not dead.

"Dad?" John had choked out the single word. He reached out to touch his father's cheek, but Liz held him back as McBundy motioned for the attendant to close the coffin.

Switt had telephoned a couple of hours before they left the motel. He said he was working on the notes and would probably have something positive within a few days.

"Just hang on a little longer, John. I promise you that all this will be worked out."

"We're going to the cabin for a few days. Afterward, we'll be back in L.A."

"Don't talk to anyone about this. It'd be too dangerous."

"I understand."

"And listen, John. I want you to know that your father and I were . . . very close. I admired that man, you know. I loved him."

"Thank you, Darrel," John had said. "Thanks a lot. I appreciate your saying so."

"Let's go back to bed now, John," Liz said, once again breaking him out of his thoughts.

He turned back to her. "In a little while. You'd better check on John, Jr., again; he's already kicked himself out of his sleeping bag once tonight."

"I already did. If he gets too cold, he'll bundle up."

"I'll be up in a bit."

Elizabeth kissed him again, then started off the dock. At the shore, she stopped and looked back. "What about the copy you made of your father's notes?"

"What about it?" John asked, his heart suddenly accelerating.

"I'd like to read them. They're by the stove."

John shook his head. "I'm going down to Duluth on Monday and put them in a safe place."

"Won't you tell me what he was working on? You think he was murdered?"

"Leave it alone, Liz."

"I'm worried about you, darling."

"Leave it be," he said more gently. "Go back to bed. I'll be up in a minute or two."

She stared at him for a moment longer, then smiled and went back across the lawn and into the cabin.

When she was gone, John lit another cigarette, drawing the smoke deep into his lungs, and exhaling slowly as he looked across the lake. He was a large, husky man, with thick brown hair and blue eyes. He was somewhat reminiscent of his father, except for the faraway, almost dreamy expression that came over him at times. He was a scientist, an organic chemist with Monsanto. Within a couple of years, if all went well, he'd become chief of his section.

Yet, standing here now, he wondered how it would be possible for him to go back. How it would be possible for him to continue with anything for that matter.

He remembered that his father told him how, as a young man, he would sleep in the boathouse. Just as the sun was coming up, he would meet his Uncle Fred down at the dock, and they would take the old fishing boat out into the middle of the glass-smooth lake.

"Those were the times, John," his father used to say wistfully. "It was simpler then."

The first time John had heard the story, he had been frightened for days that his father did not love him. That if, by some feat of science or magic, his father would somehow go back in time, leaving his wife and boys.

Later, when John was a little older, and had begun to think he understood what it was to grow old and lose your youth, he felt sorry that his father seemed unable to relish the here-and-now.

Once, cruelly during that period, he had asked his father if he had always wished for another time. Wished now for his youth, and when young, wished for adulthood.

His father had smiled and patted John on the shoulder. "It's not just a matter of misplaced time, son; it's a matter of expectations. There were troubles then too, you know, just like now. But at the time I loved Uncle Fred more than anyone else in the world."

"Why?"

"Because he was a fine man. Because he treated me well, with understanding. And, I suppose, because he needed it more than anyone I ever knew."

"Sorta like Mom," John had said.

"Sorta."

Now, as an adult, he understood what his father had meant. Those summers on this lake with his Uncle Fred had been the hitching post for his entire life, the one thing that time could not alter, that world events could never change. A constant that could be examined under the flickering lights of differing ages but which would always remain the same.

Uncle Fred had provided that constant for his nephew, and John knew that his own personal constant was his father. The memories of their conversations. The recollections of all the times his father had stood behind him, giving him his support and love. All that was his to carry with him wherever he went.

He sighed deeply several times in an effort to relieve the pressure building in his chest. There was still the unfinished business of his father's notes, naming Robert McBundy as one of the men involved in a conspiracy that touched at least a half-dozen governments.

His father had trusted Switt. But Switt was only one man and could not easily work independent of the Agency as Wallace Mahoney had.

John turned that over in his mind, amazed that he was taking his thoughts in such a direction.

Per Larsen, Chaim Malecki, Armand Arlemont, Sonja Margraff, and General David Ben Abel. All of them had been murdered for their involvement in this business.

But there were others on the list, besides McBundy, who were still alive: Leonardo Rubio with the *Servicio Informazione Sicurezza Militare;* Walther Zwiefel with the *Bundesnachrichtendienst;* and McNiel Henrys with the British Secret Intelligence Service. Among them, and several others, was his father's murderer.

The tightness in his chest returned. He was an amateur. An analytical chemist, not an investigator.

A tremendous explosion shattered the still night air. The warm pressure wave, smelling of plaster dust and wood, shoved him off the end of the dock into the shallow water.

He jumped up immediately, sputtering, his heart hammering, his mouth open as burning boards and other debris fell all around him.

The cabin was on fire. The roof and front wall had collapsed forward, flames leaping into the night sky.

"No!" he screamed, slogging through the waist-deep water to the shore. And then he was stumbling up the lawn toward the furiously burning cabin. "Elizabeth!" he shouted. "Elizabeth!"

Another explosion, this one from the side of the cabin, lifted the collapsed roof from the porch, setting it down twenty feet away on top of the small boathouse, which immediately caught fire.

There was no way for him to get close to the front of the

cabin where the fire was the most intense, so he headed in a dead run around the back. Somehow he had lost one of his shoes, and he burned his foot on a flaming timber.

Up on the porch he slammed open the back door and leaped into the main room, but the side wall had been pushed inward, blocking his progress.

"Elizabeth!" he screamed again from just within the doorway, tearing at the burning rubble with his bare hands. "Carl! Cindy! John!"

The entire cabin was on fire now, and the heat drove him back out the door, where he stumbled off the porch and fell hard to his hands and knees, mindless of his burns.

"Elizabeth!" he cried out again.

There were several smaller explosions, almost like rifle shells going off within the cabin. The flames mounted higher into the night sky, completely engulfing the cabin, so that John was forced to crawl farther away, toward the greenhouse, whimpering and crying in shock.

He finally collapsed just beside the gravel road, the stones harsh against his cheek, watching the cabin burn.

They hadn't had a chance. The first explosion had collapsed the roof over the front porch where the children were sleeping and had pushed the far wall down on the bedroom where Elizabeth was.

If he hadn't insisted they stay out here . . . if he had made them stay in town in a motel . . . if he had kept Elizabeth with him a little while longer . . . if . . . .

"Father," he cried. "Oh, God . . . Father."

The events at Geneva, Switzerland, and Shultz Lake, Minnesota, were in actuality the genesis of the inevitable end.

All through that late summer, everyone had a difficult time—even Robert McBundy moved from task to task like an automaton. Months later, when those around him recalled those days, they reminisced that he had been like a sleepwalker moving through traffic at a busy intersection.

Timing was king. From Mahoney's departure from Greece to Israel to help the Mossad, when a bomb at the Athens airport meant for him killed a small Greek boy instead, all the way through to the fact that Switt had jumped a full twenty-four hours before any of them had even thought to connect him, the timing had been critical.

Of course none of that provided any consolation to them, not then, and certainly not later when it all finally came together. But through the winter, they had to wonder how it would have been, had the timing—any of their timing—been off by just the slightest degree.

"Hindsight," McBundy had often told tradecraft classes, "is the bane of the operative, and the comfort of old men."

Chapter 3

IT WAS SOMETIME after 3:00 A.M. Saturday morning when McBundy signed out with the marine guard and emerged from a side exit of the Central Intelligence Agency complex near Langley, Virginia. The night was humid and still, and before he walked across the brightly lit parking lot to his car, he stopped to loosen his tie.

He was a man in his early fifties, of medium height and regular features, but his stocky, almost pudgy frame, his round face, his black hair and bright eyes set his appearance apart from the studied anonymity of most of his colleagues within the Agency. His two secrets, known only to his wife and a few close associates, were that he usually wore a girdle to keep an expanding girth in control and dyed his hair on a regular basis.

McBundy was a vain man in that he foisted these little deceptions on the people he worked with; he always dressed sharply, usually in London-tailored three-piece suits, and he drove a Mercedes that was never more than two years old. But vanity was simply a game with him, never an obsession.

Agency wags gossiped about almost everyone in the Company, from the DCI down, but never about McBundy. McBundy was inviolate. The Operations king. Sharp as a tack upstairs, you know. Mind like a computer, and a will and demeanor like Joseph Stalin. Not to be crossed or in any way messed with. A hard man, but with compassion, don't you see.

As Chief of Clandestine Operations, he worked his people long hours, drawing out abilities they never knew they possessed. But he had never left one of his people out in the cold. Not once.

If there was, however, any complaint about McBundy— and he had heard and ignored this one—it was that once he had a bee in his bonnet, he would never let go. Once committed, his energy was boundless, his inventiveness awesome, and his direction unswerving.

A sudden chill passing through his body—a premonition?— made him shiver as he crossed the parking lot and climbed in his gunmetal-gray 450 SL, tossing his briefcase in the back seat.

He sat behind the wheel without turning the key, reflecting on what had been happening and the next moves they were going to have to make.

"But carefully," he told himself aloud. He stared out the windshield at nothing, his hands tightly gripping the leather-wrapped steering wheel.

If any of them made a mistake now, the entire operation could blow up in their faces. The consequences would be nothing short of a disaster.

General Franklin Lycoming, the DCI, had called him up to his office yesterday, and the pompous old bastard had actually hinted at McBundy's resignation. To save the service possible embarrassment.

He hadn't said it in those words, of course, but the message had come across loud and clear from the moment he had begun talking about his days in the wartime OSS, and then the early Agency days, when their operational headquarters were split into a dozen different functional units, spread over half the East Coast. It was all before McBundy's time, and he hated nothing more than listening to the reminiscences of men he couldn't escape.

"We could do things in those days, Bob," the old man said, and McBundy had all but laughed in his face. "But ever since the Bay of Pigs, and then the Allende thing and all the other fiascoes . . . well, you know the story as well as I do."

Lycoming, who had left the young CIA to become a professor of political history at Harvard and then had come back into government service on Kissinger's coattails, should have retired gracefully and supplemented his pension on the lecture circuit. Instead, he had landed this job shortly after the election nearly four years ago. So far he hadn't bungled it too badly, nor had he done anything to distinguish the service. But now McBundy knew what was coming. Housecleaning, in government parlance.

"The Agency can't stand another shake-up," McBundy had argued.

"Just my point, Bob, just my point. They've got us under the microscope up on the Hill. Hell, you've read the subcommittee reports. Aronson and that entire gang are after blood. Ours."

For just a moment then, McBundy had become seriously alarmed that the man had been indiscreet about one or more of their current operations. "We're not throwing anyone to the wolves. Not this time."

The DCI was shaking his head, his lion's mane of hair flopping from side to side. "You've missed my point entirely." He withdrew a sheet of onion skin from a file folder on his desk, glanced at it, then handed it across. "Routine message surveillance and confirmation," he said.

The authorization stamps and initials adorned the first page like ornaments on a Christmas tree, the President's National Security Adviser's initials at the head of what amounted to several pages of a transcript of a telephone call from Israel's Menachem Begin to President Reagan. A trace stamp and voiceprint verification were marked at the bottom.

Begin was referring to Wallace Mahoney's death on the El Al jet, a fact the President had absolutely no knowledge of, although he covered himself beautifully with expressions of his understanding of Begin's concerns. He assured the Prime Minister that the United States in no way placed any of the blame for Mahoney's death on Israel. It was simply an unfortunate occurrence.

There was more, but McBundy looked up. "What's this all

about?" he asked, handing the paper back. The DCI replaced it in the folder.

"Wallace Mahoney was retired, as I understand it."

"Yes, he was."

"Needless to say, the President was embarrassed by this, and he tracked Mahoney down to us. He telephoned me personally to ask what the hell his connection was with Israel."

"We are running no operation."

"Exactly what I told the President, Bob. But then I find out from your own bailiwick that Mahoney may have been involved in the death of a senior French secret service officer in Paris a week or so ago."

McBundy could suddenly see the entire operation going down the tubes. He sat forward. "We picked it off the Interpol net. And for a short time we thought Mahoney may have been involved. But he was not."

"What was he doing in Israel and then in Paris?"

"I couldn't say, sir. Presumably a vacation."

"Why the call from Begin, then? If Mahoney was merely there on a vacation, why the call?"

"I'm sure the Mossad has our agent-identification list. He was probably spotted in Tel Aviv, and when he suffered his heart attack on an Israeli plane, they got nervous. Begin was just covering his back, that's all."

Lycoming stared long and hard at McBundy, the skepticism and indecision marked clearly on his features.

"You're telling me, Bob, that you were not running any operation with Mahoney in Israel?"

"That's exactly what I'm telling you. Not in Israel. Not anywhere with Mahoney."

The DCI nodded and looked away. "Aronson got hold of this somehow. He's calling for a closed-door investigation."

"His brother is an Israeli citizen."

"That's right," the old man snapped. "As a result, he is very sensitive. I'm throwing the doors open to him. Including your door—if you're still around."

They had arrived at the point McBundy knew was inevitable. "I hope to be around for a long time to come, but I'd like to ask one favor."

Again there was a moment of silence, until Lycoming barely nodded.

"Hold Aronson and his crew off for two weeks."

The DCI seemed startled. "What are you telling me now, Bob?"

"Only that Mahoney's death may have been something more than a simple heart attack. Before Aronson comes over here to snoop around, I want to know exactly what happened."

"How do you propose to find that out?"

"I have a few friends over there."

"There will be no operation in Israel."

"You have my assurances. But give me two weeks before you open the doors to Aronson. Can you do that?"

"I don't know . . ."

"Christ, you're Director of Central Intelligence. Aronson is only a junior Senator from New Jersey."

"Don't presume to tell me what my position is," Lycoming flared.

"Two weeks," McBundy insisted.

"I want no written reports, Bob. Not one scrap. But I want to be informed every step of the way."

"I don't expect there'll be anything to report," McBundy said smoothly as he got to his feet. "But if I find anything at all, you'll be the first to know."

"I would expect so."

At the door McBundy stopped and turned back. "Did you know Mahoney? Personally?"

The DCI looked up. "Never met him. But I've read his file, and from what I'm told, he was quite good at his job."

"He was the best," McBundy said. "The very best."

The Mercedes started with a roar of its powerful engine, and McBundy flipped on the headlights, backed out of his parking slot, and drove slowly around to the front entry road.

He had not been honest with the DCI, of course. Once this was settled and behind them, he was going to get out of the service. He would not be staying on for a long time to come, as he had said.

Wherever you went, it always seemed as if the old days were somehow better, that the way things were now—and the way everything was heading to hell in a hand basket—made it no fun any longer. As if it had ever really been any fun.

Camaraderie was the next point brought up in conversations

on the subject. In the old Agency days the work was tough, sure as hell, but everyone stuck together. They were fighting for a common cause. They knew they were right, that they were doing good things, even if everyone else didn't. But it was enough. They had their work, and they had each other. Not like today, when it's everyone for himself. The service used to be *we* back in the old days; now it had become *I*.

The parkway was all but deserted at this hour, so McBundy made good time to the Cabin John Bridge across the river, then back on River Road toward Chevy Chase. As he drove, he kept checking the rearview mirror, watching the few cars behind him. A highway patrol car hung back behind an eighteen-wheeler. Nothing suspicious.

Finally off the feeder road, he turned down a residential street and stopped in the middle of the block. He cut the lights, but not the engine, and settled down to wait.

The automobile's air-conditioning unit had pulled the temperature and humidity down to a comfortable level, and McBundy closed his eyes for a moment in an attempt to rest his mind by cutting off all outside stimuli. It didn't work, of course; he kept seeing Mahoney lying in the coffin, his skin pasty-white except where the rouge added a little color.

He kept seeing John and Elizabeth Mahoney standing there, staring down into the coffin. Never had he gone through anything like that, nor did he ever want to repeat the experience.

His mind drifted to disconnected events and places, to snatches of conversation and bits of reading—a kaleidoscope of thoughts and impressions.

His wife JoAnn had left for Los Angeles the day before yesterday to be with her sister, whose husband had died two years ago. She called it her semiannual pilgrimage, and always left amid a flurry of last-minute telephone calls and visits to the bridge club, the hospital auxiliary, and her Veterans' Help organization.

The house would still be dark now, the curtains drawn, perhaps the porch lights on; he couldn't remember if he had switched them off.

The weekend was set, of course. Anyone who needed him would know where and how to get hold of him but not why he was there. Those who didn't could wait until Sunday—Monday at the latest.

Records-keeping would not post its summary of files checked

out until Monday morning, anyway, which gave him plenty of time to cover himself.

He opened his eyes as a set of headlights turned the corner at the end of the block and slowly approached.

Had Lycoming not called him in, he would not be quite so nervous about this. And yet he was grateful for the knowledge of exactly where he stood with the man. Fighting the uncertain was impossible, whereas the known—no matter how bad— could be defended against.

The headlights materialized into a flashy-looking black sports car, a Toyota Supra, McBundy thought, which pulled up across the street.

McBundy got out of his car, then reached in the back seat for his briefcase. A tall, thin man got out of the passenger side of the Datsun and came across the street.

"No tails, sir?" he said, keeping his voice low.

"None," McBundy said. "How about you?"

"We're clean. Good luck."

"You too," McBundy said, patting the man on the arm. "But if anything blows up, or even threatens to develop, you know what to do."

"Of course."

McBundy crossed the street and slipped into the passenger seat of the low-slung sports car. His Mercedes pulled away from the curb and headed down the street to his house six blocks away.

"Let me put that in the back, sir," Bob Greene said, taking McBundy's briefcase. He swiveled around in his seat and stuffed it into the tiny luggage area beneath the sloping rear window. "No trouble getting away?" he asked.

"None," McBundy said tersely.

Greene flipped on the headlights, put the car in gear, and headed slowly down the block, then north toward the interstate.

"Don't mind telling you, sir, that I'm a little nervous about this," Greene said after they had driven a few minutes in silence. He was a tall, heavyset man with a thick shock of dark, wavy hair, and big, honest eyes. His eyes were his major asset, he once admitted. And he was probably right. Looking into his eyes, no one could possibly believe that he was anything other than what he represented himself to be: guileless, gentle, and honest as the day is long. It was a perfect combination that contributed to his expertise as the best interrogator and legman in the Company. Greene was more than good. He was nearly perfect.

"We're all nervous," McBundy said, answering his unsaid question. "And should be."

"That's not why," Greene interjected. "Although I don't particularly care for this sort of thing."

"What then, Bobby?"

"It's the direction we're worried about. None of us has the foggiest idea where this is all going. I mean, if we knew that, it might be better."

"Or worse."

"Or worse," Greene admitted. "But at least we'd know what we were up against."

McBundy thought about that for a moment. "Everyone feels the same way?"

Greene glanced over at him and nodded. "Essentially."

"Thirty-six hours, then we'll make a go or no-go decision."

"That would be fine with us, sir," Greene said. "But I can speak for all of us when I tell you that we're not trying to put you on the spot. No one wants to nail you to the wall. We all trust you, sir."

"I know that," McBundy said, touched. He understood what was troubling them. Most of them were married and had families. Most had been with the Company for a long time, so they had their careers, retirement, and all that to consider. Before they put that on the line, before they were asked to go any further, they would have to have answers to a number of questions. Then they would either dump the entire thing or draw their battle lines.

But whatever the decision, McBundy told them, it would be final. There would be no going back, no poking around.

Once they were on Interstate 95 heading northeast toward Baltimore, Greene settled back at a steady sixty miles per hour, turned on some music, and offered McBundy a cigarette.

"I was pleased when you and Leonard agreed to help with this," McBundy said, taking the cigarette.

Greene glanced at him again. "I guess I gave you the wrong impression earlier, when I said we were getting nervous."

"I understand," McBundy said.

"We're all going to help. Hell, we're all happy to help. In fact, I don't think there'd be one in the group who would have turned it down under any circumstances."

"You need insurance."

"I don't know if any of us would use that word, but it's close enough."

"And I'll give you that insurance as best I can, Bobby. But you have to realize that there's still a lot here that no one understands yet. I mean, we're still just stumbling around in the dark."

"I know that, sir. But like you said, we'll all know a lot more by the end of this weekend."

McBundy nodded, then settled back in his seat with his cigarette and his thoughts.

He had come this way before, a few years ago, filled with expectation. He had confused feelings now. And a sense of déjà vu.

The farmhouse was located five miles north of Greenwich, Connecticut, several hundred yards along a well-tended gravel road. Ostensibly it belonged to a crime-conscious New York corporate attorney, and the fifty acres of heavily wooded property were completely surrounded by a high wire fence.

In the years it had been used as a safe house, none of the local residents had ever bothered to try to get in. Most people in Greenwich enjoyed their privacy and respected that of others.

It was nearly noon by the time they pulled up at the gate. Greene jumped out of the car, unlocked the big padlock, and swung the gate open. He drove through, then stopped again to relock the gate before they continued up to the house.

McBundy had slept off and on during the long trip up from Washington. Although he had splashed some water on his face at the restaurant where they stopped for breakfast, he still felt dirty, and he had a terrible taste in his mouth from the cigarettes he had smoked.

He rolled down the window. The lovely smells of the trees instantly replaced the stuffiness of the car, and his head cleared.

The house, a large six-bedroom, two-story Colonial, was set in front of a small paddock from which bridle paths radiated in three directions. To the left, visible from the drive, was a large, ramshackle barn, and to the left of that were several small sheds and garages. Everything seemed to be in need of some repair, or at least a coat of paint.

They pulled up in front of the house, and Greene waited for McBundy to pull out his briefcase before he continued toward the garages.

For a minute McBundy stood on the gravel drive looking up at the house, smelling the fresh outdoors, listening to the birds. The day was glorious; only a few puffy white clouds gently sailed across an otherwise perfectly blue sky. Washington and its corridors of power and intrigue seemed as if they belonged to another universe, which in a way they did.

McBundy shook himself free from such thoughts. Intellectually he knew that whatever they decided here this weekend would set the course for a lot of people for a long time to come.

He started up the walk to the front porch as Greene came from the garage, and together they went in to the foyer. To the right was the small living room; beyond that was the parlor where they had worked the last time they were up here. The stairs to the second floor bedrooms were straight ahead. Doors to the left concealed the dining room and kitchen. A hallway beyond the stairs ran back to a storage area, the basement door, and the rear exit.

"Stan will be in the parlor," Greene said. "He wanted to have a word with you first."

McBundy stood stock still for another moment, listening to the sounds of the house. A radio was playing upstairs somewhere, and from the kitchen he could hear the faint rattle of pots and pans. He glanced that way.

"Larry Jensen volunteered to be chief cook and bottle washer," Greene said.

McBundy had to smile. "I suppose it's been egg foo yong and fried rice."

"It's coming out our ears. He even brought his own cooking utensils."

McBundy took a deep breath and let it out slowly in a futile attempt to settle his nerves. It was all coming together now, he thought. Or rather, it would begin in a little while, and for one terrible moment he wondered if he was up to it. If any of them were up to it.

"I know," Greene said softly, evidently reading McBundy's mood. "We all feel pretty much the same."

McBundy nodded. "Just give us a minute or two, will you? Then bring him down."

"Right. Who else do you want initially?"

"No one . . ." McBundy started to say, but then he reversed himself. "Everyone. Have everyone come in."

"Yes, sir," Greene said, and McBundy stepped lightly through the small living room, one ear still cocked to the radio playing upstairs.

Stan Kopinski, the Agency's resident historian, was seated at the long conference table that dominated the room, a huge pile of books and note pads in front of him.

He was a small man, close to retirement age, with thinning white hair and wide, liquid eyes behind gold wire-rimmed glasses. He had always seemed like an aging sparrow to McBundy; wrinkles and white hair and quick, birdlike motions. It was said of him that he never slept, that nothing but a data stream ran through his veins.

He looked up as McBundy came into the room, then rose to his feet. "Any trouble getting away?" he asked, his voice, like his body, thin.

"Went like clockwork. You?"

"No one has ever paid any attention to me, unless they needed some quick information," Kopinski said with a laugh. "How's JoAnn these days?"

"Just fine," McBundy said. "She's off to her sister's in California."

Kopinski nodded, although it didn't seem as if he had heard what McBundy said. "I wanted to talk to you before we get started."

McBundy went to the windows and threw the curtains back. The room was too gloomy for his liking.

"I've got the budget lines taken care of for your signature, just as you asked," Kopinski said, holding out a note pad.

"I'll look at them later. Are they open-ended?"

Kopinski nodded. "But there'll be questions sooner or later. I mean, we can cover this operation just so far."

"If you're asking for a time line, I can't give it to you yet, except that it looks as if we'll have to have it all wrapped up within two weeks."

"Exactly what I wanted to ask you." Kopinski seemed frustrated. "You've set up an operation here with no goal."

"We'll have a go or no-go, with an objective in mind, by the end of this weekend."

The promise didn't convince Kopinski, but he held his silence.

"I'm sorry, Stan, but I can't be more specific than that."

"All this may have been for nothing?"

"I hope so, but I doubt it," McBundy said.

"You *hope* so, but you *doubt* it." Kopinski shook his head and sat down. "Pardon me for saying so, Bob, but you've put yourself—hell, *all* of us—out on a limb."

McBundy was about to reply when he heard Greene's voice in the hall. "Just this way, sir."

Kopinski looked up, and McBundy could feel his heart accelerating as Wallace Mahoney, looking a little pale, a little tired, and a bit older than he had the last time they had met, walked into the room, stopping in midstride as he saw McBundy.

Greene and Larry Jensen were just behind him.

No one spoke for what seemed like years. McBundy could no longer hear the radio playing upstairs; Mahoney had evidently turned it off when Greene had come for him. But he could hear the birds singing outside.

"Hello, Wallace," he said at last.

"You're certainly a surprise," Mahoney said. His voice was soft, almost as if he had not used it for a long time and wasn't quite sure of the correct volume. He was wearing baggy trousers that accentuated his paunch and a plain dark shirt, open at the collar, which contrasted sharply with his thick shock of white hair. His skin hung slack on his neck and face. Were it not for his eyes, which looked very much alive and intelligent, he would have appeared to be nothing more than a burnt-out old derelict. A skid-row bum. Everyone in the room, and a great many people elsewhere, however, knew otherwise.

Mahoney had not only been the best the Company had ever known, in their book he still was.

"We're sorry we had to treat you so roughly, but it was the only way," McBundy said.

Mahoney's eyes flashed. "It was your man—the steward on the plane?"

McBundy nodded.

Mahoney looked at Kopinski, and then slowly at Greene and Jensen behind him. "Either you've brought me here, then, to recruit me into the network, or I've been terribly wrong about you, Bob. In any event, we've got a lot of ground to cover."

A lot of ground, indeed, McBundy thought, and Mahoney was the man who would lead them through it. The only man. And until just this moment he had felt pity for him.

Chapter 4

LATER, WHENEVER MAHONEY recalled that moment, he would swear up and down that they had all stood there in the safe house parlor, shaking each other's hands, and offering up simultaneous explanations for everything from the legmen who had shadowed Sonja Margraff to the precise nature of the drug that he had been given on the El Al jetliner from Tel Aviv. But in fact they stood for less than two minutes, with no explanations for anything, wearing silly expressions on their faces as if they were boys in grade school who had just won the Fourth of July footrace.

For the previous three days at the safe house, he had been told nothing. He had remembered his heart attack on the airplane, then nothing until he woke up at the Connecticut farmhouse under the care of a doctor who said not one single word.

During that time, Mahoney had mentally walked through his past as if it were a cemetery, the gravestones marking the people he had known and dealt with, the various sections, his

few strings and had you pronounced dead right there at the airport, and we got you out."

"Once we had you in the ambulance, you were given some Inderal to stabilize your heart and respiration, and then an injection of Valium to keep you under," McBundy said. "It worked like a charm."

"I'm surprised you got around the airline officials," Mahoney said. The ramifications of what they were telling him still hadn't sunk in.

"They were more than happy to cooperate. Our man in Tel Aviv said that you had been put on the plane persona non grata, which didn't come as much of a surprise, considering everything that had happened up to that point."

"What then?" Mahoney asked. "I was brought here? What about my son?"

Again McBundy looked away, and even Kopinski was suddenly busy with his notes. Mahoney had a feeling he wasn't going to like what was coming next.

"We held you under sedation in our Georgetown house for forty-eight hours."

"Why?"

"Just before we moved you we gave you another dose of Sus-Phrine, which put you back in a deep coma. You were dressed, some makeup was applied, and you were brought out to one of the chapels at Arlington."

"Arlington . . ." Mahoney started to say, but then he understood. "My funeral."

"A memorial service. There weren't many people there. Just a small squib in the papers."

"But John and Elizabeth and the children," Mahoney said, his voice rising. "What about them? You did tell them the truth, didn't you?"

McBundy shook his head. "John insisted that he see your body. Said otherwise he'd take his story—whatever that might have been—to Jack Anderson. I had to let him see you."

"He thinks I'm dead? Right now, he thinks I'm dead? Is that what you're saying to me?"

McBundy nodded. "He's closing down your cabin. But you have to understand, Wallace, that there was no other way for us to make this convincing. And I definitely didn't want to involve your son in this mess. I didn't think you would want that."

Mahoney stared past Kopinski and the others toward the window. It was a lovely day. John thought he was dead. He would be grieving. Liz would be comforting him. She had always been the strong one. Marge had loved her; she said that if anyone would be the making of the Mahoney line, it would be John's wife. She was a good mother with a sensible head on her shoulders, was Marge's pronouncement, her final seal of approval. And when Marge was dying, it had been Elizabeth who had been there, providing the comfort her husband could not.

He wondered now if John was remembering their past. Was bringing out his memories and dusting them off, just as he was going through the odds and ends at the cabin, dusting them off to be packed away. Whenever John got onto something, he would stick with it. He'd stay at the cabin until the job was done, no matter how painful it was.

Christ. But why? Why had McBundy engineered such a thing? Was he a part of the network after all? Was Switt even now searching for him?

Mahoney presumed that John had received the notes and had passed them on to Switt.

"I'm sorry, Wallace. We all are," McBundy said, finally breaking the silence.

Mahoney blinked and looked away from the window. "Why did you do it? Would you tell me that?"

"I was rather hoping you would tell us that."

"Don't play games with me, goddamnit! What are you after? You had Sonja Margraff trailed to my house, and you probably had someone on me when I left."

"Yes, we did," McBundy admitted. "We were there in Athens when the locker exploded, and I almost had you picked up. But when we realized you were meeting with Wasserman—the head of the Mossad—I held off for a bit."

"Then you knew it all."

"No, we didn't. We lost you in Athens, and the next I heard, you had shown up in Tel Aviv. From there we tried to keep up with you, but you kept dropping out of sight, and we couldn't make any sense of it, other than that you were free-lancing for Wasserman."

"Still doesn't answer my question," Mahoney said, watching McBundy's eyes.

"You were up to something for the Israelis, we knew at

least that much, although we had no idea what it might be. But I was just going to have to wait until you came home to do anything about it. But then two things happened to change my mind. Actually three things."

Mahoney waited. Kopinski and the others were watching him, waiting, he supposed, for a reaction. He gave them nothing.

"The first was your possible involvement with Arlemont's death in Paris."

"Which told you what?"

"Which told me that whatever it was you had been working on involved more than just the Israelis. The French secret service had something to do with it." McBundy was suddenly sweating, and he took out a handkerchief and wiped his brow. "The second trouble spot in my mind was when you disappeared from your hotel in Washington the day after I had spoken with you. Jensen tried to track you down."

Jensen was a fat man with a baby face. He seemed troubled now. "The people at the Marriott said you personally did not check out. The next day someone was sent for your bags, and your bill was paid. But no one saw you leave."

"Did you get an ID on whoever it was who picked up my things?" Mahoney asked.

"A description, but no ID. It turned out to be a dead end. One of many. Thought you might be able to help on the score, sir."

"And the third thing?" Mahoney asked, ignoring the question and turning back to McBundy.

"At that point I had decided to pull you in, no matter what you said. But the French were looking for you, and the Israelis had been in close contact with you for some time, so I didn't want to upset the applecart. But when you suddenly surfaced again in Tel Aviv, we decided to get you out immediately."

"But why the extreme measures?"

"That was a last-minute decision on my part. It was one of the scenarios from the beginning, but until the last moment I never seriously considered it," McBundy said. Suddenly there was a tension in the room that hadn't been there before. "Up to that point I had kept an absolute lid on the entire thing. You were breaking the law, as you damn well know. By rights you should have been arrested and prosecuted, but I wanted to see what you had come up with." He looked at Kopinski. "Stan alerted me to the problem initially. It was something he had been working on for months."

"Within the Agency?" Mahoney asked, almost certain now what McBundy was going to say.

McBundy nodded. "But first I have to ask you what Wasserman hired you to do."

"Ferret out a mole in his service," Mahoney said. There was no use lying about that part now.

"Chaim Malecki?" McBundy asked. He was sweating much harder now.

Mahoney nodded. "He was passing secrets to Per Larsen, with ININ, and to Arlemont with the SDECE."

"That's it, then," McBundy said, glancing again at Kopinski. When he turned back, his jaws were tight. "There is a mole within the Company as well. Stan has suspected it for some time now, and he's been making quiet checks on records and on data access and usage."

Mahoney knew that there was a traitor in the CIA. And everything he had learned until now had pointed to McBundy as the one. But now he wasn't so sure. Either McBundy was innocent, or he had set this entire thing up—Mahoney's fake death, his funeral, and bringing him here—for some ulterior reason. What reason?

"And?" Mahoney asked. He didn't think it was McBundy, and he was glad that his earlier suspicions were proving groundless. He and McBundy had been friends for years.

"We began to realize what it was you might be doing for the Israelis, and when Stan went looking for your case-history files, he discovered that they had been tampered with."

"How?"

"Dates changed, cross-references misplaced, indexes rerouted, a host of things. With a light touch. Very professional. Very knowledgeable."

"It appeared that whoever was doing the number on your files was setting you up for a fall," Kopinski said. "The next time Aronson and his bunch from the Hill came over for an intelligence audit, you would have been implicated in known leaks along a dozen fronts."

"That's why you engineered my death?"

"With you evidently out of the way, we would have a little time to work all this out."

"Then no one else in the Agency knows that I'm alive?"

Mahoney asked, a new respect for McBundy growing.

"Just us here in this room, along with Sampson who's standing in for me at my house, and Dr. Lewis who helped with the medical end."

Mahoney took another drink of the very good whiskey, then reached out for the bottle and poured himself another stiff shot. "You're hoping that I'll tell you what connection back to the Company I came up with."

McBundy sat forward expectantly.

If not McBundy, then who, Mahoney wondered, trying to make some sense of it, trying to put all the pieces into a recognizable order. Who had had the most access to his files and to him personally?

There was only one answer other than McBundy, of course, but the implications were too frightening.

"I want John and his wife and the children picked up and brought here. Immediately."

"We can't do that," McBundy said.

"You must. John is in danger at this moment."

"What are you talking about?"

"He knows everything. When I was in Paris I wrote it all down—everything—and sent the notes to John. He's received them by now."

McBundy turned white. "What do you mean by 'everything'?"

"I'll tell it to you, Bob, but you have to get John away from that cabin."

"Presuming he received your notes, he wouldn't have told anyone else, would he . . . ?" McBundy let it trail off. "But of course you would have included instructions on what to do with the material should anything happen to you."

Mahoney nodded.

"Who?"

"Switt."

"Who the hell did you think the mole in the Agency was?" McBundy shouted.

"You," Mahoney said softly.

A silence fell over the room as the meaning of what Mahoney had just told them sunk in.

"Oh, my God," Kopinski said. They all turned to him. "Switt is gone."

"Gone?" McBundy asked, his voice barely audible.

"Compassionate leave. He was broken up by Wallace's death. He wanted a few days off. I tried to telephone him yesterday, but there was no answer at his apartment."

"He had access to your records," McBundy said, as if he was trying to convince himself.

"I talked with him when I was in Washington. He dropped me off at my motel."

McBundy was shaking his head in amazement. "Would John have read the material?"

"He may have," Mahoney said, a sickness growing in his heart.

"I'll go, sir," Jensen said, getting ponderously to his feet. "I can be down to La Guardia within an hour or so, and out to Minnesota by early evening."

"Switt has a long head start," Kopinski said sadly. "Perhaps we should telephone the cabin."

"No," Mahoney ordered. "If John has read my notes, he'll be very jumpy. He won't trust anyone but Switt. If you telephone him, he might run."

"I don't want him on the loose..." McBundy started to say, but he stopped for lack of an alternative.

"What about Switt, then? Shouldn't we be doing something to find him?" Kopinski asked.

"He either went to the cabin, or he's gone to the network now," Mahoney said. Then he looked up at Jensen standing there. "Cover yourself, Larry."

"Switt is good, but I know his methodology."

"There are more than just Switt. There are others."

"Soon as I get them out safe and sound, I'll call here."

"Just cover yourself."

"Yes, sir," Jensen said, and left the room.

For several moments no one said anything. Mahoney got to his feet. He suddenly needed some fresh air.

"Let's go for a walk, Bob," he said.

McBundy got up. "I'm sorry, Wallace, but none of us had any way of knowing."

"I understand," Mahoney said.

They went down the hall and out the back door, where they headed down one of the bridle paths that crisscrossed the entire estate. Within a couple of minutes they were out of sight of the house. The day was warm, the trees in full leaf, the underbrush thick and green. Occasional patches of wildflowers adorned the path.

"When Switt came to me and said that you were talking with the Israelis, I was angry," McBundy began.

"So was Switt. He called me a ruthless son of a bitch."

"Ha," McBundy said, the word almost a bark. "Dedicated. Ornery, perhaps, and certainly stubborn, but not ruthless. That's without compassion, and you've never been short of that."

They walked awhile longer in silence, listening to the birds and enjoying the fresh air. Both of them knew that what they were doing at this moment was nothing more than a breather before the main round. McBundy knew there was much more, although he had no way of knowing at that time just how much Mahoney had to tell. And Mahoney was at once frightened for his son, yet girding himself for his head-to-head confrontation with Henrys and the network.

"You never had any children, did you, Bob?"

"No."

"Do you miss not having any?"

McBundy smiled. "It's hard to miss something you've never had, Wallace. But yes and no. Sometimes at night, when JoAnn and I do most of our talking, we think it would be grand to have had children. Perpetuating the line and all that. But then at other times we're definitely glad we didn't."

"Like now?"

McBundy looked at him. "Like now. And like when Michael was killed."

"There were other pains too," Mahoney said, remembering. "Broken arms, pneumonia. The usual run."

"Maybe that's why we never had any. Neither of us does well with pain. At least not of that variety." They stopped. "How in heaven's name you and Marge ever dealt with it was always a source of amazement to us."

"It was almost always Marge," Mahoney said. "She was the strong one."

They began walking again. "I almost had you arrested in Washington—when we met at the airport."

"I thought that may have been crossing your mind. What held you back?"

"Your eyes."

Mahoney looked at him but said nothing. Not until the last

few years had he ever been truly conscious of his own physical appearance. But when his hair had turned white—seemingly overnight—and when he had begun to develop a paunch, when bags appeared under his eyes, and the skin began to hang slack on his neck and on his forearms just below the elbows, then he began to understand just what kind of an appearance he presented to others. From that time on, he had become much better able to do his job. At times he was able to blend in. An anonymous figure in a crowd. A stooped old man. Tired. Slow. No threat. At other times he was able to assume other roles. Aging but distinguished banker—his silver hair a definite asset. Diplomat. Businessman. Even retired general. Yet he had never thought about his eyes.

"It was the look in your eyes," McBundy continued. "I'd seen it before. As a matter of fact the look has become a legend since you left. The young ones, just out of school, try to affect that look of determination. Used to be Bogart was king, and we damned near had to issue a directive that no one was to wear a trench coat. Nowadays, it's 'the look.'"

"I should be flattered," Mahoney said, and he wondered if his grandchildren had enjoyed the lake the last few days. He hoped John and Elizabeth hadn't brought them to the funeral.

"Yes, you should," McBundy said. "Do you want to talk about it now? I believe you said something about a network?"

Mahoney said nothing.

"Dr. Lewis is out, of course. No use involving him any further that I can see. Which leaves myself, Greene and Sampson, Jensen and Kopinski."

Still Mahoney held his silence.

"The frontline troops, Wallace. But they . . . we have to know the entire story. You're going to have to trust us. We'll do whatever you want, but first we have to know the entire story."

"I don't have all the pieces."

"Then give us what you do have, for God's sake. We're going to play ball with you—"

"No, you're not, Bob," Mahoney said, stopping to face the man. "What you are going to do is listen to whatever I have to say, and then there'll be a decision. Either I'm crazy or I'm sane. Either it's something worth pursuing, or it's not. Either it's worth sneaking around back alleys behind the DCI's back, or it's not." Mahoney shook his head.

Almost from the beginning, when he was working with the

OSS behind German lines near the end of the war, Mahoney
had understood that there was no such thing as altruism in the
intelligence community. Methods and means for a goal. Troops
and equipment for objectives. Budget lines and currencies for
cost-effectiveness. The hell with the human factor except where
it was significant to the effort.

He was just as guilty of that kind of tunnel vision as everyone
else. Even now he was playing McBundy like a fish. Leading
him on, teasing him with bits and pieces, so that when it came
time for him to swallow the hook, he'd do it with a passion.

Overriding all of that, in his mind, was the gnawing fear
that Switt had done something to John. It made it almost impossible for him to think straight.

"After lunch," he finally said. "But Greene and Kopinski
will have to be in on it as well."

"Naturally," McBundy replied, obviously relieved.

"No lies, no half-truths. Everything will be out in the open
between us."

"I'm not a Carlisle."

Mahoney clapped him on the shoulder, remembering his
many confrontations with the Agency's chief of station in Moscow. The man had been the most ruthless, unfeeling, self-
serving son of a bitch the Company had ever known. No one
liked him. "Sure you are, Bob. We all are, at least a bit."

Chapter 5

AFTER LUNCH KOPINSKI brought a small suitcase into the parlor and set it atop the conference table. Greene brought in the coffee and a bottle of cognac, and McBundy distributed yellow legal pads and pencils around.

Mahoney had gone upstairs to splash some water on his face. When he came back down he stopped just within the doorway and shook his head. Kopinski had taken a small tape recorder out of the suitcase and laid aside a half-dozen cassettes.

"This is not going to be taped," he said.

McBundy looked up. "Come on, Wallace, be reasonable."

"No tape. You can make notes, but that's it."

"That sounds a bit ominous."

"It is."

McBundy glanced at the tape recorder. "We're dealing with a deep plant in our Agency—"

"Reason enough to keep this quiet, Bob," Mahoney cut him

off. "You know better than I what a stink would arise if this came out."

"We are accountable for our actions," McBundy said, somewhat indignantly.

"That's right. And once this is over with, I'll go over the entire thing again for the record, if you want."

McBundy puffed up. "Goddamnit, Wallace, you keep talking about networks and dark secrets. Christ, isn't it enough that we have a mole in our own service? I mean, it's all well and good that you helped the Israelis with their problem. How about helping your own service?"

"It goes deeper than that. Much deeper," Mahoney said. He hadn't moved from his spot just within the doorway.

Kopinski stood with a tape cassette in his right hand, his left on the recorder, looking from Mahoney to McBundy and back.

McBundy was scowling. "I'll hold you to your promise that you'll tell it again," he growled.

Mahoney nodded.

"Put it away, Stan, but keep your ears open."

Kopinski repacked the recorder and spare cassettes into the suitcase, and set it down on the floor beneath the window as Mahoney took up his earlier position at the end of the table. He poured himself some coffee and added a dollop of the cognac, then lit a cigar from the box McBundy had brought him.

A dozen different thoughts and impressions crowded his brain as he tried to sort the story into some easily told, and therefore easily understood, order.

"My involvement with this thing started two years ago," he said after a moment.

A startled expression crossed McBundy's face. "Two years ago? August?"

Mahoney nodded. "I was content in those days, Bob. I don't think Marge and I were ever as happy as we were all that spring and summer."

It had been a lovely summer. The weather had been grand. Marge was content, especially after John, Elizabeth, and the children had come out for two weeks. He spent many of his mornings fishing, and in the afternoon he and Marge would lie on the screened-in porch, and read or talk or sometimes nap. On weekends they often went into Duluth to see a movie and go out to dinner.

They had been like little children then, discovering the world and each other anew. Sitting here now, Mahoney wondered why he had ever given it up.

But when the two legmen from the Company had come for him, come asking for help, it was a foregone conclusion that he would respond.

"She was a prize, Wallace," McBundy said. "In a season when we desperately needed prizes. We didn't want to screw it up for lack of knowledge. Hell, you knew the Komitet's organizational chart and methodology better than anyone else in the Company. We thought you'd give us the edge."

Jada Natasha Yatsyna was her name, the syllables even now soft and round in Mahoney's mind. She had been working as the KGB *rezident* in Beirut when she made her initial contact. She wanted out as fast as it could be arranged, in exchange for complete cooperation.

McBundy had said later that for an intense two weeks while the operation was being set up, everyone at Langley had sat on pins and needles, wondering when and how it would all blow up in their faces.

But it hadn't. A nuclear sub had been sent into the Mediterranean, and she was picked up north of the city.

"She was a lovely lady," Mahoney said softly, remembering clearly the feelings he had had for her. Feelings that he had never spoken about with Marge and for which he still felt a small pang of guilt.

"That's ancient history," McBundy said. "What did she have to do with it? You knew we tracked her murderers back to the Soviet embassy in Mexico City."

"No, I didn't."

"We couldn't do a thing about it. You can understand that."

"Were they actually seen entering the embassy?"

"I don't know. I would assume so. Where else would they have been going, if not the embassy?"

"She came over for two reasons," Mahoney said as if he hadn't heard McBundy. "The first was that she wanted to see where Alek was killed."

"White Sands Missile Range."

"Trinity," Mahoney said more specifically.

Jada and Alek Badim had been sent to the States sometime in early 1943 to assassinate Dr. J. Robert Oppenheimer, Jr., who was the chief scientist and guiding spirit on the Manhattan District Atomic Bomb Project, and General Leslie Groves, who headed the logistics side.

But they had been discovered, and Badim was nearly killed by Michael Lovelace, a former enlisted man in G-2 with a talent for detective work.

After that near miss, Jada and Alek had gone to the East Coast, where they took up the lives of deep-cover agents under the control of a GRU officer back in Moscow. Although the project was well within the purview of the NKVD, the Soviet Military Intelligence service had been given the job.

Their orders had been changed. It had been the GRU's intention to slow the atomic bomb project by killing its two organizers. But new information coming from Klaus Fuchs and other traitors on the project suggested that sabotage of the first test would be a better alternative.

If the first test had been a failure, according to Jada, then an invasion of the Japanese islands would have been likely, with the Soviet Union participating. In the end, Japan would have become another Germany, divided, with the Soviet presence strongly in place in the Far East.

And they had almost succeeded in that plan as well. Badim had actually made his way across the desert and onto the site, but he had been killed when the bomb went off.

Jada had been close enough to be dusted with fallout, but she managed, nevertheless, to make her way out of the United States and back to the Soviet Union, where she was given a job with the forerunner of the KGB, finally rising in rank to *rezident,* the equivalent of chief of station, in Beirut.

"She wanted to come back to see where Alek Badim, the only man she had ever loved, was killed," Mahoney said.

His cigar had burned down, and his coffee was cold, but he ignored them for the moment.

"That was the first reason she defected. What was the second?" Kopinski asked. McBundy didn't seem interested.

"She wanted to see Michael Lovelace, who was living in San Antonio, Texas."

"We all know that," McBundy argued. "But why? Was it revenge?"

Mahoney shook his head. "Not revenge," he said. "She had had plenty of time to think about what had happened during the war, and she managed to pry loose some information from the Komitet without raising too much of a fuss, but she needed more."

"From Lovelace?"

Mahoney sat forward. "It was Jada's belief that there may have been collusion at high levels between our government and the Soviets over the atomic bomb project."

McBundy's eyes opened wide, and Mahoney could see a small blood vessel throbbing at his temples. His face turned red, and for a moment Mahoney thought the man was going to have a stroke. But then he laughed, the sound totally devoid of humor.

"Collusion. Really, Wallace. What a cock-and-bull story. And you believed it?"

"Not at first. Not then, at least," Mahoney said unperturbed. "But she did draw some interesting little pictures for me. Here's a for instance: We were freely sharing our research information with the British, and yet after the war it was the Soviets who came up with the atomic bomb first. Another for instance: There were more than four hundred Soviet spies operating in this country in the forties. Not a single one of their major operatives was caught until after the war. And this: We had the men and materiel in place in Germany, so why didn't we continue east? Or better yet, why was Patton's drive stopped early, allowing the Soviets to capture Berlin?"

"This has all been hashed out in the history books. I've read them all. None of it points to so-called collusion," McBundy said. "But just for the sake of argument, let's suppose there was an exchange of information. From whom to whom? Roosevelt to Stalin?"

"At a much lower level," Mahoney said. "Probably within the OSS. Perhaps within the War Department."

"Okay, let's assume there was this exchange of information, and the Russians were getting our secrets from us, and we weren't actively seeking Soviet agents. Why were Badim and Jada sent here to kill Oppenheimer and Groves, and then later attempt to sabotage the bomb? Answer me that."

Mahoney remembered exactly how it had been in San Antonio that warm evening. He and Jada sat in lawn chairs across from Lovelace. Three old people who might have been contentedly reminiscing about their youth. They had spoken about the forties and Lovelace's work for General Groves. He had seemed genuinely pleased to finally meet Jada. He knew that she had come for information, not revenge.

"You want to know why Hoover had a bug up his ass and wouldn't cooperate," he had said. "I've been waiting for someone to show up. I knew someone would come knocking at my door sooner or later."

Jada was sitting on the edge of her chair, her eyes bright.

"Your little operation was nothing more than a double cross..." he had started to say, but he never completed the sentence.

"That's when they killed him," Mahoney said. "His last words were that their little operation was a double cross."

"And that meant something to you?" McBundy asked, unimpressed.

"Why did they kill him and Jada?"

"Come on, Wallace, you can do better than that. Comrade Yatsyna was a high-ranking KGB officer who defected. I don't know how they tracked you down to San Antonio, but they did, and they killed her. It's standard operating procedure. Lovelace just happened to be in the way. A *mokrie dela*—a wet operation. Blood will be shed by all traitors."

"What was Lovelace trying to tell us then?" Mahoney asked. He had known what McBundy's reaction would be, yet he wanted to hear it all. He wanted the man to expend all of his arguments, one at a time, as they came up, so that later he would not be able to come back on them.

"God only knows. When we got you back up from San Antonio, I personally looked into the affair. We managed to trace the men who killed him and Jada back to Mexico City, as I've already said, and I dipped into the old files on Lovelace. Frankly I'm surprised that Groves hired him in the first place. They had a term for his type in those days. Fuck-ups. Lovelace was a fuck-up."

"So you dropped it."

"We sat back and licked our wounds," McBundy said. "There wasn't much else to do."

Mahoney looked past McBundy out the windows again, his worry for his son, daughter-in-law, and grandchildren rising to

the front of his mind. He felt so goddamned helpless sitting
here like this. And yet he knew that unless he convinced
McBundy, the operation would probably end right here. He
could no longer do it on his own. He needed backup. Legmen.
Passports and other papers. Money, transportation, credibility.
In effect, a license to operate.

To do what? He suddenly wondered. A head-to-head confrontation with Henrys? Sooner or later Henrys and his people
would manage to kill him. Yet Mahoney shared the same kind
of dogged determination that drove McBundy. They were both
men who, once they had set out on an operation, could never
let it go.

Then Marge had developed her cancer, and there was a grim
four months when he watched her die, and afterward he had
almost died himself. For months he went through all the classic
symptoms of deep bereavement. For a time he could not eat,
and he had lost forty pounds. He could not sleep, and he moved
through the cabin like a zombie. During a short period he
developed an intense hatred for everyone he had ever come in
contact with, the people in the Company, and even his own
son. They were alive. Marge was dead. It was not fair.

Sitting here now, thinking about that brief but intensely
emotional period of his life, Mahoney was struck with the
sudden silly notion that he would never die: that this was all
a vast joke; that he would continue forever, living his life in
the shadows.

The others sitting down the table from Mahoney had a fair
idea that he was thinking about Marge, because of the chro-
nology of his story, and they were embarrassed for him. But
McBundy was anxious, and he wanted to continue.

"Can we get you another drink, some more coffee?"

"No thanks," Mahoney said, blinking, then sitting back. He
was getting old, he thought. Tiring easily now.

"It was a strange time for me, Bob. I think you can pretty
well guess that much," Mahoney continued his narrative.

"You would have pursued the Lovelace thing further,
if . . . ah . . . Marge hadn't taken ill?"

"Almost certainly."

"But it was a dead end, Wallace. Too much time had passed.
And I still don't see what connection you're drawing between
what the Russians were doing here in the forties, to a traitor

in the Mossad, and possibly to Switt in our own service."

"I didn't draw the connection at the time. That came much later, and in fact was drawn for me."

"I don't understand."

"You will," Mahoney said. "Suffice it to say that if the Israeli woman, Sonja Margraff, had come a few months earlier, I would never have agreed to what she asked. As it was, I really don't know why I flew to Athens."

"But fly you did," McBundy said, scowling now. "You were the receiving officer for the spotter at Tel Aviv who had flagged Sonja coming our way. Why didn't you stop her?"

"We wanted to know what the hell she was doing. Here's a Mossad officer traveling under a civilian passport. And then, when she was obviously heading out to see you, we became doubly interested."

"And concerned as well, I might add," Greene said.

The instructions for Mahoney's meeting with Wasserman were waiting for him in a locker at Athens's Ellinikó Airport. But Mahoney had been cautious and had sent a young Greek boy to fetch the things. The locker exploded, killing the boy. Mahoney went immediately into town and checked openly into his hotel, almost willing someone to make a try on him.

Wasserman found him later that night. He was just as confused and worried about the explosion as Mahoney, but he still requested Mahoney's help in ferreting out the mole in the Mossad.

"It turned out to be Chaim Malecki, Sonja's lover, and a trusted, highly respected Israeli citizen," Mahoney said.

"How did you uncover him?" McBundy asked. "You mentioned Larsen with ININ and then Arlemont in Paris. What did they have to do with it all?"

"Everything," Mahoney said. "But it was really strange in Israel. They wanted me to help them, and yet they resented the presence of an outsider. They wanted to know who their traitor was, and yet they were deathly afraid to find out."

"The Israel Beer mess did that to them," Kopinski said. "Ever since then, they've been gun-shy when it comes to that sort of thing."

"Understandably so," McBundy agreed. "But how did you turn Malecki?"

"He'd been on my list of suspects almost from the beginning. But I knew that as long as I remained on the scene, he, or whoever the mole was, would remain quiet. Unless something of such vast importance came up they couldn't help but go after it."

"And you provided it for them?"

Mahoney nodded. "I called it Operation Wrath. Cover letters, assessments, action lines, implementation timetables, budget work-ups—the works. All of it suggesting preemptive nuclear strikes on the capital cities of Syria, Iran, Iraq, and Jordan."

"Good God," McBundy said after a hesitation. "And Wasserman went along with such a thing?"

"Reluctantly. The documents were planted in the operations room at Lod Airport, where we watched Malecki pick them up and leave."

"You followed him?"

"To Brussels, where Per Larsen picked them up."

"NATO," McBundy said. "But why was Malecki passing Israeli documents to NATO? That doesn't make much sense to me."

"Nor to me at the time," Mahoney said. "I returned to Tel Aviv, where I went through Malecki's case-history files one by one."

"Looking for?"

"Connections. And I came up with them. Per Larsen with NATO's ININ and Armand Arlemont with the SDECE, among others."

McBundy had picked up his coffee cup and started to raise it to his lips when his hand stopped. "Me?" he asked.

Mahoney nodded. "Malecki attended parties wherever he went. Making contacts. Ostensibly looking for money for a number of projects back home. Your name showed up on the guest lists of several parties Malecki had attended in Washington."

McBundy nodded. "I knew of the man, but didn't know him personally," he said. But then another thought struck him and he put his cup down. "You started after the contacts then. First Arlemont in Paris. Did you kill him?"

"No. When I confronted him with what I knew, he pulled out a gun, then telephoned someone whom he called Mongoose and told him I was there. After the call, we struggled, and when he fell he apparently broke his neck."

McBundy was following that closely. "Then you came to Washington after me."

Mahoney smiled. "I wasn't quite sure about you. We've been friends for too long. But I did come to Washington to see if I could dislodge you."

"Then where did you disappear to?"

"I was drugged and taken away from my hotel," Mahoney said. "When I woke up I was in Geneva, at the summer home of McNiel Henrys of Britain's Secret Intelligence Service."

"The British are involved in this as well?"

"Henrys runs the network, as far as I can tell," Mahoney said.

"You mentioned a network earlier," Kopinski said. "Besides Malecki with the Israelis, Arlemont with the SDECE, Larsen with ININ, presumably Switt with us, and finally this Henrys person with SIS, are there others?"

"The West Germans, the Italians, the Soviets, and the Chinese Communists at least."

"Traitors in each service?" Kopinski asked, but Mahoney was watching McBundy. He was not buying this at all.

"That's right," Mahoney said. "With Henrys as a central clearing agent."

"Fantasy," McBundy said softly. "Double agents running around the world, exchanging their dark little secrets. Killing each other . . . you failed to mention that part, you know."

"Not fantasy, Bob," Mahoney said. "I met with Henrys. He told me everything. Told me they had known my Operation Wrath documents were probably fake. There *was* a conduit there. From Malecki to Larsen, and from Larsen to Henrys. In addition, when I confronted Arlemont with Malecki's name, he knew it. Not fantasy."

"So there is an international network of moles exchanging information. Why? What purpose does this little group serve?"

"I don't know," Mahoney admitted. "According to Henrys, they're out to make sure we don't muddle ourselves into an all-out nuclear war."

"Noble," McBundy said dryly. "But you don't believe it."

"I believed that part," Mahoney said thoughtfully. "But there's a lot more. There's something else there. An undercurrent . . . evil, if you will."

"Not so altruistic."

"Just the opposite."

"Where do their operational funds come from?" McBundy asked, bringing up a point that had bothered Mahoney. "Surely not out of their own pockets. Running operatives around the world is expensive."

"I don't know who funds them, or how they recruit new members, or where they come up with their frontline troops. There's a lot yet I don't know, Bob. But I'll find out. Just as I'll find out what their real purpose is."

"You're going to have to do better than that to convince me," McBundy said after a long silence.

"We've been together for a long time, Bob, and in all that while, have you ever known me to pull a stunt?"

"You suspected me as one of your moles," McBundy said sharply. He thumped his fist on the tabletop. "Come on, Wallace, for Christ's sake, you can't sit there and tell me a bullshit story like that and expect me to swallow it."

Mahoney remained silent as he stared at McBundy's mottled complexion. A certain amount of his reluctance was probably due in part to his pique at being included in the list of suspects. But a larger part, Mahoney suspected, was due to the fantastic nature of the story. Fantasy. It almost seemed so to Mahoney, and he had been there.

"Let me back up a bit, Bob," Mahoney said finally.

"Indeed," McBundy said indignantly.

"The Israelis had constructed a satellite receiving station near the town of Al Qaryūt. Supposedly a weather satellite."

"*Supposedly* a weather satellite?" McBundy asked, his right eyebrow rising again. "The ComSat project?"

"That's the one, only the satellite wasn't gathering weather data. It was a spy satellite. Infrared, broad-band electronic emissions and high-resolution photography. State of the art."

"There were rumors," Kopinski said.

"It was a closely guarded secret, from what I could gather."

"We would never have allowed that technology into the Mideast," McBundy said.

"The receiving station was destroyed. Jordanian troops from a base at Ataruz, just across the Dead Sea, made a strike on the station."

"If everyone believed it was just another weather satellite station, why the strike?"

"That's just what Wasserman asked himself. Because of that raid, and other happenings over the past few years, he concluded they had a mole highly placed within the service. I was given a list of every single person who knew what Al Qaryūt really was."

McBundy digested that for a long moment. "Hardly strengthens your case, Wallace. Malecki obviously sold out to the Jordanians as well."

"General David Ben Abel, the head of Aman, sent some of his people across to Ataruz." Aman, as they both knew, was charged with collecting purely military intelligence; it nevertheless worked closely with the Mossad. "He wanted to capture the base commander, bring him back, and find out who ordered the raid."

"And?"

"He was assassinated in his office. And everyone on the base at Ataruz, including his men, was killed. Soman. An American-made nerve gas."

"I'm well aware of what Soman is, and who manufactures it." McBundy was still annoyed. "Chaim Malecki could not have had access to it."

"That's right," Mahoney said tiredly. "And even if he had, who made the on-site delivery? And why? Malecki provided the intelligence first about Al Qaryūt, and then about Ataruz. But where did the muscle come from?"

They were all staring at him. Greene's mouth hung half open. And McBundy's right eyelid was twitching.

In Geneva, Henrys had intimated that the network had been operating since 1943 as a direct result of work on the atomic bomb.

"You brought me back," he said to McBundy. "What did you want from me?"

"Help in ferreting out *our* mole."

"And now will you go along with me? Will you help?"

"Do what?"

"Get to Henrys. To the network. Find out who brought it into existence, who funds it, who or what has held it together all these years, and what it's really up to."

McBundy got up and went to the window where he stared outside, his back to Mahoney. "As far as anyone is concerned, you're dead, Wallace. You could walk out of this house and with care you could live the remainder of your life safely in anonymity."

"Tempting," Mahoney said.

McBundy turned back. "But not tempting enough to leave this alone?"

"If you've believed what I've told you, Bob, you can't ask me that."

"What the hell am I supposed to believe? Some cock-and-bull story about spy networks involving half the United Nations?"

"Let me go out and get the information for you."

"You need a seal of approval? A license?"

Mahoney nodded.

"You'd go after Henrys? And the others in the network?"

"Not directly. Not immediately. I need more information first. I have a few ideas."

"I'll bet you do, Wallace. I'll bet you do," McBundy said, the beginnings of a wry smile creasing the corners of his mouth.

"I'd need several passports. Some operational funds. Things like that."

"I can set that up," Greene said. "And Stan can build him a background. We've done it before."

McBundy seemed battered. Mahoney knew that he was feeling betrayed by his own people, who evidently thought more of the story than he did.

"You'd have to accept me as control. Absolute control."

Mahoney nodded, his eyes half closed. Now that he was sure McBundy would go along with him, his thoughts had turned back to his son. Jensen was the best. But Switt had had a full day's head start. At this point, however, all he could do was wait.

Larry Jensen sat in his rented car at the end of the driveway, staring at the charred remains of Mahoney's cabin. He was on his way out after having talked with the fire marshal and his investigators, with the St. Louis County Coroner, and with an angry police detective. They were all still back there poking around the remains. The bodies of Elizabeth and the three children had already been pulled out, bagged, and brought down to Duluth for autopsies. Foul play, the detective kept shouting. The son of a bitch killed his own family and then took off. John had not been inside at the time of the explosion, which had apparently been caused by a faulty valve on the LP gas tanks outside. And now he was missing, his car gone. But where? What in Christ's name had happened here? And almost more important, how in hell would he ever be able to tell Mahoney?

Chapter 6

IT WAS EARLY Sunday morning, a few minutes after five, more than twenty-four hours after the explosion, when John Mahoney pulled off the highway into a roadside rest area a few miles north of Missoula, Montana. He had driven straight through from Minnesota, snatching a few hours' sleep at another rest area yesterday evening. Otherwise, he had pounded across the North Dakota high plains during the hot day, stopping only for gas, and once, near Minot, for a hamburger and a cup of coffee. The suitcases were still in the trunk of the car, and sometime during the early morning hours yesterday, he had stopped to clean up and change his clothes.

He felt battered now, the same sense of bewilderment and deep-set horror that settled on Larry Jensen yesterday afternoon riding with him like the weight of the world. It was impossible that Elizabeth and the children were dead. And yet he knew for a fact they were. Just as he knew for certain who had killed them, and why. What he was less certain of was why he had run. God in heaven, he had turned his back on them and run.

There were a couple of cars and a half-dozen trucks parked in the rest area lot. When John stumbled up the walk to the restrooms, one of the truckers emerged, looked twice at him, then went across to his truck.

Inside the restroom, John splashed some cold water on his face and looked at himself in the mirror. His eyes were red-rimmed and puffy now. He looked like hell.

There had been nothing else for him to do, he tried to tell himself. They had murdered his father, and then his wife and children. They would be coming for him next. Somehow McBundy had found out about the notes and arranged the explosion. They would protect their network at all costs. His father had said as much in his notes, and yet John had not really understood. His father had shielded them from any knowledge of his work, so espionage remained the stuff of fiction.

He closed his eyes, and he could see the thick sheaf of notes his father had sent him. He could see the writing in his father's crabbed hand. Line after line, marching down the pages; he could see the notes, and he could read them now in his mind. A photographic memory, the kids had called it when he was in school. Total recall was the psychological term. He could forget if he wanted to. But he could remember, chapter and verse, anything at all.

He turned away from the sink, relieved himself at one of the urinals, and returned to his car. The morning was crisp and clear, and before John started the engine, he rolled down his window and lit a cigarette.

"Just hang on a little longer," Switt had told him on the telephone. "I promise you that all this will be worked out."

McBundy had probably murdered Switt as well, which left no one.

"Don't talk to anyone about this. It'd be too dangerous."

Too dangerous. John repeated Switt's final warning.

He leaned forward, resting his forehead on the steering wheel, the tears coming again to his eyes. At times the rage had built up inside of him so badly that he could barely control the car. But at other times, like now, the tears streamed down his cheeks, grief consuming him. He saw Elizabeth and the children at the breakfast table. They were talking to him, asking him something, but as hard as he tried he could not make out their words. They seemed so far away. He wanted to reach out for them, but he could not.

"Say, buddy, are you okay?" someone at his shoulder asked.

John jerked up to look into the concerned face of the trucker he had passed coming out of the restroom.

"Are you all right?" the trucker asked again. He was wearing a cowboy hat and a western-style denim shirt.

John nodded. "A little tired, I guess."

"Well, you look like hell. Maybe you should stay here for a couple of hours and get some rest. Got far to go?"

"No. Not too far," John mumbled.

The trucker stared at him for several seconds. "Missoula is only about thirty miles south. But maybe you should get out and walk around for a bit. Clear your head."

"Thanks. I'll be all right."

Missoula was only thirty miles away. That was amazing. John had no conscious idea where he was. He knew that he had driven west. But until this moment he hadn't realized how far he had come. Missoula. Why? he started to ask himself. But then he recognized perfectly well why he had come here. And he was beginning to understand what he was going to have to do afterward.

It took a little more than half an hour to drive the distance, and the sky to the east was just beginning to lighten when he reached the outskirts of Missoula. Instead of continuing into the city, he headed back east to Greenough Park, where he turned off the highway and followed a secondary road a couple of miles further into the countryside, finally pulling onto a narrow blacktopped road through a stretch of thick woods.

A heavy iron gate across the road was padlocked for the night, the headlights from his car flashing off the St. Martin's Cemetery sign just before he pulled up and shut off the engine.

He got out of the car, softly closed the door, and walked up to the gate.

It was quiet here, the morning air quite cold. On the other side of the gate, the road wound its way up the hill past the small maintenance shed, beyond which were several brick buildings.

A small service entrance to the right of the roadway gate stood slightly ajar. John slipped inside and hurried up the road past the buildings, his heart beginning to accelerate.

He had not actually made a decision, but somewhere on the long drive his thoughts—no, his emotions—had coalesced, and now he felt himself propelled along an inevitable path. The network could not be left unchallenged: that would be a betrayal of his father's whole life, would render his death meaningless. To John that idea seemed more abstract than the burning desire for revenge for Elizabeth and the children that now tore at him.

No, the network could not be left unchallenged. But he didn't know how he would be able to do anything to them. He was an analytical chemist, not an operative. He needed strength. It was why he had come here. Unknowingly he had thought of this place as a refuge.

A hundred yards further up the hill John left the road and followed one of the footpaths that meandered through the cemetery. It seemed that he had spent a lot of time here over the past few years. Too much time. The place was nearly as familiar to him as his own backyard.

At the top of the hill, the gravestones stood like soldiers in rank and file. John slowed down as he approached a grouping of three of them, the tears coming again to his eyes.

His father's grave was in the center, his mother's to the left, and his brother's to the right. They were here. He could almost feel their presence in the predawn air. He could feel his mother's touch on his cheek, and hear his brother calling him. But mostly he felt his father.

"Father." The word choked at the back of his throat.

The hill was just as he remembered it, just as he saw it in his dreams, stretching away to the mountains and the forests, which were only dull, hulking shapes this early in the morning. The wind was the same too, a light breeze, but cold and mournful.

It was almost impossible to believe that Elizabeth and the children were dead. Too catastrophic for his mind to accept such a thing. And yet standing here in front of his parents' and brother's graves, he could believe it. For the first time since he had stumbled away from the cabin, he could honestly feel the fact throughout his body, only here in the cemetery, death seemed . . . almost natural. He was the intruder here. The anomaly was that he was alive, while all around him was death.

Suddenly he felt a crushing sense of loneliness, so palpable here on the hill that he had to step back a pace and turn away.

It was then that he saw a brief flash of light through the trees down the hill near the front gate. When he tried to focus on it, however, it disappeared.

The caretaker, possibly. The thought crystalized in his mind. Or the police may have discovered his car. Or worse yet, someone from the network. Either way, it meant danger.

He glanced back at his father's gravestone. Then, careful to make no noise, he started down the path toward the black-topped road, stopping every few yards to listen for sounds from below. But there was nothing.

The eastern horizon was definitely lighter now, and the trees were beginning to take on a ghostly, early-dawn appearance that played tricks on the eyes. At first, down near the road, John was certain he had seen a movement near the maintenance shed, but then he wasn't sure he had seen anything at all.

He stopped just within the deeper shadows of a clump of trees where the path opened onto the road. He scanned the area between the brick buildings and the maintenance shed. From here he could not see his car because the road curved slightly to the right, nor could he see anything out of the ordinary.

They had killed his father, and they had murdered his wife and children. Those were inescapable facts. Once they realized he had not been in the cabin, they'd come after him. They would come here. Expecting him to run this way. It had been stupid for him to come here. And yet there had been a compelling need. Just as another, harsher, much sharper feeling began to well up inside him. They had killed everyone he loved. Brutally. Without sense. And they would pay. God . . . they would pay.

He turned and looked over his shoulder back up the hill. The sky was lightening quickly. There wasn't much time left for him to make a move. Within ten or fifteen minutes it would be too light for him to conceal his actions. Impossible then to get out of there without being seen.

Again he glanced down the road, and out of the corner of his eye he was certain he had caught a movement, a flash of white around the corner of the maintenance building. Someone was there. Waiting for him.

For just another second John hesitated. He had done what his father had asked him to. He had turned the notes over to Switt. But then, after the explosion, he had run. He had not waited for the police. He could have stayed at the cabin. He

could have explained it all to them. They would probably have
found evidence that explosives had been set under the cabin.
They would have realized that someone had murdered them,
and that it had not been an accident. And yet, would they have
believed him? Wouldn't they have immediately suspected that
he was the murderer?

He wanted Elizabeth right now. He needed her comfort, her
cool head. God, he ached.

But he had run. And if there was any evidence to be found
at the cabin, it would point to him. To him as the murderer.

He turned and, keeping low, hurried twenty yards back up
the path, then headed to the right, between the gravestones,
parallel to the blacktopped road, but in the opposite direction
from the gate and maintenance shed.

As he remembered it, the road curved around the hill, making a big loop that eventually came back to the gate. For most
of its length, then, it would be out of sight of the maintenance
shed.

About a hundred yards further, John angled down toward
the road, coming on it almost immediately, but hanging back
as he looked toward the gate. Across the road there were more
graves, but to the right, toward the gate, there were trees and,
beyond them, the tall iron fence.

It was becoming very light now. Concealment was almost
impossible. But they would be watching the road. They would
be waiting for him to come down from the path.

He dashed across the road, keeping one eye on where he
was running and the other toward the direction of the gate. He
worked his way between the gravestones, some of them very
large and ornate, to the first section of trees, where he stopped
behind a larger one to catch his breath.

If they were going to kill him here, they would probably
try to make it look like a suicide. They would say he had killed
his wife and children, run to his family's graves, and then in
remorse shot himself to death. It would wrap up the mystery
as far as the police were concerned.

Neat. No questions would be asked. A simple murder-suicide.
The network would survive. His father's death would have
been for nothing.

John's heart was hammering as he worked his way through
the broad band of trees, then across an open field to another
area of pine. From here he could see the brick buildings and

the top of the maintenance shed. He had caught just a glimpse of one man on the far side of the maintenance building, but there would be at least one other. Probably near the car, to cover whatever path John took back to the gate.

Keeping very low, he raced across the narrow open area to the rear of the nearest brick building. There was a large wooden door set in the back of it, and several windows high up. A gravel driveway connected the three brick buildings with the maintenance shed another thirty yards away.

He eased around the corner of the first building and glanced out toward the road, then dashed across to the second building. Again he peered around the corner, but still he could see no one out there. His heart was hammering. He wanted to strike back. The need was becoming almost desperate.

At the corner of the last building, he looked across the open space to the maintenance shed, on the other side of which someone was waiting for him to come down the road. From there he could just see the top of the iron gate, but he could not see his car.

Whoever was waiting for him would be armed. Ready to kill him. Capable of it. Willing. A professional.

John looked back the way he had come. He could turn around and probably make his way out of the cemetery through the back gate. But then what? Hike into town and take a plane back to Duluth? Turn himself in to the police?

He looked again at the maintenance shed, its windows beginning to reflect the morning light.

They had murdered Elizabeth and the children. They were professionals working for the network. If they missed now, they would try again. And again. Until they succeeded.

For an instant he could see the cabin exploding, he could hear the dull *whump*, he could feel the pressure wave pushing him off the dock and smell the burning wood.

Careful to make no noise on the gravel driveway, John stepped away from the protection of the last brick building and hurried across to the maintenance shed, where he looked through one of the windows.

At first he couldn't see much of anything except a few vague shapes, and on the opposite wall was another window, beyond which was the fence to the left of the gate. Whoever was out there was just beyond that window, or below it, armed and ready to kill. As before, John hesitated a moment as he tried to think this out. If he turned and walked away from this now, he could probably hide until he figured out whom to contact with his information. But if he continued, it would end up either in his death or in the death of at least one man out there. Was he capable of murder? Dear God, was he?

He ducked below the window and moved to the small service door. It was open, and with no further hesitation he slipped inside, softly closing the door behind him.

He stood just within the shed, his heart pounding, his breath catching in his throat. He waited for his eyes to adjust to the darkness.

The shed was filled with tools, including several small lawnmowers, rakes, baskets, and shovels. Hanging on the wall were a couple of hoes and one pitchfork, the tines long and rusty. He stared at the pitchfork for a few seconds, his eyes drawn to the tines, to the jagged points. It was a weapon. The only weapon in the shed. His weapon. Drawing him like a siren.

He stepped away from the door, threaded his way through the lawnmowers and other equipment, and reached up for the pitchfork. For a moment he could not bring himself to touch it. He kept seeing what it would do to a man. He kept seeing the tines red with blood. But then the cabin exploded in his brain, and with shaking hands he grabbed it. He started to turn when one of the hoes that had been hanging next to the pitchfork fell off its pegs with a clatter.

John spun around. A face appeared in the window less than five feet away from him. It was a man, with deep-set eyes under bushy eyebrows. He raised a gun to the window at the same moment John lunged forward, thrusting the heavy pitchfork with every ounce of his strength. The long, rusty tines crashed through the window, the outer ones bracketing the man's neck, the center one penetrating his throat and jutting out the back of his neck. Blood gushed from the terrible wound.

John released his grip on the handle and leaped to the door, tore it open, and raced around the corner of the shed to the man who was flopping on the ground, blood everywhere, the pitchfork sticking through his neck.

Someone was running down the road, and as John scrambled on the ground for the fallen man's gun, two shots were fired at him, smacking into the side of the maintenance shed over his head.

John had the gun in hand, and he rolled to the left as a third shot was fired. He sat up, brought the pistol up, and fired four times in rapid succession at the approaching man, who jerked each time and finally fell on the grass a few yards away.

The roar of the gun echoed in John's ears as he sat there, stupidly looking at what he had done. There had been no words, no screams, no shouts, no human communication. It had simply happened.

He scrambled backward, then got up. Christ, they had been here to kill him. They either had known he would come here, or they had followed him all the way from Minnesota. They, or someone like them, had killed his wife and children, had killed his father.

The pistol was suddenly very heavy and ugly in his hand, and he made to toss it aside but then thought better of it. His fingerprints were on it. When the police came, they'd find out who did this.

It was fully light now but strangely quiet. The birds were not singing and even the wind had died. Before long someone would be up here.

Quickly, John pulled out his handkerchief, wiped off the pistol grip, barrel, and trigger, then laid the gun beside the man by the window. He wiped the handle of the pitchfork, then bent down next to the body, careful not to get any blood on his clothes, and flipped back the man's jacket and extracted his wallet.

Inside, the man's face stared up at him from a green plastic identification card, a seal on the left, a thumbprint on the right, his name at the bottom: Stewart R. Burrows, 2458 Woodhaven Road, Bethesda, Maryland. Over the top of the photograph were the words FEDERAL BUREAU OF INVESTIGATION.

John's hand shook so badly he almost dropped the wallet. He closed it and hastily stuffed it back in the dead man's pocket, then got to his feet and looked wildly around.

The FBI. Christ, he had killed two FBI agents. But why had they come after him? Why had they come here like this? Why had they hidden in ambush?

His mind was spinning as he stumbled back to the road and made his way to the gate. A gray Chevrolet sedan with U.S. government license plates was parked next to his car, and the sight of it stopped him in his tracks for just a moment. But then he sprinted to his car, leaped inside, started the engine, and spun around back down the highway.

There was no way that the local police would connect him with the two bodies. Not at first. Not until they contacted the FBI office in Washington. By then he would be long gone.

But where? There was no place in this country where he would be safe. If they had traced him to Missoula, they certainly would trace him back to Los Angeles.

Past Greenough Park, he got onto Interstate 90 for a few miles, and then headed south on Highway 93, crossing the Clark Fork River in town, and on the south side, the Bitterroot River, where he sped up. The highway led south through Idaho and Nevada, where it connected with Interstate 15, through Las Vegas and finally down to Los Angeles.

They would probably be watching his house by now, but he was going to have to risk going there. He was going to have to get out of the country somehow, which meant he'd have to retrieve his passport and get some money.

But then what? Where could he go? And whom could he turn to with his information?

The traffic on the highway was beginning to build with the morning as John drove, careful to keep within the speed limit.

McBundy was a high-ranking officer with the CIA, and apparently he was a part of the network, which meant there was a strong possibility that the two men he had killed also worked for them. If they had sent those two after him, they would send more. And more. And more. Until they were successful. They'd never let him go.

Once again the lines of his father's handwriting marched down the pages in his mind. Line by line, he followed his father's investigation into the network that had eventually killed him. There had been a gap in time, though, from when he had mailed the notes from Paris until he was murdered aboard the El Al flight. A gap during which his father must have found out more.

But there was a lot in the notes he had sent. Names such as Chaim Malecki, Per Larsen, Armand Arlemont, McNiel Henrys. And places. Tel Aviv, Brussels, Paris. His father had been on his way to see Arlemont when he mailed the package.

There were others too: Leonardo Rubio in Italy and Walther Zwiefel in Germany among them.

As he drove, John found himself wondering who was the key to the network. McBundy? Zwiefel? Perhaps the Englishman, Henrys. Whoever it was, if he could find that out, the man could provide a conduit to the others.

McBundy was out by virtue of the fact that John's face was too well known. And the police were probably looking for him.

It would have to be Europe. Rome, he thought. Rubio. If he could somehow get to Rubio, or perhaps to Arlemont in Paris, the others would come running. The real leader or leaders would come out. If that didn't work, he'd go after them all, one by one. He would kill them as they had killed his father and his wife and his children. One by one they would fall.

As he drove, his grip tightened on the steering wheel, causing his knuckles to turn white.

One by one. They had lived by the sword, and they would die by it. They understood nothing else.

Chapter 7

THE DWELLINGS AROUND Shultz Lake were called either houses or cabins, depending upon who was doing the talking. Realtors making their pitch called them houses, while the residents knew them as cabins. Actually they were little more than built-upon fishing shacks that had been put up in the twenties and thirties, in a simpler time, when shelter, a well, an outdoor privy, and an old wooden boat with a pair of oars was plenty for a vacation.

Wallace Mahoney's cabin had been sufficient for him and Marge, made to order for the life they desired to lead. And in the very short time they had lived on the lake, the place had already built up its own patina of poignant memories for him. Memories that were tied not only to his wife, but to his youth as well.

"Stop here for a moment, would you, Larry?" Mahoney said just before they reached the narrow gravel driveway that led into the place.

Jensen had telephoned yesterday with the unbelievable news,

and although McBundy still wasn't one hundred percent convinced that Mahoney's story was not a figment of an over-
worked imagination, he had demanded that no one make any
moves, at least until they had come up with some identification
for Mahoney. A background, so that if he should be stopped
out here and questioned, he would have the answers. They had
worked through the night on it. Carefully, as McBundy explained, so that General Lycoming and his personal staff of
snoops would not be tipped off. Budget lines, materials, per-
sonnel . . . it was all snarling into an impossible mess that somehow had to be straightened out and covered up before Senator
Aronson and his crowd came over for their audit. It was a
nightmare. Meanwhile, McBundy had promised that a watch
would be put on John's house and his office at Monsanto in
Los Angeles.

"But why in God's name did they kill Elizabeth and the
children?" Mahoney asked, still numb with grief. "It doesn't
make any sense. Maybe it was simply an accident. But then,
where did John run off to?"

*He's on the run now. Frightened. Alone. There's no telling
what he'll do or where he'll go in his present state of mind.*

Mahoney had flown from New York that morning in a state
of shock, and Jensen had been waiting for him at the airport
in Duluth. On the way up to the lake they hadn't spoken more
than a few words.

Jensen pulled up at the driveway and let Mahoney out of
the car. The afternoon was lovely, the sky clear, the birds
singing. From here he could not see his cabin, but he could
smell the lingering odor of smoke, and the driveway was deeply
rutted from the passage of the heavy firetrucks and other vehicles. A crow cawed from deep in the woods somewhere
across the access road, and from farther away he suddenly
could hear a tractor starting up. There was a farm on the north
side of the lake. Marge had gone over there once a week to
buy eggs, fresh milk, and sometimes a couple of loaves of
homemade bread.

The car's engine was turning over slowly, and Mahoney
looked in at Jensen.

*They were positively identified. Elizabeth and the three chil-
dren. But Wallace's car was gone, and John's body wasn't
found.*

He felt numb again. A sense of unreality. What he had been

told was simply not true. He would walk down the driveway, and Marge would be waiting for him. She would draw him a warm bath, and while he was soaking away his troubles she would pour him a stiff shot of whiskey. Then she would sit on the edge of the tub and they would talk, just like always.

"Are you all right, Wallace?" Jensen asked with compassion. It was obvious he too was suffering.

"I just need half an hour alone. I don't want anyone coming down the driveway."

Jensen wanted to say something else. Mahoney could see it in his eyes.

"What's been our story here?"

Jensen blinked. "It was the residence of a former Company officer. I have orders to keep it sealed off until our field teams come out to sift through . . . the ashes. You may have left documents. Things like that."

"They bought it?"

"They checked with Bob, but they won't hold off for too long. I figure we have today and perhaps tomorrow before they'll begin agitating."

Mahoney closed the car door. "Stay here," he said firmly, and he started down the driveway. The very tall pine trees crowded in on both sides, their overhanging branches blocking most of the sun, trying to fill the dappled air with their clean scent over the acrid odor of smoke.

The LP tanks apparently developed a leak, Jensen had told him. The gas somehow built up under the cabin, and something set it off. But where had John been? Elizabeth's body had been found where the side bedroom had been, and the children had been asleep on the screened-in porch. But there had been no trace of John or the car. Had he driven into Duluth for some reason? Had he seen something and chased after whoever had done this thing? Or had he merely run?

The trees fell away just before the greenhouse, and Mahoney was stopped in his tracks by the awful sight. The cabin was completely gone. The roof and walls had collapsed inward, and then had burned to little more than ashes. The cabin had never had a proper foundation. It had been built on thick posts driven into the soft ground. Even the floor had burned through, so that only the charred foundation posts remained, surrounding the bottom half of the natural stone chimney.

For a long time, Mahoney could not bring himself to move

closer. Beyond the cabin, his aluminum fishing boat was still tied to the dock, and on the beach he could see where debris that had been blown into the lake from the explosion had washed ashore.

To the left, the boathouse was half collapsed and partially burned beneath a section of the front-porch roof.

Mahoney tried to convince himself that if McBundy had told John the truth, instead of going through with the sham funeral, this would not have happened. But it wouldn't wash. McBundy had done the right thing, trying to insulate John, because he had no way of knowing about the notes. No way of knowing that John had suspected him as the CIA's representative in the network.

He forced himself to continue past the greenhouse to where the back door of the cabin had been, and he looked at the debris. There was little or nothing left. To the right, the heavy kitchen range was still intact, although the cabinets around it were gone. Broken dishes and half-melted pots and pans in piles mixed with the burned wood.

Across the cabin he spotted where the fireman had pulled aside the rubble to get at the iron bed, the top of its frame blackened and bent. He stared at it for just a moment, until the vision of Elizabeth lying there, beneath the burning building that had collapsed on top of her, rose up into his mind's eye, and he had to turn away, the bile rising at the back of his throat, his stomach churning.

Tell Switt to be careful with this information, he had written to his son. But it should not have turned out this way. There should have been no real danger for his son. The notes should have gone directly to Switt—the one man Wallace foolishly trusted—and that should have been the end of it for John. Not this.

John had probably passed the notes to him just after the funeral, and then he had come out here. And Switt had probably wasted no time contacting Henrys in Geneva.

But who had ordered that John and his family be murdered? Henrys, or Switt, or someone else?

There was nothing here, Mahoney thought. He walked around the cabin and past the boathouse, and went down to the dock. He looked out across the lake. On the south shore there were a couple of fishing boats, and in the bay he could see several pontoon boats rafted together, drifting in the pleasant weather.

John had probably stood here looking out across the lake, wondering about his father, worried about McBundy and about what Switt was doing with the information he had passed on.

With his back to the remains of the cabin, Mahoney could, just for the moment, forget all that had happened here. Once again he had the strong feeling that Marge would be calling him for lunch. They would sit out on the porch, and they would talk.

He hung his head, the tears coming to his eyes. Almost more than anything else, he missed his conversations with Marge. He missed their long talks about everything from the weather to their children, from music to the books she was always trying to get him to read. But she had never nagged, she had never complained despite the often nearly impossible conditions his work with the Company had imposed on their marriage. For forty years she had been his companion as well as his lover.

It was strange, too, he mused, that at this moment his thoughts had turned back to his wife, instead of to John and Elizabeth and the children. But he suspected that Marge had always been his refuge. Whenever he was tired or hungry or frightened, he always came back to Marge, and she was always able to comfort him. God, he missed her terribly.

He looked up as a speedboat towing a waterskier raced by, the skier waving, proving that he could manage with only one hand.

Mahoney waved back, then turned and stared at the cabin. They hadn't been after Elizabeth and the children. That had been an accident. They had been after John. But who? The question kept nagging at him. Who had ordered the killing?

His son had passed the notes over to Switt. That was a certainty. Switt had probably told him not to talk to anyone about the notes and had probably asked John if he had read them.

Mahoney turned that thought over in his mind. What would John's response have been to such a question? He would have answered honestly. His father had trusted Switt above all others. Switt was a man to be honest with.

John had probably read the notes and had probably told Switt as much. Still no reason to go after him . . . *unless Switt was the traitor*. Otherwise nothing would have happened.

After John left, Switt would have telephoned Henrys for

instructions. Christ! "John Mahoney knows about the network."

"He can't do anything with the information," Henrys said sharply.

"What if he talks?"

"To whom? Not to McBundy; he thinks McBundy is the man responsible for his father's death."

"Then he'll do something about it."

There was the snag, Mahoney thought. If they feared that John would not let it go, that he would want his father's murderers brought to justice, might they feel they had to eliminate him?

Yet, without proof, what could John do? He wasn't an operative. He had no credibility beyond the fact he was the son of a former CIA officer.

Tell Swift to be careful with this information. It's very dangerous. Several people have already died because of it.

John had been serious as a boy and pragmatic as an adult. But the arrival of the package of notes from Paris, followed by the announcement of his father's death, had to have shaken him deeply. Swift would have been comforting, but John would have been thinking ahead. If he had read the notes, he would be able to recite them back, word for word. Yet would he have bought himself some insurance? Would he have copied the notes?

Mahoney turned that thought over. If there had been a question as to the veracity of John's information, he would have been unable to prove what he had read unless he had made a photocopy of the notes, so that his father's handwriting could be verified. Swift could have had the paper analyzed, and he would have discovered to his horror that John had had the notes copied. A simple process could detect the effect of the strong photocopy light on the paper.

Mahoney left the dock and walked slowly back up to the destroyed cabin. If the notes were still here, it would take a week to find their ashes. If John had run, would he have stopped long enough to retrieve his notes?

If they had been in the cabin, he could not have gotten to them. But if he had hidden them someplace else?

Mahoney shook his head. Too many ifs. Too weak. He was clutching at straws.

The police or the fire department investigators had already done their preliminary search here. He could see where the rubble around the area of the north wall, where the LP tanks had stood, was disturbed. But nothing else had been moved. Nor would it be. They had probably discovered that the LP tanks had been tampered with. They had murder here, and John was the prime suspect. Yet if they searched further into his son's background, they would have to discover that there had been no motive.

He walked slowly around the side toward the back, but then stopped as he spotted a sneaker, lying in the grass. It was still laced up. It had not been untied. He bent down and picked it up. It must be John's, and it should not be here. He looked across the cabin and then back toward the lake. The explosion had forced everything toward the southeast, toward the lake and the boathouse. The shoe was lying on the north side. It could not have been blown out of the cabin. It must have been dropped here.

He fingered the tied laces, then looked again toward the dock. John had been down on the dock. Probably had not been able to sleep. The explosion occurred, and he came running, losing his shoe here. Then what?

Mahoney continued around to the back of the cabin, and stopped again where the back door had been. The fire would have been the most intense toward the front of the cabin. John would have come back here in an attempt to get in, to try and save Elizabeth and the children. But he could not get in. Everything had collapsed forward, and the flames would have been rising.

From there he would not have been thinking straight. It wasn't likely that whoever had set the explosion would have hung around out here. They would have been down in Duluth asleep. In the morning they would watch the newspapers or listen for the radio news of the explosion and *five* deaths. So why had John run? And where had he gone?

Mahoney untied the shoe, then tossed it into the cabin. The investigators had evidently missed it on their first round. On Sunday they probably had only a skeleton crew. But they would find it when they came back again, lying on the ground next to where the LP tanks had been.

Jensen was coming down the driveway, his tie loose, his coat flapping. "Anything?" he called out.

Mahoney shook his head and moved away from the cabin. "I thought he might have left something."

"Sir?"

But John wasn't an operative, Mahoney realized. He was probably frightened and on the run. He had never read the handbook. He had never been to school on the routine: When on the run, leave a signpost for your backup people. Let us help you.

But John was surely alone now. If he had thought it out at all, he would understand either that Switt had been the wrong choice or that Switt had been killed. By McBundy.

"There's nothing here," Mahoney said at last. "When is the next plane back?"

"Two hours. We're booked on it."

They started up the driveway toward the car. John had probably run home to Los Angeles. Or was that wishful thinking? His son wasn't stupid. He'd know they were after him. It was why he had run in the first place. But where?

Suddenly a stunning thought crossed Mahoney's mind, and it stopped him in his tracks. Say John had read the notes, knew them chapter and verse, could recite them line by line. He knew all the names, although he couldn't know their complete significance. Then he would probably believe that McBundy was responsible for the deaths of Elizabeth and the children. It would be a logical assumption from what John knew.

"What's the matter?" Jensen asked.

Mahoney focused on him. "Did Bob say where he was going to be today?"

"At home, I suppose. He was done at the safe house. What is it?"

"It's John. He's on his way to Washington to kill Bob. Or at least I think he is."

"Impossible."

"I think he's going to try it. Jesus. He thinks Bob engineered this."

Mahoney's mind was racing. The local police would be putting out an APB on John and the car. If John was thinking straight, he'd stay off the interstates and keep to the back roads. By now he could already be in Washington.

And afterward? Rome? Bonn? Christ, was it possible?

"Then we'd better get to a telephone," Jensen said. He started to speed up, but Mahoney held him back with a sharp command.

"No!"

Jensen turned. "But we must, Mr. Mahoney. I mean we can't just let it be. My God, if you're correct..."

"John would not be able to actually do it... I don't think he would. At least not without confronting Bob first. If that happens, Bob will be able to take care of himself. He'll convince John that I'm still alive."

"Why not telephone?"

"There's been too much overreaction here, Larry. I wouldn't want Bob to jump."

It was evening by the time Mahoney had dropped Jensen off at his apartment and taken the legman's car over to Chevy Chase, where he parked near the Chevy Chase Club just off Wisconsin Avenue.

From the car he walked west and he turned down a quiet residential street as the night deepened.

The weather was warm and sticky compared to what he had just left in Minnesota, and by the time he was in position he was sweating. A slight mist had begun to come into the heavy atmosphere, and it formed indistinct halos around the streetlights and lent a somewhat mysterious air to the night.

Jensen worked for McBundy, but he had promised not to telephone, and Mahoney trusted him. He had no other choice in the matter, actually, but it was easier this way. It was one thing off his mind, one less item to worry about. For the moment.

He moved slowly past McBundy's house, on the opposite side of the street, as if he were merely out for an after-dinner stroll. The lights were out downstairs, but the porch light was on—was he expecting someone?—and one of the upstairs bedrooms was illuminated.

Jensen had said something about JoAnn being away. Probably one of her pilgrimages to California that McBundy joked about. So whom was he expecting for company? Or was the porch light merely a habit? Or a signal to his watchers that all was well within?

At the corner, Mahoney turned north, never varying his pace, apparently a man without a care in the world.

There had been no one on the block, unless someone was set up in one of the neighborhood houses. There had been no parked cars, no vans or buses, in fact nothing else on the street. Just houses. Most with lights on. Mahoney wondered how many of his neighbors McBundy knew on a first-name basis, if any.

John could have made it here by now, Mahoney thought, if everything had gone well for him. Of course he may have holed up in a motel in some small town between here and there. Holed up, perhaps, and thinking, his grief nearly, if not completely, overwhelming him. Thinking about his wife and children surely, but maybe even about revenge for the deaths.

The network will do anything to remain intact, he had written in his notes to his son.

Would John be thinking about that, his hate building into some kind of reckless rage? An anger directed first at Mc-Bundy, the man Mahoney had named and the man John had to believe was responsible for the murders?

Mahoney ducked into the alley halfway down the block and headed back toward the rear of McBundy's house, realizing that he really didn't know his own son beyond the fact that he was a good man. He had turned out to be a good husband and an excellent father.

But what measure of man was he? Strong enough to turn into an avenging angel? Was that in fact why he had run? Or had he run simply because he was a coward? Or frightened? Or confused?

McBundy's home was a large, two-story brick structure with a detached garage at the rear that had once been a carriage house.

Mahoney opened the back gate and moved silently between a line of privet hedges and the side of the garage to the shadows just before the back of the house.

There was no one here. Mahoney was almost one hundred percent sure of it. Upstairs, he could see a dim light apparently coming from an open bedroom door and spilling out into the corridor.

McBundy would be up there in bed, reading or watching television.

Or, Mahoney thought, John had already been here, and McBundy was lying upstairs dead. His weariness suddenly left him as he understood that he could very well be too late, and he hurried away from the hedges, up the back walk, and onto the rear porch. He reached out to press the doorbell at the same moment that the inner door opened. McBundy stood there, a grim expression on his face.

"I figured you'd be here sooner or later tonight, Wallace."

Chapter 8

JOHN MAHONEY STOOD in the dark kitchen of his house in a
fashionable Mission Hills neighborhood just off Woodman Avenue, listening to his own heartbeat. He was a stranger here
now, even though every square inch of the room he was standing in was as familiar to him as his own body. The expression
on his weary face and in the haggard slump of his shoulders
was at once tense and yet sad. He was a man resigned now to
whatever would happen next. This combination of emotions,
this surrender to fatalism, had come upon him gradually as he
had driven southwest from Missoula. The deaths of his wife
and children, focused to such a fine realism at the graves of
his parents and brother, had somehow been made less immediate by the killing of the two FBI agents, and had been driven
even farther from his unconscious understanding by his distance
from the cabin.

He had not, however, operated like an automaton, as the
circumstances might have suggested. Instead he had become

wary, almost as if he too had been to the same school as his father, almost as if he had lived that kind of life in which ever present danger sharpened one's survival instincts.

In the twenty-four hours since he had left Missoula, he had been conscious of the change in his attitudes from his first frightening escape to his growing resolve to strike back at the network; to the personification of his desire for revenge in the person of Leonardo Rubio; and finally, sometime during the night, to his acceptance of his present lot.

He was no longer simply an analytical chemist. Those days had been as shattered by the explosion as surely as if he had been a victim of the terrible murder himself, which of course he was. There was no going back to his old life. That was utterly impossible.

Whether or not he wanted this drastic change in himself was a moot point. It had occurred through circumstances totally outside his control. Even back at the cemetery, he understood that he had no choice other than to meet the two men who had come for him. Part of some sort of network or legitimate employees of a law-enforcement agency—it did not matter one whit. They had been in his way, and they had to be eliminated.

Nor was John amazed at his own metamorphosis from scholarly chemist into ruthless fugitive. He took the change as a matter of course. Cause and effect. Replace hydrogen with a radical, and an ester is formed. Back any living creature into a corner, threaten its existence or the existence of its most cherished possessions, and it will fight back.

There were so many memories here. He moved silently through the kitchen and into the living room, where he carefully pushed the drapes aside and looked out. Under the streetlight he saw a blue van parked across the street, the kind with bubble windows on the sides, wide sport tires, and a scrollwork paint job. At any other time in his life he would hardly have noticed the vehicle, even at this odd hour. Yet now he knew not only that it was out of place, but he understood just what it was. One antenna for the FM radio, one for the CB, perhaps, but three was a giveaway. Three. Who inside the van was doing the communicating, and what was he saying?

There had been nothing in the *Los Angeles Times*, which he had bought and read from first page to last at the small coffee shop in Pomona, about him being wanted for anything. No stories about an explosion at a remote cabin in northern

Minnesota or the murder of two FBI agents in Montana. Nor
had any of the gas station attendants at his various stops given
him a second look.

But McBundy would be watching for him. He had been
certain of that all the way through the desert, and then down
out of the mountains and foothills into the valley. Nor had his
certainty let up for one moment as he parked the car on a dark
side street three blocks from his house and walked the rest of
the way, coming in across Soren Poulsen's backyard.

One of the back screens had a hole in it he didn't remember,
but nothing else had been disturbed, which on reflection seemed
strange. Wouldn't someone have searched his house? Wouldn't
someone from the Los Angeles Police Department or the FBI
have come out here to look through his things in order to find
a clue as to where he might have headed?

Careful not to move the drapes too quickly, he backed away
from the window and returned to the kitchen. By feel he located
the small penlight Elizabeth kept for emergencies in the drawer
by the telephone. He moved down the hall and into their bedroom, where he softly closed the door.

He took a large towel from the bathroom and shoved it
against the crack at the bottom of the door. The bedroom
windows faced the back of the house, and the venetian blinds
and curtains were drawn. But from the front of the house there
was a possibility that the watchers in the van might spot a
chance reflection of light in the hall from under the door.

When he was satisfied, he flipped on the penlight and went
to the desk in the far corner. From the bottom drawer he pulled
out the small strongbox that Elizabeth had insisted they buy
years ago. He unlocked it and extracted a bundle of papers
bound together with a thick rubber band. The title for the car,
insurance policies, an odd assortment of warranty cards for
everything from the furnace to the dishwasher, most of them
hopelessly out of date, and then his and Elizabeth's passports,
and five birth certificates.

He pulled out his own passport, stuffed it in his pocket, and
then looked at the birth certificates. His eyes blurred. It wasn't
real. It couldn't be real. Elizabeth was off at the hairdresser's,
and the children were visiting their grandparents in Minnesota.
That was it. What did it signify that he was looking at the
documents, hunched over the strongbox, a penlight in hand, a
bath towel stuffed in the crack beneath the door? That was how

one always looked at such papers. It was normal.

Carefully he folded the papers, rebundled them with the rubber band, and put the packet back in the strongbox, which he relocked and returned to the bottom drawer.

As he turned, the narrow beam of the penlight fell on the head of the bed. A terrible vision came to him of Elizabeth's burned, blackened body lying there on the clean bed. His hand shook so badly he almost dropped the light, and yet he was unable to drag his eyes away from the two pillows lying side by side; one for his head, the other for Elizabeth's.

God in heaven, he wanted to cry out loud, why this? Every person he had ever loved had been taken away from him.

The telephone on the nightstand rang, and John spun around, shining the penlight on it, the noise startling in the silence. It was no time to telephone anyone. Their friends knew they were gone. And so did the people at work. They weren't due back until Wednesday. The telephone rang again, the noise all the louder because of the darkness.

John flipped off the penlight and hurriedly grabbed the towel from the floor. He refolded it hastily and stuffed it back on the shelf in the bathroom. The phone rang a third and fourth time.

He raced back to the living room. He peeled back the drapes and cautiously looked outside.

The van was still there. It hadn't moved. No lights had come on. No one had gotten out. Nothing was happening.

The telephone rang in the kitchen, then cut off in the middle of a ring. Whoever was trying to call had finally given up.

John's heart was hammering, and his mouth seemed very dry. He had gotten his passport. He had what he needed. Why linger?

I don't know if I will be able to help, Switt had told him.

Standing here looking out the window at the van, he remembered with startling clarity his meeting with the one man his father had trusted. But that seemed as if it had happened years, not four days, ago. And in the interim, Switt had probably been murdered. Otherwise he would have done something by now. John wondered if the man had a family, a wife and children, parents who were mourning him at this moment.

Moving away from the window, John went back down the hall and opened the boys' room. Without the light he could only see the dim outlines of the bunk beds. John, Jr., had slept on the top bed, Carl accepting the bottom because, as he had explained in his most serious manner: "A bed is a bed, and I don't care if it's the top or the bottom one as long as it's soft and warm."

Their worktable and bookcases beneath the window were filled with half-finished model airplanes and cars, as well as stacks of paperback science fiction novels. John, Jr., built the models; Carl read the books. Between them they had divided the room to their own very precise measurements.

John backed out of the room, softly closing the door, then crossed the hall and opened the door to Cindy's room. Her tiny pink canopied bed with its frills and ruffles stood at one side, the tiny table and chairs at the other. Around the tea set, dolls waited for their little mistress to return.

At that moment, more than at any other, John wanted to lash out. To race out of the house, tear open the doors of the van, and crush whoever was there spying on the house. They were connected with what had happened, which ultimately connected them, however tenuously, with the actual killing of his wife and children.

He closed the door and went back into the living room, where once again he looked out the window to check on the van. There was someone there. Someone standing by the driver's side, smoking a cigarette, apparently talking with someone in the van through an open window.

It was no longer completely dark outside, John suddenly realized. The sky over the houses to the east was becoming lighter, yet he could not make out the features of the man standing across the street. He wanted to see him so that later he would be able to recognize him. He knew he was playing a dangerous game, standing here at the window, waiting, almost willing the man to come closer and show himself.

They hadn't been in the house yet, or at least they had not disturbed anything that he would notice, so there was no reason to suspect that they'd change their minds and decide to come in now. He glanced at the front door and noticed the envelope lying on the floor.

He glanced again out the window to make sure the man hadn't moved, then went over to the door and got the envelope. It had been dropped through the mail slot.

He took it back to the window where in the dim light he could just make out the writing on the front. He caught his breath. It was another letter from his father. This time postmarked Tel Aviv. But it had been sent almost two weeks ago. Evidently it had arrived while he was in Washington.

He looked up as the man by the van flipped his cigarette away and came around to the front of the vehicle. He glanced both ways up the street, then seemed to look directly at John before he started across.

John stepped back from the window, his heart racing. He wasn't ready to confront anyone. Not here and now. Not before he had read his father's second letter.

He turned and hurried back into the kitchen, then opened the back door and slipped outside, making sure the latch had caught before he went around the pool and crossed his neighbor's yard again.

Across the street he looked back a last time. He'd never come back here, no matter what was in this new letter. He was leaving his house and his friends as completely and as irrevocably as his wife and children had left him.

He turned and strode away from all that was familiar toward whatever fate his father's first letter, and now this one from Tel Aviv, had set for him.

It was fully light by the time John had driven down to Los Angeles. He resisted stopping to open and read this latest letter from his father until he could settle some place with a cup of coffee. He had returned for his passport and money. He had the first, and his elaborate plan of cashing small checks at several outlying branches of his bank in case the police were looking for him seemed unnecessary. The van had been there, but there didn't seem to be any kind of active search in progress. There had been nothing in the newspapers and nothing on the radio news broadcasts. *Killer of wife and children at large. Two FBI agents dead in shoot-out: California man being sought.*

It was around 8:00 A.M. when he parked the car in a lot just off Seventh Street and walked to the coffee shop in the bus depot. He took a booth by the window and ordered breakfast.

While he waited for his food to come, he took out the letter. His father's first package—the one from Paris—had been a thick bundle of notes, sealed in an inner envelope with a note that it was not to be opened unless his father died under suspicious circumstances. This one was not double-wrapped. It consisted only of a few pages. It seemed telegraphic, as if his father had been in an extreme hurry and couldn't take the time to go into detail. And it felt odd, almost frightening, to read a letter from his father, knowing he was dead.

Malecki had been killed by Sonja Margraff, his father had written, who in turn had killed herself. Per Larsen, the man from ININ, was dead, and the Israelis wanted his father dead.

Most of the letter, however, outlined a talk his father had had with McNiel Henrys, who was evidently the coordinator of the network. His father described the house in Geneva where Henrys and he had met, and Henrys's promise that he'd learn the entire story once the Israeli mess was cleaned up.

When he finished, an intense weariness descended upon him, making it almost impossible to go on. He wanted to find a hole somewhere into which he could crawl and sleep for a hundred years.

Yet nothing was changed for him. He was going to continue. There was no reason to quit. The Henrys his father had known had been a reasonable man. But reasonable men do not kill women and children.

Just a little while longer, he told himself as he dragged himself out of the booth and paid his bill at the cash register. The girl at the counter was young and had a bad case of acne. She seemed very bored and did not bother looking up when she wished him a good day.

Outside, instead of turning right toward where he had parked, he headed left to Main Street, then walked casually toward the Civic Center.

The Monday-morning traffic was heavy, and the day was turning out to be very hot and still, with a thick haze hanging over the city.

His brother Michael, who had chosen to live in Montana and work for the Forest Products Service, had chided him about living in the midst of pollution and high crime. John's only defense had been to tell him that as soon as a major chemical company built a research facility in the clean air of the Rockies, he'd be the first to transfer.

Walking now, he could distinctly hear Michael's voice, and he could see him leaning against a doorjamb, a toothpick in his mouth, his hands stuffed in the pockets of his blue jeans.

The children loved him. And on the rare occasions when he would come down to Los Angeles for a visit, they were almost impossible to manage.

"Uncle Mike! Uncle Mike!" they would shout, then dance

around him, wrestling him to the floor and going through his pockets until they found the treats he invariably brought for them. Sometimes it was candy or gum, but often it was something else, such as a toy. His last gift to the boys had been their own pocketknives. Elizabeth had objected strongly, but Michael had ignored her and taken the boys out to his car, where he produced several short lengths of soft pine: "Wood that was grown just for carving."

For weeks afterward, Elizabeth was picking up wood shavings all over the house. Even serious Carl had taken his knife and a block of wood into the bathtub with him one night, and clogged the drain with a mass of wood chips.

A couple of blocks up he turned toward Broadway and then stopped on the corner for the light to change. Across the street was the main branch of the Wells Fargo Bank. It was a few minutes after 9:00. The bank was open, and it already looked very busy.

There were no police cars, no uniformed officers outside. But that didn't really mean anything. If they were waiting for him, they'd be inside. Either hidden from view or disguised as bank tellers, or perhaps as the bank's security people.

The light changed, and the crowd streamed around him as he continued to stand there, staring across the street. Without money he could do nothing. There was only a couple of hundred dollars left in traveler's checks from their trip to the funeral, but several thousand dollars remained in their checking-savings account.

Someone bumped his elbow, and he started to spin around in fright but checked himself as a large black woman moved ponderously past him and stepped off the curb.

The light changed again, and the crowd piled up behind him.

They had been watching the house, but even if they believed he had made his way back here yet, they would have no reason to watch this bank in particular.

John wasn't completely sure of his logic, yet he had to have money. The longer he waited, the more likely someone would start to watch the banks.

When the light changed a second time, John moved across the street with the crowd. Hesitating only a moment longer, he stepped inside the bank and went immediately to one of the tall tables set up in the middle of the lobby.

No alarm had been sounded. No one was paying any attention to him. The bank was very busy. The single line feeding the tellers was long, and the hum of conversation was high.

If they were going to watch a bank, they'd probably have stationed their people at the Van Nuys branch, where he usually did his banking. Not downtown. He rarely came down here.

He wrote out a check for cash in the amount of twenty-five hundred dollars, signed it, then went across the lobby to wait on line.

No one was watching. No one was paying him the slightest attention.

The line moved forward. Of course they could have put some kind of a hold on his account so that when he tried to cash a check, the teller would be instructed to telephone someone. He had a vision of trying to fight his way out of the bank past the security guards by the door.

"Stop that man!" the teller would shout.

He could see them drawing their pistols, bringing them up as he ran toward the doors.

The line continued to move forward. Even if he did manage to get out of the bank, he'd still be without money, and they would know for certain that he was in Los Angeles. A manhunt would begin, and within hours, if not minutes, they'd have him.

"May I help you, sir?" someone was asking.

John looked up out of his thoughts at the teller, a woman with gray hair, her glasses dangling in front of her from a chain around her neck. He almost turned and ran. Instead he laid the check on the counter and signed the back of it.

"I'd like to cash this, please," he said, his voice soft, his stomach churning.

"I'll need to see your driver's license and a credit card," the woman said, deftly scooping up the check.

As he was digging out his wallet, she typed something into a computer terminal. The message?

She flipped the check over, wrote her initials in one corner, and then copied the numbers of John's driver's license and American Express card as he held them out for her.

"How do you want this, sir, large bills?"

"That'd be fine," John mumbled.

The woman counted out twenty-five hundred-dollar bills. John picked them up and walked back across the lobby toward the door, stuffing the money into his jacket pocket.

Still there were no alarms. But now, anyone who wanted to check with the bank would find out that he had been here in Los Angeles. They would know. It wouldn't take McBundy's or Henrys's people very long now to get on his trail.

The security guards ignored him as he stepped outside. He headed back the way he had come. He was two blocks away before he dared glance over his shoulder.

No one suspicious. Nothing. It didn't make sense.

The police in Duluth had to believe he had killed his wife and children. They knew he was from Los Angeles, so why hadn't the story hit the L.A. papers or radio stations?

And the two FBI agents he had killed in Missoula. Surely by now he had been connected with their deaths. Again, why hadn't the story broken in the L.A. papers?

Unless McBundy was behind it all. Unless McBundy had so much power within the CIA that he was able to convince the Duluth police and the FBI not to bother looking for John, to drop their investigation. Not unless McBundy was saving John for his own people.

If that was the case, would they believe he would return to Washington in an attempt to get at McBundy, the man his father had named as the traitor within the CIA? Or would they suspect that he'd try something else. Perhaps all this was an elaborate setup in order to maneuver him out of the country so that his murder, when it came, would not raise embarrassing questions. Perhaps they felt Henrys would be better able to deal with him than McBundy. Perhaps they were toying with him. Playing him like a fish.

Chapter 9

MEN ON THE RUN will either lash out, or pull back and return to their past in order to get in contact with their roots, as if doing so will give them solace. Driving past Greenough Park outside of Missoula, Mahoney understood that he had made a wrong choice. It had been fifty-fifty whether John would take the former or the latter course. His son had not come after McBundy, and now Mahoney was deeply worried that too much time had passed for him to have any reasonable chance of catching up with him. He could envision John at the cabin, the flames rising high into the night sky. He could see his son trying to get in to save his wife and children; he could feel the pain and disbelief and anger John must have felt. Just as he could understand that the only place left for John was here in Missoula. His brother, his mother, and presumably his father were buried here. John would have come seeking comfort.

McBundy had given him a scant twenty-four hours to catch up with John before the police would have to be brought in.

"You have to understand that the police in Duluth have four murders on their hands. If they're held back much longer, they'll create a very large fuss, which would ruin your cover. Henrys and the others would know damned well that something extraordinary was going on."

Mahoney knew he was correct. He knew it intellectually, and yet he was deeply frightened of the consequences of throwing his son to the wolves. On the other hand he keenly felt the pressure to stop the network before it was allowed to wreak further havoc.

It was a few minutes after noon, but a cold wind was blowing down from the snow-capped mountains in the distance. He had flown from Washington, rented a car at the airport, and picked up the interstate to East Missoula, getting off at Greenough Drive.

Reaching the long-familiar blacktopped road through a particularly dense section of woods, he slowed down, once again going over John's options. If not directly to McBundy, where would John go first? Back home to Los Angeles? To Europe?

A few hundred yards along the road, he came to the open gate, the St. Martin's Cemetery sign above it. He parked his car just outside the fence, shut off the ignition, and got out.

It was quiet here after Washington, although he could hear what sounded like a tractor further up the hill. It was probably the groundskeeper mowing the grass; there was that fresh, unmistakable odor in the air.

He remained by the gate for a minute or two, drinking in the sweetness of the countryside, the blue-tinged mountains in the distance very majestic. It was peaceful here. Mahoney remembered how surprised they had been when he and Marge had first come to Missoula to visit Michael at the Forest Products lab. "Why, it's beautiful here," Marge had said, and Michael had laughed. Mahoney could almost hear him. "What did you expect, Mother?"

Michael had wanted to be buried here, and Marge had insisted she be buried next to her son.

"You don't mind much, do you, Wallace?" she asked a month before she died. And he said he didn't. Montana was such a beautiful place for them to all come together.

Past the brick buildings, he headed up the long path to the crest of the hill, his mouth dry and his throat constricting. At the top there were three headstones set together beside a couple of empty plots. He approached them slowly.

He could see Marge. He could feel her gentle touch on his back as she massaged his shoulders; he could feel her presence beside him in the bed, or next to him in the car, or back at the cabin while he was out fishing.

She was here now, along with Michael, and his gaze drifted from Marge's headstone to Michael's, and finally to his own. Something cold stirred at the back of his mind. For a moment it was as if hundreds of hands were clutching at him, but then it passed, and he was able to look at his own name on the stone without emotion. His name here like this was not associated with death.

The tractor had come around the hill. He could hear it clearly now, below on the road, and he turned and walked back down the path.

If John had come here, he probably would have avoided contact with anyone, yet there was a possibility that he had been seen. Mahoney wanted desperately to get some line on his son's flight so that he could get some sense of what his son would do. Larry Jensen had gone out to Los Angeles to see if John had showed up there. Unless they touched base with him by tomorrow morning, it would be too late to help.

The groundskeeper was just climbing off his machine by the maintenance shed when Mahoney came off the path to the road. He looked up and waited.

"Good morning," he called out as Mahoney approached. He was an older man; like Mahoney his hair was white, but he was stooped, and his hands shook with a slight palsy as he pulled out a cigarette and lit it.

"Good morning," Mahoney said. He remembered seeing the man when they had brought Marge's body out for burial.

"Do something for you?"

Mahoney pulled out his wallet and flipped it open to the Central Intelligence Agency identification card McBundy had supplied him with. The caretaker would, he assumed, be ignorant of the Agency's charter and not question why Mahoney was operating within the United States, in the FBI's province. "Rupert Blakemore. I'm a special investigator with the Agency."

"Will Houseman," the man said, looking up from the ID, then shaking Mahoney's hand. There was something in his eyes. A hint of recognition? Mahoney wondered.

"I'd like to ask you a few questions, Mr. Houseman, if you have the time."

"You must be here about them FBI fellas."

Mahoney nodded, being very careful to keep his expression and tone of voice neutral, although he didn't know what the man was talking about. "What can you tell me?"

"Nothing much I didn't already tell the cops from town. State boys were here, and someone from the FBI, of course. Three-ring circus. Hardly fitting for a place like this." His eyes narrowed. "Surprised you boys are in on it."

"Why don't you go over it again for me," Mahoney said. He was certain the man was trying to place his face.

"Nothing much to tell, Mr. . . . . Blakemore. Lotsa people come to the cemetery on Sunday, so I come down early to unlock the gate and make sure everything looks nice. I got here around eight and found the two of them."

"Where?"

"Just around the corner here. Their car was parked outside the gate."

"Show me."

"I went over all this yesterday. Spent the whole day at it. I'm behind with my work now."

"It'll just take a minute. I want to get it clear in my head what happened out here. Exactly how it happened."

"Don't know if that'll be so easy," the groundskeeper said. "It all sorta puzzles me, you know?" He led Mahoney around the side of the maintenance shed where a piece of plywood had been nailed over the window. Glass littered the wet ground. "Had to wash the blood away. There was a lot of it. Wouldn't do for anyone to see it like that."

"There were two of them here?" Mahoney asked, prompting the man who was staring at him.

"Don't I know you?"

Mahoney shook his head. "I don't think so. This is my first time out this way. About the two FBI agents . . ."

"Right. One of them was lying just below the window. Whoever done it was inside the shed, grabbed the pitchfork, and stuck it out the window clean through the poor fella's neck. That's where most of the blood came from. I'll tell you, it was an awful sight."

"Where was the second body?"

"That's where it gets confusing, to my way of thinking. This poor fella was lying here, the pitchfork sticking out of his neck, his gun in his hand. The other fella was lying just a few feet away, just by the road. He'd been shot dead."

"How do you know they were with the FBI?"

The old man managed a slight grin. "They tried to tell me they wasn't. But I looked. Soon as I found them I called the cops, but then when I was waiting, I looked in their wallets to see who they were. FBI, plain as your ID card."

"And then what?" Mahoney asked.

"What do you mean 'and then what'? The cops came, took a lot of pictures, asked me a lot of questions, then they carted the bodies off, and left. Took the entire day." He scratched his head. "Funny thing, though, there wasn't a word about it in the paper. Wife said I must have been crazy. Imagined it all."

Had it been John? But what the hell was the FBI doing out here? McBundy hadn't said a thing about them being in on this.

"There weren't any newspaper or television people up here. Don't know how they kept them out of it."

Whoever had caused the explosion at the cabin could have followed John out here, then lain in wait for him as he came back down the hill. But what happened here would mean that John hadn't been in shock. In a daze. On the contrary, he had been on the watch. Alert. Very careful.

"Hobart, he's our chief of police, told me to keep quiet about all this. I wasn't supposed to talk to anyone. But you, of course, well, that's different."

"Thank you, Mr. Houseman, you've been a big help," Mahoney said. He moved away and stepped out to the road. He was finished here, and he just wanted to get away. Into town. But the groundskeeper glanced up to the path Mahoney had come down.

"The Mahoney family," the man said, bringing Mahoney up short. "You were up there. That's who you remind me of. Any relation?"

Mahoney looked him full in the eyes and shook his head. "Never heard of them. I was looking for you. Thought I heard your tractor up there."

The groundskeeper nodded, but it was clear he was skeptical. The feeling of recognition would fade with time, Mahoney was sure, in the excitement and confusion of finding two murdered FBI agents.

"I want you to follow Captain Hobart's instructions and not talk to anyone about this, Mr. Houseman. You do understand, don't you?"

"Yes, sir," the man said.

Mahoney walked back to the gate and got into his car. The groundskeeper remained standing on the road, watching as he turned the car around and headed back to the highway.

The killer had been John. Mahoney was certain of it. But what in God's name was the FBI doing involved in this? And had they already picked him up? Or worse, was his son lying dead somewhere?

Mahoney drove back into Missoula, where he stopped at a phone booth in a downtown gas station and placed a call to McBundy at Langley. Blakemore was an operational name that had been assigned to Sampson, who was waiting, out of sight and out of touch, at the Connecticut safe house. As far as anyone at the Agency was concerned, however, Sampson, operating as Blakemore, evidently was out in Montana. No one would question it.

There was nothing yet from Jensen in Los Angeles, but his plane had just landed there, and it would still be too soon for him to have found anything.

"John may have been here, but so was the FBI," Mahoney said.

"They haven't been called in on this, at least not to my knowledge," McBundy shouted. "Christ, that's all we need to screw everything up."

"Can you check on it from your end?"

"I'll try, but I don't want to make any waves."

"I'm going to talk with the local field-office agent, so you'll probably be getting a verification call very soon."

"What's happened out there?"

Mahoney explained about the bodies, where they had been found, and how they had died.

"You think it was John?"

"I think it's likely. The timing fits."

"What in God's name was he doing out there?"

"On his way to Los Angeles, probably," Mahoney said. Even McBundy wouldn't understand why John would have wanted to come here. McBundy had never had children. He had no idea of the emotional ties within a close family.

"If John shows up in L.A., Larry will pick him up and bring him back. But check with the local Bureau office and find out what the hell their people were doing. It'll probably turn out to be something else totally."

"I hope so," Mahoney said, and he hung up.

Around the corner and two blocks away, he parked in a visitor's slot at the Federal Building and went inside, where he was directed to the tiny, second-floor office of Jared Kraus, the FBI agent in charge.

Kraus was a short, well-built man in his late thirties, and it took him only five minutes after Mahoney had shown him his CIA identification to receive verification from McBundy himself.

"What brings you to this neck of the woods, Mr. Blakemore?" Kraus asked.

"I understand two of your people were murdered at St. Martin's sometime yesterday morning."

Kraus sat forward so fast he nearly fell off his chair. "What the hell does the Agency have to do with this?"

"Probably nothing at all. But I was here, heard about the incident, and thought I'd better check into it."

"What are you doing in Missoula?"

"I'm following someone."

"A murderer?"

"No," Mahoney said.

Kraus just eyed him for a long moment. "You're going to have to do better than that, otherwise I won't give you a thing. You're way out of your territory—Christ, haven't you guys learned anything?"

"Someone else may be following my man."

"And he may have done the killing?"

Mahoney nodded.

"Why Missoula? Why that cemetery?"

Mahoney could envision Kraus going out to the cemetery, recording all the names of the headstones, and then tracing each of them. It wouldn't take the man very long to realize that a CIA agent was buried up there, one whose son was wanted for murder in Minnesota.

"I was supposed to meet someone here," Mahoney said,

sitting forward. "And goddamnit, Kraus, I want that kept completely under your hat. What I want to know is what the hell your people were doing out there."

Again Kraus just eyed Mahoney. He was a sharp young man, and he was far from sold on the story he was being told.

"They weren't my people," he said at last.

"Whose, then?" Mahoney was afraid of this.

"I don't know yet. They both carried Bureau IDs. Forgeries. But good ones. As were their license plates. I sent their photographs and fingerprints to Washington. Just waiting for the word."

"I'd like to see the bodies," Mahoney said.

"I thought you might be asking that," Kraus drawled. "Yet you can't tell me what this is all about. It'd help."

"I'm sorry."

"Yeah," Kraus said, getting up. "They're over at the morgue in the hospital."

Mahoney followed the FBI agent over to Community Hospital on the south side of town, and together they went into the small morgue in the basement of the building.

A young attendant opened the body drawers, one at a time, and flipped back the sheets. Mahoney didn't recognize either one of them, although he had seen the types. They looked like street people, big-city hoods, hit men. The one who had been shot had probably been a boxer at one time; his nose had obviously been broken more than once. The other one, with the mutilated neck, had several scars on his torso.

"I'd say he picked those up either on the streets or in Vietnam," Kraus said. "We're hoping it was in the military, but I have my doubts."

Neither one of these men was the type that Henrys would use for his dirty work. And yet, Mahoney had to ask himself, whom did the network hire as field men when something desperate had to be done? Looking down at the two bodies, he sensed the answer.

"Don't suppose you recognize them?" Kraus asked hopefully.

Mahoney shook his head. "They're not who I expected at all."

"Which means?" Kraus asked as the attendant pulled the sheets over the bodies and closed the drawers.

"Which means I was probably on a wild-goose chase. My man came and went. What happened with these two was a completely separate incident."

At the door Kraus thanked the attendant and then turned to Mahoney.

"You don't expect me to swallow a bullshit story like that now, do you, Mr. Blakemore?"

"Doesn't matter. It's the way it's going to read in Washington," Mahoney snapped.

"Now the pressure comes."

Outside, they stopped when they got to Mahoney's car. "We have a very sensitive investigation going here," Mahoney said. "That's all I can tell you. But if you're stepped on from Washington, don't take it personally."

He got in his car. Before he drove off, he looked up at Kraus. "Sorry."

"You son of a bitch," the FBI agent said.

Larry Jensen's flight arrived half an hour late in Los Angeles, he had a very long wait at the car rental counter, and when he finally got his car, traffic had been extremely heavy all the way up to Mission Hills near Van Nuys. He was tired and on edge by the time he got off the freeway and headed to John Mahoney's house. And damn well confused, too, he had to admit.

Before he had left Washington that morning, McBundy had taken him aside. Mahoney had already left, and the chief just wanted to clear the air before they got started.

"Mahoney came to me last night. Told me everything, so I'm not holding it against you," McBundy said.

Jensen felt uncomfortable. It had been his duty to call McBundy and warn him, but Mahoney had made him promise.

"You have to understand, Larry, that Wallace isn't thinking straight at the moment. He's gotten himself off the track."

"It is his son, after all."

"I know, and there's no help for it. But I want this cleared up posthaste so that we can get on with it."

"Yes, sir," Jensen had said.

"I'm counting on you, Larry. You're the best legman we've got. Pick up John, for God's sake, and bring him in."

"Do my best, sir," Jensen had said.

The day was very hot and muggy, the smog so thick it made his eyes water even through the car's air conditioning as he turned onto Mahoney's street and slowly cruised down the block for his dry run.

Children were out playing, a small mail truck was stopping and starting further up the block, and a pool maintenance van was parked across the street from John's house.

As Jensen passed the van, he spotted a man at the side of one of the houses, doing something to the pool's filtering equipment.

At the end of the block, he turned around and came back, pulling into John's driveway and shutting off the engine.

No one seemed to be watching him, but he knew that tomorrow, when the L.A.P.D. was finally brought into the investigation, neighbors would mention they had seen a strange man at Mahoney's house.

He got out of his car, went up to the door, and pulled out his lockpick set. Within a few seconds he was able to step inside.

"John?" he called out.

The house was deathly still. Passport, gun, money, clothing. If he found them it would mean John was still close by. If he found nothing, it might mean nothing. But John did have a passport, they knew that much.

He moved down the hallway toward the back of the house. The telephone rang. A second later the doorbell chimed.

He hurried back to the living room, where he looked out the window. The pool service man from across the street stood by the door. He was holding a clipboard.

The phone rang again and so did the doorbell. Jensen opened the door.

"Good afternoon . . ." the maintenance man said.

Jensen nodded, about to ask him if someone had called to work on the pool, when the man moved the clipboard aside, revealing a small automatic pistol equipped with a silencer.

"Oh, shit," Jensen started to say, trying to move back out of the way. The barrel of the gun came up and fired twice. Both shots hit him in the head.

Chapter 10

IT HAD BEEN crisp and almost cold when Mahoney left Montana on the early-afternoon flight east. Now as he drove his rented car past the Washington Monument, the night was very warm and humid. It was quite a contrast. He was already beginning to get used to such switches, although he didn't like them. He parked just off Constitution Avenue in the staff parking lot of the National Museum of Natural History, across the Mall from the Smithsonian Institution. He walked around to the front of the huge building and peered up the wide marble steps toward the shadows in the long row of columns. If someone was up there watching, he was completely invisible from Mahoney's vantage point. Light glinted off the glass on the front doors, but the depths of the shadows were impenetrable. Of course, everything depended upon Greene. If he had mentioned Mahoney's call from O'Hare Airport in Chicago, then someone could be up there. If he had kept his word, there would be no reason for anyone to be there.

Mahoney turned back as a black Toyota sports car came up Madison Drive, then slowed down and stopped at the curb. Mahoney stepped briskly down the sidewalk and got in the passenger side.

"I don't know what this is all about, Mr. Mahoney, but I sure as hell don't like it," Greene said. He seemed shaken.

"It's nothing to be overly worried about, Bobby. I just wanted to talk to you in private, that's all."

Greene turned up Seventh Street, past the National Gallery of Art. There was very little traffic at this hour, so the humid air didn't stink of exhaust fumes.

"This is going a little fast for me, you know."

"We've managed tougher assignments."

Greene glanced at Mahoney. "It was different then."

"In the old days?" Mahoney prompted.

Greene nodded. "It was clear that we had the backing, but now it's anyone's guess." He shook his head. "Christ, I just don't know anymore. I just don't know."

"Don't know what, Bobby?"

"About anything."

"Or *anyone*, Bobby? Aren't you sure about anyone? Maybe McBundy?"

Greene flinched. His knuckles were white on the steering wheel.

"I'm not sure about Mr. McBundy, or about you, sir."

"Tell me about Bob."

"Is this what this is all about tonight, Mr. Mahoney? Is it why you called me out, to ask about Mr. McBundy? Do you still have your doubts?"

"We all have our doubts. You do. McBundy does. So do I. Didn't Bob ask you about me? Didn't he check around?"

"It's his job," Greene said defensively.

Mahoney agreed. "It is his job, just as I've made it my job to find out about the network. What makes it tick. Who runs it. Why."

Greene was silent for a long time. He seemed to wrestle with his conscience. When he spoke, he didn't look at Mahoney.

"McBundy thinks you're addled. Thinks you've gone 'round the bend."

"But he figures I've sacrificed enough for the Company that he has to give me a chance?"

"Something like that."

"How about you? Or the others? What do they think? Or don't you share your views among each other."

"Come on, Mr. Mahoney, I don't deserve that. None of us does. Not now."

"Not now? What's 'not now'?" Mahoney asked. There was something wrong with Greene. Something beyond what he'd noticed before.

"I mean, I know that you have to be hard. But Jesus Christ . . ."

"Pull over here," Mahoney said.

"Sir?"

"Pull over here!" Mahoney shouted. "Park the fucking car!"

They were nearly to Mount Vernon Square, and Greene turned onto a side road, pulled up to the curb, and shut off the headlights.

"Now, I want you to tell me what the hell is going on. What happened while I was gone? Did Jensen find my son? Is that it?"

Greene looked at him. "You don't know, do you?"

"Don't know what? What happened?"

"About Larry. He was killed. Shot down. In your son's house."

"Oh, Christ," Mahoney said. He let out the deep breath he had been holding. "Oh, Christ," he said again. "When did this take place?"

"This afternoon. Before you telephoned from Chicago. I thought you had talked to McBundy, that you knew. I thought that was why you had set up this meeting like this."

"I didn't know," Mahoney said.

"You didn't know a thing about it?" Greene asked, still incredulous. "You haven't talked with McBundy since you've been back?"

"No," Mahoney said. His mind was racing. "What happened out there?"

"Larry had just arrived at your son's house. He hadn't had a chance to look through anything, as far as we can tell. Leastwise, nothing in the house seemed disturbed. Someone came to the door. Probably rang the goddamned doorbell, and Larry just answered it, and got himself gunned down. No ID on it yet."

"How did you find out?"

Greene looked at him. "McBundy told us, of course. How the hell do you think we'd know?"

"Steady now, Bobby," Mahoney said. "How did the information originate? Who generated it?"

Greene started to say something, then shook his head. "I don't know for sure. Local cops, I guess."

"Maybe the FBI?" Mahoney asked.

"What are you searching for, Mr. Mahoney?"

"The truth, that's all. I was just wondering where Bob got all this information so quickly."

"Well, I don't know," Greene said. "All I know is that Larry Jensen is dead. I can't even face my own division chief, and you're—"

"And I'm what, Bobby?"

Greene said nothing.

"Come on. I think we're getting down to the nitty-gritty now. I'm what?"

"A ruthless bastard."

Mahoney had to smile. He had heard the term before. "My daughter-in-law and grandchildren are dead, my son is on the run and wanted for murder, and now Larry Jensen is dead, and I'm still running around asking silly questions and doubting everyone's word. Is that it, Bobby? Is that what has you bothered? Because if it is, you'd better hang on. There's more to come. Much more."

Greene held his silence.

"If I'm a ruthless bastard, how about McBundy? What's he?"

Still Greene said nothing.

"A single-minded bastard, perhaps?"

"Sir?"

"Or perhaps a ferret. Maybe a night animal? Better yet, is McBundy a mole?"

"Never!" Greene shouted. "He may be a lot of things, Mr. Mahoney, but never that. He'd give his life for his country. For the service."

Which country, which service? Mahoney wanted to ask. Just as suddenly, however, another thought struck him. Perhaps Switt, and now Greene, had been right. Perhaps he *was* a ruthless bastard. Hadn't he been single-minded all his professional life? Hadn't he been like the proverbial man with blinders on? Hadn't he sacrificed his wife and children for his job?

What a revelation, if it were true. Or was he just having second thoughts about this business? Jensen was dead out in California in John's house. Who had killed him? John? It certainly was possible. John had evidently killed the two men in Missoula who had posed as FBI agents. Why wouldn't he kill Jensen, whose identification pegged him as CIA? He already thought McBundy was after him. Perhaps he thought Jensen was McBundy's trigger.

"So, how were you recruited for the business?" Mahoney asked, pulling himself out of his own dark thoughts.

Greene blinked, and Mahoney sensed disappointment in his voice. "It was routine."

"No, it wasn't," Mahoney said. "It's not every day that the Chief of Clandestine Operations asks you to work independent of the Company."

"He said you were in trouble."

"When, Bobby? When was this?"

"I don't know. July. August."

"Before I went to Athens?"

"About the same time. He said he was going to let you have almost enough rope to hang yourself, but he wasn't going to let you go over the brink. He was going to be right behind you, to pull you back if need be."

"And is that what happened? Were you one of the ones who dogged me?"

"Not at first. Certainly not directly."

"But later?"

"I was one of the collators. Stan Kopinski helped out. There were others who provided the data."

"Who?"

"Wilson. Bogdanovich. Carlberg."

"In Tel Aviv?"

Greene nodded.

"The station chief out there, did he know? Did the ambassador know?"

"No," Greene said. "And the others didn't really know anything either. They were just instructed routinely to keep an eye on you. Low priority. Grade nine, I think it was."

Mahoney said nothing, trying to put himself in McBundy's shoes. It had to be nearly impossible for him to keep this under wraps now. A good man dead in California on an operation that did not officially exist. And an aging, recalcitrant ex-agent on his hands who refused to go away or, short of that, play by the rules.

"You have to understand how much trouble it was. With a grade nine, they weren't watching you very closely. No need to, as far as they were concerned. So we had to extrapolate a lot of information."

"Dangerous," Mahoney said, coming back. "Especially when lives depended upon the decisions you people were making."

"Bob McBundy is a good man," Greene flared. "I'd stake my life on it. All of us would. It's just that... he's under pressure."

"I can understand that, Bobby," Mahoney said tiredly. "Let's go back."

Greene made a U-turn in the narrow street and went back out to Seventh, where he headed back the way they had come.

"I'm sorry about Larry," Mahoney said.

Greene glanced over at him. "He was a personal friend. We went fishing last month."

"He's married, isn't he?"

Greene nodded.

"How's Bob going to keep it from her?" Mahoney asked, hating himself for the question. But his ass was going to be on the line very shortly. He wanted to make sure there weren't any loose ends.

Greene flared again. "I don't know! I suppose he'll have me say something to her. Some bullshit story about how he's out on an assignment. I'll get Joy to talk to her too. We'll make it a fucking family project. Jesus Christ!"

"Sorry," Mahoney said.

They drove the rest of the way back to the museum in silence.

"Mr. Mahoney—" Greene began when Mahoney opened his door.

"I'm sorry you're taking it so hard, Bobby. I've had my losses too."

"You're going to have to trust him. You can't go off leaving your back wide open."

Mahoney nodded. "Before I go off, I'll either come to terms with Bob or arrange something else." He got out of the car and looked back. Greene wanted to say something, it was written all over his face, but he held his silence. "See you later."

"Yes, sir."

The apartment in Georgetown was one of McBundy's new ones. It was on a float, so was relatively secure despite its proximity to everything. Instead of being funded on a specific budget line, as was the custom, the operational money for this place and a couple of others floated from line to line so that there was very little likelihood of it being pinned down.

It was nearly midnight by the time Mahoney arrived at the second-floor apartment and let himself in. Immediately he sensed something was wrong, and he stepped back.

"It's me." McBundy's voice came from the dark interior.

Mahoney could smell his aftershave. It's what had put him off. "Are you alone?"

"Yes," McBundy said. "Is Bobby waiting downstairs, or did you come alone?"

Mahoney stepped the rest of the way into the apartment, closed and latched the door behind him, and flipped on the light. McBundy had turned off all the lamps except one in the corner, which provided only a dim light. He sat near the window, his legs crossed, his vest still buttoned and his tie still snug despite the lateness of the hour.

"You're well informed," Mahoney said.

"The field may be yours, Wallace, but this town is mine. Is Greene downstairs?"

Mahoney shook his head. "I sent him home. He wasn't very happy."

"None of us is. Jensen was a good man. One of the better ones."

"Who killed him?"

"Not your son, if that's what you're worried about. Neighbors saw a pool maintenance man at the door. The man has disappeared."

Mahoney nodded. McBundy had a drink in his hand. He took a sip.

"Bottle's in the kitchen on the counter. I left a glass out for you."

Mahoney went into the kitchenette and poured himself a shot of the Kentucky whiskey. Then he came back into the

living room and sat heavily on the couch. His bags were still
in the middle of the room where he had left them when he had
arrived from the airport.

"Rotten stuff," McBundy said, taking another drink. "Don't
know how you can drink it all the time."

"Are you going to help, or are we just going to play this
little game of attrition until the DCI sits up and takes notice?"

"That's really up to you, isn't it? I mean, we've got a three-
way race here as far as I can see. We can either go after the
mole in our own service, who is probably Switt. We can go
after this network of yours. Or we can attempt to retrieve your
son."

"I don't deserve that," Mahoney said, stung. But the instant
he said it he recalled that Greene had said the same thing to
him.

"None of us deserves what we're getting at the moment,
Wallace, but we've been kind of desperate around the home-
stead lately."

"Does Lycoming know?"

"About what? You?"

"The mole in the service."

McBundy shook his head. "Not a glimmer that I've seen.
Unless, of course, he knows all about it, and just like you, he
suspects me."

Mahoney was not sure. "You don't believe a thing I told
you."

"Oh, yes, I do," McBundy said, sitting forward. "Oh, yes,
indeed I do. It's just that I'm beginning to seriously wonder,
Wallace, whether or not McNiel Henrys and his crowd haven't
got the right idea. I'm wondering if we shouldn't leave them
alone—leave them to their own devices."

"You don't mean that," Mahoney said. He had never seen
McBundy like this. He wondered if he were drunk.

"No," McBundy said after a moment. "But I didn't care
about any of it to begin with. We have a mole in our service.
I wanted him out, that's all."

"Any word from Switt yet?"

"None. He's disappeared."

"Geneva?"

McBundy nodded heavily. "He used two fake passports.
New York to Montreal to Paris on one. From there to Geneva
on the other."

"I hope your people haven't poked around Geneva."

"No. It's quiet over there."

"Switt's the one, then."

"My immediate reaction is to chase after him. Pull out all the stops. Accuse him of murdering your daughter-in-law and grandchildren, and now Jensen."

"You'd run into a dead end. The two men lying out in the morgue in Missoula are probably hit men, maybe from New York or Detroit. You'll probably find that they caused the explosion in my cabin." Mahoney had to stop. His heart was racing, and his breath was coming too fast. He took a deep drink of the whiskey and forced himself to calm down.

"How about Switt?" McBundy asked.

"They've either hidden him deep, or they killed him. I'd guess the latter. Per Larsen was their man, and they killed him when he got in the way. Or rather, when he began to get himself noticed."

"Christ, it's hard to believe," McBundy said, shaking his head. "Switt worked on everything. He was a jack-of-all-trades. The great fixer." He shook his head again. "Even now I wish the bastard were here. He'd be a great help."

"I know," Mahoney said, thinking back to the times he had worked with Switt. He supposed he had come close to loving the young man. He wondered how he had been recruited. That was one of the keys, after all.

"How was he turned?" McBundy asked, almost as if he had read Mahoney's mind.

"That's one of the things I want to find out before I go after Henrys."

McBundy looked at him. "And then what, Wallace?" he asked. "For Christ's sake, your entire family is wiped out, and you're planning your next moves. Is it revenge, Wallace? Or are you the coldest son of a bitch that ever walked the face of the earth?"

"Don't say that to me, Bob," Mahoney said mildly. His gut was churning. But he felt he had to keep himself together.

"I'm sorry."

"I've given my bit to the service."

"More than your bit, Wallace. For Christ's sake, give it up. Step down. Let someone else take it."

"Is that why you pulled me back from Israel? Is that why you set me up?"

"That was before your daughter-in-law and grandchildren were . . . killed."

"So we've gone through all this for nothing?"

"What the hell do you want?" McBundy shouted.

"Switt's the mole. He's gone now, probably dead, and you're going to leave it at that?"

"That's all my charter reads."

"For the service and nothing but the service. That sort of thing?"

"There's only so much I—any of us—can do. Only so much the Company can or should do."

"Well, I don't have a charter, Bob. And perhaps you're right, both ways. I *am* a cold son of a bitch, and it is revenge." He went back into the kitchenette and poured another drink. "I'm a ruthless bastard too, Bob," he added.

When he came back into the living room, McBundy was at the door.

"Are you going to help me, or am I going to have to do this on my own?"

McBundy turned back. He seemed far away in thought, but he answered nevertheless. "I told the DCI I was going to look into your death. A congressional hit squad is sniffing around, looking for scalps. I made Lycoming promise to hold them off for two weeks. That was three days ago. Leaves you eleven."

"How about operational funds? Documents? Data backup? Those kinds of things."

"Kopinski and Sampson have your background about ready. You'll be punched in on a blind budget line. One of our contingency funds. It won't hold up forever, but we're just looking at eleven days. And I do mean eleven days, Wallace. There'll be no holding back the floodgates after that."

"Thanks," Mahoney said.

"I had to do it, Wallace," McBundy said. "After all, your resurrection was my idea."

THE INVESTIGATION

Chapter 11

JOHN MAHONEY ARRIVED in Rome shortly before 9:00 Wednesday morning. The immigration control officer never blinked as he stamped John's passport and reached for the next. After claiming his suitcases, John exchanged a large amount of money into lire—he didn't know how long his business here was going to take—and took a cab immediately into the city. It had been hot and hazy in Los Angeles, hot and polluted in Mexico City, and it was already very warm and humid here. Traffic was heavy at this hour of the morning, everyone driving at unbelievable speeds, horns blaring, brakes screeching. The odor of burned clutch and exhaust was strong. The cabby recommended the Esperia, which, considering the low rates, turned out to be a surprisingly large and prosperous-looking hotel on the Via Nazionale. After he had taken a quick bath, he bought a map of the city from the newspaper kiosk outside, then walked a few blocks to the Termini railway station, where he rented a small Fiat that he drove immediately to a parking lot near the

Colosseum. The car and the overnight bag in the trunk containing a few of his things were his insurance policy. He had a feeling that by the time he was ready to leave, any normal means of exit from the city might be denied him.

This was an area of museums and ancient buildings, and much as a tourist guide might scout an area before he brought his flock through, John hurried from place to place, stopping every now and then to gaze up at some point of particular interest. All the while he was acutely conscious of his surroundings, more aware of what was happening around him—especially behind him—than he could ever remember having been in his life. But he had been raised by a pragmatic man and had been trained as a scientist. He understood what it took to survive. If not the technique, certainly the spirit.

He passed below the Forum along the Via dei Fori Imperiali, then worked his way to the end of the Via Nazionale, which ran from the Piazza Magnanapoli to the Piazza della Repubblica. It was work; he was very conscious now of the press of people and of his own exhaustion. But he felt calmer now that he had an escape route.

He made it back to his hotel, where he flopped on the bed. It seemed like months since he had last rested, and he fell into a dreamless sleep.

It was dark when he awoke, cotton-mouthed, stiff from lying in one position, his skin oily with sweat. He got up from his bed and stumbled over to the window, which looked down on the street. There were only a few delivery trucks about, and two workmen were loading boxes into a restaurant across the way.

John yawned and rubbed his eyes, then focused on his wristwatch. It was shortly before 5:00. For a moment or two he stared at the dial in confusion. He was sure he had reset it to Rome time. He had lain down around ten that morning and evidently slept through the day. But 5:00. It should still be daylight. Suddenly it struck him that he had slept almost around the clock. It was 5:00 in the morning. Thursday.

He went into the bathroom and took a leisurely shower, the sense of unreality, that he really was in Rome, growing again within him. It just wasn't possible. And yet he was here. Elizabeth and the children were dead. The two FBI men were dead. And he was here. God in heaven, what was happening to him?

After he shaved, he dressed in slacks, an open-collared shirt, and a light sports jacket, then went out on the balcony to smoke and wait for the dawn.

He had driven straight through to El Paso, Texas, where he located the Greyhound terminal and shipped Elizabeth's and the children's suitcases, which were still in the trunk of the car, back to himself at his lab, prepaid. He crossed the border into Mexico and managed to sell his car at an all-night lot in Ciudad Juárez. He then took a flight to Mexico City, where he hung around the airport until it was time for the Pan Am flight to Rome.

It wasn't real, he kept telling himself. It couldn't be real. Elizabeth and the children weren't really dead. He really wasn't a fugitive, and he had not come to Rome to kill a man. But it was true. All of it was true. They were monsters. They had killed his wife. His babies. He wanted to scream, to lash out at something . . . anything. He wanted to smash them into the ground. He wanted to hear them beg for their lives.

Sweat had formed on his brow, and his hand shook badly as he raised the cigarette to his lips. He was going to have to be careful that he didn't run amok. That he didn't suddenly go crazy. He was safe here for the moment, as long as he didn't blow it by doing something stupid. Even when the police back home found out he had been at the bank in Los Angeles, they would have a hard time tracing his movements. They might find out he had crossed the border at El Paso, but that would probably be as far as they'd get. He didn't think the dealer he had sold his father's car to would be very cooperative, because he had sold the registration and tags as well. Sooner or later the car would be spotted and the game would be up, but that would take time. By then, John figured, he'd be long gone from here.

Sometimes he thought about what had happened to him as a deep wound that would need a lot of time and rest to heal. Each movement he made tore the flesh just a little more. Sooner or later it would become too deep to heal, and it would begin to fester. Eventually, he knew, it would kill him, just as it had killed his father.

He pulled the cigarette smoke deep into his lungs, enjoying the first of the day as he watched the workmen finish across the street, get back into their truck, and drive away. A cab pulled up to the curb, and a man and woman got out. They were dressed in evening clothes, and their laughter floated up as they entered the hotel.

To the east the sky was beginning to lighten, and after a bit John went back inside, got his key, and went downstairs.

"Our café opens in one hour, *signore*," the sleepy desk clerk said. "If you would care to wait. It is still too early. Or there is a workingmen's café around the corner."

"Perhaps for lunch," John said. He found the café and ordered a couple of sweet rolls and some strong coffee.

He was finished around eight, and he walked two blocks before picking up a cab to the main telephone exchange. The doors were just opening when he pulled up, paid the cabby, and went inside to the tables that held the city and province directories. When he had inquired upon checking in at the hotel, he had been directed here by the operator. He knew that he was carving a path for himself that even a child would be able to follow, but that didn't matter to him. He felt a certain sense of recklessness now, as if he didn't have anything to lose, which in effect he didn't. He had already lost everything of value to him.

He began with federal government listings in the main directory, which was contained in four fat volumes. At first he went through the law-enforcement agencies, but there was a bewildering array of offices, investigators, and laboratories here and outside the city as far away as Farfa. He went halfheartedly through the magistrate listings next, his search hampered by his knowing only a little Italian and even less about the organization of the government.

After about an hour, two things occurred to him. The first was that Leonardo Rubio worked for the Italian secret service, not just some federal police agency. And the second was that the secret service would not have a listing in a telephone directory showing its staff members.

He also tried Rubio under residential listings, but there was none with the same first name.

He pushed away from the table, got up, and went outside. He stood on the sidewalk, staring across the street, not really seeing much of anything.

It had never occurred to him that he would have trouble finding Rubio in Rome, either at his office or his home. The trouble was supposed to come when he actually confronted the man.

He turned after a minute or two and walked unhurriedly down the street as he tried to think this out. He was in a country and a city he had never been to before in his life, he couldn't speak the language, he was a wanted man at home, and he could not just walk up to someone and ask how he might find a man by the name of Leonardo Rubio. "He works for the Italian secret service, you know. I'd like to find him."

The first question would be: Why would you want to find him?

If he were a foreigner in the United States but knew that a man by the name of Robert McBundy worked for the CIA, how would he go about finding him?

His name certainly wouldn't be in a phone book. Nor would any government agency give out any information.

He thought immediately of former CIA agents, such as Philip Agee and others, who had published books naming names. McBundy's could be listed in such a book. But if such a book had been written about the Italian intelligence agency, he had never heard of it.

His name might also be known by some of the antiestablishment underground newspapers in the country. Such publications had ways of finding out such things. In the sixties and seventies the SDS, the Weathermen, and a host of other fringe groups published their underground newspapers in which they named names.

Antiestablishment. He tried to think it out. Rubio was a high-ranking member of the Italian establishment. Who would be opposed to him?

Suddenly he had it. He stopped short and hurried back to a newspaper kiosk he had just passed. The man inside looked up at him and smiled.

"Signore?"

"Newspaper," John said breathlessly, looking at the bewildering array pinned up.

"Sì?" the little man asked hopefully.

"Communist," John said. *"Communista."*

"Sì," the vendor said again. *"Il Martello."* He pulled a thick tabloid newspaper from one of the stacks and handed it over. John paid for it, then hurried down the block into a park, where he sat on one of the benches.

The newspaper's address was on a middle page, along with the names of the publisher and editors. According to his map, he was only a few blocks away.

If anyone within Italy would be against Rubio, and men like him, it would be the Communists. Or at least John hoped so.

He hurried out of the park, and within minutes he had come to a tiny alley off the Corso Vittorio Emanuele. At the end was the entrance to the newspaper, which was housed in a four-story yellow building.

Just inside the door was a filthy lobby. People were coming and going in a constant stream, all of them obviously in a great hurry. A desk manned by a surly-looking fellow was off to one side, and John approached him.

"I'd like some help," he said slowly.

The young man looked up and his lip curled. "What do you wish here with us?" he asked cautiously in English.

"I am a writer," John began, but the young man jumped up.

"A writer!" he shouted.

"I need information."

The young man leaned forward, his eyes flashing. "You are an American. Here to make trouble while your President is off on another nuclear adventure in Europe. Is that it?" The man's English was surprisingly good. But John thought he was going to lose control.

"I am not here to make trouble for you. I am here for information. I need to know about a man called Leonardo Rubio."

The transformation in the man across the desk was startling. It was as if someone had thrown a bucket of cold water on him.

The Communist Party was very large in Italy, from time to time holding seats in the Cabinet. John remembered reading about that. But he didn't think the party or this newspaper was a friend of the Italian government or its agencies. Rubio, therefore, if he was known, would not be well liked.

"What do you want with him, *signore?*"

John looked around the lobby. No one was paying them the slightest attention. He leaned forward. "I need to know where he lives."

"It is not known."

"Where he works then. Where his office is. You must know that," John said. "And perhaps you have a recent photograph."

"Why do you want this information?"

"I'm a writer. I'm doing a story."

"And you come to us? Are you crazy?"

"I am no friend of Rubio's."

"Or of me," the young man said. He came around the desk. He had a very bad odor, but his clothes were reasonably clean. His shoes were run-down at the heels. "Come with me." He grabbed John by the arm, dragged him around the corner, up a flight of stairs, and into a large office that was stacked seemingly floor to ceiling with books, papers, maps, and the accumulated debris of years.

"Pietro," he cried as they came through the open door.

An older man, heavily built, with wild hair and equally wild eyes, came out of a bathroom buttoning his trousers.

"Sì," he said irritably, eyeing John.

The young man who had dragged John up there spoke at great length in rapid Italian to the older man, from time to time gesturing his way, and then downstairs. When he was finished, the older man seemed pensively amused. He waved the young man away.

"Sit down, please, Mr. . . . ," the journalist said in English, waving John toward a chair.

"My name is of no consequence at this point," John said. He cleared a few books off a chair, then pulled it up to the desk, and sat down as the older man settled into his chair and lit a pipe.

"Yet you come here to my newspaper to ask for help."

John shrugged. "I began here. But if you do not wish to help, I will go elsewhere." He started to get up, but the journalist waved him back.

"Do not be so impetuous. All Americans are the same. Especially the young ones," he said. "You mentioned that you are a writer. What kind of a story on Signore Rubio do you wish to do?"

"A personality piece," John said, saying the first thing that came to his mind.

"A personality piece. I see. An exposé?"

John nodded, very unsure of himself now. Perhaps this hadn't been such a good idea.

"For whom are you doing this article?"

"No one. That is, I have not yet been commissioned."

"You are free-lance, is that what you are trying to say?"

"Yes. Free-lance." John was very uncomfortable. He was

beginning to sweat. He wanted nothing more than to get the hell out of there. Now.

The man looked at him for a long moment. "If you wanted to speak with Signore Rubio, why did you come to us? I still do not understand why you did not turn to the Ministry of Public Information. They would have set up an interview."

For an equally long moment John stared back at the editor. How far could he take this? The man ran a Communist newspaper, but he still was an Italian. Presumably he loved his country no less than any other citizen. Yet if not here, where else would the information come from? John could smell the fire from the burning cabin, and he could imagine that he was hearing Elizabeth's screams.

"Rubio is a high-ranking secret service officer. Are you aware of that?" John asked.

The man nearly dropped his pipe. *"Che?"* he sputtered. "What is it you are telling me?"

"Leonardo Rubio. He is an officer in the secret service."

"You have proof of this?"

"Yes," John said, looking at him. He was feeling cornered again.

"Vittorio," the old man called out.

Someone clattered up the stairs a second or two later, and the young man from downstairs at the information desk came in. He had a thick envelope clutched in his hands.

The editor's eyes narrowed. "Rubio?" he asked.

The young man nodded and handed it across.

The older man opened the envelope and took out a batch of news clippings and several photographs. He selected one and handed it across to John.

"Is this the man you are seeking?"

The photograph was of a man in his early forties with dark hair, deep-set dark eyes, and a pleasant-looking face. He was dressed in formal attire and seemed to be in front of a palace or some ornate government building. John had no idea if this was the man. All he knew was that the man he sought was named Leonardo Mazzini Rubio, and that he was a high-ranking officer in the Italian secret service.

He turned the photograph over. The label on the back read: RUBIO, L.M., QG NATO, BRUXELLES. His heart skipped a beat.

"This is the man," John said, looking up. His mouth felt dry. He turned the photograph back and studied Rubio's face again. He was a part of the network. He and others like him had caused his father's death, and the deaths of his wife and children. And now he had a face.

"But you say he is a secret service officer?"

John nodded. "He also has some kind of a post with NATO," he said, grabbing at the information he had just read.

"He's on the ININ Review Committee," the older man said. "Which could mean there is some validity to your charge."

Inter-NATO Intelligence Network. Per Larsen. Another of the men mentioned in his father's notes. This definitely was the correct Rubio. John placed the photograph on the desk. The journalist handed him a clipping.

"I don't read Italian," John said. But he could see that Rubio's name was mentioned in the first paragraph, along with something about the army.

"That is too bad. This man you claim is an officer in the secret service has worked for the army."

"Has worked for the army?"

The older man nodded. "This week he was appointed Minister of Defense."

"Jesus," John breathed.

"A very important position within the Italian government. A very sensitive position. Easily as dangerous a position as the Premier's"

John couldn't say a thing.

"But you are not a writer. I understand that. So I ask myself for what other reason could you be here seeking information."

John just looked at the man. If Rubio was a part of the network, as his father had written, then now, more than ever before, he had to be stopped.

"What are you after?"

John flinched, and the older man got to his feet.

"You will please leave this building. Immediately, before I call the police."

"The police?" John asked, getting up. "I don't understand. I haven't done anything."

"Why have you come to me? What do you want?"

This was all wrong. Christ, he had blown it. "It's not what you think," he blurted.

The editor turned away and went to the window where he stared down at the alley.

John looked down at the photograph and the newspaper

articles, very conscious of his beating heart and his ragged breathing. He looked up at the young man from the lobby desk, who shook his head. Christ! "I . . ." he started, but then he cut himself off. He turned and ran down the stairs, leaving the building the way he had come.

At least he now knew who Leonardo Rubio was. And as stunning as that information had been to him, it would make it relatively simple to find out where the man maintained his offices, and from there he could wait and watch until Rubio led him to his home.

But it would take time, something he did not know if he had enough of. If the editor became too suspicious of John's motives, he might tell the police what had happened in his office. They would have his description. Rubio was Minister of Defense. They would protect him. It could become impossible to get anywhere near the man.

At the corner, he turned left up toward the river. Half a block away he stepped to the curb and raised his hand to hail a taxi just as the young man from the newspaper walked past him.

"Across the street. The Caffè Emanuele," the young man said urgently. He stepped out in the street and expertly dodged traffic to the other side.

John lowered his hand and hurried down to the corner, where he waited with the other pedestrians for the light to change.

He went back to the sidewalk café in the middle of the block, but the young man was nowhere in sight.

One of the waiters came up to him. "Just this way, *signore*," he said in English.

John was led inside to a small table in the far corner. The young man from the newspaper was there, nervously waiting for him.

"Is it true what Pietro said?"

John sat down. "Is what true?"

"That you are not a writer."

"I want to talk with Rubio," John said. His heart was hammering.

"I will help you. I have the information you need—and something else." He pulled a hastily wrapped package from beneath his jacket and held it under the table for John to touch.

There was something hard in the package. It was a gun, John realized suddenly.

"Yes," the young man said, reading the understanding in John's face. "Directions for finding Rubio's estate are in the package as well. If you are interested."

John hesitated only a moment. "I am," he said. He took the package. "Now tell me more about him."

"Basta!" the young man said, and he jumped up and rushed out of the café.

The waiter came up as John stuffed the package beneath his jacket. *"Signore?"*

John looked up at him. "A cognac. A large cognac."

Chapter 12

MAHONEY WAS DRIVING up the long, gentle hill outside of Beersheba, the lush green farmland around him dark in contrast to the desert. It was night, and he could not see much except for the lights of the city he had just passed through, and the strings of lights along the fence of kibbutz Gan Haifiz above him. He had never been here at night, and it almost seemed as if he were approaching in an airplane, but coming up for a landing instead of down, the long line of fence lights the runway markers.

The desert air was clear and cold, in sharp contrast to the muggy weather of Washington over the past few days. And although he had left Israel only eleven days earlier, it seemed as if it had been years and years since he had been here last.

That feeling had to do in part with the unreality of everything that had happened in that terribly short time: his bogus death; the deaths of his daughter-in-law and grandchildren; and the disappearance of his son. But it also had to do with the fact that when he had left here, it was to have been for good. He had not come up with all the answers, but they had been locked out from him here. His work here had been finished as far as Ezra Wasserman, head of the Mossad, was concerned. Malecki was the mole in the Israeli intelligence service, and he was dead. There was nothing left but the embarrassment of picking up the pieces, and the Israelis did not want a foreigner standing around gaping at them while they did it. And finally, his sense of distance had to do with McBundy's warning that there were less than two weeks remaining to clean up the mess and get back to the barn. He couldn't help but compare the time scales. He had been away from Israel for eleven days, and now that he was back, he had eleven days in which to finish up. It hardly seemed possible.

Mahoney looked in his rearview mirror again, but there was nothing behind him except the dark ribbon of narrow highway leading back to Beersheba, and beyond that, Tel Aviv.

He had arrived late this afternoon on one of three passports McBundy and the crew had supplied him with, which identified him as William Morrison, vice-president in charge of sales for the Des Moines Desalination Equipment Company. He had had a difficult moment at passport control, where the uniformed officer had detained him long enough to make a telephone call. But it had been nothing. The man had merely wanted to make sure that Mahoney's firm was not on any restricted list. It wasn't. Mahoney's passport was stamped, and within an hour he had gotten something to eat, rented a car from the Avis counter, and started south.

Once, when he was about halfway down to Beersheba, he had had the terrible thought that Wasserman might be dead. That he'd come to the kibbutz in time to find Wasserman lying in his office with a bullet hole in his skull, much the same as they had found David Ben Abel. But there'd be no reason for Henrys to pull the trigger on Wasserman. Not now that Malecki and the others were dead, and the dust was beginning to settle. If Wasserman were killed, it would raise too many questions. No, he had reassured himself, Wasserman would be all right.

Wasserman had been spotted leaving Tel Aviv five days ago, and although McBundy had admitted they had no idea where he had disappeared to, Mahoney knew. Wasserman had told him that the kibbutz director, Carl Margraff, would soon be retiring and the job would be open. It was logical that

Wasserman would have to come down here to forget, to lick his wounds, to allow himself to heal from the terrible mauling he had taken. Like Mahoney, a number of people he had loved and respected were dead because of the network. And the Mossad chief would need time to mend. Near the end of the Sonja Margraff-Chaim Malecki thing, Wasserman had confided in Mahoney that when it was finished, and all the pieces had been picked up, he was opting for the simpler life of a kibbutz director. "Margraff," he said, "leads an idealistic life. I want that for myself, and for my wife."

Mahoney had understood perfectly well what the Mossad director had spoken of.

At the crest of the hill, Mahoney slowed the car and cranked down his window. The main gate was open, and the kibbutz, which looked very much like a military camp, was all lit up. There were dozens of cars and Jeeps parked in the central square, and he could just hear strains of music coming from the Community Center. He passed under the kibbutz sign and entered the compound, which consisted of little more than a dozen buildings, all facing the square. To the right were dormitories and apartments. Straight ahead, near the back, were the machine shops, tool sheds, generators, and wells. And to the left were the Community Center, dining hall, and kibbutz offices, along with more living quarters. At the center of the square was a small patch of well-tended grass bordered by white stones. A bare flagpole jutted from the lawn. During the day the flag of Israel flapped in the breeze.

Mahoney parked his car on the far side of the Community Center, away from the other cars and partially in the shadows of the next building. After he had shut off the lights and engine, he sat for a while listening to the sounds of the party in progress. He could hear, in addition to the music, men shouting and young women laughing. A terribly off-key man's voice was singing along with the music, which was some Israeli folk song, Mahoney supposed. But he was struck by the immense happiness in the man's voice. He sounded oblivious to anything but the joy of the moment.

Mahoney glanced toward the party, then got out of his car and went around to the kibbutz office. He mounted the steps and went inside without knocking.

A young man of eighteen or so was seated at the camp secretary's desk, textbooks and notes spread out in front of him, a cassette recorder playing classical music beside him. He looked up, the smile on his face dying as he realized that it was not someone he knew. He sat up straighter.

He said something in Hebrew.

Mahoney smiled. "I'm sorry, I only speak English." He could almost see the young man shift mental gears.

"Ah . . . yes. May I help you with something, sir?"

Mahoney took out one of his business cards and handed it to the young man. "I'd like to talk with Carl Margraff, if I could. And perhaps Mr. Ezra Wasserman, if he's here."

The young man looked at the card, then glanced past Mahoney toward the window overlooking the square. "Mr. Margraff isn't here, sir."

"Will he be back soon?"

"I'm not really sure. He's out of the country. He went to Germany. His family. A cousin, I think."

"I see. He'll be in Berlin then. Do you have his address there?"

"Yes, sir," the young man said. He referred to a note on the desk, wrote it down on a slip of paper, and handed it up.

"And Mr. Wasserman? I was told that he might be here."

"Well . . . in that case," the young man hesitated. "I can check, Mr. . . . ah"—he looked at the card—"Morrison."

"Please do."

"Does Mr. Wasserman know that you're coming to see him?"

"No."

"Maybe the morning would be better," the young man said hopefully. "If you don't have a place in Beersheba, I can assign you a room here for the night."

"That would be nice," Mahoney said. "But I'd still like to see Ezra tonight if it's at all possible."

"Yes, sir," the young man said. He picked up the phone and dialed three numbers. "It's Michael," he said after a moment. "Just fine. There's someone here to see Ezra. A Mr. William Morrison." The young man looked up at Mahoney. "Kathy is getting him."

"Fine," Mahoney said.

It was a minute or so before the young man turned back to the telephone. He stiffened slightly. "This is Michael at the office, Mr. Wasserman. There is a gentleman here by the name of Morrison to see you, sir."

The young man nodded. "Yes, sir," he said. "Of course, sir. I'll tell him."

Mahoney stepped forward quickly and motioned for the young man not to hang up.

"Just a minute, Mr. Wasserman."

"Let me talk with him."

"I . . ." the young man hesitated, but Mahoney was reaching for the phone, and he relinquished it.

"Michael? What is it?" Wasserman was saying.

"Good evening, Ezra. I'm here at the kibbutz office. We must talk. I'll explain everything."

Mahoney could hear nothing but the shocked silence.

"Ezra?" he said after a moment.

"My God." Wasserman barely breathed the words. "Oh, my God."

"The old business isn't finished, Ezra. We're going to have to talk. Tonight."

There was another long pause, and Mahoney could almost see Wasserman desperately trying to gather his wits. "I'll be right over. Put Michael on, please."

Mahoney handed the phone to the young man.

"Yes, sir?" he said, and then his face lit up. He said something in Hebrew, hung up the phone, and started gathering his things together. "Mr. Wasserman will be over in just a minute."

Mahoney had to smile. "And you're going to the dance, after all."

"Yes, sir," the young man said. He stuffed his books, notes, and tape recorder into a rucksack, then hurried out the door. "Nice to have met you," he said over his shoulder as he left, leaving the door open.

Mahoney sat on the edge of the desk, listening to the music drifting from next door and thinking about when his own Michael and John were young men in school, studying. He was thinking about youthful exuberance and innocence when a very haggard Wasserman appeared in the doorway. He was a small man with a dark complexion and very dark, intense eyes. He had a habit of cocking his head to one side, as if he were listening very closely to the sounds around him. He was wearing khaki trousers, a short-sleeved safari shirt, and thick boots.

"Then it is true," he said. His voice was soft.

Mahoney nodded. "I'm here under a different passport though. William Morrison."

Wasserman nodded. "Doesn't matter. No one is looking for you." He shook his head and came the rest of the way into the room, closing the door behind him. "Mr. Begin telephoned your President to apologize. That was nine days ago. If I hadn't resigned, I would have been asked to do so."

"That bad, Ezra?"

"Worse. The damage to our service was immense. It may take years to pick up all the pieces and cover ourselves again."

"Who is your successor?"

Wasserman's eyes became flinty. One of the most closely guarded secrets in Israel was the identity of the Mossad chief. He crossed in front of Mahoney, letting the moment pass, opened the door to the inner office, turned on the light, and disappeared inside without a word.

Mahoney pushed off from the desk and followed Wasserman into Margraff's office. Margraff's memorabilia was still on the shelves and walls. Mahoney closed the door behind him. Wasserman was pouring them both a cognac.

"That was an interesting maneuver on the plane. Would you mind telling me if it was one of our people, or one of yours?"

"Neither," Mahoney lied. "It was nothing more than a misunderstanding. But that's not why I came here. I came to exchange information with you. That, and to warn you."

Wasserman held out the snifter to Mahoney. They sat down, Wasserman behind the desk, Mahoney across from him.

"A warning?" the Israeli asked. "I would have thought it was all over now, with the deaths of Chaim and Per Larsen."

"It's still very much alive."

"Why'd you come back here, Wallace? What do you want from me?"

"Information, just as I've said."

"What kind of information? Information to do what? It's all over. It's finished."

Mahoney shook his head, then took a sip of cognac. It wasn't very good, but it was drinkable. "When I was in Paris, I wrote it all down—everything I had learned up to that moment—and then mailed it to my son in California."

"You thought you needed insurance. From whom? Us?"

Mahoney shook his head. "They tried to kill my son for the notes."

"They weren't successful, evidently, whoever *they* might be. Did you recover your notes?"

"No. They missed my son, but they killed my daughter-in-law and my grandchildren."

"Oh, no, Wallace," Wasserman said, genuine pain in his eyes. "Why in God's name? Why would they do something like that?"

"They thought I was dead. John had the notes. He was the only one left who knew the entire story."

"He's safe now?"

"No. I have no idea where he is."

"He's on the run?"

Mahoney nodded.

"And whoever they are, they think you're dead, so you can't openly go after him without blowing your cover."

"That's right."

Wasserman sat back in his chair. "I think, Wallace, if you want help from me, you'd better start from the beginning and tell me everything. Then we can get to what you want."

Mahoney set his glass down on the desk, pulled out a cigar, unwrapped it, and went through the business of getting it lit. "You know most of it. You've just refused to understand what was happening."

"A network. Is it the *they* you are talking about?"

"Malecki here in Israel. Per Larsen with ININ. Armand Arlemont with the SDECE—"

"Wait a moment," Wasserman interrupted. "Arlemont is dead. He was killed. By you?"

"It was an accident."

Wasserman digested that for a moment, but he did not pursue it. "In the CIA. Who is it there?"

"We're not completely sure. But I think it's a man named Darrel Switt."

Wasserman had a blank look. "Don't know the name."

"There are others. With the West Germans and the Italians."

"Five or six countries, plus NATO?"

"More," Mahoney said. "England. East Germany. The Soviet Union. Both Chinas."

Wasserman had been holding himself steady, first against the shock of seeing Mahoney risen from the dead, and then against the things he was being told. But this last bit seemed to deflate him. "That's a bit rough to take, Wallace. Even just speculating. How certain are you of all this?"

"Very," Mahoney said.

Wasserman looked away. "That means everything—all our grubby little secrets, all our dirty laundry—not only got to NATO, but over to the other side."

"It was all there, you know, in Malecki's contact files."

"The ones I brought you out of the archives?"

"Yes."

"But you had to know what you were looking for," Wasserman said defensively. "I mean, you couldn't just ramble through all that without having some preconceived notions. Something to go on."

"I had a fair idea," Mahoney conceded. "Malecki got around. I was looking to see who his contacts were. The regular ones."

"And Per Larsen and Arlemont were on the list?"

"That's right. Along with Leonardo Rubio from the Italian secret service, Walther Zwiefel from the West German—"

"And the KGB and the Communist Chinese? Were their names on the contact sheets as well? Was Chaim that open about it?"

"They were at various functions Chaim attended in Washington," Mahoney said. "But no, I don't believe Chaim was ever that open about meeting them. I think Per Larsen may have been one of the clearinghouses."

"Larsen. NATO. My God, that means they all had everything. Instantly."

"So did you, Ezra," Mahoney said gently.

Wasserman looked sharply at him but said nothing.

"You knew, for instance, the tactical strength and deployment of most of our forces in Europe long before the CIA ever told you. And you got that information from Malecki."

Wasserman held his silence, but Mahoney could see that he had hit the mark. Malecki had proved his worth a hundred times over to the Mossad. His money-raising successes were only the ostensible excuse for his decorations by the Israeli government. His fact-finding for the Mossad—including spying on the United States—had been the real reason he had been so well thought of.

"If Per Larsen was the clearinghouse, then your network is dead. Unless there is another clearinghouse."

"Per Larsen was only one of many," Mahoney said. "Even now I'd guess there is someone new in NATO."

"And in the SDECE?"

Mahoney nodded.

Wasserman got up from his chair and poured himself another drink. "More?" he asked.

"I'm still good," Mahoney said.

When he was sitting down again, Wasserman held the cognac snifter in both hands. "They have someone else in the Mossad?"

"It's likely. If not already, then very soon."

Again Wasserman paused to think it out. "And if we get around to flushing this one out, there'd be another?"

Mahoney nodded.

"And another, and so on? We'd never know whom we could trust."

"Something like that. But you would not be able to turn down verifiable intelligence information."

"Our most able people would become the most suspect."

Wasserman was beginning to understand, and it wasn't pleasant to witness. "Your own agency arranged your apparent demise?"

"That's right," Mahoney said. "But I've come back to ask about Chaim Malecki. I think he's the key to all this."

"He's dead."

"What I'm talking about is Chaim's background. His personal history. The things that were not in his dossier."

"The records were complete—" Wasserman started to protest.

"No, they weren't. I read them. There was nothing there by or about you and Sonja. And yet you were very big in Chaim's life. You two were the closest to him in Israel."

"You'll have to talk to Carl about Sonja."

"I will," Mahoney said. "Meanwhile, I'm here with you, and I want to know about Malecki."

"Why, for God's sake?" Wasserman cried. He jumped up. "What can you possibly hope to gain by going over all that again?"

"Not again, Ezra. There's no *again* here. You never did tell me about Malecki. You never did tell me how close you and he were. How close he was with your wife, and how Sonja fit into all of it."

"He wasn't!" Wasserman said, and it sounded more like a cry of anguish than a denial.

"I wasn't completely sure before. There were too many other things happening. But when I began to think about my own son, I understood a little what you had done and why."

"What are you talking about?" Wasserman asked, looking down at Mahoney. His complexion was mottled now, his eyes wide, and his lips compressed. "He was no blood relationship to me. In fact, I had never even heard of him until he came to Israel."

"He wasn't your son in blood, Ezra. No. That's true. But you covered for him. Right along you covered for him. He was a good man. Well thought of in the highest circles, not only because of his fund-raising work, but because of the quality of the intelligence he was bringing in from his trips. But there was even more to it than that, Ezra."

"I don't know what you're talking about," Wasserman said. He was beginning to sweat.

"Chaim Malecki may not have been any blood relation to you, but you looked upon him as your son nevertheless. Both you and your wife did."

Wasserman backed up a step, but he did not deny it.

"And Carl Margraff was a family friend. A very close family friend, and therefore his daughter Sonja was almost a part of the family as well."

"We've known them since after the war."

"That's right. So that when Carl came asking about Chaim Malecki—about an older man seducing his daughter—he felt very safe and certainly satisfied by your recommendations. Chaim Malecki is a wonderful man. He'd make a great son-in-law for Carl. And Sonja would become even more like a daughter. It was going to be one big happy family."

"No!" Wasserman cried. "I mean, yes! I don't . . ." He buried his face in his hands and turned away as he wept noiselessly.

Mahoney could hear the music from the Community Center, so bright, so young and happy. Across the way was life and joy. Here was death and misery. He just wanted to see this end. He just wanted to finish what he had begun a very long time ago.

Chapter 13

WASSERMAN WAS MUCH more subdued now. Malecki was out of his system, or at least his relationship with Malecki was now out in the open, and he had nothing to hide any longer. He poured himself a third cognac; it was the most Mahoney had ever seen him drink, and it was a small measure of just how badly he was taking all of this. He came back to the desk and sat down, his eyes moist and red, the bags beneath them pronounced.

"I may have been as close to Chaim as you say, but I never consciously covered for him," Wasserman said. "And don't ever say that to me again. I never knew what he was, and I never gave him any alibi."

"That goes without saying. I never accused you of that." Mahoney looked away momentarily. "Malecki buffaloed everyone, including you, but especially Sonja. She was in love with him, after all."

"I want to ask you about her . . ."

"Don't."

Wasserman blinked. "What?"

"Let's stick with Malecki."

"You have something on Sonja?"

"Malecki. He's why I'm here. He was recruited into the
network. I want to know how. Or at least I want some sense
of what must have happened at his turning."

Wasserman stared at him long enough to pass the unspoken
message that he would not forget about Sonja Margraff, that
they would get back to her. And then he seemed to gather
himself together. "What do you want to know? I met him at
Sharon's house. The Knesset had just come out of session, and
Golda was there, along with Dayan and Begin." Wasserman
smiled. "Begin was still something of a wild-eyed radical in
those days. Chaim didn't think much of him. Yet they got
along. I guess that's what impressed me most of all."

"You were impressed," Mahoney prompted. "Do you mean
to say that Chaim was a conservative?"

"Yes, he was. But he wasn't the run-of-the-mill conservative." Wasserman stopped. "I don't know if you completely
understand what is happening in our political structure here:
the difference between the conservatives and the liberals; between the educated European Jews and the Oriental Jews; and
the moderates versus the radicals. I could go on. But it's much
more complicated than your system."

"I understand that, Ezra."

"So when I say Chaim was a conservative, I mean to say
that he was a very special animal. In your government you
might call him a person who had the ear of everyone—and
who understood everything."

"A conservative Democrat or a liberal Republican."

"Not quite, but you have the general idea. Chaim was concerned about Begin's politics, but he understood them. And he
was among only a handful who were convinced that Begin
would rise to power."

"That's all after the fact, Ezra. How did you actually meet
Chaim? Did someone introduce you, or what?"

Wasserman's lips pursed. "I'm not sure. That's been a number of years ago." He steepled his fingers. "I'm just not sure.
I remember the get-together up in Sharon's home outside Jerusalem. There were a lot of people there. Everyone talking at
once. A lot of arguing going on. And I was just with Chaim.

We were comparing notes. I thought he was a very bright young man."

The contact method was nothing more or less than Mahoney had expected. "When did he come to work for you?"

"Almost immediately," Wasserman said without thinking. But then he looked up. "I mean, he dropped by my house one afternoon with a story about . . ." Wasserman broke off.

Mahoney smiled. He didn't feel particularly happy, though. Wasserman was beginning to lose control. "Came to you with a story about something he heard in Washington. Something having to do . . . with the Middle East."

"It was about Iran, specifically. About Khomeini in Paris. That there was a CIA plot to have him assassinated. He seemed to know Khomeini's significance to the future not only of Iran, but of the entire Middle East. And it was important, with the Soviets ready to back Iraq anytime she wanted to attack."

"So what?"

"Anything to do with Middle East stability has to do with us."

"I don't mean that. I mean, so what that Chaim Malecki . . . he hadn't become an Israeli citizen yet, had he?"

Wasserman shook his head.

"So Chaim Malecki, an American newspaperman, tells you something about an Iranian religious leader. So what? You believed him?"

"Not at first," Wasserman said uncomfortably. "But the things he said made sense. I had been looking for just that kind of information for some time. It was of vital interest to us."

Mahoney held his breath. It suddenly occurred to him just what must have happened. It was brilliant. "Just how close were the things Malecki was saying to you, to the thoughts you had been having about Khomeini and his Paris exiles?"

Wasserman flared. "It's not what you think."

"Yes, it is," Mahoney said. From low-grade spies within the Israeli government, basic information was gathered on nearly every government official so that Henrys could direct more intelligent, more penetrating inquiries. From the thousands of questions, asked of hundreds of people, a matrix of information was built, pinpointing a very few government officials—such as Wasserman—for targeting. Further information was gathered about the select few until only one at a time was selected for final infiltration. The operative was given an extensive briefing so that he could befriend his target in a knowledgeable fashion.

It explained how Malecki had gotten close to Wasserman and therefore into the Mossad. But it still did not answer Mahoney's primary questions: How had Malecki actually been recruited, and, therefore, what was the network's methodology for recruitment in general? And what exactly were they trying to accomplish? Something made them tick. They had to have some ultimate goal in mind. A supremely important goal, judging by their ruthlessness.

"Even if it is, how was I to know?" Wasserman said, and Mahoney had to wonder if the man wasn't finally losing his nerve. He hoped not.

"You weren't. But you did run a background check on him."

"An extensive one. You know that. And he came out clean as a whistle."

"Too clean?"

Again Wasserman visibly held himself in check. "A verdict of lack of judgment on my part I'll accept. But incompetence on the part of my people I will not."

"I never meant to imply any such thing, Ezra," Mahoney said. "I think you know in what high regard we hold the Mossad. It's about the best operational service in the world."

"Infiltrated at the top," Wasserman said bitterly.

Mahoney got up, fetched the bottle from the cabinet, and poured Wasserman another drink. He moved slowly and with care, much as a hunter moves so as not to disturb his game. Wasserman was in a mood, and Mahoney did not want to break him out of it—just bend it and maneuver it to his advantage.

He sat down. "How did you come to suspect a mole in the first place, Ezra? I mean, before you called me?"

"Al Qaryūt," he said. "You know that."

"No, I mean much earlier. Al Qaryūt had to have been the straw that broke the camel's back. How about the first few glimmerings?"

"Tradecraft, you'd call it, but Andabo and his crows from the Knesset called it plain blind luck."

It had started as a cross between an idle-hour game and a legitimate reorganization, Wasserman admitted. His voice and manner for the moment were matter-of-fact, much like the attitude of a criminal who's been interrogated to the point that he wants nothing more than to get it all over with. He becomes merely a tape recorder on playback. Once the reel is empty, the switch can be cut off.

Wasserman had begun studying Libyan, Syrian, and Lebanese intelligence-service organizational charts, which he built into a system. To get the order of things, a sense of the timing.

"Sometimes that's even more important than the raw data itself," Wasserman stopped unnecessarily to explain.

It wasn't long before he came to the startling realization that every time he reorganized the Mossad—shuffled an expert here, revamped a branch for effectiveness there—the Libyans, Syrians, and Lebanese did exactly the same thing with their counterparts. The Mossad was being shadowed; paralleled, as he came to think of it.

Which got him to thinking about coincidences. And he went searching the Mossad's archives, where he found them. Dozens of them.

Six months prior to construction of an observation post at Asha, the Syrian secret service began ordering up quantities of cement, steel, and wire, along with other materials for construction of an opposite number.

Three and a half months before the Strategic Planning Center at En Gedi was built, the Jordanians ordered the construction of their staging post at Ataruz.

Coincidence? Wasserman not only began to seriously doubt it, he began looking for specific proofs to nail it solid.

"Al Qaryūt came along almost on cue," he said. "About the time I was seriously beginning to doubt the veracity of our own records, Al Qaryūt came along and clinched it."

"Al Qaryūt was a big blow," Mahoney prompted after a silence.

Wasserman smiled despite himself. "The biggest," he said. "Everyone who knew about it, from the top on down, was devastated."

It was to have been for Israel what the AWAC aircraft surveillance system was for the Saudis, only in greater depth. The satellite, in a stable orbit several hundred miles above the Mediterranean, would keep watch on the entire Middle East. Its infrared, electronic, and ionization detectors would continuously monitor enemy military activity; its high-resolution television equipment could provide a visual reference for the area. They could not lose with the satellite system, whose receiving station had been constructed near the tiny town of Al Qaryūt not far inland from the Dead Sea.

"No one, absolutely no one was to have known the real purpose of Al Qaryūt or the satellite," Wasserman said. "Except for a select few at the highest levels of government." It had been kept secret—although deliberately not a closely guarded secret—that a weather satellite had been sent aloft and that the telemetry station would be constructed near Al Qaryūt. The fact that the supposed weather station was really a Mossad data acquisition center was the deepest of all secrets.

"Yet we had been compromised," Wasserman said bitterly. "You can imagine the blow. We knew it had to be someone at the highest level, but we didn't know whom to trust to carry out the investigation."

"So I was hired."

"Sonja suggested you, actually."

Mahoney looked at the butt of the cigar he had smoked and wished for another. But he had already smoked too many today, and he could feel the heaviness in his chest. He would wait.

"She wasn't a traitor," Mahoney said. "Not really. She was guilty of nothing more than loving Chaim Malecki too deeply."

"Even knowing what he was?"

"Despite what he was. You can understand that, can't you?"

Wasserman looked away, but he nodded. "You know that it was Chaim who made the first contact with ComSat, Limited, don't you?"

"Yes," Mahoney said thoughtfully. "It's the one thing in this entire affair that doesn't seem to fit with everything else." It was an anomaly, and Mahoney had not yet come to understand its significance. Malecki had been spying for the network, and it was within the realm of Henrys's logic to believe that they might wish to maneuver Israel into a spy-satellite system. It would make the network's job all that much easier. So why was Al Qaryūt destroyed? It had to have been engineered by the network, otherwise there would not have been the presence of the American-made Soman gas at the Jordanian staging post at Ataruz, from where the attack had been mounted. The network had led Israel into putting up the satellite and building the station at a cost in excess of fifty million American dollars. So why maneuver the Arabs into destroying it?

"He was a traitor to Israel, so why have us build a satellite in the first place if he never really wanted us to have it?"

Mahoney was still lost in thought, so he said nothing, but he could hear Wasserman saying something to him.

"Probably just to make us spend our money. If we used money for a project like that, which was going to be immediately destroyed, it would be that much less money we'd have for something else."

Mahoney looked up. "What'd you say, Ezra?" he asked softly.

"I was thinking out loud, trying to make some sense of Chaim's contacting ComSat for our satellite. If he was a traitor, why maneuver us into building the thing in the first place?"

"Go on," Mahoney prompted.

Wasserman shrugged. "Unless it was an exercise merely to make us spend money."

Spend money. ComSat had profited heavily from the satellite deal with the Israelis. Or at least Mahoney assumed they had.

"But if Chaim was spying for some sort of a network, as you say he was, then it doesn't make much sense. You'd expect they'd've welcomed such a surveillance tool."

"What was Chaim's tie with ComSat?" Mahoney asked.

"I'm not completely sure, but it was my understanding that it involved a friend of the family, or something of that nature."

A friend of the family, Mahoney thought. McNiel Henrys, the supposed head of the network, was in reality Chaim's uncle. If Malecki was related—even in some distant way—to an executive of ComSat, Ltd., it would mean Henrys was also related.

He was out on thin ice now. And yet it was all beginning to fit.

If that indeed was the case, it could very well lead to the conclusion that the attack on the satellite receiving station at Al Qaryūt, and the subsequent murders of the Jordanian troops who had mounted the attack, could have been a completely separate operation from that of the network.

That could mean that Malecki had dual loyalties: to the network, and to his family.

But where had they gotten the American-made nerve gas? McBundy was running supply checks on the gas, but so far he'd come up with nothing.

A sudden burst of laughter from next door brought Mahoney

out of his thoughts. He looked up.

Wasserman had his head cocked. "They're having a good time over there."

"What are they celebrating?"

"A wedding," Wasserman said. He got up and put his glass back on the sideboard. "You said you came here to exchange information, and to warn me." He turned back. "I've told you what I could. Has it helped?"

"Yes," Mahoney said. But in a far different way than he had expected. He was still trying to work out the significance of the construction and then destruction of Al Qaryūt.

"And my warning?"

"It's still active, Ezra. The network is still alive."

"What can I do?"

Mahoney wrote down McBundy's private number at the Agency on a piece of paper and handed it across. "Bob McBundy. Tell him you'd like to speak with Rupert Blakemore."

Wasserman looked at the number, then burned the paper.

"If you have any glimmering of who your new mole is, or might be, telephone."

"Meanwhile?"

Mahoney got up and smiled wanly. "I'm dead and buried at Missoula. I've not been here."

"How long can you keep it up?"

"As long as need be."

Wasserman came around the desk. "The last time you left . . ."

"I understand, Ezra. You were doing your job. But I also understand what you did for me. Your superiors wanted me eliminated."

Wasserman nodded. "This time, though, I want to wish you luck." He shook Mahoney's hand.

"Thanks, Ezra."

He left the office, went back outside, and climbed into his car. Wasserman had come to the door, and he watched as Mahoney started toward the gate. The man would be back in Tel Aviv within twenty-four hours, Mahoney thought, his retirement cut short. It was too bad. But God only knew how this was going to turn out for any of them.

Although it was very late, Mahoney drove all the way back to Tel Aviv, where he checked into the Sheraton Hotel. The last time he was here he had stayed at the Dan. But then his name had been Wallace Mahoney. As soon as he had showered the desert grime off his body, he telephoned McBundy's special number at the Agency. McBundy answered on the first ring, and later, when Mahoney thought about it, it seemed to him that McBundy had sounded a bit breathless.

"This is Bill Morrison. I just talked with the folks at the kibbutz about our project," Mahoney said.

"I see," McBundy said guardedly. It was possible that someone was listening, although it wasn't likely. Unless their operation had been completely blown, there was no reason to suspect anyone would be interested.

"I'm calling from Tel Aviv now. I'll be leaving here later in the day."

"Anything interesting come up? Any confirmations?"

"A lot of interesting things," Mahoney said. "But nothing conclusive as of yet."

"Where are you off to next?"

"Berlin, to see another old friend. How about at home? Anything new from the West Coast?"

McBundy hesitated a moment. "Your car showed up in El Paso. An illegal southern friend was driving it. Swore he bought it from a dealer in Juárez."

Mahoney swore.

"John sold it to the dealer, then took a plane to Mexico City yesterday."

"And from there?"

"No word yet. Friends are checking on it now."

"He's on his way to Europe."

"You're damned right he is!" Again McBundy hesitated a moment. "Bonn, Rome, or London, I'd say. One of the three."

"You haven't alerted any of those stations, have you?" Mahoney asked, suddenly frightened that John would be targeted by a sudden increase in activity.

"Not yet."

"Don't," Mahoney said, relieved. What he had said to Wasserman was true. Now that Malecki was gone, there'd probably be another mole within the Mossad within a short time, if not already. Wouldn't the same hold true for the CIA? Switt was their man. He was gone. Wouldn't there be another ready to take his place? And if there was, and McBundy alerted their West European stations, word would get back to Henrys very quickly. And John would be dead.

"What then?" McBundy asked.

"I'll check with you tonight. I'll be in Berlin by then. I'll intercept John myself."

"I don't like this," McBundy said.

"You think I do?"

Frascati was a very small town less than fifteen miles southeast of Rome in the Alban Hills. It was Thursday night. John Mahoney, driving his rented Fiat, followed the main highway for a mile or two beyond the ancient town and then turned north onto the Via Coronele, as the instructions he had been given indicated. The narrow road wound its way up into the hills, and after a very short distance, John began to see the lights of the houses above him.

This was an area of very expensive homes. Modern structures clung to the hillsides. Rubio's, according to the notes he had been given, was on the Via Coronele, at the crest of the hill.

"There is an iron gate at the entry to Signore Rubio's home," the notes indicated. "The gate will be recognized by the Italian flags that fly over it by night as well as by day."

A low-slung sports car came around a sharp curve from above him and passed in a flash, its lights very bright, its tires screeching slightly on the pavement.

John climbed around the next curve, and a hundred yards above him he could see a huge house, its front face almost all glass, perched on thick steel girders. Then he was around another curve, his view blocked for the moment.

It was Rubio's home. He knew it was, and the closer he came, the more his heart pounded. His mouth was dry and his stomach rumbled. He was not an assassin. He was not cut out for this. Yet the compelling need to strike back was growing to frightening proportions within him.

He came around the last curve and had to slow down to a crawl to get past a half-dozen police cruisers, their blue lights flashing. The road divided here, the left-hand lane leading to another way down the hill; to the right, a road led toward the police, into a driveway. An ornate iron gate was open. Two tricolor Italian flags flew over it. Just within the gate, well illuminated by all the strong lights, was a Jaguar XKE sports car, its top down. A woman was in the passenger seat. John could see her long, light hair. But behind the wheel was Rubio. John was certain of it. He was less than twenty-five yards away. There was no mistake. Rubio seemed to be talking to the guards at the gate.

No one paid any attention to John as he passed slowly, and then he was around to the left, heading back down to the main road.

He had to wait at the bottom of the hill for several cars and a truck to pass, and then he drove back into Frascati, a very shaky feeling in the pit of his stomach. Rubio was up there. And within twenty-four hours—forty-eight at the most—John was going to kill him.

Chapter 14

Margraff Gold und Silber, which apparently specialized in bars and medallions for investment savings, was housed in a small but well-maintained shop just off the Kurfürstendamm. It was closed due to the lateness of the hour, but through the heavy steel mesh that protected the windows, Mahoney could see cardboard signs and cutouts depicting young blond women, obviously very happy, holding smallish bars of gold up to their cheeks. A small sign to one side of the doorway indicated that the P. Margraff residence over the shop could be reached around the corner and through the alley. He had been surprised when he had learned that Carl Margraff had a cousin here. During the time he had worked with Carl's son, Peter, in Berlin during the sixties, the young man had not mentioned that he had relatives in the city. The door around back was marked with a small plate, below which were a door buzzer and a tiny speaker behind a grille. Mahoney pressed the buzzer, and moments later a thin, metallic voice answered.

"Ja? Wer ist das?"

"Gutend Abend. Hier ist Wilhelm Morrison, für Carl Margraff. Ist er hier?"

"Moment, bitte," the woman said.

Mahoney stepped back a pace and glanced up toward the street as a car passed. It was after eight o'clock, but still somewhat early for the action to begin along the Ku-damm. That would come around ten, peaking sometime after midnight. Berlin, like a lot of large cities, had its fast-lane district, but here the people had always seemed to Mahoney more frantic than anywhere else. He supposed it was because of the city's special circumstances; not only was it divided, but it was deep within enemy territory. At any moment the Soviet tanks could be rolling.

Someone came down the stairs and fumbled with the lock. The door swung open.

"Gott in Himmel," Carl Margraff said, his face ashen in the light in the stairwell. "I thought you were dead."

"May I come in?" Mahoney asked. "I'd like to talk with you."

"Of course," Margraff said, struggling to get over his initial shock.

He was short, thick-necked, and very stocky, his build and weathered face witness to years spent building the kibbutz in the desert. He wore shapeless gray trousers, a wide-collared shirt, and a light cardigan despite the warmth of the evening. His eyes squinted out of habit. He gave the impression of being very much out of place here in the city, away from Gan Haifiz. It was an impression that was strengthened when they came upstairs to the better light. The man's hands shook with a slight palsy, his lips were thin and compressed, almost bloodless, and his eyes were moist beneath their lids.

A door from the hallway to the left opened into a small sitting room where an elderly man and woman sat on a sofa watching a huge television set. They looked up as Mahoney passed the door; he caught a glimpse of concern on their faces.

"Carl?" the man asked.

"Moment, Peter," Margraff called over his shoulder. At the end of the corridor, he opened a door, reached inside, and flipped on a light. "Wait in here. I'll be right back."

Margraff hurried back down the hall and into the sitting

room as Mahoney went into what appeared to be either the office for the downstairs business or a small, much-used study. He suspected the first. A large desk was placed at an angle in one corner; in the opposite corner were a small table and lamp between a pair of wingback chairs. There were books, catalogs, newspapers, and files scattered everywhere. Mahoney sat down in one of the wingback chairs, and in a moment or two, Margraff was back. He closed the study door, then pulled the desk chair around and sat down to face Mahoney.

He shook his head. "You gave me quite a fright," he said, his voice soft, his British-accented English very good.

"I talked with Ezra yesterday."

"You were at the kibbutz? How is everything?"

Mahoney smiled. "There was a wedding. Everyone seemed to be having a good time."

"Paul and Debra. I wanted to be there. I sincerely did."

There was a long silence between them, and Margraff just stared ahead as if he were looking at something in the far distance.

"I never got a chance to tell you how sorry I was about Sonja," Mahoney said softly.

Margraff did not look up, but nodded slowly. He no longer seemed in a hurry as he had back at the kibbutz. "She's why I came to Berlin. Peter is buried here, and I brought Sonja's body back to lie next to his. They were very close. She had a great deal of respect for him. Looked up to him almost like a god." He paused. "But I already told you their relationship."

"She wasn't the mole, Carl."

"Ezra explained it to me, or at least most of it. She just picked the wrong man. We all did. It's incredible."

Mahoney noticed that Margraff was wearing carpet slippers, and they seemed oddly out of place on him. The last time they had spoken, he had been dressed in desert clothes with heavy, thick-soled boots on his feet. The slippers made Margraff seem very old and frail.

"What happened to you?" he asked. "Why the subterfuge about your death?"

"Chaim Malecki was the mole in your service; we have one in ours. They may have worked together. Someone in the clear was needed to look after it."

Margraff looked at him. "Don't we still liaise?"

"Yes. But this is different."

"And they had to fake your death," Margraff said gravely. He shook his head again.

"Tell me about Sonja and Chaim," Mahoney said. "Where did they meet?"

"Ezra could tell you more about that than I could."

"I want to hear this from you."

"At a party, I think. In Jerusalem. For some government official. Sonja was there with the Mossad, and as a friend of Ezra's."

"What did she tell you about him?"

"Not much. Not at first. We didn't talk much in those days. I think I told you that as well."

"There must have been something, Carl. Something she said, or perhaps did. Maybe she took a trip with him."

"She took a lot of trips with him. They were gone two or three times a year together."

Wasserman had never mentioned that, nor had any note been made of it in Malecki's contact sheets and files. He had been the fair-haired boy in all respects: a sacred cow whose private life was sacrosanct even to the Mossad.

"Did they ever go to Geneva together?"

"I don't know. I don't think so. Washington, mostly. Rome, and maybe Paris once. Then of course England three or four times."

"England?" Mahoney asked, suddenly very alert but keeping his voice calm.

"London, I think. And then some other little town to the north."

"Can you think of the name of the place?"

Margraff started to shrug it off, but then he read something in Mahoney's eyes. "It's important?"

"Perhaps."

Margraff got up and went to one of the bookcases. He pulled down an atlas, which he opened to a map of England. He studied it for a moment, then looked up. "St. Albans. North of London."

Mahoney had never heard of the place. "What was there? At St. Albans?"

Margraff replaced the atlas but remained standing. "I don't know, for sure," he said. "A house, or an estate. Family, I think. Or friends."

"She never talked about it?"

"Not at any length."

"Later?" Mahoney insisted. "When she and Chaim had gotten very close and she began talking to you more?"

"She was very closemouthed. If she wanted to tell you something, she did, voluntarily. But no amount of prodding would get anything out of her if she didn't want to talk."

"Not even with you?"

"Certainly not with me," Margraff said. He came back and sat down on the edge of his chair. "Listen to me, Wallace. There were only two people in all of Sonja's life she ever talked to...I mean really confided in. The first was her brother, Peter, whom she looked upon as God. And then there was Chaim."

"When was this, Carl? When did these trips take place?"

"All through their relationship."

"I mean the ones to St. Albans."

Margraff looked away, trying to think. "I don't know," he said, letting his voice trail off.

"How about just the last trip or two?"

"A year ago. Maybe a couple the year before that." He looked back. "But I'm guessing, mind you."

"None since a year ago?"

Margraff thought again, then shook his head. "None that I can recall. Of course, Sonja could have gone without telling me. I wasn't her keeper. Far from it."

St. Albans, Mahoney thought, relaxing slightly from the tension that had been building. A year, and then two years ago. The timing was right for the Al Qaryūt satellite project— or was that nothing but coincidence?

"These trips with Malecki. Did you ever discuss them with Ezra? You two did get together from time to time."

"Yes, we had lunch or sometimes dinner together once a month. And occasionally he'd come down to the kibbutz to visit. But no, we never discussed Sonja and Chaim, other than in the most general terms."

"Isn't that unusual?"

"That friends wouldn't discuss a daughter?" Margraff retorted. "Not at all, when one of the friends happened to be the head of the Mossad, and the daughter was a Mossad operative. It would have put Ezra in an untenable position."

"I suppose," Mahoney said. He hadn't expected any other

answer, yet he was disappointed. Christ, it was a cold, uncaring business.

"We're not just discussing case histories here, Wallace," Margraff said. He appeared on the verge of anger.

"I know that."

"This is my daughter who is buried here next to my son. Both of them dead in operations that in one way or another involved you."

"You're not thinking that I—"

"No, I am not implying anything of that nature," Margraff interrupted.

Mahoney thought it best to let him go on. Let him get it out of his system. So he said nothing.

"But even now—they are both dead and buried—even now you are coming after me. Sonja is dead, Wallace, what help can she possibly be to you now?"

Mahoney held his silence.

"Can you answer me that?"

"As I said, Carl, Malecki evidently worked with the deep-cover agent in our service."

"And the other? The NATO officer?"

Mahoney wondered how in hell Margraff had heard about that? Wasserman? "Yes, him too."

"So now you want to backtrack and pick up all the pieces. At the expense of my family's name. Of my daughter's. Is that what you want to do?"

"No, I don't want to do that. But it does have to be done. And this is the only way I know how."

"What else do you want from me? What else can I give? The service . . . my country . . . I've given everything I have to give. Can't you understand that?"

Mahoney could feel pity for him. He too had given nearly all there was to give. But he was continuing because he had to. Because he could think of no alternative other than lying down and dying.

"Does the name Al Qaryūt mean anything to you?" he asked after a bit.

Something flashed across Margraff's eyes, but then it passed. "It's a town, east of Tel Aviv. Not very large."

"That's all?" Mahoney asked. "Sonja never mentioned it to you?"

"In what context?"

"You know damned well."

"What the hell are you talking about?"

"Ezra never mentioned it? Sonja never mentioned it? You never heard the name, not even when you were in Jerusalem at Government House? Never?"

"I still don't know what the hell you're talking about."

Mahoney was suddenly sick of the lies and evasions. He had liked Carl Margraff. He had thought he was the only man in this entire mess who had been straight and honest, who had nothing to hide. He wasn't so sure any longer. But he wondered whether it was deceit, or grief.

He got to his feet. "I was talking about the satellite receiving station at Al Qaryūt. It was central to all this, including your daughter's death."

"A weather satellite."

"Don't tell anyone I was here. Don't tell anyone I'm alive, or that you even suspect I'm alive."

"What do you want from me, Mahoney?" Margraff cried, jumping up.

"I want the truth, Carl. But it doesn't matter now. I think I got something anyway. Something to go on."

They went to the door, down the corridor—the old man and woman were still watching television—and then downstairs to the alley door.

"You've known from the beginning what Al Qaryūt was, haven't you?" Margraff asked.

"Not from the beginning," Mahoney replied. "But for some time now."

"And have you told your government?"

"Malecki knew about it, Carl. So everyone knew about it."

Margraff was silent for a moment. Mahoney opened the door. "When do you return to Gan Haifiz?"

"Day after tomorrow. But I'm starting a new kibbutz. I think Ezra will be taking over Gan Haifiz."

"Good luck," Mahoney said.

"You, too." They shook hands. "But where do you go now?"

"Probably back home," Mahoney lied. Bonn, Rome, London. Probably in that order, he thought. Afterward, whatever happened or didn't happen would depend upon a lot of things— among them, finding John.

"Take care."

"You, too," Mahoney said, and he stepped outside. Before

Margraff could close the door, however, he turned back. "When you were in the service . . ."

"Yes?"

"Did you ever worry about your family being dragged into any of it?"

"Constantly," Margraff said. "And it's exactly how it turned out."

He closed the door, and Mahoney walked out to the street in search of a taxi.

He took the flight from Tegel Airport to Bonn, where Bob Greene was waiting for him. His morose mood had deepened after talking with Margraff, yet he was able to see from Greene's eyes that something was wrong. But he said nothing until they were driving into the city along the Rhine. Then he asked Greene to bring him up-to-date.

From Ciudad Juárez they had traced John's movement to Mexico City; that part Mahoney had been told by McBundy. The rest was disturbing.

"From there, where'd he jump to?"

"He took a Pan Am flight to Europe via Kennedy," Greene said. "He got there yesterday morning." His husky frame almost filled the Ford Cortina.

"Bonn? Frankfurt?" Mahoney asked hopefully.

Greene shook his head. "Rome."

"Rubio," Mahoney said, his breath catching in his throat. "Sampson is down there. Has he got him yet, for God's sake?"

"I'm afraid not, Mr. Mahoney. In fact, we don't think he's in Italy any longer. Either here or London, and I'm guessing here, because Zwiefel is the most exposed, the easiest to get to, and he doesn't know about Henrys."

"Give it to me straight now, Bobby."

"We had his hotel on the Via Nazionale pegged within twenty-four hours, and we went up to his room. He wasn't there, although it seemed like most of his clothing was still in his suitcase."

"His passport?"

"He had picked it up from the hotel desk," Greene said. "We stuck around there for a few hours, but he never did show up."

"Is that when you came up here?"

Greene nodded. "We figured Len could handle the situation

down there, while I took care of the preliminaries here."

"How about Rubio? Have we got any kind of a line on him? I mean, is Sampson on top of him? If John is still in Italy, he'll try for Rubio."

"It's a little more complicated than that, sir," Greene said. "Len is down in Frascati, where Rubio has his house, waiting for John to show up. And he'll stay there until something happens—or as long as you want him to."

"But?"

"We don't think John would have a chance in hell of getting close. Besides the fact that he probably doesn't have a weapon, he may or may not know that two weeks ago Rubio was appointed Italian Minister of Defense."

Mahoney whistled. "Jesus."

"There's a guard on him all the time now. It's why I don't think John is there any longer."

"What do you mean?"

"He's rented a car, a small Fiat—we have the tag number— and presumably he'll have found out by now just who Rubio is. If he's driven up to Frascati to look things over, he'll see the security arrangements, and he'll back off if he has any sense. Henrys in London or Zwiefel here in Bonn would be easier targets."

Mahoney thought about that for a moment. He wanted to believe that Greene was correct—that chances were that John would be either in Bonn or on his way here—and yet he wanted to make damned sure all their bases were covered.

"How about Frascati itself? Has Len done any checking there?"

"Not too deeply. It's a small town. If Rubio is a part of the network, his people might get jumpy if they found out that someone was sniffing around. He's been moving around a lot, but so far he's come up with nothing."

"When did you last talk with him?"

"About an hour before you came in. There's some kind of a wine festival going on down there, so he's been able to move around pretty freely tonight."

Sampson was very good, Mahoney thought. One of the best in the business. If John was down there and did make some kind of crazy try on Rubio, Sampson would catch up with him. But then, Mahoney thought, Jensen had been very good as well. And he was dead.

"I'll show you the setup here," Greene was saying. "But for my money I think we should snatch Zwiefel and put the heat on him."

"The network would just go deeper, Bobby," Mahoney said. "I want the opposite to happen. I want to draw it out. I want its main nerve—whatever that might he—exposed."

"How?"

"We'll get to it."

Chapter 15

IT WAS VERY late, nearly two in the morning, and John pretended drunkenness as he weaved his way in and out of one café after another. It was wine-festival time. Early, one sodden drunk had told him. But that made it the best of all. Later, all the wine festivals across Europe became like all the other wine festivals. This one was different because it was so early. They had the best wines as well as the worst wines from last year, along with the early sugar wines for some of the women and most of the children. But nearly everyone was drunk, gloriously, uproariously drunk. Except for John, who was getting jumpy.

It was going to be tonight, he kept telling himself. Not tomorrow or the next day. Too many things could go wrong. Christ, he could get run over by a bus in that time, and then Rubio would never be brought to account. No, he told himself, he would wait no longer. Tonight it would happen. He would make it happen.

About half an hour ago he had settled himself at a sidewalk

table at the Caffè Fiorelli, just off the town square. Across the way, the clock on the ancient church tower was coming up on the hour, and as he watched, a man came onto the sharply pitched church roof and began climbing toward the peak. The climber was carrying something pink. From here it looked like a bed sheet or a tablecloth. No one else in the brightly lit square, where the wine-tasting stalls and long tables had been set up, paid any attention to the climber, but John's eyes were riveted on the drama. That a person could risk his life merely for pleasure once had been totally beyond him. One slip, and the man, whoever he was, would fall to his death. It had to be at least eighty or ninety feet from the roof to the cobbled square. But now John found himself rooting for the climber. He could understand what the man was going through. Or at least tonight he thought he could understand, and he felt a kinship. Higher and higher the man went, until at last, reaching the apex, he draped the pink cloth over the facade of the church and then worked his way back down to the opening and dis-appeared.

John finished his wine, then went inside where the rotund bartender was holding court. The bar was crammed. Waitresses scurried back and forth.

John motioned for the bartender, and when the man came over to him he leaned forward. "Telephone?" John asked.

"Telefono?" the man repeated. He looked closely at John. *"Cinque mille lire."* He held up his hand, all five fingers spread.

John nodded, and pulled out the money.

"Sì," the bartender nodded, astounded at his good fortune. Almost four dollars for the use of the telephone. He pocketed the money, poured John a glass of red wine, then motioned for him to come around to the back of the bar, where he showed him through a door into the apartment behind. It was small and garishly furnished. The telephone was on a stand between the doorway and the kitchenette.

"Telefono," the bartender said happily. He too was drunk. He had a huge grin on his face.

"Grazie," John said. *"Molto grazie."*

The bartender looked at him for another moment, then lurched around and went back out into the barroom, the noise level rising, then sharply falling again as the door was closed.

John took a deep breath, let it out slowly, and picked up

the telephone. When he had a dial tone, he dialed the private number at Rubio's home that the young man at the newspaper had supplied. It rang a half-dozen times before it was answered by a sleepy man's voice.

"*Si?*"

"*Signore Rubio, per favore,*" John said, trying to inflect his voice with an Italian accent.

There was a silence on the line for a moment. "Who is this?" the man asked in English, very much awake now.

"Leonardo Rubio?"

"Who is this? Who is calling me on this number?"

John took another deep breath, and again let it out slowly. "I want you to listen to me very carefully. I know about McNiel Henrys, and about Al Qaryūt, and about a lot of other things. Do you understand?"

"What are you talking about?"

"Unless you listen to me, and comply with my wishes, *signore*, I will go the newspapers with this. I will tell it all. Robert McBundy. The death of Wallace Mahoney. Everything."

"Who is this?" the man asked again, but this time his voice was subdued. "What do you want?"

"It doesn't matter who this is," John said, "but we must meet face-to-face."

"Never!"

"You will come at once. But you are being watched, *signore*. If you telephone Henrys or anyone else in the network, the meeting will be off, and I will go immediately to the newspapers. They will believe me—I have the proof."

"What proof?"

"You will come at once. Alone. Down to Frascati. To the festival," John said. His heart was hammering. "You will park near the east side of the square, and then you will walk around the square in a clockwise direction until you are given other instructions. Do you understand?"

"How do I know this isn't a trick to have me assassinated?"

John somehow managed to laugh. "Why should I kill you, when I could expose the entire network?"

"What do you want of me?"

"To talk. I want information, *signore*. Nothing more."

The man hesitated. "I cannot come now. It will be at least two hours. It would create too much suspicion otherwise."

"Now, or don't bother to come. You will be able to read all about it in the morning—from your jail cell." John knew he was being melodramatic, but Rubio—or whoever it was on the phone—was apparently swallowing it. Christ, if it wasn't Rubio, all this would have been for nothing.

"What guarantees do I have that I will not be harmed?"

"Enough," John snapped. "I will hang up now! Be at the square within twenty minutes. No policemen. Neither the ones at your gate nor the ones in town. Come alone!"

John hung up the phone, sweat pouring off his brow, his legs shaking, his stomach quivering. He stood on the dock, smoking, when all of a sudden there was the terrible explosion behind him. He was being propelled into the water, but somehow at the same moment he was at the cabin, looking through a hole in the wall as the burning ceiling collapsed on top of Elizabeth in the back bedroom. Christ! She never had a chance.

He blinked and looked up out of his thoughts. He wasn't cut out for this. He wasn't a killer. A spy. An operative. And yet, he had no other choice.

Finally he went back into the bar, where he ordered a cognac. The bartender, now even drunker than before, gave it to him on the house, slopping half the drink over the bar. John drank it down, then made his way out of the bar and across the square. Two blocks away he retrieved his car from where he had parked it in a public lot behind the police station.

He carefully pulled out of the lot and drove down a series of back streets until he came to the main road. Within a few minutes he was back at the Via Coronele.

He hesitated awhile at the turn. Instead of going up the hill, he could drive straight ahead. He could return to the States. He could go to the newspapers. Perhaps the *New York Times*. He didn't have to do this tonight.

A car was coming from the town. He could see its headlights in his rearview mirror. He put his car in gear and turned up the hill, driving slowly, carefully looking for just the right spot.

It was very dark away from the lights of the town, and a thin mist was beginning to form as the temperature dropped. At irregular intervals along the steeply winding road were driveways that led further up to houses perched on the hillside. He could see some of the houses through the trees, but most were either dark or hidden from view.

About halfway up the hill, John found what he was looking

for. He pulled over to the side, swung his car around in the wide driveway so that it was facing downhill, then shut off the lights and motor. He felt for the gun in his pocket. Hunching up his jacket collar, he got out of the car and went around to the thick clump of trees at the end of the driveway. From here he could see about a hundred yards up the road to the next curve.

Within seconds after he was in position, headlights flashed in the trees up the road, and John tensed, crouching in the shadows, his hand once again going to the gun in his pocket.

A car was coming fast; he could hear its engine on the steep hill. He was about to step out into the road when the car came around the curve, blue lights flashing. He stepped back. It was the police! Rubio had informed the police after all!

The police car sped by, and moments later another police car came into view and screamed past him.

Rubio had told the police, just as John had suspected he might. They would be going down to the town to position themselves around the square. Behind them would come Rubio. When the contact was made, the police would swoop down. John would probably be shot and killed in the confusion.

He took the pistol out of his pocket. It was a small .30-caliber revolver, its nickel plating worn away in spots and its handgrip cracked. But it was loaded, and John had no doubt that it would fire.

Another set of headlights flashed in the trees above, and John could hear the car. This one was not going as fast.

He stuffed the gun into the waistband of his slacks, made sure his jacket was buttoned over it, then stepped out into the roadway as Rubio's low-slung Jaguar came around the curve.

John staggered out into the middle of the roadway, holding his side as if he were hurt. Then he stumbled and fell to one knee as the Jaguar began to slow down. He was taking a very large chance that Rubio was alone, that the police weren't right behind him, and that he'd even stop.

John looked up into the glaring headlights as the car came to a complete stop. He tried to get to his feet but stumbled again.

The car door opened, and a man came around, shouting something in Italian. It was Rubio. John recognized his voice from the phone.

He pulled the pistol from beneath his jacket and jumped up

as Rubio reached him. It was definitely Rubio. John recognized him from the photograph.

"Madonna," Rubio breathed, moving back.

John grabbed his arm and raised the pistol to the man's face. "I said no police!"

Rubio muttered something in Italian.

"In English!" John hissed.

"You didn't honestly expect me to comply with a terrorist?"

At any moment someone would be coming down the road, probably more police. When that happened, it would be too late for John to make his escape. But now that he had come this close—now that he was face-to-face with one of the murderers—he found he didn't care what happened to him. He wanted this moment to last. And he wanted to make sure the network knew what was happening to it.

"Do you know who I am?" John shouted. He could see that Rubio was listening for someone to come down the hill. If a car did come, he told himself, he'd kill Rubio instantly.

"I have a fair idea," the man said smoothly. He was a handsome, well-dressed man. Very self-assured. But from what his father had indicated in his notes, the members of the network were nothing but the best.

"Then you know why I've come," John said.

Rubio nodded. "Revenge. Only we didn't kill your father."

"Who did?"

"We don't know for sure, but I suspect it was the Israelis."

"Why them?"

Rubio smiled. "He was rutting about on their turf. They didn't like it."

"They hired him."

"Don't be tiresome. They were finished with him."

John jammed the barrel of the pistol into the man's cheek. It was all he could do to stop himself from squeezing the trigger. He had to keep telling himself that no matter what they did, *he* was not a cold-blooded murderer.

"What about my wife and children, you bastard?" Oh, but it would be so easy to pull the trigger.

"What about them?" Rubio said, shying back. But John held his arm in a vicelike grip.

"Why did you kill them?"

"I didn't. That is to say, we didn't order it. Good heavens, what do you take us for?"

John's hand was shaking. He pulled the hammer back, and Rubio's eyes went wide.

"The truth," John said. "Why did McBundy have my wife and children killed? What good did it do your network?"

"Whatever happened, it wasn't McBundy, for God's sake. Switt is our man in America."

Switt! My God, it had been Switt! John didn't think Rubio was lying now. There'd be no reason at this late date to protect McBundy. But could his father have been mistaken about McBundy? And if he had been mistaken about one man, how about the others?

"That's right—Switt," Rubio was saying.

"I want him," John said. His insides were churning.

"He's dead. We killed him."

John had let go of Rubio's arm and lowered his pistol. Darrell Switt. The one man his father had trusted, the man John had gone to for help. He had been responsible for the murder of Elizabeth and the children. Good Lord, he had been so solicitous. So understanding. Everything would work out in the end. God, he must have had a laugh.

"Who ordered all this . . . ?" John started to ask, looking up. But Rubio had stepped back and was reaching inside his jacket.

"Don't!" John shouted. But Rubio was pulling out a gun, his eyes wide, his nostrils flared, his lips pursed.

John raised his pistol and fired twice. Both shots hit Rubio in the chest, driving him backward. He stumbled and fell into the grille of his car.

The silence came back at John like a huge, crushing weight, and he took a step forward. Rubio was dead. There was no doubt about it. He had killed another man. Looking down at him, however, John did not derive the satisfaction he thought he would. No matter what Rubio had been, it was still murder.

Murder, John thought, stepping backward. He looked up again, very conscious of just how precarious his position was at the moment. Someone could have heard the shots and might be calling the police. Or at any moment now someone else could be coming down the road.

He turned and ran back to his car, tossing the gun on the passenger seat. He got the car started with shaking hands, flipped on the headlights, and pulled out of the driveway. The headlights from Rubio's car, parked in the middle of the road, illuminated the crumpled body. John turned down the hill and raced to the next curve, rounded it, then reached the main road a minute later. There was no traffic as John turned north toward Rome and accelerated through the gears. Nor had anyone noticed him leaving in the dark-colored Fiat.

Rubio was dead. And next was to have been Zwiefel in Bonn, except that now everything was different, drastically changed in his mind. If Rubio had been telling the truth, Robert McBundy had been his father's friend all along. McBundy would have helped. Even now it was possible that he might want to help. He could get on the next plane for the States, then make his way to Washington and telephone the CIA.

This is John Mahoney. I want to speak to Robert McBundy.

They would deny there was anyone by that name working for the Agency, but the message would get to McBundy. Of that he was certain. The next time he telephoned from a different place and mentioned his name, they'd put him through.

Why didn't you come to me before? McBundy would ask.

Because my father suspected you were the deep-cover agent in the Central Intelligence Agency. Because my father thought you were responsible for all that happened.

It could have helped, McBundy might say. I could have prevented the deaths of your wife and children.

He was afraid of hearing that. Almost anything else would be bearable, but not that. *I could have prevented the deaths of your wife and children.*

If Rubio had been telling the truth, then his father had made a terrible mistake about McBundy. Faced with that choice, John was certain Rubio was telling the truth, which once again brought him back to the question: If his father had made a mistake about McBundy, who else had he been mistaken about? Zwiefel? Henrys?

But Henrys was the key. His father had spoken with the man in Geneva. Spoken with him at length, according to his second letter. He was the one man in this mess whom his father could not possibly be mistaken about. The one man he was totally sure about.

It was only about 3:30 Friday morning when he made it back to Rome. He would have liked to retrieve the rest of his things from the hotel, but he thought it best to stay away, on the off chance that someone could have traced him there. McBundy may not have been a part of the network after all, but John doubted if the man could save him now from prosecution, or even assassination. He had murdered three people. Dear God, it didn't seem possible, but he had. And the police would be after him now. In the United States and here in Italy. There was no way McBundy could stop that.

Which left him only one option. He was going to have to finish what he started to do—what his father had tried to do. He was going to have to go after the network in the person of McNiel Henrys. From Henrys he would get the truth.

He drove around Rome until sometime after four, throwing the gun off the Ponte Cavour bridge, then parked the Fiat in an all-night lot a couple of blocks from the railway station. He remained there in the car until five, then took the bag he had put in the trunk and covered the rest of the distance to the station on foot.

Inside the station, he went to the ticket window for a consultation with the sleepy agent who had just arrived. The best train to Paris via Geneva, he learned, was the Lombard Express out of Venice, leaving from Milan at ten o'clock that night. It stopped in Lausanne, which—on an express train—was as close to Geneva as John could get. Since John said he would like to spend some time in Milan—something an ordinary, even if early-rising tourist might say—the agent offered the next departing train, leaving in a little over an hour at 6:40, with a change in Bologna. John bought first-class tickets on the Rome to Milan train and for the Milan to Paris run, and paid for them in cash. He was uneasy as he gave his name for the reservations, but it was unavoidable.

How fast would the Italian police be? he wondered. He went into the coffee bar, bought coffee at the counter, and found a table near the back exit.

The Minister of Defense was shot dead. There would be questions about Rubio's behavior. About answering the phone call on his private line at that hour of the morning, about sending his police ahead and then going to a clandestine meeting without bodyguards.

There'd be questions, but by now the Italians were used to terrorists. They might put Rubio's strange behavior down to extortion. Maybe a threatened kidnapping. Whatever. The police would probably not stop to mull over Rubio's actions at first. They'd be too busy trying to track down the killer or killers. They'd be searching the town.

The bartender would almost certainly remember the tall American who had paid well to use the phone. The time would match when Rubio had received his mysterious call. But the bartender had been drunk. How much would he remember? And had anyone seen the Fiat? John doubted it.

They might suspect he had somehow run to Rome. And they might even check the airports and the railway stations and the bus depots. But surely not this soon. Surely it would take more than a few hours for them to come this far.

They'd have his description. But no one could identify his car.

Rubio had been the Minister of Defense. They'd pull out all the stops to find his assassin. *Assassin*.

John suddenly felt panicky, his gut churning, his hands shaking again.

He jumped up and crossed to the entrance. At the doorway, he looked out across the main hall of the terminal. Everything seemed normal. Soon the station would be filled with commuters hurrying off the trains and into the city to their jobs. But now the station was mostly empty. Nothing was out of the ordinary. But his stomach throbbed with pain, and an intense feeling of claustrophobia was coming over him.

He turned away from the stairs that led down to the trains and walked quickly across the terminal, out the front doors, and down the street toward the parking lot. He kept telling himself that they did not yet know what the car looked like. It was his one consolation.

Sirens were sounding in the distance. A lot of sirens.

Most likely they weren't checking the train station, he told himself as he headed out of town toward the A1 *autostrada* to the north. But he wasn't going to hang around to make sure.

Chapter 16

THE HOUSE ON Kuhlstrasse reminded Mahoney of No. 10 Downing Street in London; it had the same surprising shabbiness to it, the same hemmed-in look, and the same brooding darkness, and yet it housed an important person. Important, that is, to the politics of Bonn, the capital of West Germany. Walther Zwiefel was a power within the government structure. As Greene had explained earlier that evening, Zwiefel was one of the "clean" Germans who had not been involved with the Nazis during the war. The fact that he had been on the young side during that time meant nothing. He had not been involved in the Hitler Youth—a very difficult decision for his parents, considering the times. But a decision that reflected positively on him these days. As a result of that good fortune and the fact that he was considered an intellectual, his rise within the German government could have been spectacular, except for one thing: Herr Zwiefel's wish to be nearly invisible. From all accounts, he craved and enjoyed wielding power, but he preferred to do it from behind the scenes, as much as that was possible. Perfectly suitable for a man of his intelligence, the German body politic felt. And certainly it was perfect for his role in the network.

The back entrance to the house was closed off by iron bars across the alley, and the front entryway was well illuminated.

Mahoney and Greene, stationed in a corner room of a hotel at the end of the block, could just see the doorway through a powerful set of binoculars. It wasn't the best of setups, but it was adequate.

Mahoney had gotten a bit of sleep in the early hours, but now as the sun came higher into the sky and the rush hour was in full swing on the streets below, he was once again watching Zwiefel's house.

There was a lot of activity there this morning, a great many cars coming and going—again strengthening the 10 Downing Street impression. Mahoney and Greene both watched carefully.

"Herr Zwiefel is a busy man," Mahoney said.

"It was the same yesterday," Greene replied. "Looks like he conducts most of his business from his house. A potentate."

Mahoney had to chuckle, but his gut was tight. He felt as if they were on the verge of something.

Part of it, he knew, was due to his tiredness. And part was due to his concern for his son. But another part had to do with the things Wasserman, and then Margraff, had told him.

Money. St. Albans. A pair of anomalies.

"Oh-ho, what have we got here?" Greene said.

Mahoney focused again on the doorway. A crowd of what appeared to be journalists had materialized around a large Mercedes limousine that had pulled up to the curb, police cars in front and in back of it. The driver got out of the car and came sharply around the back, where he opened the curbside door. A tall, husky man got out, said something to the news-people, then went inside.

Greene and Mahoney both lowered their binoculars at the same time and looked at each other. "Was that who I thought it was?" Mahoney asked.

Greene nodded. "The Chancellor." He looked back at the house. "Jesus H. Christ, Zwiefel travels in high circles for the Chancellor himself to come to his house."

"We're wasting our time here," Mahoney said.

Greene looked back. "I'm sorry, sir. I didn't think Zwiefel had this kind of setup. I mean, it wasn't like this yesterday."

"John would never get close."

"No," Greene said. "And Len thinks Frascati is out as well. What about London? He knows Henrys is a part of the network. Would John go there?"

"Probably, although I don't know how he'd find Henrys."

"He'd figure out a way, sir. But have you any idea how well Henrys is looked after in London?"

Mahoney shook his head. "None. In Geneva, when I was there, he was practically wide open. There was his daughter Caroline—twenty-five or so—and then a manservant and a household staff. I don't know if that's any indication, though."

"I can stick around here, and Len can remain in place at Frascati, on the chance that John will show up after all."

The telephone rang and they both turned away from the window to look at it. It rang a second and a third time, then stopped. A minute later it rang twice, and Greene answered it.

"Yes," he said softly. All of a sudden his complexion went ashen. "Christ," he swore. "You'd better talk with Mr. Mahoney. Yes, he's right here." Greene held out the phone, and Mahoney came across to him. "It's Len. He's in Rome."

Mahoney took the phone. "Is he there in Rome?" he asked without preamble.

"He was," Sampson said. "He managed to get to Rubio. He killed him."

"What?" Mahoney's stomach turned.

"He must have been in Frascati all along. He apparently called Rubio out, because sometime after midnight the local cops showed up at the square. I knew something was happening, so I stuck around. I was hoping to spot John before he did anything foolish. I thought I might be able to snatch him and get him the hell out of there."

"Did Rubio show?"

"No, sir. About half an hour after the cops showed up, there was a big commotion, and they all took off out of town again. I followed them. Rubio was shot dead on the road just down from his house."

Was it possible? Lord, had John actually stalked a man, set him up, and then gunned him down in cold blood? His John? "Was it John?"

"I don't know where he got the gun, but I'm almost a hundred percent sure it was John. He's on a train right now for Paris."

"Paris? Did you see him?"

"No, sir. But the ticket agent here recognized his picture."

Paris. Rome to Paris. There was something drastically wrong. Why would John go to Paris? London perhaps. Why Paris? "Listen, Len. Does the train stop anywhere between Rome and Paris?"

"Quite a few places," Sampson said. "Florence, Bologna, Milan—"

"Geneva?" Mahoney asked.

There was a silence on the line while Sampson consulted the timetable the ticket agent had given him.

"Does the train stop at Geneva?" Mahoney repeated.

"Lausanne, sir. About thirty miles away."

"When does it get there? What time?"

"Let's see . . . two twenty-two tomorrow morning."

Mahoney looked at his watch. It was nearly 9:00 A.M. In less than eighteen hours John would be in Geneva. It was an impossibly short time, and yet everything else that had happened had gone by at lightning speed. And with all that had happened, Henrys would certainly have a watch posted at the airport and all the terminals around the city. He'd have to now, for his own safety. Which meant the moment John arrived in Geneva he'd be a dead man. Yet Mahoney did not want to get near Geneva himself. He didn't want to run the risk of spooking Henrys.

"Where are you calling from?"

"I have a room at the Esperia on the Via Nazionale under the name of Labelle. It's one floor up from John's room."

"All right, Len, we're going to have to intercept John before he makes it to Geneva."

"Geneva?"

"He's going there. I'm sure of it. Henrys will probably have someone at the station watching for him."

"According to the ticket agent, he caught a six-forty train to Milan. It's due there at one fifty-five. He must be planning to spend the day there. I could fly up and try to intercept him when he gets off the train. If that doesn't work, I can still catch the train to Paris—it's the Lombard Express. It would give me plenty of time to get him off before we reached Lausanne."

"Good. Do it. We'll meet you there."

"What about John's things? He never returned to his room."

If he took them and someone from the network was watching, they would know that John was being shadowed by someone else. If he didn't take them, the hotel would sooner or later turn the things over to the police, and John would be pegged as a suspect in Rubio's shooting. His name would show up on the international wire as wanted for questioning in connection with murder back in the States. The police would be slower and the easier of the two to handle, Mahoney figured.

"Leave them there," Mahoney said. "If for some reason we don't make it in time to meet the train and you have to do it alone, Len, get him off before Geneva."

"I understand, sir," Sampson said, and he hung up.

Mahoney broke the connection, then telephoned Alitalia at the Cologne airport, which served Bonn as well. The next flight to Milan left in two hours. Flying time, he was assured, would be less than an hour and a half, putting them in Milan around 12:30. There'd be a lot of time to spare before the Lombard Express left.

The Autostrada del Sole was as anonymous as any superhighway as it followed the Tiber River Valley, but John appreciated the opportunity to dispel some of his tension by driving at speeds greater than he was used to at home. He drove for a little more than an hour, then pulled into an Agip station with a snack bar next to it. After filling his tank, he parked and went in for some coffee. The counterman offered him toast, John thought, but it turned out to be what he would have called a grilled cheese sandwich. Tourist maps were for sale in a wire rack, and John found and bought one for Florence.

The scenery improved as the road entered the Tuscan hills, but John was not really looking at it. He was tired, deeply frightened at what he had done, and even more terrified at what he was becoming. Killing the two men back in Montana had been purely self-defense. But Rubio . . . he had gone searching for the man. He had set him up. And when the time had come, he had pulled the trigger. That, by any stretch of the imagination, couldn't be called self-defense.

The drive was giving him plenty of time to think not only about what he had done, but about what he was going to do. Henrys had been his primary target all along. He had gone after Rubio and had intended going after Zwiefel only to frighten—to shake up—the British traitor in the network. Put the man on notice that his turn was coming.

It was foolish and foolhardy, but John wanted to strike back very hard for what the network had done to him.

But that didn't seem to matter any longer. John was beginning to feel less like someone bent on revenge and more like a mechanic out to do a disagreeable job that nevertheless had to be done. There was no one else who knew all the details about the network. And even if Rubio had been telling the truth, and McBundy was innocent, what could the man do? He was bound by the Agency. He did not have the freedom John had.

If the sirens he had heard back in Rome had been the police looking for him, and if they had checked at the railway station, they would have found out that, although he had purchased a ticket for Milan, he was not on the train. By now they would have checked the bus depots and airlines, and it was very possible they could have traced him to the hotel. From there it was conceivable they could have found out about his rented car and figured he left Rome in it.

He was stretching credulity to the limit, he knew, and yet he wasn't willing to risk his life on a bet that he was wrong.

A train would be safe now, he reasoned. They'd have no reason to look for him on it. None whatsoever, any longer.

John left the highway at the Florence exit and waited behind a small station wagon to surrender his toll ticket. In front of him, children's hands reached out of the windows, and the booth attendant placed something in each. John smiled to himself. Then he saw the faces of his own children and was shot through with pain.

The station wagon pulled away, and John rolled forward. The attendant took his ticket, and John held out a bill. He was startled to receive in return several small bills and two hard candies. The attendant explained in English that the government couldn't mint coins fast enough to keep up with demand, and small change was given in candy or, if John preferred, stamps or telephone slugs. He couldn't bear to accept the candy, so he asked for the stamps instead.

Just beyond the tollbooth, he pulled over and consulted his map. He wanted to get rid of his car as soon as possible. He found an easy route to the railway station and left the Fiat in a parking lot in its piazza. He went into the terminal and purchased a first-class ticket on the 5:10 train to Milan. Keeping his head down, he mumbled his name to the clerk, who confirmed the reservation in the name of Moloni; since it was a local train, he did not have to show his passport.

He now had about six hours to kill, and he figured he would be most invisible as a tourist. So he checked his overnight bag in a locker and wandered out of the station and toward the Piazza Santa Maria Novella. The green and white marble facade of the church was stunning, but John had no desire to go in, so he strolled through the adjoining Cemetery of Patrician Families. It was cool and green, but it brought unwelcome memories, so he consulted his map and hailed a taxi to the Piazza della Signoria. He followed the crowds of summer tourists into the Palazzo Vecchio, bought a ticket, and climbed the stairs to the Hall of the Five Hundred. Vast frescoes triumphed Cosimo de Medici's martial enterprises, and John found it all horrible. He fled back to the entrance hall, where a guide in a visored cap was permitting his obviously American flock a few minutes to buy postcards. John went up to him and asked if he could recommend something more peaceful.

"A peaceful place, or peaceful art?" the guide asked.

"Both, I suppose," John replied.

"My favorite place in all of Florence is the Church of the Carmine. The art is the most beautiful we have, and the tourists don't get there as much, only the students." He showed it to John on the map.

Thanking him, John went back into the square and crossed to one of the sidewalk *trattorie* that was just opening. He chose a table against the wall—in case anyone was looking for him—but which afforded him a good view of the sculptures. A waiter took his order, and John dawdled over his lunch until the press of waiting customers forced him to ask for his check and leave.

He walked past the Uffizi and along the river to the Ponte Vecchio, where a few enterprising shops had stayed open during the lunch hour to take advantage of the tourist season. On the far side, he was as fascinated as any tourist at the narrow streets and small shops selling not souvenirs or leather or jewelry, but the essentials of everyday life.

The Church of the Carmine had reopened after its midday closing, John was relieved to find, and he located the Brancacci

Chapel the tour guide had told him about. He fished in his pocket for coins to illuminate the frescoes. As the lights came on, he was amazed. Here were the paintings by the Renaissance masters he had seen in books and slide lectures when he had taken an art history course in college, but in life they were breathtaking. He walked around slowly, studying them, returning to feed the machine more coins as the lights flicked off.

When he finally had enough, he returned to the nave and sat in a pew. He had not felt so well since the explosion at Shultz Lake. But he knew it couldn't last; he had work to do.

At length he deposited an offering in the box at the front of the church and walked back to the river, where he crossed at the nearest bridge and hailed a taxi back to the Piazza Santa Maria Novella. There, he killed time standing in a coffee bar, Campari in hand. He checked his watch and found that it was time to go to the station and retrieve his bag from the locker.

With his single overnight bag in hand, John purchased a package of Marlboros at the kiosk and went out to the tracks. He had to show the uniformed gate attendant his ticket, but the man barely glanced at him in the crush of people, and John was past.

People and luggage crowded the waiting areas beside the tracks. Everyone seemed to be talking at full volume, and a continuous stream of announcements in Italian, French, and English came over the public-address system. Porters scurried back and forth. Vendors with carts sold everything from newspapers and candy to flowers and wine, oblivious to the obstructions they caused.

John waited tiredly off to one side, keeping out of the way of the press of people as much as possible. He hadn't slept in what seemed like days. But after Milan he would have a private compartment and a few hours to rest. Once he had reached Geneva, however, he was going to confront Henrys immediately, no matter what the hour. The man would never expect him to show up there. And certainly not so soon.

He leaned against the pillar that supported the overhang across the tracks as he thought about the coming confrontation. Henrys would be forced to explain. And then he would be made to pay. But beforehand, he would tell what he knew about the network. Everything it had done. Its remaining members. John needed to know because he was determined to exterminate the network forever.

His father had always wanted to keep the family totally insulated from the business. Of course he had failed in the end, but it hadn't been his fault. His family hadn't been drawn into the business because of his mistakes. It had come about only because he had been loved. By his wife, and certainly by his sons. Now John felt so lonely. There was no one left.

The noise level in the station rose appreciably as the electric train from Rome slowly pulled in and came to a halt. The crowd pressed forward as the doors opened, and a few people got off the train. Porters came with bags, and the conductor waived the ticket-holders aboard.

John climbed aboard the first-class car, found his compartment, tossed his bag onto the rack, and slumped down in his seat.

He looked down at the platform still teeming with people. Most of them seemed happy. Excited. They were leaving on a trip, at least for the weekend. Perhaps it was a vacation for many of them. Wasn't it wonderful?

He closed the shade, then sat back and shut his eyes. A picture of Elizabeth swam into his mind's eye, and a terrible ache for his old life rose in his chest.

Mahoney and Greene had arrived half an hour after Sampson at the central railway station in Milan, and they met at the information counter. Sampson had been just in time to meet the 6:40 train from Rome, on which John had a reservation, but as he reported to the others, John hadn't been among the passengers. Their only hope, he concluded, was to assume he still intended to take the Lombard Express.

The newspapers in the stands screamed with tall headlines about the assassination of Minister Rubio. But there was no mention in any of the stories about John, or even about an American suspected of complicity. Which meant they were safe, at least for the moment, unless the police were being purposely coy to lull John into a false sense of security. The Italians had become expert at handling such incidents, because they had been happening with increasing regularity during the past ten years or so.

They had taken a room at the Excelsior Gallia just around

the corner from the station, and Greene and Sampson got some rest while Mahoney sat by the window looking out across the city, smoking his cigars, and sipping a surprisingly good whiskey that the bartender downstairs had found for him.

A half hour ago they had checked out and had walked back to the station, where they sat themselves down at the depot restaurant for a light meal.

The station wasn't anywhere near as busy as it had been earlier in the day, but there were still plenty of people coming and going. The commuters had already left the city; the remainder were stragglers, the overtime people and the tourists taking the late trains to somewhere.

Sampson pulled out his train timetable and compared it with a map to see which towns they would be going through between here and Lausanne.

"If we're going to get him off the train before it reaches Lausanne, we're going to have to find him rather quickly."

"We're not going to get him off the train," Mahoney said. "We'll keep him aboard until Paris. But we're going to have to find him before Lausanne to prevent him from leaving. Once he gets off the train, it'll be too late."

"It's going to be quite a shocker for him—seeing you, Mr. Mahoney," Greene said. He poured them more red wine.

Mahoney nodded. "You two can run him down. When you have him, bring him back to me. I'm going to stay in my compartment. If he spots me out in the open, there's no telling what he might do. He believes I'm dead. He might think I'm a double sent to catch him. Anything is possible. But we would not have control of the situation."

"He's not likely to come to us with open arms, in any event," Greene said. "He's on the run. He's spooked."

"You'll just have to be careful, that's all."

"Yes, sir," Greene said glumly.

Sampson was toying with the remains of his spaghetti. He looked up. "What'd you find in Israel, Mr. Mahoney? Anything to go on?"

Mahoney didn't answer immediately, and Sampson fidgeted. Greene looked up, surprised at the delay.

"I mean, are we getting close? It's only been a few days, but we'd like to know the score."

"I'll let you know when we're ready to make our move, Len," Mahoney said. "I won't let it sneak up on you. We'll have a lot of setting up to do when the time comes. There'll be plenty to do. Too much for me to pull anything on you, if that's what you're worried about."

Greene and Sampson looked at each other. Ever since Jensen had been killed in Los Angeles trying to catch up with John, they had been wary, rightfully so. But Mahoney could have almost predicted the next question.

"What if John's not on the train, or we miss him?" Sampson asked.

"We can't let him get to Geneva."

"What if he does?" Sampson insisted.

"Henrys and his people will kill him."

"Or he'll kill Henrys like he killed Rubio," Greene said. "Your son is capable."

"We can't let that happen."

"I understand he's your son, Mr. Mahoney, but we're either running an operation or we're not . . ." Greene let the sentence trail off.

"In this case it's not my son, Bob. Not really. It's Henrys. I want him protected—insulated—for the moment. Without him, we don't have an operation."

"At all costs?" Greene asked, his voice like a whisper.

Mahoney stiffened at the question, even though he knew it was legitimate. Greene and Sampson had the right to know what the limits of this operation were. Jensen had given his life without knowing—because of not knowing—and all of them had become very nervous as a consequence.

"No," Mahoney said. "Not without certain limits."

Both men looked at him. They didn't seem surprised. Perhaps it was because they knew him so well, or perhaps it was nothing less than they would do.

"I don't want my son in Geneva. I don't want him anywhere near Henrys for a number of reasons. Among them, I don't want my son killed. Nor do I want Henrys spooked."

Mahoney paused, and again the other two just looked at him, waiting for him to tell them exactly how far they could go.

"But if he does somehow make it to Geneva," Mahoney said carefully, "I'm not going after him. Nor will I warn Henrys."

"You'd let them work it out?"

Mahoney had a sudden, intense vision of the cemetery outside Missoula. It was late evening. In the fall. The sky was deeply overcast, the wind was raw from the north, and a light rain was falling. He stood looking down on the graves. There was a fresh one next to Marge and Michael. But he was having a hard time focusing on the headstone inscription.

"We understand . . ." Greene started, but Mahoney wasn't listening.

"I don't know, Bobby. We'll just have to see when it comes down to it. We'll just have to see, won't we."

Greene finished the last of the wine. It was time to go. They had purchased their tickets for Paris, so they went directly downstairs to the tracks, where they were admitted through the gates, trackside. There were a lot of people there, and the big round clocks on the steel girders that held up the roof over the tracks read 9:45.

Chapter 17

MAHONEY HAD BOUGHT himself a large felt hat. He put it on and pulled it low over his eyes. There was no sign of John in the confusion on the platform, and uniformed conductors were trying to herd passengers aboard. Mahoney crossed the platform to the first-class cars and climbed up behind Greene and Sampson. They had been assigned three separate compartments, but they all crowded into Mahoney's.

When they had the door closed, Mahoney took off the hat, tossed it aside, and opened the window.

"One of you watch the other side of the train."

"Yes, sir," Sampson said. He left as Mahoney sat down by the opened window and stuck his head out.

A few people who had boarded at Venice were still getting off the train, but more were getting on. Not one of them came even vaguely close to John's looks or build.

"He may not be on this train, you know," Greene said.

Mahoney looked at him. "I know. But unless something

spooked him, I still think he's going to try to get to Geneva."

"Could he have had a change of heart?" Greene suggested.

Mahoney turned back to watch out the window. He shrugged. "After Rubio, and everything else, I don't think my son will have a change of heart. Once he gets something in his mind, he sticks with it. At least, he always used to be that way."

"Yes, sir," Greene said. There had been a lot of yes, sirs in the past few days, and it was starting to get on Mahoney's nerves. But he said nothing.

A couple of last-minute passengers, including an older lady, hurried down from the terminal, scurried across the platform, and got aboard the train. At the last car, the conductor waved, then he too swung aboard, and the train began to pull out of the station.

The edge of the building came up, then passed, and they were outside, rumbling through the switching yards, factory pollution thick in the air.

Just fifty miles to the northwest were the Alps. Soon they would be climbing out of the Lombard Valley into the clear, crisp mountain air. And then it would be very difficult, if not impossible, for John to jump the train—assuming he had managed to board without any of them seeing him. It would be either within the next few minutes, or not until just before Lausanne.

The train began to gather speed as they came away from the switching yards and passed through the suburbs into the open countryside. Mahoney closed the window, got up, and took off his jacket, which he hung in the tiny closet.

"As soon as Len gets back, I'll want you to start at opposite ends of the train, seat by seat, compartment by compartment. I want the entire train searched. Carefully. As soon as you find him, bring him back here."

"His ticket was first class."

"Which doesn't mean a thing. He might be anywhere on the train," Mahoney said. "What's the matter, Bobby?"

"If he's on the train at all."

Mahoney splashed some water on his face. "Even if he isn't, we have to give it a shot."

"Yes, sir," Greene said. Someone knocked at the door, cutting short the retort that came to Mahoney's lips.

Greene opened the door and Sampson slipped inside. "Nothing."

"That probably means he suspects he's safe for the moment," Mahoney said. "But I want you both to be very careful. I don't want any accidents."

"He knows what we both look like," Greene said.

"It's been years since he's seen either of you. He was only a young man then. Now, under stress, thinking about Henrys, I don't think he'll understand who you are until you're close enough to control the situation."

Greene and Sampson looked at each other. They had been partners for years, so they understood what was going on in each other's mind.

"I want you both to be careful," Mahoney repeated.

"Do you want us to tell him that you're alive? Or do you want us to bring him in here cold?" Greene asked.

"That'd be quite a shock for anyone to handle," Sampson said.

Mahoney finished drying his face and hung the towel back on the rack. "You're going to have to use your own judgment. If it looks like he'd be able to handle it, and he'd believe what you're telling him, then go ahead and prepare him. If it looks as if he'll make a fuss, then bring him here cold."

"He's going to be dangerous," Greene said.

Mahoney looked at him. Greene was a good man, but it was John they were talking about. Greene was right, however. "I know. Just be careful, please."

"If we have to defend ourselves?" Greene insisted.

"Goddamnit, Bobby, do whatever it takes to get him back here without creating a fuss," Mahoney flared.

"He'll be unpredictable."

"Do the best you can. It's all I'm asking. Just do the best you can."

Sampson opened the door, and he and Greene started out, when Mahoney spoke again.

"We've got a long way to go yet, and a lot of people have been killed already. I don't want to screw this up any worse than it already is."

"We'll do our best, Mr. Mahoney," Greene said.

Mahoney nodded, and they went out the door.

If John had actually killed Rubio, and if he was on this train, then it was very possible that he still had the gun—wherever the hell he had managed to get it. Mahoney just hoped to God that there'd be no accidents now. He wanted to hear the knock and, when the door opened, see a dumbfounded John there. "Father?" his son would say, and it would be all right.

John stood with his back to the bulkhead beside the dining-car door. His heart was hammering, his knees were weak, and his mouth was suddenly dry. The man talking to the steward was one of his father's old friends. Although he had only gotten a brief glimpse of the man's face, he was almost a hundred percent certain he knew him.

He turned around and eased a little closer to the window in the door and looked into the dining car again. The man was still there. He was looking around at the other people in the car.

John moved back. Christ. It *was* one of his father's CIA cronies. Leonard something or other. And he was obviously looking for someone. The coincidence was just too great to be ignored. The man was here looking for someone, all right. He was a member of the network. They had traced him this far, which meant they knew he had killed Rubio, and they knew that he was on his way to Geneva.

The sirens he had heard in Rome had not been meant for him. The police had not been as quick as the network. But Rubio was dead, and they must have figured that John would pick either Zwiefel in Bonn or Henrys in Geneva. They had gone to the railroad station in Rome, had inquired of the ticket agents, and had come up with the fact that their mark had bought a ticket to Paris. To Paris via Switzerland.

They'd be searching for him, car by car. But they'd had more than an hour. They'd be nearly finished by now.

He tried to slow down, to think this out. There were probably others. They would know he was in first class. But no one had been to his compartment yet, which probably meant they had started from the end of the train in a methodical search. They might expect he'd be on the move.

John crossed the enclosed coupling platform and looked through the glass into the first-class car forward. Two women stood near an open compartment door a couple of doors down from his. They were talking. Other than them, there was no one else.

He opened the door, entered the car, and made his way down the corridor, squeezing past the women with his apologies. He entered his own compartment, where he grabbed his passport and the rest of his money from his overnight bag, stuffed them in his pockets, then raised the shade on his window.

They had climbed up into the mountains and were passing over a bridge that spanned a gorge. It was too dark to see the bottom. There'd be no getting off here.

He lowered the window and stuck his head out to try to see what was beyond the bridge.

There were mountains rising steeply from the tracks; huge boulders and sharp rocks were everywhere, making a jump impossible, especially at the speed at which they were traveling.

They were still in Italy, but it would not be much longer before they'd be crossing into Switzerland, and then he'd have to deal with a passport-control officer.

He pulled back and closed the window, then the shade. It had looked like a lunar landscape out there, except for the trees. Forbidding, cold, isolated. Even if the fall didn't kill him, he could very well break a leg, and unable to go for help or shelter, die of exposure.

It was that or the network, he told himself, facing the door. They were looking for him. But were there others? He wasn't cut out for this. He couldn't do it. He couldn't keep going this way. No one could. But they weren't going to back down from him. They'd killed his father, his wife, and his children. And he'd killed their people. They'd never let him live.

He cracked his compartment door and looked out into the corridor. The same two women were still talking. He slipped out as nonchalantly as possible, considering he was shaking inside, again brushed past them with more apologies, and went out to the connecting platform.

There was only one thing he could do, God help him. And none of this would end until he had gotten to Henrys. Henrys was the key. His father had believed Henrys had all the answers. Although he had been mistaken about McBundy, John knew his father had been correct about Henrys. His second letter had told how he had actually met with the man. They had spoken. Henrys had admitted the existence of the network and had even told his father what its purpose was. The only questions Henrys hadn't answered were who created the network, who funded— and therefore ran—it, and how its members were recruited. Before Henrys died, he would answer those questions.

He looked in the dining car. Sampson had disappeared.

Quickly John checked his corridor, where the two women were still stationed a couple of doors from his compartment, then turned and fumbled with the outside door latch until he had levered it open. Then he pulled the heavy door open. A blast of cold air and a great rumbling noise suddenly filled the connecting platform. The rocks and mountainside seemed so close he could reach out and touch them.

He turned back and positioned himself in the shadows between the dining-car door and the open door to the outside.

If anyone but Sampson happened by, what he wanted to do would be impossible. He almost hoped the two women would decide to come to the dining car so he wouldn't have to go through with this.

The dining-car door opened. Sampson hesitated for a moment as he looked around, then stepped out and over to the open door, his back to where John was flattened against the bulkhead, his right hand loosely grasping the handrail. Sampson bent forward and tried to look outside.

Switt had been a traitor to the service. And so was this man. They had both worked for the network. Both of them had fooled his father.

John stepped silently forward. Bracing himself, he kicked out with his right foot, the blow deflecting off the man's back.

Sampson fell sideways, one foot over the edge, one hand flailing in the air, his right hand slipping on the rail.

"No . . ." Sampson shouted, his voice almost drowned out by the roar of the wind.

John stepped back and slammed his foot against Sampson's hand, but the man grabbed John's leg with his free hand and pulled hard.

He was getting up! Sampson had managed to grab the rail with his other hand and was pulling himself up. John scrambled around, doubled up his fist, and swung. He connected solidly with Sampson's face. The man's head snapped back, but he refused to let go of the rail. Again John hit him in the face, splitting his nose, blood gushing.

Sampson tried to shout something, but John kept hitting him in the face, again and again, putting everything he had into it.

Suddenly Sampson's hands were grabbing the air, and his scream was lost as he disappeared.

John grabbed the handrail and leaned out so that he could see behind the train. But there was only darkness.

He shuddered as he got to his feet, closed and relatched the door, then stepped back and once again leaned against the dining-car bulkhead. He lit a cigarette and inhaled deeply.

The man had not wanted to die. He had fought back. He had held on against all hope. Christ! One moment he had been a live human being, and the next.... John refused to think what had happened to the man when he had fallen. Instead, he could hear Elizabeth and the children screaming in the fire.

The door from John's car opened, and he froze. But it was only one of the women who had been talking in the corridor. She nodded and smiled at John, then went into the dining car, leaving him alone again.

If there were others looking for him aboard this train, they'd have to be disposed of as well. And very soon. Before they discovered that one of their number was missing.

John raised the cigarette to his lips with shaky hands, but then stopped. He had vaguely recognized one of them, but that did not mean he'd recognize the others . . . if there were others. He wouldn't know who his enemies were until they raised a weapon to him, and by that time it would be too late.

He crushed his cigarette on the floor, then hurried back into his own compartment and locked the door.

If there were others, they'd be coming after him. They'd intensify their search once they realized one of their people was missing. They'd start again at each end of the train and work their way to the other.

They'd want to get to him before he reached Geneva. They knew what he was after, and they'd want to protect Henrys at all costs. The man was their leader.

There was another problem now, as well. The train was due to arrive in Domodossola, according to the schedule, in a few minutes, and from there it was only ten minutes to Iselle and the twelve-mile-long Simplon Tunnel, the longest in the world. Iselle was going to present a problem. He had been worrying about the immigration and customs inspectors who would board the train there, but now his greater fear was for his pursuers from the network. He could try to hide, but if the train were delayed when the inspectors found his empty compartment, the network men would have no difficulty finding the source— and location—of the delay. It wouldn't much matter who found him first. He had to be off the train by then.

Could he jump? Even though the train was taking the curves

slowly, he was not at all sure he could survive a jump. But he could not stay where he was, a sitting duck for anyone who came to look for him. And maybe the network men could be made to think he had jumped.

He quickly opened his window wide, left the compartment, and made his way to the dining car unobserved. The staff had finished for the night, and only dim wall lamps still illuminated the car. But the door to the serving pantry was unlocked, and John slipped inside.

Hopefully they would believe he had jumped. But they would have no idea when. There could have been a wide spot on the tracks somewhere, or there could have been a lake or river. He could have sneaked off when they'd stopped at Arona. As long as they believed he was gone, he'd be safe.

Geneva and McNiel Henrys. They were all that really mattered.

Mahoney sat by the window, smoking a cigar. His left leg was crossed over his right, and he rubbed at the knee with his left hand. He had bad heartburn, and his eyes felt hot and dry. It had been a long time since Greene and Sampson had left, and Mahoney was worried. Several times he had gotten up and almost gone out to join the search. But each time he had thought better of it and sat back again.

He was considering it again when someone knocked and the door opened. He looked up as a white-faced Greene slipped in, softly closing the door behind him.

"Len is gone," he said.

Mahoney jumped up. "What?"

"Len is gone. I've been from one end of this fucking train to the other, and unless he's hiding, he's gone. So is your son."

Greene was very agitated. Mahoney led him back to the seat and poured a stiff drink from the bottle the porter had been good enough to bring. Greene drank it down.

"His window was open. The stupid son of a bitch jumped."

"John?"

Greene nodded. "But he did something with Len."

"I don't think so, Bobby. Len is very capable."

"So was Rubio!" Greene shouted. "I mean, Jesus Christ he had half the Italian army guarding him. But John got to him nevertheless. Christ. He's a wizard."

"We don't know what happened to Len. For all you know

he may have gotten off the train going after John."

"The hell," Greene flared, but then he forced himself to calm down, swallowing hard several times. "I managed to bribe the porter and got his compartment number. *Someone* had occupied it—there's a bag on the rack, but it's got no ID. It could be his. And the window was open. And Len is gone."

Mahoney said nothing, although he was thinking that just because a man bought a ticket didn't mean he had boarded the train. In the next tick, however, he remembered his insistence that he had *felt* John's presence near.

"Len was working his way up from the back. He should've been here long ago."

"You're a hundred percent certain Len is gone? They're both gone?"

"He's not trying to hide, goddamnit! I've been all over this train. Len is not aboard, and neither is John."

Greene was among the very best in the business, and however much Mahoney wanted to believe that he wasn't thinking straight, he could not. Greene would not fall apart like that, nor would he lie or make that kind of mistake. If he believed Sampson and John were both gone, then the chances that they were still aboard were slim to the point of being miniscule.

"He's gone, Mr. Mahoney. Your son is gone from this train, and so is Len."

"Would you stake your life on it?"

Greene looked at him. He was hurt. "Not my life, but certainly my reputation."

"Let's look for them. We'll start at the front and work back."

Greene stared into his eyes, then shook his head. "Whatever you say, sir, but they're gone."

And if they were? Mahoney asked himself. If they were really gone? If he and Greene started at the front of the train, and worked their way all the way to the back, and if they found absolutely no trace of Sampson or of John—if they were truly gone—what then?

Mahoney sat down next to Greene and poured more whiskey for both of them. For a few moments he was more conscious of their speeding toward Switzerland than of the other man's presence next to him. He was so obsessed by his nearness to Henrys that he had to force his mind back to the fact that they would have to look for Sampson and John.

Yet Mahoney understood that Greene knew what he was

talking about. If he said John and Sampson were gone, then they were, and Greene had to be hating John by now. They would get off the train at Domodossola and look. But it would be futile.

For a very long time this moment would haunt Mahoney. He would always look back on this period as the time he abandoned his son. But the fact of the matter was, he could not take the chance. They were coming close to Geneva, too close now to make any kind of a fuss.

If Henrys even suspected something was happening around him, it would queer everything.

John, he grieved.

Chapter 18

WHEN THEY PULLED into Iselle, there was a lot of commotion in the dining car for several minutes, but gradually the noise died. He opened the serving-pantry door. There was no one there.

For several long moments he hesitated. He'd be a hell of a lot less conspicuous traveling with luggage than without. But he just could not risk going back to his car to retrieve his bag. If they thought he had jumped, going back for his bag would tip them off.

He stepped off the train onto the crowded platform as nonchalantly as he could manage, then ducked into the station where he hid himself in one of the stalls in the men's room. Ten minutes later the train pulled out, and he went back up into the station.

Extra late-night trains had been scheduled because of the heavy summer traffic. The ticket agent could not understand why people came all this way to view the scenery and then were stupid enough to go through it in the dark. He sold John a ticket on the next train to Brig, due in less than half an hour. John found the currency-exchange window and changed some of his lire to Swiss francs, then cleared customs in the station without any trouble. He went outside to wait for his train, staring down at the tracks.

It reminded him of when he was a kid. He and Michael used to walk the tracks looking for loose track pins and other junk. They would put pennies and sometimes nickels on the tracks when trains were coming, and once they even put down a .22 bullet. But nothing happened.

Brig was a small town of less than five thousand people. Except for passengers from the train John had arrived on reclaiming their cars, it was almost deserted at this time of night. Parked in front of the station was a yellow bus, and as John approached he saw several people from the train, suitcases in hand, climb on board. No one paid him much attention as he came up to the driver and smiled.

"Do you speak English?"

"Yes, of course," the driver said. "You have your ticket?"

"No, not yet. Does this bus go to Geneva, or is it a private charter?"

"We are not a charter; this is a postal bus."

John had no idea what the man was talking about, and it must have shown.

"The Post Coach system?" the driver said hopefully. Then he shook his head good-naturedly. "This is the Swiss postal bus system, sir. I can take you as far as Sion; from there you must transfer to the Lausanne-Geneva bus. You understand?"

John nodded and pulled out his wallet. The driver smiled that the American had finally been made to understand such a patently simple fact.

Sion was thirty miles away, and the fare was incredibly cheap. John took a seat near the rear, next to an old man who slept the whole way despite the distinctive klaxon—the first notes of the overture to *William Tell*—the driver sounded on every curve.

The road followed the Rhône River, and it was nearly two o'clock when they reached the much larger town, where the driver directed John to a ticket booth in the terminal. The last bus to Geneva had left some time before, but there would be another first thing in the morning, arriving in Geneva in time for lunch.

John bought a ticket and then was directed to a small hotel around the corner where he took a leisurely bath and had, what was for him, a good night's sleep.

He was awakened early, as he had requested. The hotel staff lent him shaving gear and fed him a good breakfast. His bus left exactly on schedule, and he arrived in Geneva, on a gloriously warm, sunny morning, just before noon.

The bus depot was situated between the Rue des Alpes and the Rue du Mont-Blanc, a block from the lake and the city harbor. Although he was still tired, John walked over to the lake, and stood, mesmerized by the Jet d'Eau. The famous plume of water—the world's largest fountain, rising to five hundred feet—glistened in the sun. Pulling himself together, he strolled along the quay as if he were a tourist without a care in the world. It seemed like such a terribly long time since his life had been normal; since he had Elizabeth and the children.

He passed a small park at the water's edge. Little children were skipping stones, their parents seated on nearby benches. Lovers strolled hand in hand. Gaudily dressed tourists, cameras around their necks, snapped photographs.

As he walked, he tried again to slow his beleaguered mind; tried to think everything out, especially his next moves. He desperately needed a real rest, and yet he knew that if he checked into a hotel he would have to surrender his passport. As soon as the police got a look at it during their routine checks, word would probably get to Henrys. There was no doubt in John's mind that this was Henrys's town. He would have some line into every corridor of power. But that brought up another thought. Why Geneva? Why Switzerland? Henrys was a high-ranking officer with the British Secret Intelligence Service.

The first answer that leaped to mind was money. Switzerland was the financial center for all of Europe. If Henrys was the banker for the network, might not its business be conducted through a Swiss bank? Such things were quite common, he knew, because of the Swiss penchant for secrecy in financial matters.

That might explain why Henrys spent time here, but John suspected there was more to it than that. From the description of the house in his father's second letter, Geneva was not merely Henrys's vacation home. John remembered an English chemist he had worked with explaining the very favorable British tax laws for nonresident citizens; it was possible, according to him, to live out of the country for a certain number of months every year and completely escape the ruinous income tax. It was very appealing to Englishmen with large incomes, and from what his father had written, Henrys lived in style.

John stopped and leaned against the stone wall above the lakeshore walkway, gazing across the inner harbor and beyond toward the open lake. There were several sailboats out, and dozens more tied up along the docks or moored to one side of the harbor. Happy people. A city filled mostly with happy people. He felt very much the intruder here.

One part of him ached for revenge against Henrys and the network. Yet another, saner part wanted nothing more than to turn around and go home. McBundy evidently was clean. Once John got back to the States, he could call his father's old friend, set up an appointment, and tell him everything. Then the CIA could handle it, and John could return home. But to what? What was there for him to return to?

He turned away from the lovely scene below and looked across the quay up toward the casino, his entire body aching, his mind screaming for peace.

There was nothing for him to return to. Even if the network would leave him alone—which he was certain it would not—there was nothing for him any longer. He was a murderer now. Besides his legal problems, he could never return to his house or his old friends. He would not be able to stand either the emptiness, or the sympathy or condemnation he would receive.

Pushing away from the wall, he crossed the street and strolled a few blocks back to the Rhône, which divided the city north and south. He bought a Paris *Herald-Tribune* at a newsstand, then had lunch at a small restaurant. Returning to the lakeshore park afterward, he sat down on one of the benches and opened the newspaper. He nodded off a half hour later and did not awake until nearly six o'clock, a gummy taste in his mouth. The sounds of traffic, of people talking, of people running and laughing, came to him in waves as reality returned. At length he got up and went off in search of a place to clean up, and to have some dinner.

McNiel Henrys's home in Eaux-Vives came as something of a surprise to John as he passed slowly by it in a cab. From his glimpse through the gate between the carriage houses, it was older, smaller, and definitely shabbier than he had imagined. Lamps in the mews cast a glow on its facade, but all the windows were black. He supposed the interior would be much nicer, but from the outside it did not look like much.

"Where is it you wish to go, *monsieur?*" the confused driver asked John again. It was a little after nine o'clock, and night was falling quickly.

"This is the wrong street," John told the driver. "I think it may be around the corner. Behind these houses."

"There is nothing behind."

"What do you mean, nothing? I think my friend is around the corner. In the next block."

"There is no next block, *monsieur*," the driver said, raising his voice. "It is two blocks to the next street."

"Just drive around the corner, please," John said. He wanted to know what was to the rear of Henrys's house. No mention had been made of that in his father's second letter.

The driver shrugged and turned right at the corner. Two blocks up, the next street was a wide thoroughfare, with a lot of traffic. Beyond it was a very large park.

"The Avenue William Favre," the driver said.

"Turn right," John said.

"*D'accord*," the driver replied, resigned to the antics of American tourists. As long as they paid, who cared?

Along the avenue, facing the park, was a line of low buildings, some containing shops, others offices. They were all dark at this hour. As the cab slowly moved up the avenue, John watched for Henrys's house, finally spotting what he thought must be it, far behind a photographer's shop.

"Is this what you are looking for, *monsieur?*" the driver asked. "Is this where you are supposed to meet your friend?"

"No," John said. "No, apparently I was mistaken."

"*Naturellement*," the driver said, nodding. "And where would you like to be taken now?"

He couldn't just walk up to the front door and ring the bell. He'd get to the house from the back. Through the photographer's studio, perhaps.

"*Monsieur?*" the driver asked, looking over his shoulder.

"Sorry," John mumbled. "Is there a bar nearby?"

"A bar?" the driver asked.

"An inn. A pub. A place for drinking."

"*Mais oui,*" the driver said. He turned around at the next corner, and a half-dozen blocks further, the cab pulled up in front of a small hotel. A doorway to the right of the main entrance was lit with a sign for a Swiss beer.

John paid the man, got out of the cab, and entered the hotel bar, stopping just within the door. The room was very dark, with only a few red lights above the bar itself and a small white light over a raised platform where a young, heavyset woman was playing a guitar and singing what sounded like a sad song in French. No one paid him any attention.

He looked back out the door as the taillights of his cab disappeared around the corner. Then he went outside and walked the way they had come, toward the photographer's shop.

Be very careful, John. They'll stop at nothing to protect their network, his father had written.

All this will be worked out, Switt had promised. *I want you to know that your father and I were very close. I admired the man, you know. I loved him.*

There was no pedestrian traffic, but there were a lot of cars and cabs along the main streets as John walked back up to Eaux-Vives. The closer he came, the more he realized just how foolish he was being. He had come this far, and now there was a good chance it would all be ended tonight. For nothing. He had no weapon, so even if he did get into Henrys's house, and even if he did come face-to-face with the man at last, he'd have no way of forcing Henrys to talk or of defending himself against any weapon. But even if he could deal with Henrys— kill him with his bare hands—then what? He had no car. No way of getting out of the city. This wouldn't be like Rome. Here Henrys was expecting him. He'd be waiting. He might get in the house, but he'd never get out alive.

He waited for a break in the traffic, then crossed the boulevard, turned down a side street of apartments, and continued deeper into the residential district.

There was no way he was going to back off now. Not having come this far. Not after all that had happened to him.

He could envision the look on Rubio's face just before he died. The man had been so cocksure of himself. So certain that he was right—or at least that he was superior. Misplaced? Probably not, John decided.

He came to one of the streets he recognized, then turned

up toward the Avenue William Favre, where the photographer's shop was located. Now his step was quick but even. He was very close, and he wanted to get it over with.

The streets were cobblestoned, very narrow and dark, until he came to the avenue. He had walked more than a mile, circling to the east, so that he could give Henrys's house a very wide berth. By the time he had come to the small shop in the middle of the block, he was sweating lightly, his heart was thumping, and his knees felt weak.

During a lull in the traffic, John ducked into the doorway of the shop. He pulled off his jacket, wrapped it around his arm, and quickly smashed one of the glass panes in the door.

The noise was very loud, and for several terrible seconds he stood listening for the sound of an alarm or for running footsteps. But there was nothing, and after a few more moments he unwrapped the jacket from his arm, reached inside the door, and unlatched the lock.

Inside the shop he pulled his jacket back on, checked again to make sure no one was coming, and made his way through the store, around the display cabinets and the counter, into the back rooms. Just behind a curtain was a small, untidy office. The darkroom was beyond it to the right, a tiny storeroom to the left. Straight ahead was a metal door with a bar across it.

He pulled the bar out of its slots, set it aside, unlatched the locks, and carefully opened the door. The night was clear and the moon almost full, and John saw that three feet behind the shop was a brick wall about eight feet high. The very narrow alleyway between the backs of the buildings and the wall seemed to end a couple of hundred feet on either side.

The area to the rear of Henrys's house was just over the wall, and for a minute John stood there, studying the top of it. As far as he could see, there were no alarm wires or anything else to deter someone from coming over. But then Henrys would not expect anyone from the direction of the closed alley.

To the right, where the darkroom was located, was a high, barred window, blacked out from the inside.

John closed the door, then climbed on a wooden crate to reach the window ledge, bracing himself against the wall. From here he easily reached the top of the wall, and he managed to heave himself onto it. He caught a glimpse of the house a hundred yards away, and then he dropped over the far side onto a footpath, narrowly missing a marble bench set against the wall.

He was in a huge garden, and as he picked himself up he looked again toward the house. From here he could see nothing but the very tip of the roof and chimneys, his view of the rest of the house blocked by trees and shrubs.

The ground sloped upward toward the house, and John worked his way through the maze of paths, stopping every few steps to listen for sounds from above. But there was nothing except the sound of trickling water from somewhere within the garden. He felt very lonely in the moonlit garden. If anything happened to him now, there was no one on this earth who would have the slightest idea where he was. Nor was there anyone who would care.

He passed another marble bench somewhere near the middle of the garden, and a few feet away he saw where a bed of roses had been recently disturbed. It looked as if they had been dug up and were waiting to be replanted. He took the next path, and within a couple of hundred feet he spotted the stairway that led to the patio. The house towered above that.

He stepped back into the shadows of a large tree and caught his breath. He was here. He had finally made it. But it all felt vastly unreal.

There did not appear to be anyone on the patio, nor were any of the windows in the house lit. The place looked deserted. Henrys must know that John was on his way, so maybe he had left.

After a minute or so, John crept to the foot of the stone stairs, keeping his eye on the patio. Again he stopped to listen, but still there were no sounds from above, so he started up, one hand trailing on the iron rail, the other brushing against the stone wall. He kept very low and as deep in the shadows as possible.

He was nearly at the top when he heard what sounded like the crackle of a two-way radio. He flattened himself against the wall and froze where he was.

For several seconds there was nothing else, and John began to wonder if his imagination was playing tricks on him. But then he heard it again, from above and slightly to the left.

He eased up a few more steps. From here he could distinguish someone talking softly. Up two more steps, his head was just below the level of the patio. He held his breath to listen better.

"Yes . . . it is Caroline," someone radioed.

"Has she spotted you?" the speaker just above John whispered. His accent was English.

The radio crackled again. "No. But what the hell is she doing back here?"

Who was Caroline? John wondered. Henrys's wife? Perhaps a secretary?

"You'd better call the old man."

There was no reply.

"Roger. Are you there? What's happening?"

"Bloody hell, she's spotted the car. She's coming your way. You'd better get out of sight—right now!"

"I'll go into the study. Don't think she'll come in there," the man above said, and John could hear him run across the patio. Then there was nothing.

He eased up another couple of inches so that he could just see over the balustrade. The patio was a large area. To the right were a table and a half-dozen chairs. To the left was a grouping of lounge furniture. Along the back of the house were several doors. As he watched, a light came on behind the glass-paned center door, and moments later it was opened by a tall, thin woman wearing blue jeans and a sweatshirt. She seemed to be searching for something or someone. From the light coming from the house, John could see her closely. She was young, probably not yet thirty, and she was very good-looking. Perhaps Henrys's wife, he thought, but more likely his daughter. John ducked his head and listened for her movements.

Henrys was gone, apparently, but John decided that he was not leaving empty-handed. One way or another, he was going to confront Henrys. One way or another, they were going to come face-to-face. And John knew now how he was going to accomplish that.

Chapter 19

THE YOUNG WOMAN hesitated at the threshold of the patio doors, then stepped the rest of the way outside. John remained frozen where he was, not daring to move a muscle lest she spot him.

She came across to where the man with the radio had been standing and leaned out over the balustrade. She was just above and to the left of John. All she had to do was turn her head slightly and she would see him. He felt very exposed, almost naked, crouched on the stone steps.

Finally she straightened up and sighed deeply—John could hear the sound clearly—then turned back toward the open door. Something changed her mind, however, and she veered to a set of French doors to her left, opened them, and stepped inside. A light came on, but from where John was crouched he could not see inside the room.

Moments later he heard her voice raised in anger, although he could not quite make out what she was saying. Only the tone of her voice was clear. A man's voice, much lower and calmer, answered, and the woman shouted at him again.

As far as John knew, there was no one else in or around the house except for Caroline and the guard she was evidently confronting in the study at this moment, plus the one out front somewhere.

Once again he was faced with a clear choice. He could turn around, go back through the garden, climb over the wall, make his way through to the photographer's shop, and take a cab out to the airport. Or he could go ahead. If he did, there'd be no going back. This, he was sure, was the last fork in the road.

Caroline and the man were still arguing when John rose up, stepped onto the patio, and hurried across to the open door Caroline had come through.

He found himself in a wide hallway that ran toward the front of the house. To his left was a set of double doors, evidently leading into the study where the guard had gone. Through them he could hear the faint sounds of Caroline's voice.

He could not stay here, in this exposed position. He hurried down the hallway, passing a narrower hallway that led off to his right. Just beyond it, an arch separated the hallway from the front foyer, illuminated only by the soft glow from a chandelier. He looked around, every one of his senses acutely attuned to the sounds of the house.

To the left of the front door, a wide staircase ascended to the second floor. To the right the light from the entryway revealed a large living room with a huge stone fireplace. And facing the stairs was a tall, stained-glass window, dark and somber-looking now.

John ran up the stairs, taking them two at a time. At the top he hurried down the corridor to where the banister ended against the wall. Standing in the shadows, he was able to see to the front door and the living room.

He had the impression he was in a museum. He was surrounded by luxury—but of a consciously subdued variety. McNiel Henrys certainly had not earned all this on his salary as an officer with the British secret service, no matter how high a rank he held. This house—what he had seen of it so far—represented old money, very old money, and a lot of it.

A door below was flung open, and he heard someone come out, then halt.

"I will not be dictated to in my own home, you bloody bastard!" a woman shouted.

"Miss Henrys, please," the guard said placatingly. "It is for your own good. Believe me."

"Rubbish!" Caroline shrieked.

"Your father will not be happy . . ." the man started to say, when Caroline stepped forward and slapped him on the face, the noise sharp, almost like a pistol shot.

"Now get out of my house, you son of a bitch," Caroline said evenly.

"I'm sorry, Miss Henrys, if I said or did anything to offend you. But I repeat, your father stationed me here to watch over the house, and here I will remain."

"I will call him."

"That is your privilege, miss."

"Meanwhile, get out of my house. If you are to guard, you can do it outside."

The guard's footsteps sounded down the large hallway in the direction of the door to the patio.

John stood where he was. The woman was strong-willed; in that way she reminded him of Elizabeth. Almost immediately he heard her voice again.

"Give me the overseas operator," she snapped. Then, moments later, "I want London. The number is 205.67.78. . . . Yes, I'll stand by, operator, but surely there cannot be a delay at this time of night."

John could tell that she was just barely controlling her anger.

"I can hear that," she shouted after a few seconds. "But let the bloody thing ring. It'll be answered—" She stopped and the tone of her voice changed. She was calm now, in control. Almost meek. "Hello. This is Caroline Henrys. I'd like to speak with my father. I am at home in Geneva. Please see that he gets the message."

She hung up the phone and walked into view below, stopped a moment, then hurried down the hall to the back. She was gone only a few seconds, and then she was back in the hall. She went to the front door and turned the bolt. She was locking out her guards.

She came slowly to the foot of the stairs, looked once again down the hallway toward the patio, and then started up, her right hand trailing on the banister.

John stepped back out of sight, nearly knocking into a hall

table on which was a grouping of framed photographs. He turned and hurried down the corridor, opening the first door he came to and slipping inside.

He was in what appeared to be a very large, well-furnished guest room. He held the door open a crack and watched as Caroline came to the head of the stairs, walked slowly past him, and entered a room two doors down and across the corridor. She closed the door, and a second later a shaft of light spilled out beneath it.

John's insides felt as if they were filled with hot steam. When he confronted this woman, he did not want to hurt her. He didn't want that—although it would be a blow Henrys would never forget. But she didn't deserve that. Just as his children had not deserved it. Just as Elizabeth should still be alive. . . .

He opened the door, crossed the corridor to the room next to Caroline's, and entered, softly closing the door so that it latched.

This was apparently another guest room, but it was furnished for a woman, with satin at the windows, velvet-covered chairs, and a canopy over the bed. A bathroom was to the right, a large armoire to the left. Near the far wall was another door under which spilled light from Caroline's room. The rooms were adjoining, as he had hoped they would be.

At the door he listened. Caroline was humming some tune. Then he heard water running in a bathtub. He felt like a voyeur. He moved away from the door and went to the window, which looked down on the patio, the gardens, and, beyond that, the brick wall and the photographer's shop. There were blue lights! Although he could not see the street, the reflections of blue lights flashed from in front of the shop. The police had evidently discovered the broken glass at the front door.

He looked down at the patio but did not see the guard. Christ, when the police discovered that the back door was open, and that there was no other way out of the alleyway except over the wall into the garden, they'd be coming around here. The guards were waiting for him, on Henrys's orders. They'd put two and two together, and realize that he was either somewhere on the grounds or in the house.

He was running out of time.

The water in the bathroom stopped, and John could hear Caroline getting into the tub. He did not want to do this, but it was going to have to be now.

The connecting door was unlocked. John opened it and moved noiselessly into Caroline's room. A single light shone on the nightstand, and her jeans and sweatshirt were lying in a heap at the foot of the bed. A nightgown was laid out.

The bathroom door was open to the left. John took a deep breath and let it out slowly to calm the flutters in his chest. Stepping around the corner into the large bathroom, he stuck his right hand in his jacket pocket as if he had a gun there.

Caroline looked up and nearly leaped out of the tub as she opened her mouth to scream.

"Don't make a noise, Caroline, or I will kill you," John growled menacingly.

"Get the hell out of here! I told your partner—"

"I'm not one of your father's guards. I want you to get out of there now and get dressed," John said, keeping his voice low. He grabbed a bath towel from the bar with his left hand, then stepped forward and laid it on the edge of the tub, trying to avert his eyes from her nakedness.

"I will not," Caroline snapped, very much in control, although he could see in her eyes that she was frightened. She did not try to cover her small, lovely breasts. Even in his present state, he could admire her courage.

"I don't want to hurt you, Miss Henrys, but I will if need be."

"Christ, an American. If you're not one of the guards, what the hell do you want? My father—"

"Your father is a murderer who killed my wife and children," John blurted.

Caroline was too stunned by John's words to do anything more than blink her eyes.

"Now get out of the tub and get dressed. I'm not here to hurt you, I promise you that. As long as you do as I say."

"What do you mean my father killed your wife and children? What do you mean?"

"Your father didn't actually murder them, but he ordered it."

"Nonsense. My father is not a killer."

"He is. And I'm going to prove it, then bring him to justice." Even to himself, John sounded like a character in an old Western.

"You're going to kill him, aren't you?"

John said nothing. He could not find the words . . . any words.

"Get out of here, or I'll call the guard. He's just downstairs."

John nodded. "There's one out back on the patio, and one out front somewhere. But you locked them out."

Her eyes widened. "You came in past them."

"Get out of the tub and get dressed," John ordered again. He was very conscious of the fact that he was rapidly running out of time. As soon as the Geneva police showed up here, he wouldn't have a chance of getting away. "Now!" he barked.

She stood up slowly, wrapped the towel around her, and stepped out of the tub. Her legs were long and very graceful, her shoulders tiny and rounded.

John let her pass into the bedroom, where she took clean slacks from the armoire, and a pullover and underwear from her bureau.

She looked defiantly at him, and then turned her back, dropped the towel, and quickly dressed.

"Why would my father want to kill your wife and children? That doesn't make much sense," Caroline challenged John when she was dressed.

"He wanted me dead because I know about his precious network. He had my cabin blown up. My wife and children were inside sleeping at the time. They didn't have a chance."

Caroline winced. "I don't believe you—" she started, but John cut her off.

"He also killed my father a couple of weeks ago, after my father found out about the network. He was here, and talked with your father."

Caroline started to say something, but then an odd expression came into her eyes as she studied John's face. "Your father is an older man? White hair?"

"You've seen him? Here?" John asked.

Caroline nodded her head.

"He's dead now," John said bitterly. "Your father had him killed."

"No," Caroline said, still shaking her head. She backed up a step.

At any moment the police would be here, yet John felt that he owed it to this lovely young woman to explain his actions. He owed it to someone. Someone had to believe in him.

"Why do you think he posted guards downstairs? Is that normal?"

Caroline started to answer him but then held her silence. It had been enough, however. The seed of doubt had been planted. He could see it in her eyes.

"I thought not," John said. "They're down there because of me. Your father knew I would be coming here. They have orders to kill me."

"No!"

"Where is your father now? Where'd he go?"

Caroline just looked at him, her nostrils flared. She did not completely believe him, nor was she yet ready to cooperate. It was what he had expected of her from her performance downstairs. She was a very strong-willed woman.

"We're leaving here," he said.

Her eyes widened, and she backed up a step. "I telephoned my father. He'll be coming after me."

"The Secret Intelligence Service in London. I know. But you're not supposed to be here. I'll bet your father made sure you were safely away before he left."

The telephone on the table by her bed rang, and they both looked at it.

"Does anyone know you're in the house, except for the people you called? Friends? Anyone?"

The telephone rang again, and Caroline shook her head.

John went across the room, keeping his eyes on her, and picked the phone up on the next ring. "Yes?" he said softly.

Time. He was conscious of passing time, yet he was certain he knew who would be on the other end.

"Who is this?" a man demanded. His voice was British, definitely cultured.

"John Mahoney. I presume I'm speaking with McNiel Henrys."

"My God! What do you want, Mahoney?"

"Caroline and I will be leaving in a minute or two, and if you send your people after us, it will be a terrible mistake. I want the truth. And I want it from you—face-to-face, from you."

"If you leave, how will I be able to arrange a meeting?" Henrys pleaded. John could hear the desperation for his daughter's safety in the man's voice.

"I'll contact you. I have your number in London. The one Caroline used to contact you at the secret service."

"I didn't kill your wife and children, Mahoney, you must believe me," Henrys said urgently. "Darrell Switt arranged it. It was him."

"That's what Rubio said."

There was a silence on the line for a long moment. Then Henrys's subdued voice: "It *was* you, after all."

"Who'd you expect?"

"The Italian police—they're after you. And so is someone else. The CIA, I think."

"Haven't you anyone to replace Switt in the Agency?"

"Let me talk with my daughter."

"You haven't answered my question, Henrys."

"And I won't answer anything else until I've spoken with my daughter."

John hesitated. Caroline was watching him closely. He held out the phone. "Your father wants to talk to you."

Caroline came across and took the receiver from John. "Father?" she said in a small voice.

John could hear Henrys's voice, but he could not make out what the man was saying.

"I'm sorry. Albert and I... quarreled. I thought it best I come home," she said. She glanced at John. "No," she said, and suddenly her entire bearing changed, the color left her face, and her knuckles turned white where she gripped the phone.

John pulled the receiver away from her. "We'll meet, Henrys, and when we do I'll want the truth."

"If you hurt my daughter, so help me God, you'll be a dead man."

"You've already got a contract on my head. What more can I expect to lose?" John hung up, suddenly angry because he didn't really know what he was going to do when he met the man. He wanted to smash him, to pound him into the ground, grind him into the dust. Yet, even after all he had done, he did not honestly know if he had the strength or the ruthlessness.

Caroline read the torment on his face. "If you get out of here right now, I'll convince my father to leave you alone."

John just looked at her.

"Leave now. I'll call him back and tell him you're gone. He'll call off his people."

"He told you, didn't he? He told you that his watchdogs

downstairs were here to kill me."

"Leave now, Mr. Mahoney, before you do something you will regret."

"It's too late for that, Miss Henrys," John said, grabbing her arm. He propelled her to the door. "Where are your car keys?"

"In the car—" she blurted out before she realized what she was saying.

Before John opened the door, he looked deeply into her eyes. "I'm going to tell you this only once, Caroline. And I want you to understand that I'm a very desperate man. I've nothing to lose—absolutely nothing. Everything I love has been taken away from me."

She swallowed, then nodded.

"We're going downstairs, we're going to get into your car, and we're going to drive away from here. If you make any attempt to call out, or to attract the attention of the guards, or later, the police, I will not hesitate to kill you. Do you understand that?"

Again she nodded.

"Good," John said. "Let's go." He hurried her downstairs and into the small kitchen hallway under the staircase. Realizing subterfuge was useless, Caroline pointed to the door that led down a flight of stairs to the garage.

A Rolls-Royce Corniche convertible, a small MGB sports car, and an Alfa-Romeo were parked side by side.

"The Alfa is mine," Caroline said, resigned.

They went around the gunmetal gray sports coupe. John motioned Caroline in on the driver's side, then climbed in and hunched down as best he could below the level of the windows.

She looked down at him.

"Now," he said.

She activated the automatic garage door. Seconds later she put the car in gear, and they were moving slowly up the ramp and through the tunnel to the mews. Then they were out on the cobbled driveway, and she was slowing down as she cranked down her window.

What could he do? He was suddenly like a fish in a barrel. It was as if an electric current had shot through his nerves, momentarily stunning him into inaction. The guard would have to see him!

"The house is yours," Caroline shouted without actually stopping the car.

One of the guards shouted something, and John just caught a glimpse of him as Caroline sped up, and they slid around a corner.

She accelerated through the gears, and they turned several more corners before she glanced down at him.

"We're clear now," she said. "I don't think they'll catch up with us." She seemed frightened.

He sat up and pulled his hand out of his pocket. She was convinced about the nonexistent gun. At least for the time being. Once they were settled in somewhere, outside of Geneva, he would call for her father. And the man would come. Oh, yes, he would come prepared to talk.

Chapter 20

GREENE HAD STEPPED off the train during the stop at Brig, hopefully searching the platform for any sign of John or Sampson. When that proved fruitless, he and Mahoney decided to continue to Lausanne, which had the advantage of being a large city and a better center of transportation.

It was evening in Washington when Mahoney telephoned McBundy at home from the Lausanne station, and he hated what he had to tell him as much as he knew McBundy was going to hate to hear it.

They had two urgent problems, he explained: the first was to get to Geneva before John got to Henrys; the second was to square the Italian and Swiss police before they found Sampson's body lying on the tracks.

"Forget John," McBundy said. "I had a watch put on the airports, and Henrys was seen coming into England yesterday afternoon, so John isn't anywhere near him."

"Christ!" Mahoney swore. "I told you to keep the Agency

away from Henrys. If he spotted any of your men—"

"I used some of our new people, so I don't see how he could recognize them. And if he did and it comes back to us, I'll say it was a training exercise—a joke, service to service. Though if the DCI ever hears about it.... Anyway I'll take care of the police, but you'd better arrange a search yourselves. Have Bobby call some people down from Bern to help him. Between us, we're going to have to convince the authorities that Len was just what his papers show he was: a cop from Long Island on vacation.

"As for you, Wallace, I meant what I said about the deadline. You've already used up one week, and you can either go after John or go after this network. You're just going to have to make up your mind."

Mahoney felt an enormous sense of relief to know that his son was safe—not safe from whoever was after him, he amended, but safe from himself. Henrys was out of his range, at least for the moment.

"Hold yourself together, Bobby," Mahoney said just before he left Lausanne. He had to be out of there before their people started showing up and the fuss began.

"Soon as this is all cleared up, I'll be back, Mr. Mahoney," Greene said. Sampson had been like his right arm for the past twenty years. They were closer than most brothers.

"We'll be ready to go then," Mahoney said.

"I hope so. God, I hope we can strike back."

Mahoney found a taxi to drive him to Geneva's Cointrin Airport, little more than half an hour away. He had carried Greene's expression with him on the short flight over, and he carried it in his mind's eye now as he drove north toward St. Albans, which was, the car rental people informed him, barely an hour's drive from the airport.

McBundy was beginning to feel the pressure. First Switt's disappearance, then Jensen's murder, and now Sampson's death. The DCI wasn't blind. He wouldn't appreciate being lied to. But McBundy had assured them all that if they included the old man in on any of this, the operation would come to a screeching halt. A blue-ribbon commission would he appointed to find out where the blame should *not* be placed, and the entire mess would, in time, be turned over to a Senate investigatory committee that would make an even bigger—and certainly more public—mess of it.

McBundy had a dim view of academics-turned-politicians, of which Franklin Lycoming was one. From the things Mahoney had witnessed over the past few years, he was coming to the same opinion.

Mahoney was beginning to think of McBundy and Henrys as two poles between which he oscillated. Two main streams were moving now, he thought. On the one, the deaths had convinced McBundy that there was something to Mahoney's allegations; McBundy was now firmly on his side. And on the other, Henrys was getting nervous. He had to be. It had been his people who had been killed at the cemetery in Missoula. By John. John might not be enough of a threat to worry Henrys, but if Switt was alive, and if he had identified the man Henrys's people killed by mistake in Los Angeles as an Agency employee, it would have told Henrys that the CIA was on the chase.

Then there had been Rubio's death. No one could doubt that John had been behind that. And finally, if Henrys was privy to the correct channels of information among the Swiss and Italian police, he'd have to be suspicious about a dead American cop. If Sampson's description got to Switt, the Agency would be pegged once again.

Mahoney felt like a dog sniffing after a bitch in heat. He had been going round and round in circles ever since this investigation had begun at the behest of the Mossad. Only now, at last, his circles were becoming increasingly compact. He was getting wind of his prey, and he wondered if Henrys were starting to feel crowded—looking over his shoulder, readying his bolt hole.

St. Albans was a lovely old town, its ancient Roman pastoral appearance all the more surprising because of its proximity to London. It was past 6:00 P.M. when Mahoney drove the two miles off the M1 to the St. Michael's Manor Hotel, which had been recommended to him by the car rental agency. He was given a room on the top floor beneath a dormer, which looked out over five acres of parkland and a little lake. On a sunny day it would be idyllic here, he thought, unpacking his suitcase.

He sent his suit down to be sponged and pressed, then had the desk clerk send up the local newspaper, along with any tourist guides they might have.

When the things came, he drew a hot bath, poured a stiff

drink of the bourbon he had bought at Heathrow, and settled into the tub with the newspaper and the half-dozen guides, including Baedel's *Walking Tour Map of Hertfordshire Homes of Note*.

He quickly scanned the front page of the paper, which was mostly taken up with a Town Council meeting on a rezoning ordinance, the weather, and the conviction of a local for driving while intoxicated. He almost missed the caption under a small photograph of five old men. One was holding a shovel at what was obviously a ground-breaking ceremony.

HEATHROW SERVICE CENTER TO OPEN SOON, the boldface type read. An extensive helicopter-landing area and VIP processing point was to be constructed south of St. Albans off the A6. Businessmen, instead of slogging through crowded Heathrow Airport, would have their own baggage, customs, and passport-control facilities here at St. Albans, and would be helicoptered to and from Heathrow.

The bellman came with Mahoney's suit half an hour later, and Mahoney shaved, dressed, and went downstairs for dinner. Afterward, he drove into town, past the antique shops of George Street, past the cathedral and abbey, and then south on A6, the London road.

Two miles from the center of town, a dirt track led into a field to the left. Heavy construction and earth-moving machinery was parked in the field, where work had already begun. A chain was stretched across the road, and a tall plywood sign was tacked up:

HEATHROW SERVICE ANNEX
CONSTRUCTION BY HARCOURT INTERNATIONAL, LTD.

Idling at the side of the road, Mahoney stared up at the sign with some surprise. Harcourt International was one of the largest construction firms in the world. They built skyscrapers and airports and dams. Yet here they were building a tiny heliport for traveling businessmen. Near St. Albans, of all places.

Beyond the field, Mahoney could just make out a rising hill and a large section of dark woods, with a grouping of lights pinpointed through the trees. Someone was up there. Looking down on all this. Watching? Mahoney had the impression that whoever was up there was also waiting for something.

He put the car in gear, turned around on the highway, and

headed back to his hotel. Thunder rolled ominously in the distance, and the rain, which had been little more than a drizzle, began to fall in earnest.

Back in his room, Mahoney took off his coat and tie, rolled up his sleeves, and poured a stiff shot of the passable whiskey.

Chaim Malecki had come here. More than once. Even more significant than that, however, was the fact that Malecki had brought the woman he loved here. To what? To meet whom?

He opened the guidebook to the local *Homes of Note* and scanned the table of contents for the names of the old men in the heliport ground-breaking photograph. He came up with Patton.

"Hillside Meadows," the guide read, "is one of the loveliest 19th-century pre-Victorian estates in this area of Hertfordshire. It boasts the finest, most extensive collection of rare Persian rugs in all the U.K."

Mahoney followed his finger down the gushing description of the home, which was not open to the public and could only be seen from either the fields bordering the A6 or the Timmons Road on the hill.

The home was owned by Lawrence and Kathleen Patton. Mahoney held the newspaper up to the light. Patton was a tall, thin man with glasses, fairly old, if the newspaper photograph could be trusted.

The guide listed the Patton family background, finally coming to the present. Lawrence Patton was chairman of the board of Woroco—World Oil Company—the largest privately held oil firm in the world.

He lowered the book to his lap, then set it aside for a moment as he poured himself another drink and relit his cigar.

The service center could, with sufficient reason, have been constructed for Patton himself. He could be a very busy man. His time valuable. Especially in light of recent developments in the oil industry.

Malecki had come here often to see someone. The Pattons? Or, as Mahoney suspected, someone connected with ComSat, Ltd.?

The guide listed estates and owners' names but not their occupations, so he was forced to begin on the first page of the descriptions and work his way through them all, one by one.

Within half an hour he had come up with a German's name. Alois Reichert, who owned Morning Rise, an ultramodern estate to the north of town, was president and majority stockholder of Kreuger Steel, A.G., which, if Mahoney's memory served him correctly, was the fifth or sixth largest steel firm in the world, with plants in England, France, and Germany.

The third and fourth names came within a few minutes of each other an hour and a half later.

George Panagiotopolous, whose home incorporated the ruins of a pre-Tudor abbey, owned Harcourt International, Ltd., with offices in Athens, London, and New York. And Sir Rudyard Jonstone, who had one hundred and fifty acres to the east of St. Albans and whose estate had been in the family for nearly two hundred years, was chairman of the board of ComSat, Ltd.

Bingo, Mahoney thought. ComSat, Ltd., the company that had designed and put up Israel's spy satellite and had installed the receiving-station equipment at Al Qaryūt.

The name wasn't all that surprising. Mahoney had thought he might find it here. Malecki had probably come here to see Jonstone. It proved the connection between Malecki and the firm. Wasserman had said the Al Qaryūt project was initiated at Malecki's suggestion. But how about others with whom Jonstone was associated here in St. Albans? Were there others connected with Malecki, and thus the network? And why had Malecki brought Sonja here, like a young suitor might bring his intended to meet his family? These people weren't Malecki's family. Or were they?

Mahoney continued to work his way through the guidebook, coming within twenty minutes to a second name in the newspaper photograph. Aubert Holmes, president and chairman of the board of Inter-Continental Technologies. It was a new one to him.

It was incredible, but the leaders of four—maybe five—of the world's largest and most powerful firms had their homes in or around one tiny town north of London. Coincidence, he asked himself? He doubted it. But if they were indeed working together, or if they were somehow connected with the network, perhaps through ComSat, then their close proximity to each other like this—out in the open, with no attempt to disguise the connection—was a blatant piece of arrogance. They must be supremely confident that no one would deign to suspect them.

More likely he was chasing after a will-o'-the-wisp, and

there was someone else here Malecki had brought Sonja to meet. If they weren't just pleasure trips after all.

Yet Wasserman's words—that it had been Malecki's idea for the satellite system—kept coming back to him. It had been his idea. ComSat had put it up. And Malecki had brought Sonja here. Like a supplicant bringing an offering to the altar? He hadn't merely come here alone, he had brought the woman he loved—a woman who was a Mossad operative. And she had evidently been so impressed that she later risked her life to cover for him.

He thought about Marge, and about the things he had done in his early days to impress her. He remembered that he would hold up for her approval the things that were most important to him. Achievements, insofar as he could discuss them outside the Agency. Friends.

Had Malecki done that with Sonja? And if so, who or what here did he list as his proud achievement?

He looked at his watch. It was after eleven and he was incredibly tired, yet his mind refused to shut down. A kaleidoscope of images and thoughts raced in a jumbled pattern. There was danger here, extreme danger, even though no one could possibly be expecting him. He was dead. Yet he felt there were eyes watching his every move. Waiting for him to make the one mistake that would reveal his real purpose.

There'd be others, of course. This was the citadel. That is, if he were correct in his assumptions. He sincerely hoped he was wrong, because the implications were far more frightening than anything he had previously imagined. It was like being in the control room of a nuclear reactor and hearing the alarms go off.

He went and lay down on the bed, where he looked up at the ceiling, his eyes refusing to close. William Morrison was a tourist in St. Albans, which meant he could leave in the morning without attracting attention. But he could not leave tonight. It would be noticed.

Mahoney turned the thought over. His concern was not for his own physical well-being. Rather he was afraid of being cheated of the final satisfaction of exposing the network. Too many people had died—his family, his friends—to deny him that.

In the morning, he told himself, and he let his mind drift. In the morning he would find out. He fell asleep on that thought.

* * *

The morning was dreary, but the rain had stopped. Mahoney rose very early, had tea and toast sent up to his room, packed, checked out, and drove back to Heathrow. As he drove he wondered if he were being an old fool. Everything that had happened so far could have an alternate, less ominous explanation. There was a network, of course. He had heard it from Henrys himself. But perhaps it stopped there. Perhaps it was merely a collection of operatives who performed tasks for Henrys.

He was clutching at straws, and he knew it. Even Henrys had admitted there was more to it. He said that the network was begun in the 1940s because of the American success with the atomic bomb. It had been started so that there'd never be an all-out nuclear war. But there was obviously more . . . something larger.

There was almost no Sunday-morning traffic, and Mahoney had time to wonder if perhaps Henrys weren't correct after all. Perhaps peace at all costs was a valid philosophy when the alternative was nuclear war. For nearly forty years the threat of nuclear war had hung over the world, but it had not come. There had been Korea and Vietnam and a host of other shooting matches, but never the dreaded nuclear confrontation. In God's name, was he right after all?

Mahoney turned his car in at the rental agency, then booked a seat on Pan Am's midmorning flight to Washington, which left in an hour. At the bank of public telephones, he dialed the international operator. He had wanted to make these calls last night, but it would have been far too risky from any telephone in St. Albans.

He gave her his international credit card number, told her he would be making three calls, and gave her the first number, then settled back with a cigar to wait for the call to go through.

A woman answered after two rings. *"Ja?"*

"This is Mr. Morrison. I would like to speak with Carl, if he is there," Mahoney said in German.

"Morrison?" the old woman repeated, confused. She was Carl's cousin.

"Yes," Mahoney said. "I was there the other night visiting with Carl. It is very important I speak with him."

"Just a moment, please."

A few moments later Carl Margraff was on the line. "Mr.

Morrison?" he said very carefully.

"It's me," Mahoney said. "There was one last thing I forgot to ask you."

"Leave me alone," Margraff said. "I don't want to hear any of this. I spoke with Ezra. He's back in Tel Aviv."

"I expected that," Mahoney said. "There is still a lot to be done. And I do need your help, this one last time."

There was a short silence. "All right," Margraff said. "What is it? What do you want?"

"After these trips to St. Albans, did Sonja ever mention anything—anything at all—about the people she met?"

"I told you before, nothing. She just didn't talk about it."

"You told me she never talked *at length*, Carl. Which means she must have mentioned something. A first name, a dinner engagement. Anything, no matter how inconsequential. I don't have to tell you the drill. You've been through it before."

"There's nothing—" Margraff said, then stopped short.

"What is it?"

"It's not much, but I do remember Sonja raving about rugs. Persian rugs, I think it was. She and Chaim had just returned from England, and she had this frenzy all of a sudden for Persian rugs. Does that mean anything to you?"

Mahoney was back in the guidebook. The Pattons' home just off the A6 held the most extensive collection of Persian rugs in the country. "How about a name or names? Lawrence or Kathleen Patton?"

"No," Margraff said. "There's nothing more. Honestly, she never talked about her private life. Not really. Just that she and Chaim had gone to England. And the rugs. Nothing else."

"Thank you, Carl. Thank you very much."

"*Don't* keep me posted," Margraff said. "But good luck just the same." He hung up.

His next call took nearly ten minutes to go through, and when it did, a woman answered with a single word, "Yes?"

"Tell Ezra that it is extremely important that Mr. Morrison speak with him immediately," Mahoney said, and he gave the Mossad operations clerk in Tel Aviv the telephone number of the phone booth, then hung up.

The airport was surprisingly busy this morning, and as Mahoney waited for Wasserman to return his call, he smoked his cigar and watched the people going by.

Wasserman's call came less than five minutes later.

"Morrison?"

"It's me," Mahoney said.

"What are you doing at Heathrow?"

Mahoney was impressed. Wasserman's staff had researched the telephone number rather quickly. "On my way back home. I need one more piece of information before I go."

"No."

"ComSat provided the electronics. Who provided the on-site construction? An Israeli firm?"

Wasserman said nothing.

"It'll happen all over again, Ezra. The very same thing. I'm trying to prevent it."

"Not an Israeli firm. ComSat recommended a firm they always use. We hired them."

"Harcourt International?"

"That's a matter of general knowledge," Wasserman said, "but yes."

Athens, Mahoney thought. So long ago, it seemed, but it was connected. The gigantic construction conglomerate had its offices in Athens, where a bomb meant for him exploded in the airport locker. "Thanks," Mahoney said.

"What have you got? Anything that can help me?"

"Not yet. But soon, I hope. Very soon."

With barely twenty minutes to go before his flight was scheduled to take off, Mahoney got his last call through, this one to McBundy at his home.

"Are you on a secure line?" Mahoney asked. "Has it been swept recently?"

"Every week," McBundy said. "But it's not even five o'clock in the morning here. Where are you calling from? Greene has got his hands full over there, and the shit is just about ready to hit the fan."

"I'm on my way in. I'll be at the float house later today."

"I'm calling a halt to this today."

"No!" Mahoney retorted a little too loudly. He looked around to make sure he hadn't attracted any attention. "You said another week. We're almost there, goddamnit!"

"It's costing too much."

"What do you think it's cost me? John is out there somewhere. . . . Christ, Bob, you're not going to back down now. Not now!"

"We'll talk when you get back."

"You're goddamned right we'll talk. But meanwhile, don't do anything, Bob. I need your promise on it."

"I'll wait until you're back. But it's over."

"One question first. I'll need something on it by the time I get back. Who manufactures Soman?" It was the nerve gas that had killed all the troops at Ataruz, the strike force that had destroyed Al Qaryūt.

"Christ," McBundy said. "This is an open line."

Mahoney waited.

"Inter-Continental Technologies," McBundy said at long last.

Everything, every last piece fell neatly into place for Mahoney. All the anomalies were gone. There was only one last operation now, which would give them everything they needed.

"Have Kopinski there. And we'll need a couple of legmen," Mahoney said.

"They found Len's body," McBundy said. "On the Italian side of the Simplon Tunnel."

"How's Bobby holding up?"

"I've called him back. Len...was in pretty bad shape. There wasn't much left."

"I'll be back this afternoon," Mahoney said. There was still a lot to be done, and he was acutely conscious of the fact that time was very short for his son. For all of them. Greene was going to have to pull himself together. They were going to have one shot at this, and only one shot. It either worked, or they'd never get another chance. In forty years the network had made only one mistake. If they didn't pounce on it, they'd not be making another very soon.

THE GENEVA COVENANT

Chapter 21

IT WAS COMING very nearly to the end, although it was not until much later that historians could look up over the rims of their eyeglasses and pedantically intone that these were the last phases. Mahoney was of a single mind in those final few days. There wasn't a moment in his waking hours when he wasn't working on what came to be known as "the project." Such a silly, mundane title, actually, but one that later came to stick, as if *the project* were magic words that could sanctify the entire messy operation.

In the main it was not a particularly contemplative time—except for the one very brief period in Missoula—and ran contrary to Mahoney's usual behavior prior to a difficult and complex operation. Rather, as he expressed it, it was a busy time of juggling.

McBundy and General Lycoming had to be juggled off each other. McBundy wanted to call a halt to the entire affair, and the DCI was nearly, but not completely, ignorant of the pro-

231

ceedings. The DCI had to remain that way, and McBundy's motivation to see to it had to constantly be shored up.

There had been trouble, to that end, from the moment Mahoney had returned to the States and moved back into McBundy's new safe house, in Washington, another float.

Mahoney had been back scarcely half an hour, and had just taken off his jacket and poured himself a drink, when McBundy showed up.

"We can go to Lycoming right now, or we can talk it out and go first thing in the morning."

Mahoney was tired and in no mood for McBundy's bullshit. "I'll either do this with your help, Bob, or I'll do it alone. Your choice."

McBundy glared at him. "I'd have you arrested for treason."

"You don't want that kind of a mess. I wouldn't back down, and that'd mean a trial. An embarrassing, long, messy trial."

"I could have you shot."

"Shit," Mahoney said. He liked McBundy, but at the moment he had the almost overwhelming urge to smash the man in the face. "Are you a hundred percent sure I haven't sent off another letter to someone somewhere? Or how about my son? Would you kill him as well?" Mahoney shook his head. "There are a lot of loose ends, Bob."

McBundy drew himself up to his full height, his stomach unnaturally flat for a man his age, and told Mahoney exactly what kind of pressures he was under with the DCI and Congress breathing down his neck. The next day, when he thought back on it, he couldn't quite remember what he said. But he did remember clearly Mahoney's next words.

"We've only a few days to go. And when it's over, the network will be smashed, for better or for worse. If you can't go along with me on this, then I'll have to do it on my own. Because it has to be done. Just don't get in my way."

Kopinski had to be juggled as well when he balked. His job was to act as banker for the short but intense operation, and as such he was going to have to perform some sleight-of-hand in the Agency's computer center.

"What you're asking me to do, Wallace, is grossly illegal," Kopinski said with his birdlike motions.

"But think of where we've come from, Stan," Mahoney said. Kopinski had come to the float house later that same evening. They were going to have to work very fast, Mahoney explained. John was on the loose, and there was no telling for certain what warping effect he was having on their time lines. But it was a certainty he wasn't helping matters any.

"Besides," Kopinski told his wife the next week, "the man was dreadfully frightened for his son. Every hour that went by, the certainty that his boy would wind up dead rose a thousand percent or more."

Kopinski cooperated, of course, with the financial arrangements, which included housing, travel, cars, provisions, and equipment. The entire gamut for such an operation.

A pair of Larry Jensen's old teammates, Thomas Jones and Jim Carron, were brought onto the team, and it was very late that same Sunday night when they came around at McBundy's request. Neither knew what was happening, and it took a bit of time for them to recover from the shock of seeing Mahoney alive. More time was wasted bringing them up-to-date on everything that had happened so far, including all the deaths.

Jones and Carron were both young, in their thirties. Both were built, Mahoney commented at the time, like small mountains. But they were bright. Sharp as tacks. They caught on almost immediately, but then it became a juggling job just to keep them reined in. They wanted to hop on the next plane and start the operation immediately. Mahoney was glad that the operation was to be put into effect within the next seventy-two hours, because he did not think he could have kept those two down much longer than that. He sent them off to arrange transportation at both ends, as well as phone links and communications equipment for operational use.

Then came the confrontation he had dreaded most, the main act in the juggling revenue, in the person of Bobby Greene, who flew in from Milan Monday morning and demanded to see Mahoney even before going home to clean up from his trip.

Greene was beside himself with fury. When he came into the float house, his body seemed to fill the doorway and then expand so that there was little or no breathing space in the living room for anyone else.

He and Mahoney did a little dance together, shaking hands almost as if they were posing for photographs. Then they went for a walk, at Mahoney's request. It was before noon and the streets were busy. Mahoney had hoped that being in public would in some small measure help to calm Greene down.

"We found Len," Greene said, carefully controlling himself for the moment.

"I heard," Mahoney said.

"He was on the Italian side. Outside Domodossola. He was in pretty bad shape. I mean really terrible condition. He fell under the train. He was dragged then, for a long ways."

"We knew he was dead, Bobby. The main thing is that we'll have him back. He'll be home."

"Your son killed him."

"Yes, he did."

"He's running scared. I know that. In his position I would have done the same thing. But God Almighty, I don't really know if I can handle this operation much longer. I mean, I don't know for sure if I can hold myself together. I'm afraid I might go berserk at the wrong moment and ruin everything."

"You're not going to go berserk, Bobby. And this operation does have to be done, otherwise the same things will keep happening over and over again."

"From what you've said, I wonder if it would be so bad," Greene said, not looking up.

His voice was rising again, and Mahoney was becoming worried for him. "Easy."

Greene shrugged. He was having a hard time caring about the network, which was for him distant, and impersonal—not the real thing like Sampson's mangled body. Given time, of course, his thinking would reassume its normal balance, but at that moment he seemed to be fighting Mahoney's logic.

They crossed the street with the light, and the man McBundy had sent to follow them had to dodge traffic in the middle of the block in order to keep up. McBundy was going along with Mahoney, for the moment. But as he had said in the past: "With delicate operations, the divisional chief would be wise to cover himself. It's like building a house of cards; the most elaborate structures are inherently the most dangerous. Build a solid framework, hidden out of sight, but there, nevertheless, for your protection."

Mahoney and Greene came to the next light, and then the next, without saying anything to each other, until Greene pulled up short.

"What is it we're trying to do here?" he said. "I mean, *exactly* what. You have some sort of an operation planned, evidently, and that I can respect and understand. But what have we been doing for the past week? Why the delay? What have we been waiting for?"

"I knew what had to be done, but I wasn't a hundred percent sure."

"Are you now?"

"No," Mahoney admitted. "But close enough."

"So now we mount an operation."

Mahoney nodded.

"McBundy says you've brought in the whiz kids, Jones and Carron, along with Stan and me. With you, that makes six. Enough?"

"Dr. Lewis will be joining us. That makes seven, plus our people from Bern."

"Let's bring someone else in on this, if you're not sure. Jesus, let's not have a repeat of Larry or Len. I still don't know why they killed Larry."

"A mistake, probably."

They started walking again, making a large circle around the float house. It was a lovely morning. The sun was shining, and it was warm. Quite a contrast, Mahoney thought, to St. Albans, which was another world of money and power and death, the dismal weather somehow appropriate. Ever since he had come to what he assumed was his understanding of the network, he had fought a glum mood that threatened to take over his being, to make him turn his back on the entire affair and walk away. But he could no more do that than he could abandon his son, still out there on the trail of Henrys. Mahoney only hoped that Henrys's monumental ego was monumental enough so that he'd want to play cat and mouse with John for a time. Lead him along. Toy with him. If he did that, they'd have enough time to set their operation in place and run it.

"What have you got in mind for me?" Greene asked at length.

"We're going to need two houses. One in Geneva itself—hotel will do—as an operational headquarters, and the other some distance outside the city. The first would have to be tight, the second absolutely sacrosanct."

Greene nodded.

"There can be no screw-ups on the second place. We'll not have a lot of time. It'll be very tight."

Again Greene nodded but held his silence.

"Look, Bobby, I'm sorry about Len. Really sorry. But there's nothing I can do to bring him back. There's nothing I can do to bring my grandchildren or their mother back either."

Greene stiffened with the chastisement. "They're bastards," he said with great emotion. "They're all bastards. But we'll get them in the end, won't we?"

"We will, Bobby. We will. You can count on it."

They decided to use McBundy's house as the most logical place for the final, most crucial of Mahoney's meetings. JoAnn McBundy, back from California, was told nothing more than that their home would be used for a meeting that evening. And, being the good Agency wife she was, she went out to a movie and afterward had a late dinner with friends.

Kopinski, with the help of Greene, had set up a taping system in the study, this one at McBundy's insistence. "After all, we do have to cover ourselves," McBundy said, and Mahoney offered no objections. In fact, he was almost amiable.

Jones and Carron played chauffeur from Washington National Airport, while Mahoney, McBundy, and the others waited in the study, silent for the most part, a bit grim as the early evening wore on.

The doorbell rang and McBundy jumped up as if he had been shot out of his chair. "This is it," he said, rubbing his hands together.

Kopinski calmly reached over and flipped on the table lamp, which activated the recording devices, and he and Greene went into the other room, softly closing the door behind them. From where they would be sitting, they would be able to monitor the entire conversation.

"All set then?" McBundy asked. Mahoney crossed his legs and nodded. McBundy went out into the corridor, and Mahoney could hear him opening the door and then greeting their guest.

The study was large, with traditional furniture, including huge, handcarved desk that had belonged to McBundy's grandfather. There were a lot of books and a few photographs. The only things conspicuously missing from the walls were awards and certificates. "We're in the wrong kind of business for that," he had once explained to his wife.

"Just this way," McBundy said. Wasserman appeared in the doorway, blinked several times, then stopped in his tracks when he saw it was Mahoney.

"Good evening, Ezra," Mahoney said, standing and coming across the room. "So good of you to join us." They shook hands. When they were seated, McBundy poured them each a snifter of cognac.

Mahoney was very conscious of the ticking of the clock in the hallway and of his own breath, which he suddenly realized he was holding. Wasserman *was* the key, after all, the plum, the prize, the raisin in the cake. He was the one bait at this moment that Henrys could not resist. Yet, like a silly schoolboy faced with asking his first girl to a dance, Mahoney found himself in difficulty.

"He knows it all, Ezra," he finally managed to say. But there was so much else to say.

Wasserman and McBundy both flinched as if they had been snapped with a rubber band. They looked at each other, and McBundy nodded.

"I can't say as I approved of your methods, Wasserman," McBundy said pompously, referring to his hiring of Mahoney. "But I suppose in your position I'd have done the same."

"And your government? What position has it taken?"

McBundy shrugged with just the correct degree of disregard. "There has been no *official* view developed as of yet. It'll depend, I suppose, in a large measure on you."

"I see," Wasserman said, and he turned his gaze to Mahoney. "How about me, Wallace? Do I know everything?"

"Not yet, Ezra, but you will if I can get your promise that whatever is said in this room will go no further unless we all agree that it can."

"You want me to play traitor to my own service?"

Mahoney had to smile. "You asked the same of me."

"It's different . . ." Wasserman sputtered, but then he let it lie. "If it involves putting my country or my service at risk, I will not cooperate."

"Your service and your country are already at risk."

"There is no evidence of another traitor—"

"Yet," Mahoney interjected harshly. "Yet, Ezra. Are you willing to take the risk that the status quo will last indefinitely? Or will you help us now?"

"I would be missed."

"What I'm proposing would only take two or three days of your time. There'll be more work later, but your participation would not be required."

Wasserman again looked to McBundy for confirmation, clearly no longer trusting Mahoney's motivations—if he ever had.

"I don't know the entire plan yet, myself," McBundy said. "But I'm committed to this. It's the only way out of what has become an impossible situation for us." He straightened his already straight tie.

"For all of us..." Wasserman turned back to Mahoney. "You do have a mole in your service?"

Mahoney nodded. "And they'll be wanting a new man in the Mossad. Someone special. Someone who knows the territory, who understands the political climate."

Wasserman was listening to Mahoney with growing horror.

"There are only two men at the moment like that in Israel," Mahoney went on. "One would be the logical choice based on his tragic losses, the other based on his position."

"Carl Margraff is one. He could come back into the government. Everyone trusts him."

"And you are the other."

"Why me?"

"Carl has had his share of troubles. First losing his son, and then his daughter. He's given his share to the business. More than his share." Mahoney took a sip of his drink. "Will you help us, Ezra?"

Again Wasserman looked from Mahoney to McBundy and back, vacillating, his troubles clearly marked on his face. But in the end he nodded his head, the movement barely perceptible but there nevertheless.

Twenty-four hours, Mahoney told them. They'd a scant night and a day to get things ready. To come up with the equipment, the funds, the paperwork, the time schedules. They were going to have to be quick but thorough.

On Tuesday he took the early-morning flight out to Denver over McBundy's vehement objections. From there he took a feeder airline flight to Missoula, arriving in the early afternoon having gained two hours flying west.

As he explained to McBundy, it wasn't something he had to do, but it damn well was something he was going to do.

"Sort of like looking one last time at your cards just before you make the big bet," he said. In truth he needed reassurance of the kind he could only find from his wife.

From the airport at Missoula, he rented a Ford Escort and drove out to Greenough Drive to St. Martin's Cemetery, where he parked near the maintenance shed.

The caretaker was nowhere around when Mahoney got out of the car, walked up the road, then turned onto the path that led up the hill. A few puffy white clouds scudded across the crystal-clear sky from the west, and a light breeze sighed through the treetops. The smell of the pine and the sweet, crisp bite to the air gave Mahoney a deep nostalgia for an entire host of times from his past: from when he was a boy in Duluth to his courting days with Marge; from the times when Michael and John were young and they'd go camping as a family; to the cabin at Shultz Lake where he and Marge had planned on spending the remainder of their lives.

At the top of the hill as before, he stared down at his wife's grave and tears came to his eyes. A heavy feeling passed his chest, and he had to shake his head for the disbelief of it.

He ran his fingers through his thick white hair as he looked up from the grave and past the hill toward the east. There were mountains all around him, snow clinging to the upper elevations. They gave him a strong sense of the majesty of people, of relationships, of the good things.

"It *is* you," someone said behind him, and Mahoney spun around. Will Houseman, the groundskeeper, stood there, his billed cap dirty and slightly awry, a wide-eyed expression half of disbelief and half of knee-slapping surprise on his face.

Mahoney nodded. "Your memory is correct, Mr. Houseman."

The man's eyes strayed to Mahoney's headstone. He pointed. "Who's buried there?"

"No one," Mahoney said.

The old man's jaws worked. "I suppose there's a reason for it," he said. He laughed. "You're not a ghost, are you?"

"Not a ghost, but I'd be obliged if you wouldn't say anything to anyone for a few days," Mahoney said. After that it would not matter.

"You work for the government, do you?"

Mahoney nodded.

"You're on some kind of a mission? Like on television?" the old man was excited.

Mahoney nodded. "Just like on TV."

The old man smiled. "Why, then, come on down to the

shack, and we'll have a drink. 'Less you're in a hurry."

Mahoney's plane did not leave for a couple of hours yet, and spending that time with the old caretaker made more sense than standing over two graves. Marge would understand, and that was all that really mattered.

Chapter 22

SUNDAY WAS A living nightmare for John Mahoney. With Caroline Henrys in tow, he was not able to sleep. He had warned her that if she bolted, she could probably escape easily enough, but there would be terrible consequences for her father. Shaken as she was by her conversation with him in Geneva, she was inclined—for the moment—to believe him. But he did not know how long that would last, how long before she might decide that his threat was as empty as his nonexistent gun.

In the small hours of Sunday morning, they had driven up to the yachting town of Morges, where they spent the early morning at a lakeshore park, leaving at first light. They breakfasted at a small wayside inn, then continued up the lakeshore to Lausanne, where they purchased a few toilet items from an open pharmacy.

Keeping to the smaller roads, John spent the rest of the morning driving toward the walled university town of Fribourg. He found a parking place in the old town, under the shadow of the fifteenth-century tower of the St. Nicholas Cathedral, and held Caroline's arm firmly while they bought supplies for a picnic lunch. Except for the lack of a camera, they might have been any couple come to gape at the elaborate national dress of the local farmers and their wives who were in town for church.

They picnicked a few miles west of town, and then continued through Schwarzenburg and the mountainous roads beyond, to Bern, the capital, where John figured they could make their call to London from an automatic cabin in the busy main post office across from the railway station.

John had had Caroline telephone her father's contact number in London Sunday morning from Lausanne, to arrange for a telephone conference at three o'clock that afternoon. But when they called at three, a recorded announcement told them that the number had been disconnected. Caroline swore she knew of no other number where she could reach her father when he was away from the house, and a call there produced no answer.

It was at this point that both of them began to get frightened: John because he knew he could not keep going without sleep for much longer, and Caroline because she feared that sooner or later John might become desperate enough to do something really crazy.

From Bern they headed southwest, past the bear pits just beyond the Nydegg Bridge, where tourists and locals alike were tossing food to the bears, and on through medieval Thun. John was too bleary-eyed to admire the scenic north shore of Lake Thun as he drove toward Interlaken, where he had hoped to spend the night. When he stopped for gas and information just outside the town, however, he was told to his dismay that although there were nearly ninety hotels in the small town, now, at the end of August, there were still enough tourists to fill all of them. Caroline was growing even more nervous, and John thought it would be only too easy to lose her among so many people. So, instead of trying his luck in Interlaken, he consulted his map and pushed on in the direction of the Jungfrau.

That was probably a mistake, but he was too tired to think it out. The road twisted and turned as it climbed higher and higher, and John, who had not driven a standard-shift since his college days, except for the tame Fiat he had rented in Italy, found it difficult to control the powerful Alfa-Romeo. It w twilight when at last they stopped in a small village near the Jungfrau which, at more than thirteen thousand feet, towered above everything.

The village boasted several hotels that catered to summer skiers; all were full, but John was finally directed to an inn that could take them. It contained only five guest rooms, with one communal bathroom for three rooms on the second floor, and another for the two rooms under the wide eaves.

They got an upper room, and John waited outside the door while Caroline took a long bath. When she was finished, they went back to their tiny room. The owner's wife brought them some dark bread, slices of cheese and sausage, and two bottles of Hurlimann beer.

John locked the door and checked to make sure it was too far a drop from the window for Caroline to escape that way. Then he took one of the pillows, laid it against the door, and sat down on the floor, facing her, a bottle of beer and a sandwich next to him. If she was going to escape, she'd have to go through him.

Their conversation during the long drive had been mostly limited to discussions about stopping for gas, rest stops, and food. From time to time, though, to calm her down, John had asked her questions about her background. From what he could gather, they had always been rich, the house in Geneva was an old family summer estate, and she had attended the best private schools. At the moment she was living at home after a particularly nasty divorce, and was more or less running the Geneva house and acting as her father's social secretary. John had only volunteered that he had been very much in love with his wife, and that it was impossible for him to believe that she and their children were dead. They avoided, for the most part, any discussion about her father and the present situation.

Caroline opened the window a crack for some fresh air, then crawled into bed, fully dressed. She looked very much like a freshly scrubbed little girl.

"When you're finished eating, I'll turn off the light," she said.

"You can do it now," John replied tiredly. His tongue seemed thick. It was difficult to form words.

It took a minute or two for John's eyes to adjust to the darkness, but when they did he was able to see Caroline sitting up in the bed. She was watching him. It was very quiet. Out the window he could see the vague, hulking shapes of the mountains in the distance, and he could smell the odor of pine trees.

"How long are we going to keep this up?" Caroline asked, breaking the silence after a time.

John sighed deeply. He had almost been asleep. There was a deep heaviness in his chest. He had been smoking too much the past few days. Without the cigarettes, though, he didn't think he would have kept awake this long. "As long as it takes," he said hoarsely.

"Don't be stupid," she snapped. "To do what? Corner my father and kill him? Are you looking for revenge?"

"No! But what would you do under the same circumstances, Caroline?"

"Well, I'm sorry, but I wouldn't go trying to murder some-one. It'd make me the same as the killers."

"You'd let the police handle it?"

"My father's not guilty of anything. He's not a murderer, no matter what you say, or what you think you know."

John leaned his head back, not much interested in the food now. He was so tired that he ached everywhere. "I've kid-napped you."

"You bloody well have," she flared.

"Your father knows who did it."

"And he won't stop until he finds me."

"If I were your father, I wouldn't. I'd have every law-enforcement agency throughout Europe looking for you. I'd probably call out the military. I'd call the CIA; after all, this does involve an American citizen. I'd surely put up roadblocks. Every town across Europe would have our photographs. They'd have a description of your car and its license number. And, of course, being a high-ranking officer of the SIS, I'd have the entire secret service working on it. There'd be hundreds—more likely thousands—of people looking for us now. There'd be newspaper headlines. Radio broadcasts, television. Christ, I'd have it put up on billboards, run airplanes around the country with banners."

Caroline had the oddest look on her face. Twice she started to say something, but both times she held her silence.

"Of course, when the police come around first thing in the morning to get our names from our passports downstairs, they'll have us immediately. Won't they?" John took a drink of the cool beer as he let what he had just said sink in. He wanted her to think about it the way he had, to really stew over it. To agonize over her decisions, as he had his.

He had not been surprised that there were no newspaper headlines or radio warnings about them. He didn't think Henrys would warn the police. It would be too dangerous. Henrys knew that if John was brought in alive and kept alive, although the police would not believe such a wild story, the seed of doubt would have been planted among his own colleagues in the SIS. If John were allowed to talk to McBundy, or at least get some word to him, then Henrys's position and that of the network's would become very shaky. They'd never allow John to remain alive to stand trial. But in the meantime, he'd be able to do a lot of irreparable damage.

Henrys's people would be conducting the search themselves. Of that, John was certain. But John was not clear on why Henrys had cut off his only line of communication with them: the SIS number in London. Why had he shut that off? Was he trying to tell them something? Or was he merely trying to protect his own position within the SIS, thereby abandoning his daughter?

There was more than was outwardly apparent, John thought. But he could not focus his mind enough to reason it out coherently at the moment. He could feel the beer bottle slipping from his hand, and he saw Caroline looking down at him with a terribly strained expression in her eyes, her mouth pursed, and then he was sleeping.

The sun was streaming through the window at a long angle when John awoke nude beneath the covers in the very soft bed. He sat up with a start and threw the covers aside. His watch showed that it was late afternoon. Caroline was gone. She had evidently undressed him and put him to bed, although he had absolutely no recollection of it.

He got out of bed and padded across the room. Atop the bureau were the toothbrushes and other things they had picked up in Lausanne, along with his wallet and his passport.

He opened the passport and looked inside. His photograph, several years younger, stared up at him. Caroline must have retrieved it and brought it back up here. But why? It didn't make much sense. If she had wanted to get away from him and make sure he wouldn't follow, she would have taken his money and his papers, as well as his clothes. Unless she was so frightened she hadn't been thinking straight.

Why put him to bed? Why bring back his passport?

He took a towel from the wardrobe in the corner, wrapped it around his middle, and looked out in the tiny corridor. Caroline was just coming up the stairs. She was carrying a bundle wrapped in brown paper, and his jacket and trousers on a hanger.

At the head of the stairs, she spotted him standing at the half-open door. She stopped, a look of childish guilt crossing her face.

"I took your clothes to get them cleaned," she said.

John stepped back into the room, away from the door. Alarm bells were jangling along his nerves. Something was wrong, drastically wrong here. Kidnap victims simply did not go out and do favors for their kidnappers, and then return to them.

She came into the room, closing the door behind her. They stood facing each other for a long time.

"Did you have a good sleep?" she asked.

"Where did you go?"

"To have your clothes cleaned. They were a mess."

"What did your father have to say?"

Caroline's nostrils flared and her eyes widened. She held up his jacket and slacks and the package. "I went out to have your clothes cleaned," she repeated, raising her voice.

"Why didn't you run? Why did you come back?"

"I . . . don't know," she stammered.

She was lying. Christ, she had called her father. She did have another telephone number where she could reach him. She had told him where they were. He had probably ordered her to remain with him. The bastard.

John leaped forward, and Caroline stepped back as he grabbed his clothes and threw them down on the bed. He glanced up at her as he opened the package and got dressed as quickly as he could. Her complexion had turned pale and her lower lip was beginning to quiver as she stood, her back to the door watching him.

"You can't get rid of me," she said. "You're going to try to kill my father. I'm going to be there to stop you."

"You called him, didn't you?" he said, not really expecting an answer. "What the hell do you expect will happen? He'll come out here, we'll have tea and sit around and chat about my wife and children? About my father and everyone else he's killed, or has had killed?"

"My father is not a murderer!" she shouted. "You bloody bastard, you don't know what the hell you're talking about!" She sprang at him, raising her fists as she came. John had just enough time to spin around and defend himself as she leaped on him, pummeling his head and shoulders with all her strength.

They fell back on the bed and wrestled for several intense seconds until he managed to grab her wrists and wrap his left leg around her legs to stop her from kicking. Their faces were inches apart. She smelled sweet and he could feel her breasts through her sweater. She was breathing hard, and he could feel himself responding to her sexually.

"Bloody hell," she said, feeling it too.

"I mean your father no harm . . . if he's innocent," John said, his voice husky.

"He is," Caroline said heavily. "You'll see."

They looked into each other's eyes for what seemed like a very long time, until John let go.

When they parted they were both acutely embarrassed. Caroline got to her feet as John sat up. She stepped back.

"You bloody pig," she said.

"I'm sorry," John said. He quickly finished dressing, and got his things from the bureau. The car keys were missing. He turned back to Caroline. "Your car keys," he said, holding out his hand.

"We're staying here," she said, stepping back.

"Why?" John asked, disappointed that he had been right about her. He stepped forward, snatched her purse, and before she could do much of anything, found her car keys. He tossed her purse back to her.

She fumed for just a moment, then started after him again. But this time he only backed up a pace, then stopped, flat-footed, waiting for her to come. She instantly sensed that he would not be pushed any further, and she backed down.

"Now what?" she hissed.

"We're getting out of here before your father's goons show up and I end up dead," John said. He went to the door and looked out into the corridor. There was no one coming.

"All right, I called him," Caroline admitted.

John turned back. "I know that."

"He promised that he would come alone."

"You told him that I wasn't armed?"

"He wants to talk."

John looked at her for a long time. She was so goddamned naive. But then, so was he when it came to this business. He'd do the same for his father, if he were Caroline.

"If your father were actually coming here to talk with me, I'd agree to it. But it just won't happen that way, Caroline. He's going to send his frontline troops after me. And they're not coming to talk."

"No!" Caroline screeched.

"How long ago did you call him?" John asked.

She balked at answering.

"Christ. You called him this morning," John said with a sinking feeling. He threw open the door, then turned back and grabbed her by the arm, pulling her out into the corridor. "I'm going to check out and pay our bill. If you make any wrong move, so help me God, I'll..." He let it trail off. He didn't know what he'd do.

She followed him downstairs without resistance and stood at his side, meekly smiling as he paid their bill, thanked the owner for the meal last night, and volunteered that they were on their second honeymoon; they were spending a few days at Interlaken and had come down here on an impulse—hence their lack of luggage—and would be going on to Zurich after that.

At the door, John hesitated and looked outside across the tiny square. Caroline's Alfa was parked around the back of the bakery, across from the inn. There was some traffic out there now, several canvas-covered trucks and a parked delivery van, as well as pedestrians everywhere.

John was looking for a car or a man out of the ordinary, someone neither a local nor a tourist. Someone with "the look" he was learning to spot. But there was no one like that, and he stepped outside, guiding Caroline along with him.

"I thought you wanted to talk with my father?" she asked desperately as they crossed the cobbled street.

They passed a statue of a man on horseback. "On my terms,"

John said. "At a time and place of my choosing, so that he can't bring along any of his people without me knowing about it."

"And if you're wrong? If my father shows up alone? If no one else comes along?"

"Then we'll talk."

"Will you believe him? Will you at least give him a chance, or are you just going to shoot him down?"

They stopped. "You still don't understand, do you, you spoiled little bitch," he snapped angrily. "You really don't give a good goddamn about anything. My wife is dead. My children . . . my babies are dead. Some son of a bitch killed them." John shook his head and looked around a moment as he tried to clear his mind. "My father sent me a letter in which he told me that he spoke with your father. Your father admitted to him, goddamnit, Caroline, that he was the head of some kind of a spy network, which had killed and would continue to kill anyone who got in its way. Including my father, including me and my family."

"No!" Caroline shouted, pulling away. She held her hands to her ears. Several people looked curiously their way.

John grabbed her arm again and hurried her the rest of the way through the square, across the street on the opposite side, around behind the stores to the cobbled parking lot that the inn shared with other businesses.

He pulled up short when they came in sight of the car. There were a dozen other automobiles parked in two rows behind the buildings. Beyond them a narrow rocky area sloped down to a small, fast-moving creek, across which were several chalets. The scene was very picturesque, but John wasn't noticing any of that. His concentration was centered on the other cars in the lot. No one was sitting in any of them. At least, not as far as he could see from where he stood. No one was lounging around, waiting. The only person in the lot was an older man getting into a battered Volkswagen. The car started up, backed out of its slot, and then left through the far exit.

John tightened his grip on Caroline's arm and started across the parking lot, the Alfa's keys in his left hand. If she had called her father sometime this morning, there would have been plenty of time for his people to get up here from Geneva. Any window now could contain a sniper's rifle, he thought, looking up. Any of the innocent-looking cars could contain an assassin hunched low. Or at any moment there could be a squeal of tires and a car could come around the corner and bear down on them.

"My father hasn't called the police because he knows what happened to your wife and children, and he doesn't want to make things worse for you," Caroline blurted. She *had* been thinking about what he had said.

"He wouldn't sacrifice his daughter for another man's feelings, unless he's a worse bastard than I think he is."

"I don't believe this..." Caroline started to say, when a man dressed in a dark suit stepped out of the back door of the bakery about twenty-five feet away and came toward them.

John saw the man out of the corner of his eye, knew exactly what he was, and shoved Caroline aside as he ducked low and to the left.

The man carried something in his right hand. He raised it as John came in fast from his right. A hot poker stitched his shoulder, just below his neck, spinning him around and causing an instant wave of dizziness and nausea to wash through him.

Caroline was screaming in the background, and everything seemed to slow down, and get easy. It was strange.

John had been thrown backward, but he managed to regain his balance and start forward again. His vision was almost surreal. He could see someone else at the far end of the parking lot looking their way. He watched, almost detached, as Caroline leaped at the man, grabbing for his gun hand.

The man fired at the same moment that Caroline bodily shoved him around, so that the shot ricocheted off the cobblestones.

John was on top of him in the next instant, all three of them falling together.

Caroline had the man's gun hand as John scrambled to extricate himself, finally getting enough room for a clear swing. His fist connected with his assailant's jaw with every ounce of strength he had. The man flopped backward, his head bouncing on the stones, his eyes fluttering.

Caroline scrambled back, the man's gun in her hand. She got to her feet as John stood up shakily, blood streaming down from the wound in his neck. They looked at each other for what seemed like hours but which was only seconds, and he hung his head.

"I can't fight you any longer," he said tiredly.

"Bloody hell," Caroline swore. She grabbed his arm and led him forward. She stopped to pick up the car keys he had dropped in the attack. Then she was helping him climb into the passenger seat of the Alfa. She got in behind the wheel, and they headed out of the parking lot, tires squealing, as people began streaming into the lot to see what happened.

Chapter 23

MAHONEY HAD STRESSED coordination and speed, and Mc-
Bundy had been magnificent in setting this all up on such
terribly short notice.

Everyone but Mahoney had gotten to the operational safe
house, which had been set up in a large cabin just outside
Céligny, north of Geneva on the lake, within twelve hours of
each other, but by totally different routes.

McBundy and Kopinski, the most conspicuous of them all
had flown to Paris, where they were picked up at Charles de
Gaulle Airport by a very confused embassy staffer, who had
no idea of what was going on. But he agreed to keep the affair
off the daily logs in return for a large, though unspecified
favor at the next promotion cycle. He drove like crazy across
France, coming into Geneva and finally to Céligny around 6:0
Wednesday evening. He turned around and headed back im
mediately. McBundy had told him it would be best if he di
not get involved nor talk to anyone—absolutely anyone–

about this. The staffer wholeheartedly agreed.

Jones and Carron, unknowns as far as Henrys and the network were concerned, chanced coming in on the same flight to Geneva from New York. Jones, however, rented a small Ford Cortina at the airport, while Carron rented a windowless Volkswagen van from an agent downtown. They arrived within half an hour of each other at the Céligny cabin.

Dr. Paul Lewis, who had been in on what he called the Mahoney caper from the beginning when Mahoney had been drugged on the plane from Tel Aviv, flew in to Zurich, took a bus up to Basel, then flew from there down to Geneva, where he took a Swissair bus up to Lausanne. Jones went to fetch him with the car, and reported later that the normally very taciturn doctor talked his head off all the way. "The man was excited. Like a kid at Christmas, for Christ's sake."

Greene flew back to Milan, where he rented a Fiat Spyder convertible. He took the *autostradas* as far as he could, traveling west from Milan to Aosta, then going through the Mont Blanc Tunnel at Courmayeur to Chamonix, picking up the highway along the Arve River into Geneva, and finally arriving at Céligny.

Each of them had his own tasks to perform in preparation for "the snatch," as they were calling it, so there was very little socializing going on.

It was an intense period, they all would agree later. But at the time, they were so busy no one ever stopped to think about how hard he was working.

The cabin was very large by European standards. It had been Kopinski's idea. He had been here several years ago, staying at the main house further up the hill, across the road. He remembered the great cabin overlooking the lake and the fleet of small sailboats that the resort maintained. "If worst comes to worst," someone had quipped, "and all hell breaks loose, we could always sail out of here."

Kopinski had found out the great cabin was available. He had rented it through the first of the year to avoid suspicion. It was one of the bits of tradecraft McBundy's teams always made standard procedure. Short-term rentals of anything provided a bright track for anyone watching. "No use handing them a road map," McBundy would say.

There was a large natural-stone fireplace in the main room on the first floor, which also contained a kitchen, pantry, dining room, and a surprisingly large bathroom. Upstairs, four bed-rooms all faced a balcony overlooking the main room. There was a second bathroom—another unusual feature. Outside was a long front porch, supported by pillars made of the same stone as the fireplace facing. A wide path ran down through the woods from the house, joining paths from the other cabins, to the lake. Behind, to the right, the cabin had its own private drive-way from the highway.

Later that evening, carrying three large pieces of luggage, Carron drove the Cortina down to Geneva where he rented a room on a lower floor at the Hôtel des Bergues. It was one of the luxury hotels downtown on the river with a distinguished atmosphere, where nothing out of the ordinary could possibly happen. Mahoney had recommended the hotel as their primary contact location for that very reason, as well as for the build-ing's innumerable ways in and out.

Carron parked the Cortina himself in an out-of-the-way spot not too far from the hotel, then went up to his room. He had registered under the name of Hubson, an executive in the Mis-souri Lutheran Synod, diminishing further any suspicion that might fall to the operation if Henrys was watching too closely.

Later that evening, Jones drove the Fiat into Geneva, reg-istering under the name Vanderhof at the new Ramada on Rue de Zurich. Henrys would be somewhat skittish at the moment, and with Wasserman coming in like manna from heaven, he might jump any which way. Jones at the Ramada was going to have to be the backup if Henrys got spooked at the Hôtel des Bergues. Although the Ramada wasn't as conveniently located, it was large, and a veritable maze of hallways, stair-wells, and exits. As a backup, it was nearly perfect.

Thursday morning, Greene and Dr. Lewis drove into Ge-neva, where they checked into the Moderne on the Rue de Berne, a down-at-the-heels hotel very near the Cornavin rail-way station. They parked the van nearby.

Then they all settled down to wait "for the stars to arrive," Greene would later write.

McBundy had made it clear to them all that there would b absolutely no contact with the people from Bern, men fror the embassy there he was calling his "pristine" team. Ther were four of them, and they had not been told about Mahone or about the real nature of the operation. Henrys, an SIS office was suspected of some kind of hanky-panky and a watch w to be put on him. Under no circumstances were they to say anything to anyone about this, and even more important, they were to make absolutely certain that they were not spotted. "And, no," McBundy had lied to them, "it has nothing to do with the death of that Long Island cop off the Lombard Express several days ago."

Mahoney, traveling under the name Walton, wearing thick glasses and walking with a limp, flew into Geneva that morning and took a cab downtown to the railway station. He got on the shuttle to Lausanne, arriving there, after a delay, around noon. He rented a yellow Opel, which he drove to Céligny after lunch. It was a little after three in the afternoon when he pulled into the driveway of the cabin. He got out of the car, stretched, and took his suitcase into the house.

Kopinski was upstairs on the balcony. One of the bedroom doors was open, and it looked as if he had been napping.

McBundy came from the kitchen, a cup of coffee in his hand. "You made it," he said tersely. He was nervous.

"No trouble," Mahoney said, putting his bag down. "The others are off?"

"They're all in place," McBundy said. "Greene called from a phone booth not more than an hour ago."

"Good. Any word yet from Wasserman?"

"None." McBundy looked at his watch. "He should be coming in any minute now on the Paris train. It's sometimes late. There's still enough time for a run-by, if you want to look things over. There's been quite a bit of activity over there."

"I don't think it's necessary. Have any of our team double-checked?"

"Jones made a pass late last night. And Carron called a 'wrong number.' Someone with a British accent answered. Sounded 'distraught,' as Jim put it."

There was a boar's head mounted over the fireplace. One of its large, yellowed fangs was chipped off. Mahoney went over and gazed up into its eyes. It was a mean-looking creature. Some local huntsman had tromped through the brush, with his dogs and maybe some companions, until this animal was flushed out and shot to death. The adrenaline would have been pumping in the men. Afterward, when they had dragged the carcass back to their camp or even this lodge, there would have been a celebration.

But time for adventure like that had always been so elusive to Mahoney. He had seldom been able to take his sons anywhere. They had never gone hunting together, and only rarely had he taken them fishing.

Mahoney turned back. McBundy still stood under the balcony. Kopinski above. They were watching him. Knowing damn well what he was thinking.

"Any word yet about John?"

"None," McBundy said. "At least not directly. No one has seen or heard from him."

Mahoney's stomach did a little flip-flop. "What do you mean 'not directly'?"

"Just what I said, Wallace. He hasn't been spotted by any of our Bern people coming into or leaving Geneva. I had them watching for him as well, at first. He was on the train Friday night, we know that for sure. And he jumped off somewhere after the Simplon Tunnel; we're reasonably sure of that."

McBundy was stalling, and it made Mahoney angry, but he waited for the man to spin it out.

"Beyond that, we know nothing about his movements, although we're assuming he is or was on his way to Henrys."

Mahoney nodded but said nothing.

McBundy seemed uncomfortable. "There was a police report. A breaking and entering of a photographer's studio Saturday night. The place is directly behind Henrys's home. Nothing was taken, but they did find a back door open in addition to the forced front door. They checked at Henrys's house, but his security people there said they had had no trouble."

"Anything on the security people?"

"Nothing," McBundy said. "It was just a routine item on the police log. Someone broke into the shop, found nothing worth stealing, and left. They put it down as vandalism."

"It could have been John. He could have gotten to Henrys."

"Not very likely. Henrys is there, all right. He was spotted coming from the airport last night. In a bit of a hurry, it seemed like. The breaking and entering was five days ago."

"Our people haven't been spotted? You're sure of it?"

"As sure as we can be," McBundy said irritably.

"It'll work out, Wallace," Kopinski said from above, and Mahoney looked up. "John may have gotten to the house, found Henrys was gone, and got out of there to wait for another chance."

"It's all the activity you say is going on over there that bothers me," Mahoney said. "What kind of activity?"

"No one seems to be sleeping, for one thing," McBundy said. "Lights on all night. Cars coming and going. He's called in a lot of troops."

"John must be close, and they know it. They're after him," Mahoney said. "Is there a drink in the house?"

"Sure," McBundy said. He turned and went back into the kitchen.

Kopinski came downstairs. "We'll have Henrys in twenty-four hours or so. After that, we'll be able to wait for John to show up."

It wouldn't be that easy, Mahoney thought. Although his son wasn't a pro, he had certainly eluded capture by professionals. He had even killed several of them. He was thinking on his feet as he ran. He was a frightened amateur, afraid for his life, so everything he did was instinctual. And it was all correct, so far.

It also wasn't going to be as easy as Kopinski thought it would be, because once they had Henrys, it still wouldn't be over. Henrys himself was going to have to give them the key for breaking the network and making sure it wouldn't rise from the ashes. Mahoney had a couple of ideas about that, but he was going to have to play it on the wing. There was no other way. There simply were too many variables, his son among them.

McBundy came back with his drink, and they were about to sit down when the telephone jangled. They glanced at each other, then McBundy went across to the table behind the couch and answered it.

"Yes?" he said. He nodded a minute later. "Yes. Thank you." He hung up. "Wasserman's train from Paris came in a half hour ago, and he checked into the des Bergues ten minutes ago. He's got a suite three floors above Carron's room. The monitoring equipment will be in place within a few more minutes."

"Ezra can make his call anytime after that," Mahoney said. "And then we'll know."

There was a tension in the room now. "Either hotel will work fine," McBundy said.

"Henrys may want to meet somewhere else, in which case Ezra can stall him and Greene can get ahead of them. But that's not what's got me worried."

"What, then? John?"

Mahoney nodded. He sat down on the couch and took a sip of his drink. "Henrys's people were there. If John got onto the estate from the photographer's studio, they could have nailed him. He could be dead by now."

"Or he might have spotted them and turned around," Kopinski said. "Or he might not have been at the photographer's studio. He might not have gotten that far. Good Lord, Wallace, what do you want us to tell you?"

"We didn't find him on the tracks," Mahoney continued. "He's in Geneva. Or at least he went there. And that was days ago." Another thought struck Mahoney. He turned to McBundy. "Anything on Henrys's daughter, Caroline?"

McBundy shook his head. "She wasn't with her father, and she doesn't appear to be at the house. But our hands are fairly well tied from making any direct inquiries."

"She could be anywhere," Mahoney said.

"I don't think she's important," Kopinski said. "At least not at this stage of the game, unless you think she knows about the network and has helped her father."

"I can't imagine that," Mahoney said.

There was a lull, and McBundy glanced over at the telephone.

"Ezra has agreed to cooperate," Mahoney said. "He won't go back on his word."

"We're way out on a limb here, Wallace. But I guess there's no need to tell you that again. You know that score. This will either work, and work brilliantly, or we're all going to jail. Misappropriation of government funds and property. Operating illegally in three friendly nations, including one neutral. Quashing a civil murder investigation. Exposing our people to needless risks . . . risks in which two of our people have been killed." McBundy shook his head again. "Do you realize the strings I've had to pull to keep the lid on this so far? The favors I've had to call in? The fudging of paperwork? The outright lying on a daily basis to everyone from the janitors all the way up to Lycoming, who has unknowingly lied to the President for me? Christ, Wallace, they'll probably have me shot for all of this, even if it does work."

"I'll be there with you, to explain it all. We'll see the President himself. Lay it all out for him. If there'll be any decisions to be made, he'll have to make them."

"Were you there when I talked to Jensen's wife? Will you be there when I tell Sampson's family . . . ?" McBundy didn't finish. "I'm sorry," he mumbled.

Mahoney reached over and patted him on the arm. "It's all right, Bob. We're all under pressure here. It'll be over before too terribly long."

"Is Henrys going to go for it?"

"You'd better believe it. He'll take it hook, line, and sinker. If Wasserman calls him soon, he should be moving tonight."

"None of them has a chance to rehearse adequately, but it should work smoothly. Bobby will make sure of it."

"Dr. Lewis understands what he's to do if Henrys becomes difficult?"

"Don't worry about it, Wallace," Kopinski said. "They all know the verses as well as the chorus."

Bobby Greene remembered Mahoney's words from the Washington safe house quite clearly. "The problem is that once we begin showing up in Geneva, the clock starts ticking. It's Henrys's town. We're not going to have many hours before he gets wind that he's been surrounded. There'll be no run-throughs, no rehearsals, no length of time for surveillance for cataloguing his habits and movements so that we can find just the right time for the snatch. We're going to have to do it right the first time, or not at all."

It was night. He lay on the narrow bed in the tacky hotel, listening to his radio playing softly on the table next to him, while Dr. Lewis sat in front of the television, which was playing without the sound while he read an American medical journal.

"Bring them with me everywhere I go. Like to keep up-to-date," said the doctor who had set up Mahoney's conversion to dead-man status.

The telephone rang. Before Dr. Lewis could turn around, Greene had it. "Yes?" he said, making his voice husky.

"He went for it. He's on his way to the primary. They're to meet at the bar." It was Carron, three floors below Wasserman.

"Did Henrys's muscle get the room number?"

"Yes."

"They'll front for him, then. They'll be taking apart the room. Get our stuff out of there."

"Will do."

"We're on our way," Greene said. "We'll be on Tac One when we're in range." He hung up.

Dr. Lewis, his eyes wide, his mouth half open, had gotten to his feet, dumping his journal to the floor. "This is it?"

"Right," Greene said, already on his feet and throwing on his jacket. He pulled a small .380 Beretta automatic out of his bag, checked to make sure the clip was loaded and firmly in place, and stuffed it in his jacket pocket.

Mahoney had said no weapons, but Greene had decided he was not going to end up like Larry or Len. He was going to fight back if it came to that, and worry about the nasty repercussions later.

The doctor got his small medical kit, and they left the hotel, retrieved the van where they had parked it, and drove over to the des Bergues, parking behind the hotel in the shadows near one of the service entrances.

From one of the cases they had left in the back of the van, Greene got their small, powerful walkie-talkie. He flipped it on and made sure the channel-selector switch was on the Tactical One channel. He keyed the talk button.

"Unit three here."

"Two on line," Carron radioed back. "He just went downstairs."

"Anyone show up yet?"

"Not yet. I'm at the end of the corridor in the stairwell."

"Is the room clean?"

"Just pulled out our things," Carron said.

"Standing by."

Dr. Lewis lit a cigarette with shaking hands. He had worked for the Agency for a number of years now, but he would admit to anyone who cared to listen that he never got used to this part of an assignment. The preparation was fast-paced and usually interesting. After it was all over, the feeling of accomplishment was great. But during the actual operation, his nerve gave him hell.

Usually at this point Greene bantered with whomever he was working with. But this time he remained silent, although he was excited. It wasn't that he disliked Dr. Lewis—as far as he was concerned, the medico was a good man—but there was so much at stake for him personally. This one was for Sampson.

Before they had left the States, Mahoney had taken him aside one last time, looked him in the eye, and made him promise that there'd be no personal vendettas against Henrys. Greene had reluctantly agreed. But it didn't stop him from thinking about it now. Thinking about the satisfaction he'd get from squeezing Henrys's neck, watching the man's face turn purple and his eyes bulge out.

Carron had called at 9:00 P.M. to say the meet was set up. It was now only twenty after, when he came back on the Tactical One channel.

"Unit three."

"Here," Greene said into the walkie-talkie.

"They just showed up. Two of them. They got in there like real pros. No fuss, no bother."

"We're on our way," Greene radioed. He stuffed the walkie-talkie beneath his jacket and pocketed the van keys, then he and Dr. Lewis entered the hotel. They found their way to one of the service elevators and took it up to the ballroom level on the third floor. They took the regular guest elevator up to the top floor, then the stairs back down two levels to Wasserman's floor. Carron was waiting by the stairwell door, the walkie-talkie hidden beneath his coat. When he saw who it was, he relaxed.

"I figured you'd be coming that way, but I wasn't sure," he said.

"They left yet?" Greene asked. He looked out the small window to the corridor.

"About a minute ago. They were quick."

"Let's go," Greene said. He threw open the door and the three of them hurried down the corridor, Carron pulling out his lock-pick set.

Within a few seconds he had the door opened and they were in Wasserman's suite. The doctor and Carron hid in the bathroom, and Greene took up position in the bedroom, the door slightly ajar so that he could see the sitting-room couch, the television, the writing desk, and, beyond them, the door.

Chapter 24

ALTHOUGH JOHN HAD merely been spinning out a story to the innkeeper, Caroline assumed that he wanted to get to Zurich. Stopping in Interlaken only long enough to purchase bandages for his neck wound and a sweater-jacket with a high collar to cover them, along with some whiskey to dull his pain, she drove straight through to Zurich. She was at home at the wheel of the Alfa-Romeo, and they made good time, arriving there in less than two hours.

Caroline pulled into the driveway of the Baur au Lac, an elegant old hotel in its own small park next to the lake. John waited in the car while she went inside, listening to the noise of the diners in the hotel's outdoor restaurant behind the greenery on the other side of the drive. Caroline was back in a few minutes and asked John for his passport, then helped him out of his seat and turned the car over to the doorman. She left their passports at the desk, and they were led immediately to their suite.

As soon as the bellman, who had not raised an eyebrow a

their lack of luggage, had left, Caroline undressed John, bathed him, and changed the dressing on his wound. She kept telling herself that she was merely doing what her father had asked of her: "Stick with him no matter what, until I can get to you." Yet who had tried to kill John? One of her father's people? She also told herself that she was staying with him so that if and when he tried to kill her father she would be there to stop him. Yet she wasn't completely sure those were her only motivations. In fact, she had to admit to herself, she had no real idea why she was doing any of this. Yet his story was so compelling. And there was his wound. Fortunately the bullet had not lodged in his neck, nor had it broken any major blood vessels. He would have died otherwise or at least been beyond her meager first-aid skills. But his weakness frightened her. He had slept through Monday night and most of the next day and night. Whenever he woke up, she fed him soup from room service.

John had awakened that morning—Thursday—ravenously hungry and impatient to finally force the issue with her father. But Caroline had been out purchasing bandages and painkillers. She also brought back several newspapers, including the ones from Geneva. John refused the pills, telling her he was ready to move on to Geneva.

"You can't go. I won't let you," Caroline said shrilly. She was tired from caring for him, and confused. "You're not well enough. And besides, even if he is there, you'd never get close to him."

"I just want to talk, honestly," John replied patiently. She was frightened that now, more than ever, he wanted to harm her father. And she remained terribly confused about her father's actions, and frightened by them as well.

"That can't happen. He won't allow it."

John shrugged and let the argument drop for the moment.

It was late afternoon now, and John was browsing through the train schedule the hotel provided in the desk. The *Schweizerische Bundesbahn* ran intercity trains to Geneva every hour. There was one at 8:00 P.M., and he meant to be on it.

Caroline, watching his face, knew that he had not changed his mind. She knew that he intended on trying to get to Geneva.

"You can't take the Alfa; the police will recognize it," she pleaded. "You'll be stopped. They'll search you and find the gun. You'd never even get close to Geneva."

"I'm taking a train."

"And then what? Are you going to take a cab to the house? Walk up to the front door and ring the bell, hoping my father will answer the door so you can gun him down?"

"I'm not going to kill him, Caroline," John shouted. They stood facing each other in the middle of the room. He reached out and grabbed her by the shoulders. "But is he going to be allowed to continue the killing?"

"He's a good man," Caroline cried. "When my mother died he took her place in my life. He can't be what you say he is."

John glanced over at the newspapers on the desk. They had both looked through them. "There was nothing in any of the papers about a shooting incident. Nothing about an American being wounded while being sought for a murder or a kidnapping. Nothing. Yet half a dozen people witnessed the incident."

"He's trying to protect us!"

"That's why he lied to you?"

"No!" she cried. "He's not a murderer!" She began to cry in earnest, her body shaking.

At first John just stood there, but then he put his arms around her shoulders and held her close to him. He was not very steady on his feet. He had lost a lot of blood and eaten very few proper meals in a week or more, yet once again he found himself responding to this woman in his arms. It was crazy—it was worse than crazy, it was terrible—that so soon after his wife's brutal murder he could even think of a woman, let alone hold one. Yet Caroline was here, alone and very frightened.

They were alike in many ways. The thought occurred to him as he held her while she cried it out. He had lost his father, and now, in a way, she had lost hers. Both fathers were somehow involved in the world of secrets, cutting off their children from a large part of their lives. He was alone, no family now to rely on. So, apparently, was she. And they were both very frightened of what might happen next.

In addition, John was troubled about her. He had wanted to get away from the hotel before she came back so that he wouldn't have to face her. And yet he had purposely lingered until she had returned. He told himself he had to make sure that she wouldn't call her father when she discovered he was gone. But if she had wanted to do that, she could have done so at any time in the past few days. So it wasn't that.

Holding her now in his arms, feeling her body against his

he knew damned well why he had stayed back, but he blotted it out of his mind. Forced it away. It didn't make any sense.

Her crying subsided, and she looked up at him. "At least let me come with you."

John shook his head and disengaged himself from her. "No. I'm going alone," he said.

"You don't know your way around Geneva like I do."

"I got in the first time."

"That was luck. They won't allow that to happen again."

"Wait a minute, Caroline. Are you telling me now that you'd...help me get to your father?"

She looked deeply into his eyes. "Yes. I'll help you get to my father. To talk to him."

"He may not want to hear what I have to say."

"And you don't want to talk to him. You want to kill him!"

"He wants to kill me!"

"Bloody hell," Caroline said, frustrated. She put her hands on her hips. "You have a choice, then. You either take me, or I'll call my father and tell him you're on the way."

John started to flare up, but then he backed off. It didn't really matter if she called her father or not. Henrys had not responded to his daughter's kidnapping in any way except violence. He would not understand now about talking. He understood only death and destruction. It didn't matter if she told her father John was on the way. Henrys already knew that. Somehow, in some fashion, he would get to Henrys.

"You may do whatever you want, Caroline. I don't give a damn any longer," he said. She started to protest, but he held her off. "I'm sorry that I kidnapped you."

Caroline was speechless.

John hunched up the collar of the jacket that Caroline had cleaned for him as best she could, then left the room and strode down the wide, plushly carpeted corridor to the elevator.

She came to the door, hesitated a moment, then ran after him. "You have to take me with you, John!"

He pushed the button for the elevator. "I don't want you here."

"Why?"

"I don't—"

"So that I won't stop you from killing him? He's my father, or God's sake."

John turned to her, grabbed her by the shoulders, and bodily shook her. "Because if something happens, I don't want you to get hurt."

The elevator doors slid open. Two older women on the car looked at them disapprovingly.

"I'll follow you then," Caroline said, distraught. "You won't leave me behind."

"No, Caroline."

One of the older women coughed. John glanced at them as the elevator doors closed and the car continued.

Caroline threw herself into John's arms. "We have to do this together," she cried. "You, because you want to know about your family, and me, because I want to know for sure."

"One way or the other?" John asked softly.

She looked up at him. "One way or the other."

Still he hesitated as once again he tried to examine his feelings. But it was all so confusing. Nothing was simple. Nothing was as it seemed to be. Nor would it ever be.

He looked at his watch. "It's just six now. The train leaves in two hours."

The clock at the Grossmünster cathedral across the Limmat was striking nine when the sleek black Mercedes sedan pulled up at the entrance to the Baur au Lac. Two very large men dressed in stylish business suits jumped out of the car, not bothering to shut off the engine. They raced into the hotel and across the lobby to the desk. The manager, who had received a call from the police, was waiting for them.

"What room are they in?" the slightly larger of the two men asked. He had a large, bulbous nose and very high cheekbones. A wicked-looking scar ran jaggedly from his left eyebrow, across the bridge of his nose, then halfway down his cheek. He spoke in French. His impatience arose from the fact they had been searching for some sign of John and Caroline all week, but it had never occurred to anybody that they would run to ground in a deluxe hotel where Caroline was known. Only when Henrys finally asked friends in the police for a bit of discreet help did it emerge that their name had appeared on the passport list from the Baur au Lac. Henrys was furious.

"It's on the fifth floor, monsieur, but they are not there now."

"When did they check out?"

"Oh, they didn't check out. They just went out. Perhaps to dinner."

The bigger man held out his hand. The concierge got the room key from its slot and passed it over. "Five-oh-three," he said, but the two men had already turned and were marching to the elevators.

The manager looked after them, pulling his collar away from his neck. These were not the sort of people Caroline Henrys had associated with since she had been coming to this hotel.

It seemed to John and Caroline that they had the entire train practically to themselves for the three-hour journey. They were due in Geneva at 11:09 P.M., with only one major stop—a few minutes in Bern—sometime after 9:30.

It was approaching that hour now. He and Caroline left the dining car, where they had eaten a light meal and shared a half-bottle of Pouilly Fuissé.

John's neck and shoulder still ached terribly from his wound, but the pain no longer dominated his every thought, not after what Caroline had told him. No longer were his reasoning abilities numbed as they had been. Now he was thinking ahead of himself, he was planning ahead, figuring the situation, analyzing the options, just as he had analyzed chemical equations in the lab.

Over dinner, he had closely questioned Caroline about her father's normal day-to-day routine. At first she had been reticent about giving him very much information until he promised again that he would just talk. No violence. But in order to do that, he was going to have to get close enough to Henrys so that he could not call his bodyguards. From the things she was telling him, it began to appear that her father led two almost completely separate lives.

His position within the British Secret Intelligence Service, as far as Caroline knew, was as senior political adviser and analyst. While in England, he spent much of his time either in London—"dispensing wisdom," as Caroline put it, to 10 Downing Street—or relaxing at her aunt's house in the tiny town of St. Albans, just north of London. She was an aunt by marriage, actually, very stuffy and not much fun at all.

It amazed John to realize that Henrys—who had become a nearly mythical villain to him—was of flesh and blood. He had a sister-in-law and probably other relatives as well.

"But lately, over the past three or four years, Daddy has spent more and more of his time at our Geneva house," Caroline explained. "Semiretirement, I always supposed. But he's always denied it. Said he could work just as well, and perhaps even better for the lack of distractions, in Geneva."

"Any friends in Geneva? Relatives?"

Caroline smiled. "No relatives, although we've tons of friends," she said. But then she stopped as if she had thought of something else.

"What is it?" John asked.

"I was just thinking about something I learned a couple of weeks ago. The family was evidently once much larger, with relatives in England, the States, and of course, Geneva. They built the Geneva house a couple of hundred years ago."

John was impatient with the story about her ancestors. He wanted to know about her father, the here-and-now. He desperately wanted to find some clue as to how he could approach the man without being gunned down. "The Henrys name goes back that far?" he asked curtly.

"Not Henrys, actually," Caroline said with a faraway look in her eyes. "We're part Jewish, actually. One branch of our family was Malecki. Thank God that part was years ago."

John nearly dropped his glass, slopping some of the wine on the tablecloth. Caroline blinked.

"What is it?" she asked. "What'd I say?"

"Malecki?"

She nodded. "Tons of years ago, actually. But there nevertheless. There was the main branch in England, from what I understand, and some of them evidently emigrated to the United States. The British branch built the Geneva house as a summer getaway."

"Does the name Chaim Malecki ring a bell?" John asked. He was treading on dangerous ground now. If he didn't watch his step, Caroline would clam up, and he'd have to start all over again.

"No. I don't think so," Caroline said. "Was he one of my relatives?"

"I don't know. Probably not."

"What is it, John? Where'd you hear the name?"

"From my father. But it doesn't matter now. The man i dead." There obviously was a connection, though, John wa thinking. Malecki—the Henrys family name—working for th network under Henrys. The coincidence was too sharp for there not to be a connection. John wondered if there was a way in which he could use the information. At length, however, he decided against it.

The upshot of his conversation with Caroline, as their train sped toward its brief stop at the Swiss capital, was that her father almost always had one or two bodyguards with him. *Almost always.* He called them his traveling companions, although they had always remained strictly in the background.

"Unless you knew they were there—unless you had been told—you'd never know they were watching," she said.

"That good?"

"I've seen various of them around, most of my life, and I've gotten to know them all. But when we're traveling I'm never able to spot them, even though Daddy says they're there. That's why I was so surprised to see ones I'd never met stationed so obviously at the house the other night."

"Does he ever go anywhere without them?"

Caroline started to say no, but then she changed her mind. "Sometimes he goes off alone," she said slowly, carefully. It was almost as if she were revealing something she was not supposed to.

"When is that?"

Caroline looked at him, then glanced around at the few other diners in the car. She shrugged. "Mother's been gone for a long time. And he . . ."

John suddenly understood. He either had a mistress tucked away somewhere, or he went to prostitutes. "Okay, I understand, Caroline." Again it gave him an odd feeling in the pit of his stomach to again think of Henrys in such human terms.

Their seats were three cars forward of the dining car, and they stopped between cars before they reached them.

"What is it now?" Caroline asked.

"We're going to be stopped at Bern for a few minutes," John said. "I want you to get off the train and telephone your father. Try him first in Geneva."

"To tell him what?" Caroline demanded.

"That you're alone. That you've gotten away from me, and that you want to talk with him."

"That's silly. Why would I say such a thing? If I escaped from you, why wouldn't I simply return home?"

"Because your father hurt you," John said, winging it. "Because he promised to come to us, but instead he sent someone to kill me. You want to know why."

"That's bloody well stupid. He'd never believe me."

"That you're hurt, then. That you don't trust his bodyguards. You're hysterical."

"He'd send them anyway. Order me home."

"You don't trust him any longer. There were things I told you—disturbing things—that you must have the answers for."

"He's my father. I love him. I couldn't distrust him..." She let it trail off as if she were no longer sure about that.

"Then tell him you're afraid I'm following you. I got in once past the bodyguards, and you're afraid."

"And if he agrees? Where do we meet?"

"I don't care," said John. "You pick the place. Anywhere that's neutral. Anywhere that's open, so his bodyguards can't come along without us knowing about it."

"That would be somewhere along the lakeshore."

"That's as good a place as any," said John.

"And you'll be with me? At my side, so I can make sure you won't try to hurt him?" Caroline asked. "Will you throw away the gun you have?"

"I won't throw away the gun, but we'll be side-by-side. I promise not to hurt your father unless he or his people try to hurt me."

Caroline looked at him for a long time. "I want to believe you, John. God only knows why... but I do."

They became aware that the train was beginning to slow down. John went to the window in the door and looked outside. He could see that they were coming into a fairly large city. He looked at his watch. It was just about 9:30. Bern. Caroline was going to have to make her decision right now. He felt badly about lying to her. But Elizabeth and the children were dead... as impossible as that seemed.

He turned back. "I just want to meet with him when no one is shooting at me." His hand went involuntarily to the bandage on his neck.

Caroline looked sympathetically at him and finally nodded. "I'll do it," she said. "I'll telephone him. We'll meet and talk. And he'll have an explanation, you'll see." She said the last without much conviction. •

* * *

They announced the stop in four languages—German, French, Italian, and English—and when the train came to a complete halt in the station, Caroline jumped off and disappeared into the crowd.

John stood on the platform, just off the boarding stairs of their car, watching the scurrying crowd, while he waited for her. Of course, if she wanted to take off, she could. But, as back in Zurich, he knew he could do nothing other than trust her. If she had wanted to betray him then, she could have. Just as she could run away from him now. He did not think she would, though. Caroline was his key to unraveling this entire mess. And he was Caroline's key to understanding her own father.

The minutes passed very slowly, and John kept checking his watch, then searching the crowd for her face. But she did not come.

The train whistle blew and the electric doors began to close as the train started down the platform. John jumped up into the car, and when the doors were fully closed, he pushed the override bar, and the door slowly slid open.

"Caroline!" he shouted.

She realized the train was moving, and she began to run as quickly as she could.

John was half out of the car, hanging on with one hand, and stretching out his other.

Caroline caught up with the train, and he pulled her aboard.

"I didn't think you were coming," he said.

Caroline was breathless. "He wasn't at home," she gasped. "He was gone."

John's heart sank. "Where?"

"He's in Geneva. He's at a meeting. They're at the Hôtel des Bergues. Very posh. I know where it is."

Chapter 25

KOPINSKI APPEARED ON the balcony from the bedroom where he had set up the recording equipment. "Wallace, Bob, could you give me a level check?"

Mahoney, who had been pacing the room, looked up. "Is it finally ready?" There had been a last-minute malfunction with the recorder, and Mahoney had become agitated.

"I believe so."

Mahoney turned to McBundy, who stood by the fireplace. "I'll have him sit on the big chair with his back to the door. Initially," he added. The evening was surprisingly chilly, and they had laid a fire. It was burning gaily now.

McBundy drained his glass of liquor, put it down on the table near the fireplace, and came across to sit in the easy chair. "How's this?" he asked.

"The rest of us might move around the room from time to time," Mahoney said, glancing up at the balcony as he moved in front of McBundy, then went across the room to the window.

He was worried that this would not work out. He was worried about Greene holding himself together. And he was nearly out of his mind with worry about his son. Where in hell had John disappeared to? No one had seen or heard anything of him. There was nothing on any of the police wires. He had disappeared . . . almost as if he were dead.

Kopinski came back onto the balcony. "It's working fine," he said. "I'll rewind both machines and get everything ready."

"Thank God for at least one small favor," Mahoney mumbled, but Kopinski heard him.

"No news is good news, Wallace," he offered.

Mahoney glared at him.

"Sorry," Kopinski said, and he went back into the bedroom.

"Don't take it out on poor Stanley," McBundy said. "He's along for the ride, but he didn't invent the game."

Mahoney looked at his watch. It was a few minutes after ten. "What the hell is keeping them?"

"Bobby has Carron for backup."

Henrys had gone for it too easily, Mahoney thought, staring at his reflection in the dark window. Maybe he knew the entire setup. Maybe his people had watched them coming in from Washington. In that case, they'd have this house pegged, as well as all three hotels and the vehicles. Maybe Henrys had brought along some heavy artillery. Maybe he had refused to meet alone with Wasserman, and at this moment it was going sour.

The operation was basically a simple one. But even during the easy ones a dozen things could go wrong. He could have totally misread Henrys, or misunderstood Wasserman's acquiescence. Greene could blow up the moment he saw Henrys and kill the man on the spot. Such things had happened before. It took no stretch of the imagination to think that such things could happen now.

He turned around and gazed at the telephone, almost willing it to ring. They'd telephone when they were on the way. Wasserman would remain in his room along with Carron to act as his backup in case Henrys's people got suspicious and came up to investigate. One of them would telephone with the news. In addition, Jones was coming over and would be covering the front entrances to the hotel. He'd be able to see anything developing in time to get word to Carron to get the hell out of here.

It was foolproof . . . or nearly as foolproof as possible, given the short time they had in which to set it up.

The worst part of it all was that getting Henrys out here was the easy bit. The difficult business would begin then.

It had been forty-five minutes since they had taken their places, and Greene was unhappy. He'd stay here in the bedroom until hell froze over if that's what it took to nail their mark. He did have a great deal of patience, but that didn't mean he had to like it.

He pulled his automatic out of his jacket pocket for the tenth time, checked the clip, checked to make sure a round was in the firing chamber, and checked to make sure the safety was on and working. Then he put it back.

Twice he had risked stepping quietly away from the door and going to the window. Geneva was beautiful, lit up at night, but he wasn't seeing any of that. Instead he had searched the street below in an effort to pick out someone, anyone out of the ordinary. Maybe Jones, down there somewhere, waiting, watching. Maybe Wasserman and Henrys leaving in a cab. It certainly was within the realm of possibility that Henrys would insist they go somewhere else for the meeting—somewhere other than up here to Wasserman's room. If Henrys was spooked or running scared, if he thought they were closing in on him, he'd make such last-minute switches. It was routine, good tradecraft. Any operative worth his salt would do the same. Jones was out front, just in case, but it wasn't foolproof.

"We'll just do the best we can," Mahoney had told them before they left Washington. "It's not perfect by a long shot. But it's good, considering the time we had to set it up."

Which was less than Len had had riding with him when he bought it. Christ, he was just following Mahoney's son. A friend of the Agency's. Untrained and supposedly nonaggressive . . . at least toward the guys in the white hats. And yet Len was dead. Parts of his body were all over the tracks just before the Swiss border.

The bile rose from Greene's stomach as he thought about seeing Len's body. It was hardly recognizable as human, except for the tattered clothing still clinging to the remains. Blood and bits of tissue had been dragged along the tracks for more than a hundred yards.

He closed his eyes tightly, and he could hear the Italian

police shouting back and forth. They had brought a handcar up the tracks, with a body bag and the medical people, and scraped up what was left of Len. All the while they were talking, jabbering incessantly, as if this were all so very routine.

The lights came on in the sitting room, and Greene opened his eyes, ready to ask what the hell Carron or Dr. Lewis was doing out of the bathroom. But it was Ezra Wasserman and McNiel Henrys. Greene would have been able to identify Henrys anywhere, under any circumstances, he had studied his file photographs so intently. He was on the tall side, in his late fifties, a bit of gray at his temples and in his neatly trimmed mustache. He was dressed in a gray tweed jacket and light trousers, his shirt collar open. He looked like a very distinguished statesman.

Greene leaned closer to the partially open door so that he could hear.

"You're certainly going to have to do better than that, Wasserman. A whole lot better," Henrys was saying. They stood facing each other, and he seemed nervous, upset; Greene could see it in his face and hear it in his voice. But Wasserman, by his bearing, was in control.

"It wasn't difficult to get your name, between what Wallace Mahoney told us and what we learned at St. Albans."

Henrys laughed. It wasn't convincing.

"Have a seat," Wasserman said. "I'll get you a drink. We're going to be here for a bit. I hope you warned your people downstairs. There is a lot of ground to cover that Chaim couldn't possibly have known about."

It was their cue. Greene pulled out his automatic, flipped off the safety, and barged out into the room. He quickly stepped to the left so that he was clear of the table and lamp.

"Good Lord," said Henrys, spinning around.

Greene held the gun up. "Don't you move, you bastard! Don't you move or I'll pull this trigger."

"Easy, now," Wasserman said. He stepped back, nevertheless, out of the line of fire.

Henrys's complexion had gone pale, and he raised his hands over his head, as Carron and Dr. Lewis came out of the bathroom. He looked at them.

They were all held in tableau for several long seconds. Greene felt almost paralyzed. He knew what to do next, yet he was having a hard time making anything work.

Carron took out his gun and pointed it at Henrys. "Bob?" he said.

Greene blinked. "Check him for weapons."

"You're Americans," Henrys said, amazed.

"That's right. Just want to talk," Carron said, pocketing his gun and efficiently patting Henrys down. He straightened up when he was finished. "Nothing."

Greene nodded, and Dr. Lewis came forward, opening his medical kit as Carron stepped behind Henrys and suddenly pulled his jacket off his shoulders, pinning his arms back.

"Here, what do you think you're doing?" Henrys protested, but Dr. Lewis had pulled out a hypodermic syringe, checked it for air, and without ceremony jabbed the needle into Henrys's left arm, just below the shoulder.

"Christ . . ." Henrys shouted, trying to struggle out of Carron's grasp. But within seconds the Demerol began to take effect, and Henrys's struggles rapidly weakened.

"He shouldn't go out on us," Dr. Lewis said. "But he'll certainly become very tractable."

Greene put away his gun, and after a minute or so, Carron pulled Henrys's jacket back up.

"We shouldn't have any trouble with him now," the doctor said.

Greene took one arm, and Dr. Lewis took the other. They led the unresisting Henrys to the door.

"Where are you taking me?" he asked, his speech slurred.

"Someone would like to talk to you," Greene said. Before they left, he turned back to Carron and Wasserman. "We'll get him back as soon as possible. Meanwhile, Jones will keep you posted."

"Henrys's people are downstairs waiting for him," Wasserman said. "I spotted two of them in the lobby. There may be more."

"Yes, sir," Greene said. "If anything—anything at all— seems like it's developing, just get out of here. We'll take care of picking up the pieces."

"I'm booked on the afternoon flight. We've plenty of time unless his people downstairs begin to get worried."

"Yes, sir."

"Good luck," Carron said.

Greene nodded, then he and Dr. Lewis slipped out into the

corridor with the very loose Henrys, who was mumbling something about his daughter.

They took the main elevator back down to the ballroom level, then took the service elevator again to the ground floor, where they made it out to the van with absolutely no trouble. Within a couple of minutes from the time they had left Wasserman's room, they were driving toward Céligny, Greene at the wheel, Dr. Lewis in the back with their patient.

Once they had passed the Botanical Garden on the north side of town, the doctor began injecting a totally unresisting Henrys with a drug that would counteract the Demerol, thus bringing him back to near normal consciousness.

Mahoney had been very specific about the last bit. "As soon as it's possible, I want Henrys's head clear. When he walks into that cabin and sees me, I want him to know who he is seeing. No doubts in his mind. It'll be then that he'll understand he's been outmaneuvered."

Dr. Lewis listened to Henrys's heart, and took his pulse and blood pressure. Then, satisfied that all was well, he put his things away and took the automatic Greene handed back to him, as Henrys began to come around. As far as he was concerned, the tough part was over. The rest would just be a matter of technicalities.

Carron had telephoned half an hour earlier to say they were on the way, and now Mahoney was beginning to get impatient. There couldn't be much traffic at this time of night, and he couldn't imagine what was keeping them. The drive up took barely thirty minutes under medium conditions. Where was the delay?

He sat, a notebook in hand, a bottle of cognac and two snifters beside him, in one of the easy chairs that he had pulled up near the fireplace. A .30-caliber snub-nosed revolver was stuffed in the cushion beside him, at McBundy's insistence. There was no telling what Henrys might do when confronted.

A second easy chair faced Mahoney's. The fire was still burning in the grate—McBundy had added a few additional logs twenty minutes ago—but the lights in the main room of the great cabin had been switched off. The only illumination now was from the flickering flames. The room smelled pleasantly of woodsmoke.

They had two choices, he thought, going over them again. They could either put the heat on Henrys immediately. Burn him into revealing absolutely everything he knew about the network. Or they could talk him into giving them the means for unraveling it.

If the first, Dr. Lewis had assured them that he had the drugs in his little bag of tricks that would quickly unlock everything Henrys ever knew. Of course, the drug-aided interrogation would have a deleterious effect on Henrys's mind. It was even possible that he'd never be the same again. Yet, as Greene put it, "So we fry the bastard. So what? Think of the ones he's wasted."

No finesse. The thought kept running through Mahoney's mind. So they fried Henrys. Put him totally out of commission. What would prevent someone else from stepping in and taking his place? Zwiefel and all the others still part of the network, would be out, of course. But it would start up again with new faces. New leaders.

"We want to end the network permanently," Mahoney had told them. "We want to find out its reason for being. Its rationale. When that comes out we can treat the cause, not just eliminate the symptoms."

Which brought up the second choice: reaching Henrys and reasoning with him into providing them with the means for the network's dismantlement. Not its destruction, but rather a disbanding. If Henrys could be made to believe such a proposition, then a major motivation for resistance would have been removed; he'd not have to stand fast in order to save his comrades in arms with whom he had worked for God-only-knew how long.

For that, Henrys's initial cooperation would have to be managed somehow. If they could successfully snatch him from a hotel in *his* town and whisk him away, and furthermore, if they could confront him with a totally impossible situation, a real shocker—Wallace Mahoney's resurrection from the grave—it might be enough to tip him over the edge.

Henrys would probably be upset. John had managed against all odds to kill a couple of his people in Montana, then had come to Europe and killed Rubio. And now he might well be in Geneva, or on his way. No doubt Henrys was feeling a bit pushed at the moment.

Kopinski came onto the balcony. "They're here," he called down.

Mahoney glanced up at him. "I don't want to lose a word."
"You won't."

McBundy came around the corner from the kitchen as headlights flashed through the windows, then were extinguished. He held his hand in a thumbs-up gesture, then moved out of sight.

Mahoney poured himself a drink as he listened. The van doors closed; footsteps came up onto the porch and hesitated a moment; and then the front door opened.

"What is this place?" Henrys's voice was unmistakable. Mahoney could just see his silhouette framed in the doorway.

"Inside. By the fireplace," said Greene harshly.

Henrys stepped the rest of the way into the great room, then headed directly, almost resolutely, toward where Mahoney was sitting, his features still in darkness.

"Who is it?" Henrys asked. "Who's there?"

Greene and Dr. Lewis hung back by the door. They were to go into the kitchen, but they wanted to catch Henrys's reaction when he saw who it was.

Henrys came into the area lit by the fireplace, and Mahoney, who had been sitting back so that his face was in the shadows, sat forward. "Good evening," he said.

Later Mahoney would describe Henrys's first reaction as one of "instant bloodlessness." It seemed as if every last shade of color was drained from his face, except for a very slight blue tinge around the lips. His mouth opened, but no sound came out. His eyes were wide, his nostrils flared, and a slight tic made his right eye jump. He held up a hand as if he were trying to ward off a blow. Finally he staggered a little to the left.

Dr. Lewis rushed across the room and helped him into the facing chair.

"Thank you," Mahoney said.

Dr. Lewis nodded. He glanced down at Henrys again, and then he and Greene, broad smiles on their faces, went into the kitchen.

Mahoney, his motions very slow, very deliberate, leaned forward and poured Henrys a cognac. "I must come as something of a surprise to you."

Henrys passed a hand across his eyes. "It's been you all along, directing it all."

"I've been to St. Albans, if that's what you mean."

"You bloody bastard!" Henrys suddenly screeched like a man demented. "You bloody bastard!"

Behind him, Mahoney could see that Greene and McBundy had come around the corner.

"You were dead. I saw the autopsy report. The funeral. Switt, your son, everyone thought you were dead."

"They were mistaken, as you can see," Mahoney replied calmly. He continued in a reasonable tone. "The last time we met, you promised to tell me everything once I successfully took care of a little matter in Tel Aviv."

"What are you talking about?" Henrys snapped. He was still deeply shocked, but Mahoney could see that he was recovering fast. He was very good.

"Malecki is gone, which means the Mossad is clear for the moment. Switt is gone, so we're clean. Rubio is dead, which means SISMI—and in fact the entire Ministry of Defense—is clean. Now we've burned you, which means we can talk with the SIS."

Henrys glanced up toward the balcony, then over his shoulder toward the kitchen. Greene and McBundy had stepped out of sight again.

"It's finished, Henrys," Mahoney said. "I've been to St. Albans. Patton. Reichert. Panagiotopolous. Sir Rudyard. I could go on." Mahoney was, of course, guessing that those names held some significance. And it paid off.

"They'll never let you live!" Henrys shouted. He started out of his chair. Mahoney snatched the pistol out of the cushion and held it up. Henrys stopped in midstride. Greene was at the corner again, this time holding his automatic. Whatever composure Henrys had managed to muster had deserted him again and now his lower lip was quivering. He seemed on the verge of a breakdown. That was bothersome to Mahoney. Henry had more going for him than that. There had to be something else troubling him. Something deep.

But the first clue had come. Henrys had said: They'll never let you live. *They.*

"Sit down," Mahoney commanded.

"You're smart, Mahoney. And you've won this time. But it doesn't really matter what you've done to me and my family

That's of little consequence. The network's been operating nearly forty years. I told you that. It started before my time, and it will continue long after I'm gone."

"There are others?"

"There will always be others. There's absolutely nothing you can do about it."

Mahoney opened the small notebook and looked at it. He had written the names of the people from St. Albans, prominent names, internationally famous companies, along with the connections from the town to this puzzle. Henrys and Malecki were related, apparently with ties to someone in the town. ComSat, the firm that had put up the spy satellite for Israel, was there, as was the construction firm that had built the receiving station at Al Qaryūt. Soman, the nerve gas used to kill the troops at Ataruz that had destroyed the station, thus eliminating evidence, had its representation at St. Albans. Everything seemed to come back to that one place. *Money. Power. Greed.*

"Perhaps there isn't a thing I can do about the network," Mahoney said, looking up. "But you can."

Henrys shook his head. "You have some of the names. What more is there? Do you think the Soviets or the Communist Chinese are going to cooperate with you? Hardly. So what have you got? Nothing."

"I have you, and I understand St. Albans."

"You have nothing, and you understand nothing," Henrys hissed.

Mahoney sat there a moment, eyeing Henrys. "I mean to dismantle the network. I don't want to cause any further harm to you or the others. I don't even want to see anyone in jail or exposed to his own government, although God knows you people deserve to be punished for the destruction you've caused." Mahoney shook his head. "But that wouldn't accomplish a thing."

"You're mad."

"You, my dear Henrys, are going to provide me with the means to do just that. Together, you and I are going to come to a complete understanding."

Henrys looked toward the door, gauging his chances for a successful dash. He knew Mahoney had a gun, and he knew that at least Greene and Dr. Lewis were somewhere in the back of the house. No doubt within earshot.

"You once told me that violence is a part of the human condition. I agreed. But neither you nor your mentors at St. Albans have the qualifications, or the right, to act as the puppet-masters of us all."

Still Henrys said nothing.

"What did they offer you?" Mahoney asked. "Money? Power? The house in Geneva?"

"You bloody fool. You bloody, bloody fool. Not only don't you understand, you have no conception of what is happening ... what has been happening all these years."

"No," Mahoney said calmly. "Tell me."

Henrys seemed to be on the verge of making some kind of decision. "My daughter," he said.

Mahoney hid his instant joy. There comes a point in every interrogation when the subject crosses over from hostile to cooperative. He thought that point was coming now. "What about her?"

"I want her back."

Mahoney had no idea what the man was talking about. But he was going to have to play along. At least for the moment. "That will depend, of course, on your cooperation."

"This is my daughter we're talking about, for God's sake! I want her back. She's not been a part of this."

"I might remind you of my losses as well," Mahoney said sharply, but he held himself back from saying any more. His daughter had evidently wandered off, and now Henrys was running scared thinking that Mahoney had taken her. It wasn't cricket, but it definitely was a lever.

Henrys hung his head. "It wasn't my fault. It was Switt. He was running scared. He overreacted, for God's sake." He looked up. "But we took care of it. The network cleans up its own messes. Only now ... your son ... he's taken Caroline."

The news was stunning. John *had* got to Geneva after all, at least Mahoney assumed his son had snatched Caroline from the house. But now where was he? And what effect was this going to have on their operation?

"You must understand why I tried to strike back at him. I was to protect my daughter. But I never realized that he had help. None of us realized it. We thought he was working alone in retaliation for what ... happened to his wife and children.

At that moment it was all Mahoney could do to keep from raising the pistol and shooting the miserable son of a bitch.

God, what arrogance, what inhuman gall. "Why did you kill Jensen?"

"It was a mistake," Henrys said matter-of-factly, as if it hadn't meant a thing to him.

McBundy came from the kitchen in a hurry, a very stern expression on his face. Henrys looked up. "You," he said.

Control, Mahoney thought. Henrys was on the verge of going one way or the other. He would either retreat deeply, or open up and help them. Mahoney wondered how he was going to manage it either way.

"Why don't you explain it all to Bob, as well, and we'll go from there," Mahoney said. He could hear the quaver in his voice.

McBundy came across the room, pulled one of the footstools a little closer to the fire, and sat down, stretching his legs out in front of him as if he had all the time in the world for a fireside chat.

"My daughter . . ."

"We'll get back to her," Mahoney said. "But first things first, shall we?"

Chapter 26

AND STILL IT was the same night, although by now they wer[e]
into the very early hours of Friday. Dr. Lewis made a pot o[f]
coffee while Greene telephoned Carron in Wasserman's suit[e]
to confirm that nothing untoward had happened in town. [It]
hadn't. Everything was status quo. How is it coming out there[,]
Carron had asked, to which Greene replied he hadn't the fog[-]
giest. Kopinski remained, all the while, in the upstairs bedroo[m]
with the tape-recording machine, making damned sure, as h[e]
put it later, that not a single word was missed. "Not a singl[e]
word, mind you. We were being told history from the lips [of]
one of the participants."

Once Henrys was convinced—he had convinced himsel[f]
really—that his daughter's well-being was on the line, and th[at]
she was, for the moment, beyond even his reach, he open[ed]
up one hundred percent. No one said a thing as the man flitt[ed]
here and there, as if he were offering up bits and pieces

sweets in an effort to find out what it was that whetted their appetites.

Someone had told Mahoney a long time ago that in his business, family was never, never to be involved. When that began to happen, no one would be safe, and the entire structure might come tumbling down. Leave the innocents alone.

Mahoney had suffered in this respect. Suffered deeply. But Henrys was under the gun now, and it was destroying him.

Henrys's testimony was centered on four areas: the history of the network, including its beginnings; its recruitment tactics; its operations; and its ultimate objectives.

The organization got its start, as Henrys had previously explained to Mahoney, shortly after it became apparent to a number of powerful people that the United States would be successful in its efforts to construct an atomic bomb.

"It was a new era. They all knew it," Henrys said.

"When you say *they*, by that you mean..." Mahoney prompted.

"T. Carter Winslow, chairman of the board of U.S. Industrial. His company was doing a lot of work on the bomb project, particularly on gas-diffusion techniques, in liaison with some of our British firms. But previous to the war, U.S. Industrial had also had firm contacts with such companies as International Computer, Ruhr Steel and Metal, and Conners, Ltd., along with a host of big firms in other countries."

"The beginning of the multinationals," Mahoney said. It fit closely with what he had already guessed.

"The very beginning, actually, of an exclusive club," Henrys said. "Of a financial nature. Money, not national boundaries, was what counted, don't you see. With nuclear war possible—and often likely—with total destruction of civilization as we know it, there would be no businesses, no factories. More important, no consumers."

"No profits," Mahoney said.

"Exactly," Henrys agreed. "So the network was born as a guarantee against nuclear war. The U.S. began by sharing its nuclear secrets with its allies—at least with enough of them to insure a balance of power. After the war, the list of nations joining the membership—not the nuclear club, but just the exchange of intelligence information group—was expanded."

"We were already sharing nuclear secrets with the British

government during the war," Mahoney said.

"Right. So the Soviets were brought into it. Of course the Axis powers were not given the information."

"Nagasaki and Hiroshima must have been terrible mistakes, then."

"Terrible mistakes. But it was just the beginning of the network. We had cooperation with the NKVD in the Soviet Union and some cooperation with the OSS in your country, along with MI6 in mine. But it wasn't until 1955, when the West German BND was formed from the Gehlen Organization, that we had any real cooperation from that quarter."

Gehlen had been the creation of the Americans, Mahoney remembered, so the BND had played catch-up. "Before then, what happened?" he asked. He had worked in Germany and had a special interest in hearing about it.

"In West Germany?"

Mahoney nodded.

"Very little intelligence of the hard sort was passed back and forth, at least directly, though we did glean a lot from OSS and then CIA reports. We were still fledglings then, you know. And you have to bear in mind our lingering distrust of the Germans for a long time after the war. When the Soviets set up the East German K-5, for example, they sent Colonel Makurin, who was a network man. His successor then helped form the *Ministerium für Staats Sicherheit*—the Ministry for State Security. Then there was China, with Chiang Kai-shek's people at first, but later Mao's. There was BOSS in South Africa. The SNB in Czechoslovakia—"

"How were you recruited?" Mahoney asked, cutting into Henrys's narrative. Henrys blinked.

"Kim Philby."

There was a silence in the room. McBundy sat forward.

"Philby? He was one of you?"

Henrys nodded. "His communism was an aberration. Long before he was exposed, he knew it was coming. Just as we all know it'll happen eventually, so he recruited me."

"And you have your successor picked out?" Mahoney asked.

"Naturally."

"And Switt?"

Henrys nodded. McBundy and Mahoney looked at each other. With Switt's disappearance, someone else had stepped

in to take his place. There was another mole within the CIA.
Christ!

"Once a man, or a woman, is recruited, the first task—
besides covering his own tracks—is to think about recruiting
the next person."

"Isn't that dangerous?"

"It can be," Henrys said matter-of-factly. "It has created
some operational problems from time to time. There have
been—"

"Accidental deaths of key operatives?" Mahoney finished.

"We're fighting a war here, Mahoney," Henrys said in defense.

"Surely you don't do the physical things yourself?" Mahoney asked.

"Some of it."

"Who delivered the Soman to the base at Ataruż? Who killed
those troops?"

"An oil-field engineer and his assistant. It was quite easily
done, actually. Flew it in aboard a small helicopter, right under
their radar. They were prospecting."

"British?"

"Americans."

The arrogance of the man was awesome. Dozens of soldiers
had been murdered at the Jordanian base, not merely to protect
the network from exposure, but to protect that particular operational goal.

"The two men in Montana, with FBI identification?"

"They were hired in Detroit through blind intermediaries.
They've done other jobs for us. They do a job, they get paid,
no questions are asked. If they happen to get burned, it's no
loss. If they happen to get arrested, there is no way they could
be traced back to us. No way. We have men like that in Moscow, in London and Paris, in Athens. Even Peking."

"You're the directors."

Henrys nodded.

"Funded by a group of multinational corporations."

"It was quite clever of you to have come this far," Henrys
said patronizingly. "But this is as far as it goes. You have the
information you came seeking, so now release my daughter,
and be done with it."

"One last bit," Mahoney said. And those who knew Mahoney—the archivists, the historians who collected all the pieces and put them in order, the legmen who had to put everything back together and smooth the ruffled feathers of several European governments—had nothing but praise for him. "To that moment, all they had was a lot of wind, with little or no substance," one of them said. "It was Mahoney's intuitive leap that made everything else that followed, and is following, possible."

Greene and Dr. Lewis had come out of the kitchen, and Kopinski leaned against the rail on the balcony above.

"That's all there is, except of course for the actual details. Names, dates, and places, that sort of thing," Henrys said.

"I don't mean that."

"Won't do you much good," Henrys plugged on.

"Your ancestral name was Malecki, I believe."

Henrys looked at him and nodded. "You know that."

"There is a branch in Great Britain that changed its name to Henrys. Another branch, which retook the name Malecki, emigrated to the United States. Chaim was one of them."

Henrys nodded again, a hooded look coming to his eyes.

"But there never was a Swiss branch of the Maleckis, was there?" Mahoney said quietly. "You have no connection here?"

"I never told you there was."

"Which means the family house in Geneva—the place you seem to spend an inordinate amount of time and protection on—is a fairly recent acquisition."

"It's been in the family for years."

"In the morning we can check with the registry of deeds. I'm sure we'll find the coverup, records tampered with. But think we'll be able to prove that you've had the house—or the family has had the house—only since, let's say, 1943 or '44."

"What are you getting at?" Henrys snarled.

"I want it."

"You want what?"

"It's hidden in your house somewhere. Or perhaps very close by. Perhaps in a bank. A safety-deposit box that can be approached and opened only under very special circumstances."

"What the bloody hell are you talking about?" Henrys protested. "I've done my part, now I want my daughter."

"Which is it, Henrys? A bank? You are the guardian of the seal or the document, or whatever it is. That's why you're here in Geneva."

Henrys turned to McBundy. "I demand that this charade be terminated."

McBundy said nothing.

Henrys glanced up at Kopinski on the balcony, over his shoulder at Greene and Dr. Lewis, then back to Mahoney.

"My daughter," he said.

Mahoney got up and lit a cigar, then poured another drink. "We're discussing the most highly competitive conglomerates in the world here, Bob," he said, ignoring Henrys. "Companies such as U.S. Industrial and International Computers and Conners, Ltd., which helped fight the war. Companies that helped construct the guns and tanks and bombs—including the atomic bomb. Companies that manufactured such things as Zyklon-B, which was used to kill millions of Jews. And companies so large, so vastly important to the survival and well-being of their countries that, no matter their activities during the war, they had to be rebuilt from the ashes afterward."

"Oil, steel, electronics," McBundy said, playing the game, although he seemed bewildered. Henrys looked from one to the other.

"Exactly," Mahoney said. "The multinationals that never do anything without a contract. The most fiercely competitive of all companies. It's what brought them to international status in the first place."

Mahoney turned to look at Henrys. "But they don't trust one another. They cannot. Their avowed aim is to make a profit. If any one of them gains an edge over another..."

McBundy was watching carefully.

"If Winslow began it, if it was his idea, don't you think he would have drawn up a contract? Something in writing that he and the other multinationals could have signed?"

"You're insane. Why would anyone commit himself to such an extent? Folly," Henrys said.

"They could not trust one another, of course, to honor any kind of a verbal agreement. They'd have to have it in writing. Have incriminating evidence that they could use against any one of their members who decided to stray."

"That makes absolutely no sense."

"Oh, but it does. Such a document would insure that no one backed out, that no company would betray the organization. With each new chairman of the board would come a message. The document would be read and honored. If it weren't, it would mean the end of that company. And if any company decided to break away, the other would insure compliance or ruin."

McBundy had gotten to his feet, Henrys all but forgotten now. "If such a document existed...my God, think of its power. It could wreck the world economy."

"In the wrong hands," Mahoney said. "If it came out. But it mustn't."

They both turned and looked down at Henrys. Mahoney's insides were churning. They were close. So goddamned close.

"We'd destroy it, Henrys," he said.

"No!" Henrys screamed. "You're all crazy! Every one of you!"

"You *will* help us," Mahoney raised his voice. "You will in the end, you bastard."

"Get away from me..."

"If need be, we'll bring your daughter here."

"Caroline...?"

"We'll bring her here, Henrys, and kill her in front of you, just as you killed my son's wife in front of him."

Henrys's mouth worked, but no sounds came out. His Adam's apple was bobbing.

"I'm officially dead, Henrys," Mahoneys said. "I can...and will do anything I want." He turned away. "Son of a bitch..."

"Wait," Henrys cried.

Mahoney spun around. "You'll fetch it, we'll destroy it. Then the network can be dismantled."

"Impossible," Henrys said in a small voice.

Mahoney hid his triumph. "It is in Geneva."

"The Banque de Genève."

"In a safety-deposit box?"

"In a special place. Gesgarde—he's the bank's director—knows where. Only he."

"Isn't that dangerous? If something were to happen to him?"

"There are sealed instructions for a number of banking matters, in that case," Henrys said. "Our routine banking affairs plus—"

"Plus what?" Mahoney interrupted. He sat on the edge of the chair so that Henrys would not have to look up at him. There was a heavy sense of drama in the room. Even the fire in the grate had flared.

"The Geneva Covenant," Henrys said, very softly.

"What? I didn't quite hear that," Mahoney said.

"The Geneva Covenant," Henrys repeated. "They all signed it. Everything is there. The original operations. The first pay-offs. The first contacts with the secret services from the original member nations. Then the others. The new businesses, the new nations." Henrys seemed on the verge of collapse. "But you'll never get it. Gesgarde will never release it. Not without confirmation from all the directors that it is coming out."

As soon as it was discovered that Henrys had been interfered with, the order would go out for his elimination, Mahoney knew. So they had very little time. It was going to have to be done tonight.

"You have nothing to threaten them with, Mahoney, don't you see? You can accuse them of anything you like, all day long, but without proof they wouldn't even have to answer your charges. I'd just be another casualty, another Kim Philby. Another Burgess or MaClean. A traitor to my country. But no one would believe a story about a network, financed and run by the biggest, most respected companies in the world."

This morning. Immediately, while they still had the slight edge of surprise, Mahoney thought. He focused on Henrys, put his cigar and drink down, then pulled the English traitor to his feet.

"Wallace?" McBundy said, alarmed.

"You're going to telephone Gesgarde," Mahoney said harshly.

"It won't do any good. I've already told you that."

"You are going to inform Gesgarde that you must make contact immediately with the directors, or *your* directors, or whatever you call them. From the bank, where Swiss law protects the security of your communications. Now, this morning."

"No."

"Oh, yes, Henrys. Oh, yes, you are. If need be, we could have you on the square in St. Albans within hours, a sitting duck. Failing that, your daughter . . ." He didn't have to finish.

"Oh, you bastard. You bloody bastard."

Chapter 27

LIVING THROUGH THE events of those final hours Friday morning was like riding on a very frightening roller coaster. It was nearly three o'clock when, under Kopinski's close scrutiny, Henrys telephoned Emile Gesgarde, the director of the Banque de Genève, at his home. Kopinski, whose French was excellent, listened to every word, his finger poised to sever the connection in case Henrys said something to warn the banker. Onerous as it was, Henrys did cooperate, fearing for his daughter's safety. Gesgarde would meet with Henrys in front of the bank at 6:00 A.M. sharp, a full hour and a half before any of the other bank employees showed up.

While that was going on, Mahoney took Greene and McBundy into the kitchen, where, with one ear cocked toward the living room, Mahoney answered the inevitable questions and issued his instructions.

"What the hell was that all about?" McBundy asked, almost as if on cue. "How did you know?"

"I didn't. I was guessing."

McBundy looked at Mahoney in amazement. Greene was shaking his head.

"I don't believe any of this," Greene said.

"It's going to be very tight," Mahoney said after a brief pause to make sure there were no more questions or objections. "Once it gets out that Henrys has been contacted, he'll be done, and we'll have to start all over again."

"His bodyguards at the hotel—" Greene said with alarm.

"Call Carron and make sure nothing has happened. If everything is still all right, you and Dr. Lewis will get Henrys back to Wasserman's room the same way you brought him in. From there we'll let Henrys go. His bodyguards will pick him up, and Jones will follow them home."

"Meanwhile, we stake out the bank?" Greene asked.

Mahoney nodded.

"What would prevent Henrys from telephoning Gesgarde and calling it all off, then contacting whoever he works for and telling them everything?"

"Two things," Mahoney said. "The first is his daughter, Caroline. John evidently has her. And the second is this: when it comes out that Henrys has spoken with us, he'll be finished. They'll probably kill him."

"And if John should show up?"

"I don't know," Mahoney said. "It would make things difficult, if not impossible. He could be almost anywhere by now." He looked at his watch. "All we need is another three hours."

"And once we have the document—this Geneva Covenant or whatever he called it—what are you going to do with it?"

"Destroy it," Mahoney said. He could hear that Henrys was off the phone.

"We can't!" McBundy protested. His voice was high-pitched, strangely out of key.

"Oh, yes, we can, and we will. Right there on the spot," Mahoney said. He went back to the great room.

Henrys looked up. "He'll be there at six. But no matter what you say to them, they'll never release the Covenant."

"You will be returned to Ezra's room at the des Bergues. From there you'll be on your own. But I expect you to show up at the bank. It's your only hope."

"And you?"

"One of us will meet you there. You can explain that you

have an associate from Woroco who will prepare the messages."

"It won't work."

"Leave that to us."

"They've been at this for nearly four decades. They know what they're doing. You'll never get away with it. They'll have us all killed."

"When we're finished, there'll be no reason to eliminate us. No reason whatsoever."

"What about Caroline?"

"She will be returned to you as soon as we've completed our business."

Henrys looked deeply into Mahoney's eyes, wanting to believe him. But it was difficult. He had lived with lies for so long, it was hard for him to believe in anyone anymore.

"I'll hold you personally responsible for her safety. After all, it is your son who has her. And one way or another, no matter how this turns out, if she is harmed I will kill you."

Chapter 28

THEY HAD MANAGED to rent a Fiat from the agency at the train station just before it closed. By morning the network would know that he was back in Geneva, but it didn't matter to John. His business with Caroline's father would be finished. He turned and looked at her. She was asleep, her head back on the seat, her lips slightly parted, and her breasts rising and falling with her breathing. She looked haggard, as he was sure he did. They had been through an ordeal. At first she had worried for her own safety: John was a kidnapper with an insane story about spies and murderers. And then, when she began to have her own doubts, she started to worry for her father's safety.

They were parked across the street from the hotel, in a line of cars along the river. Twice police cruisers had come slowly by, but John and Caroline had ducked down and were not spotted.

He had wanted to storm right into the hotel. Demand to

speak with Henrys, then confront the man in the lobby. But Caroline held him back.

"You'll never get close enough to my father to talk to him that way," she said.

"He couldn't refuse me. It would make a scene. I don't think he wants that at this point."

"His bodyguards are right across the street. There'll be another pair inside."

John looked across to the brightly lit hotel entrance. The doorman, resplendent in his uniform with its gold buttons, stood with his hands clasped behind his back. The black Mercedes was there. Two men inside.

There had been a lot of activity earlier; gaily dressed people coming and going as Friday night turned into Saturday morning. Around two o'clock, however, the traffic had begun to taper off, and by three there wasn't a soul in sight, except for the two men in the Mercedes across the way.

Maybe he was gone, John thought. Maybe the servant Caroline had spoken with had lied to her. Maybe her father had not come here at all. Or, if he had, maybe he had been alerted that Caroline and therefore John were on their way.

A white Volkswagen van passed them and turned left at the end of the block. John got just a brief glimpse of the driver. The man was vaguely familiar. He had seen the profile before. A long time ago. But where? Or were his nerves just jumpy?

For several seconds he toyed with the idea of following the van. But then he decided against it. Henrys's bodyguards were still in the Mercedes across the street. He could see their figures silhouetted by the bright hotel lights. And Henrys was most likely still inside.

Still, the face in the van bothered him.

He looked at his watch. It was nearly four o'clock, and a light mist had begun to form from the river, making halos around the streetlamps. It was chilly, and John shivered.

The white van reappeared at the far corner a few minutes later, having evidently turned around on the Rue du Mont-Blanc. John sat up. It crossed the quay and continued onto the bridge, its taillights bright. Then it was gone.

It had come from around the corner. From the back of the hotel? Had it delivered something and then left? Nothing out of the ordinary. Delivery vans usually began making their rounds about this time of the morning. But this van was plain; ther

was no sign or company logo on the side. And the driver of
the van. . . . The more John thought about it, the more he was
sure he knew him. But from where?

Caroline woke up and stretched. He turned to look at her.

"Anything?" she asked. She looked beyond him toward the
hotel, and suddenly she stiffened.

John spun around. One of the bodyguards from the Mercedes
had gotten out and was opening the back door. A tall man,
dressed in a sports jacket and light trousers, came across the
sidewalk and got in the car, followed by two other husky men.

"My father," Caroline said.

John started the Fiat as the Mercedes's parking lights came
on and it pulled away from the curb. He pulled out and, keeping
as well back as he dared, followed.

"If he doesn't come, if he runs, then what?" McBundy asked
Mahoney.

They sat with Dr. Lewis in the back of the Volkswagen
van. Greene was at the wheel. Jones had followed Henrys
home. And Carron was still at the hotel with Wasserman.

"He won't run."

"If he does?"

"Jesus, Bob. If he does, he does. We'll have to find John
and get the hell out of here. Start again."

"They know you're alive."

"We won't have to start from the beginning. We know who
they are, and we know what holds them together. From that
we could go after them." Mahoney got up and went forward
so that he could look down the block at the Banque de Genève.
It was housed in a nondescript stone building in a row of similar
four-story structures. The street was very narrow and curved
out of sight at both ends. Sitting here, fifty yards from the
bank, they could not see much beyond the bank, nor could
they see very far behind because of the way the street curved.

The fog had deepened, making the street seem even narrower than it was, the buildings closer together, and the single
streetlamp in front of the bank weak and ineffective.

"He'll come," Mahoney said softly.

Greene looked at him. "I think he will."

Mahoney smiled and patted him on the arm. "We're close
now, Bobby. Very close."

Greene looked away, toward the bank. "I hope it's all been

worth it, sir. I hope all the deaths, all the disrupted lives and destruction . . . I hope it's all been worth it."

"Me, too—" Mahoney started to say, when lights emerged from the fog at the end of the street.

"This is it?" Dr. Lewis asked.

Mahoney glanced at his watch. It was a minute before six. "Possible," he said.

The lights materialized into a Citroën sedan that pulled up in front of the bank. The lights were doused, and the car door opened, the domelight illuminating, for just a moment, a small man. He was alone.

He unlocked the front door of the bank and went inside. A light came on behind one of the curtained windows.

"Gesgarde, the banker," Greene said.

Lights appeared from behind, and moments later a Mercedes passed them and parked behind the Citroën. The door opened, and Henrys got out. He too was alone.

"This is it," Mahoney said. "Wish me luck."

"Don't go," McBundy said. "It's a trap."

"Maybe not," Mahoney said. He got out of the van and hurried down to where Henrys stood waiting for him. His hand was in his jacket pocket, his fingers curled around the butt of his .30-caliber revolver.

Henrys was highly agitated. "I was followed! Christ, your people were too obvious."

"No bodyguards this time?" Mahoney asked, glancing up the cobbled street. Where the hell was Jones?

"No. But I'm sure Robert—my man—has telephoned his control by now. But we've got another problem."

Mahoney said nothing.

"I don't know what the hell you're trying to pull, but Caroline called last night. Wanted to know where I was. One of the silly servants told her the hotel."

"She didn't show up."

"Of course not. She's with your son. We'd have spotted them if they had tried."

"Inside," Mahoney said.

"You lied to me, Mahoney. You don't have my daughter Your son has her. He's been working independently of you."

"You'll get your daughter back. I promise you that."

Henrys was a man whose back was against the wall. Bu Mahoney was getting the impression that he wasn't doing thi merely for his daughter. There was something else.

They crossed the sidewalk to the bank door and Henrys pressed the buzzer. "If anything has happened to her, I will hold you responsible."

"Yes?" a thin voice came from the speaker.

Henrys lurched forward. "McNiel Henrys."

The door buzzed and they went inside. Gesgarde, a slight, dark man, was waiting for them in a small anteroom. He didn't seem surprised by Mahoney's presence.

"My associate, Monsieur Landon," Henrys said, making up a name on the spur of the moment.

The banker started to bow, when Mahoney pulled out the gun and pointed it at him. *"Mon dieu!"* the little man said.

"I want the Covenant," Mahoney said.

The banker was aghast.

"We cannot release it," Henrys said. "I have explained that to you. Not without all the directors' approval."

The banker was nearly in a state of apoplexy; but Henrys's words, more than the gun in Mahoney's hand, were making it worse.

Mahoney stepped a little closer to the banker and raised the revolver. "I hate these things," he said. "They are loud and very messy. But I will shoot you dead unless you comply immediately."

"I do not know what you are talking about, *monsieur*."

"The Geneva Covenant. Originated by U.S. Industrial's Winslow, and signed by a number of very influential men. Get it for us, or die here and now."

The banker looked to Henrys for help.

"And then what?" the Englishman asked.

"I will destroy it."

Henrys looked at the banker. "Get it," he said.

The banker shook his head and backed up a step. "No."

Mahoney cocked the gun, the noise very loud. "Five . . . four . . . three . . ."

"It is impossible!" the banker cried.

"Two," Mahoney said evenly. He raised the barrel a little higher so that it was pointing directly between Gesgarde's eyes. "One . . ."

"Wait!" Gesgarde shouted, raising his hand.

"The document," Mahoney said.

"It will be all right, you will see," Henrys said. "When it

is destroyed, everything will be all right."

"It will be the ruin of my bank. A matter of confidence. We have kept this for so many years. And there are accounts because of it."

"The accounts will not be removed, I promise you," Henrys said soothingly. "All will be as it has always been, except there will be no further need for messages to St. Albans."

"They will not forget this."

"They will thank you for it. I do not lie."

Mahoney motioned with the gun toward the stairs.

The banker was wavering. "The time lock . . ."

"It is not in the vault," Henrys said. "I know that. It has been brought out at all hours of the day and night."

"Do it," Mahoney said. He felt as if he were on the edge of a cliff. One false step and they'd all plunge to their deaths.

"We haven't much time," Henrys said. "We must have it now."

Gesgarde abruptly turned and scurried to the stairs. They followed him up one level to an office at the back of the building. He flipped on the desk lamp, first making sure the window curtains were tightly drawn.

He hesitated a moment longer, then, shaking his head, went to a cabinet that he slid aside to reveal a wall safe. He turned around. "Please," he said. "There are other, sensitive documents here."

Mahoney and Henrys both stepped back so that they could not possibly see the combination. Gesgarde quickly opened the large safe, withdrew a thick book bound in brown leather, and handed it to Henrys.

"Is that it?" Mahoney asked.

Henrys nodded, almost reverently.

Gesgarde closed and locked the safe, then slid the cabinet back in place.

"Say nothing to anyone about this, and you will never be bothered," Mahoney said.

"My fate has been sealed one way or the other," the banker said with a shrug.

"Remain here in your office for at least fifteen minutes. Then go about your business as usual," Mahoney instructed. This was it. The very thing dozens of people had died for in the past six weeks was now within his grasp.

He motioned for Henrys, and they went down the stairs and

across the anteroom. They paused by the front door.

"You're going to destroy this?" Henrys asked.

"Yes," Mahoney said. "I want to look at it first, of course. But it will be destroyed. We can return to Céligny and finish this there."

"I have not read all of it. But thank God it is over," Henrys said.

The comment was startling. "You wanted out?"

Henrys nodded. "For years. Ever since Vietnam. Most of us wanted out, actually," he said. "They engineered the war, by the way, you know. After the French gave up, they engineered your involvement."

"For money?"

Henrys nodded. "Your government was spending upward of a billion dollars a month on the war. Huge profits were being made."

"Money is their god."

"A false prophet, but their only one," Henrys said.

"Now it's over."

They went outside and started down the street, Henrys slightly ahead and to the left. McBundy jumped out of the van and ran toward them.

"Did you actually get it?" he called out.

"What the hell—" Mahoney started to say, his stomach sinking, when Henrys held up the book as if it was some kind of a trophy . . . or signal.

McBundy took something out of his pocket and lobbed it underhanded toward Henrys.

Mahoney instinctively rolled right as a bright magnesium flare lit up the darkness. It enveloped Henrys, who screamed once, then fell writhing on the street in the middle of an intense fire.

McBundy was racing away from the van. Mahoney brought his revolver up and fired two shots. The second hit home.

A woman was screaming hysterically at the end of the street, but Mahoney ignored her as he ran around the fire to where McBundy was lying on his side. Blood was leaking from a hole in his chest, forming a large pool on the cobblestones, but his eyes were still open and aware, the flames reflecting their moistness.

"Why, Bob?" Mahoney asked, kneeling down beside his old friend. "Christ, why?"

"We couldn't let it out," McBundy said, his voice barely audible.

Mahoney leaned closer. "What is it, Bob? What'd you say?" Jones was there, staring down at them.

"St. Albans. They sent me. The book had to be destroyed." His words were like a hammer blow. "*They* sent you? Who did? Who's 'they'?"

"Doesn't matter," McBundy croaked.

"But why, Bob? Why?"

"They...wanted it to end. It was no good any longer. They...it had to end, no matter the cost..."

"We could have worked together."

"No one was supposed to know. I didn't tell them about you, Wallace. But Henrys had to be destroyed. He knew too much. I didn't..." McBundy grabbed Mahoney's arm. "You're safe, Wallace...we're all safe..." A great pain wracked his body, and when it passed he slumped back on the street, his eyes open, his chest still.

What had been in the book that McBundy had not wanted anyone to see, at all costs? Mahoney was aware that there were people standing over him, but it didn't matter. McBundy had been a friend for a very long time. And he had been a traitor as well. They...whoever *they* were...from St. Albans had sent McBundy to destroy Henrys and the document.

A woman was crying.

"Dad?"

Mahoney looked up into the eyes of his son, who was holding a young, good-looking woman. She was sobbing, looking toward the dwindling magnesium flames. "Hello, son."

"My God. Oh, my God, is it really you?"

Mahoney got slowly to his feet. He reached out and took his son's free arm. Greene stood by the open van door. Mahoney gestured toward him. "We have to get out of here. Before the police come."

Dr. Lewis came up the street, and he gently pried Caroline from John and led her back to the van.

"Caroline Henrys?" Mahoney asked. He had seen her briefly when he had been at Henrys's home, but she looked different now. Older. Haggard.

"All this time," John stammered. "All this time, you've been alive."

They could not remain there much longer, but John looked

as if he were on the verge of collapse. There were bandages around his neck, and he seemed very pale. He had lost weight as well. Mahoney's heart went out to his son.

"I didn't know," John said, tears welling up in his eyes. "Christ . . . Christ . . . Dad, they killed Elizabeth . . . and the babies! The bastards! Oh God . . . the bastards!"

And then his son was in his arms, his shoulders heaving as he sobbed.

"It's over now, son," Mahoney said, barely able to control his own emotions. He kept seeing Marge, how she used to be there when he came home. She'd have a drink waiting for him, and they'd talk. They'd be together, and she knew the right things to say and do at the right times to comfort him, to take away the pain and the hurt. But she was gone now. Just as Elizabeth and the children were gone for John. They had only each other. Another image welled up in Mahoney's mind, an image of when the boys were little . . . John and Michael. They had gotten into some trouble—Mahoney forgot now exactly what—and after they had been spanked, he had overheard them pledging each other never to separate. They were the two musketeers. When he had told Marge about it, she had smiled and said that none of them would ever be truly apart from the other.

But, God, it was so lonely now.

John nodded. "She hasn't been a part of this. She's innocent."

"I know," Mahoney said.

John stared at his father. "All this time. You've been alive."

"We've won, John," Mahoney said. "The network has been smashed."

"Oh God, Dad," John said. "Was it worth it?"

"I hope so," Mahoney said. "I truly hope so."

It was dark as the limousine hurried across the Roosevelt Bridge into Washington and continued up toward Georgetown. Mahoney took out a cigar but almost immediately decided against it. He put it back in his pocket.

The DCI, Franklin Lycoming, his face illuminated momentarily as they passed under a streetlamp, looked at Mahoney, his left eyebrow raised. He seemed disdainful. But Mahoney was too tired to notice, too worn out.

"The Swiss aren't happy, but they'll settle down," Lycoming said. His voice was as soft as the whisper of a southwest wind across a wheatfield just before a tornado.

Mahoney shrugged. He turned to look out the window. It was over. The network's foundation was destroyed. He had seen it done with his own eyes. The glue that had held them together—the fear and blackmail that the information contained in the Geneva Covenant represented—had been elim nated. There'd simply be no good reason for them to revive the network.

The two painful surprises in this affair had been his son and, of course, Robert McBundy. Although, thinking back, he acknowledged his on-again-off-again suspicions of McBundy. He shouldn't have turned them off.

John had developed some sort of affection for Caroline Henrys, which could not possibly lead to anything. They were too dissimilar, worlds apart. John was merely reacting to the deaths of Elizabeth and the children. In time he would understand his mistake. But, after all they had been through, Mahoney conceded, if they found solace in such a relationship now, it would not be so terrible.

His mind kept returning to McBundy. An old friend. A confidant for years. At one time a friend of the family; Marge had liked him. Yet he had worked for the network.

Mahoney still wasn't quite sure what McBundy's role in this affair had been. Evidently, however, he had worked directly for someone from St. Albans. Probably T. Carter Winslow. Winslow had a home there, they had learned. McBundy had wanted the Geneva Covenant destroyed before anyone had a chance to look at it. But his death seemed so useless. It served no purpose. They could have brought the Covenant back to Céligny, and the book could have been destroyed.

Mahoney sighed deeply. It would not have worked out that way, and McBundy had known it. Too many people had died, including Elizabeth and the children. Mahoney would have wanted his revenge.

They turned up Wisconsin Avenue past Georgetown University, and a few blocks later the driver turned down a narrow cobblestone street of very well-to-do homes. They stopped in front of a large red-brick Colonial. Lycoming's. The driver jumped out and came around to the DCI's door, but Lycoming waved him off for the moment.

"An extraordinary business," Lycoming said. "But as I have already indicated, it is over as of now. Do you understand at least that much, Mr. Mahoney?"

Mahoney looked at the man. Lycoming had always been one of those elusive characters . . . always at the fringe of the public's awareness, always being appointed to one position of importance or another, but no one ever seemed to know his *story, his real measure. Mahoney nodded.* "Senator Aronson and his people are coming over to the Agency for an intelligence audit. They'll be looking for scalps."

Lycoming's lip curled slightly. "Aronson is a fool. He knows nothing, nor will he learn a thing at Langley. This was a Company affair, and it will of necessity remain a Company affair."

"And the President, will he be told?"

"To make political mincemeat out of this?" Lycoming snapped. "Of course not. He'll be told nothing. It's not his business."

That was all wrong, and yet Mahoney found he did not really give a damn. He was too tired. He had lost too much. He had been so mangled in the battle he no longer had any feeling for the war.

Lycoming leaned a little closer. "We're in the middle of SALT II and the MX missile business. And on top of that, the Soviets are hinting that they're ready to try again to place nuclear warheads in Cuba."

"What are you telling me?" Mahoney said.

"Simply this, Mr. Mahoney: As far as your involvement is concerned, this investigation is completed. I will arrange to have the pieces picked up and swept under the carpet if need be. If you pursue this further, I will have you arrested and charged under the Secrets Act."

Mahoney said nothing. It no longer hurt. The network was gone.

"Is that clear?"

"Yes, it is."

Lycoming opened his door. "My driver will take you wherever you wish. Good evening."

Mahoney nodded. It was finally over. Charges would never be brought against John, and now perhaps, he and his son could attempt to regain some semblance of normalcy in their shattered lives. They could rest, and most of all they could begin the very long process of forgetting.

Tales of International Intrigue and Riveting Suspense from

SEAN FLANNERY

☐ 10819-1	EAGLES FLY	$3.50
☐ 34232-9	HOLLOW MEN	$3.50
☐ 82402-1	THE TRINITY FACTOR	$2.95

Available wherever paperbacks are sold or use this coupon.

 CHARTER BOOKS
Book Mailing Service
P.O. Box 690, Rockville Centre, NY 11571

Please send me the titles checked above. I enclose _____ Include 75¢ for postage and handling if one book is ordered; 25¢ per book for two or more not to exceed $1.75. California, Illinois, New York and Tennessee residents please add sales tax.

NAME_____

ADDRESS_____

CITY _____ STATE/ZIP_____

(allow six weeks for delivery.)

A–3

Bestselling Books for Today's Reader

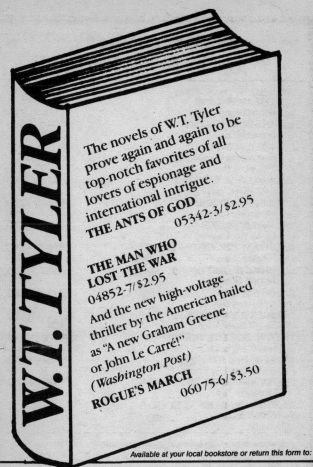

Bestsellers you've been hearing about—and want to read

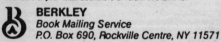